# BLOOD RUSH

## BOOK TWO OF
## THE DEMIMONDE

# ASH KRAFTON

Red
Fist
Fiction

Cover art: Red Fist Fiction

Interior design/formatting: Red Fist Fiction

First edition published 2013
Second edition published 2016

Contact Information can be found at www.ashkrafton.com

ISBN: 1-946120-01-4
ISBN-13: 978-1-946120-01-4

BLOOD RUSH
BOOK TWO OF THE DEMIMONDE

BY
ASH KRAFTON

ASH KRAFTON

# DEDICATION

To my Beloveds—
My husband, my children, my family

Dear Sophie,

I've read your articles on relationships so I know you'll understand my situation. My own relationship ended several months ago when "John" woke up one day, a completely different person.

We haven't spoken since we split, but recently I changed jobs and discovered he works for the same firm. Seeing him again awakened so many feelings I thought I'd conquered. I realize, despite the pain he'd caused me, I never stopped loving him.

Our contact is purely professional right now, but I want to reconnect with him on a personal level. Sometimes it seems like a good idea. Other times I worry he'll run away, or say something to devastate me again.

Should I take the chance? I mean, I don't have anything left to lose. Do I?

Signed,
Lonely yet Hopeful in Harborview

*Dear Sophie,*

*This is another fine mess you've gotten us into. How are you going to help that lady when you can't even help yourself?*

*Sincerely, Sophie*

I don't believe in happily ever after. These days, I'd settle for alive until sunrise.

I never thought I'd become a nine-to-fiver. Certainly never thought I'd be too preoccupied to make fun of myself for being one. Sometimes the irony was too great to appreciate.

While I waited for the elevator to arrive at *The Mag*'s foyer, I smoothed my scarf along the back of my neck and hefted my tote bag a little higher on my shoulder. Every chime increased my trepidation, tightening the fist of anxiety in my chest and the sensation of bees swarming in the top of my stomach. I hated quitting time.

More underappreciated irony. Why not?

People chatted around me but I fidgeted with my zipper, keeping my gaze lowered and my mouth closed. Leaving at five in the afternoon meant more than crammed elevators and crowded buses; it meant the light would fade soon and with it my peace of mind. The autumn wasn't a happy golden foliage time of year for me anymore.

Although it was only early October, already the longer nights and shorter days made me feel nervous and brittle. Bad enough I didn't have a sweetheart to share the long nights but even worse now that I knew what came out when the sun went down. Although I hadn't had any problems with vampires over the last year, the threat never left my mind.

Vampires were out there. It was just a matter of time until I had to deal with them again.

Halfway during our descent, I felt a vibe. It was a mild one but, over the past year, my empathy had become sensitive to the point of being squirrely. The thin thread of power wound its way around each of the passengers as the Demivampire who owned it checked out who else was in the car. When it reached me, it felt like a poke on the arm. I glanced over my shoulder, catching the eyes of an older dark-eyed woman near the back. She sent a tiny pulse of apology-laden power and lowered her eyes.

I smiled politely and concentrated on tugging my scarf loose. The DV didn't approach me in public where any old human could see. We kept our dealings distant and private. That was the way I preferred.

The door opened and I flowed out with the crowd, sunglasses on and scarf over my hair. I hoped everyone would more or less continue on together today so I could hide in the crowd a bit longer.

Without turning my head, I saw a rail-thin guy, his scruffy head and jeans out of place amongst the exiting office employees. He leaned against the wall, scanning the people emerging from the other elevators. Seemed to have missed me—good. Taking shelter behind a taller woman and her chatty companion, I hustled out the front doors.

Outside, my luck ran out. My camouflaging crowd of coworkers suddenly scattered like roaches when the kitchen light is turned on. I hesitated, taking too long to pick a direction.

It was all he needed to spot me. I looked back through the glass into the foyer of *The Mag*'s building. He was on the move, eyes locked onto me.

I bolted.

Startled faces blurred past as I hurried through the five o'clock exodus, bumping into one man, dodging another, and rounding the corner at a speed unfitting for heeled pumps. Steve Madden would be horrified if he knew what I did in his shoes.

Well, Steve could kill me later. Right now, I was facing a much more immediate threat.

At the corner, a bus was loading and at this point I didn't care if it was mine or not. An elderly lady with a big shopping bag struggled on the steps and I danced behind her like a first grader with a full bladder. Once she cleared the last step I leapt up, slamming my token into the fare box.

The door closed behind me just as my pursuer caught up. For once I was glad for the driver's rude efficiency. The bus leveled and lurched forward. I grabbed the bar, almost swinging into the laps of the front seat passengers. As we pulled away from the curb, I met the man's stare through the grimy glass of the door.

Rusted-orange eyes with wide pupils.

Non-people eyes.

*Werewolf* eyes.

I sank onto an empty seat, heart thumping, gradually slowing. Glancing up at the sign over the driver's seat, I realized I'd ended up on the round-about route. Close enough for me. I tugged my necklace out of my shirt and kissed the pendant, my good luck charm, and offered a silent thankful thought to whatever divine powers had saved my behind, yet again.

Reaching into my bag, I pulled out a book of poetry and readied for a long ride home. Ironically, when I'd flipped to a random page, I opened to one of Dylan Thomas's poems.

*Do not go gentle into that good night. Rage, rage against the dying of the light.*

I had no energy left for rage. All I could muster was a thankful thought because at least today's escape had gone better than most.

A beast of a different sort met me at the door once I got home, but I was prepared for this one. Since moving to my current apartment, Euphrates had become a one-hundred-percent-indoors cat and poor kitty was not coping well.

I squeezed through the narrowly-opened door and blocked his escape with my tote bag. He'd made it out into the hall twice since moving here, which could have caused major fallout. The other apartment on this floor was occupied by a *No Pets Allowed* vigilante who seemed intent on catching me with the furry goods. Mrs. Petterson already suspected Euphrates wasn't a television and frequently warned me something dire would happen should I dare bring in a dog.

As if. I definitely didn't swing that way.

Luckily, Euphrates wasn't up to any cat acrobatics so my bag was enough to contain him. He accused me with a heavy-lidded glare and a toothy wail that made me pity his near-solitary confinement.

Scooping him up, I dropped my bag on the couch and glanced around with dismay. Stacks of cardboard boxes exaggerated the tight fit of the room. I'd begun to unpack when I moved in three months ago but quickly grew disheartened by the lack of space. If I'd had time when I was planning the move, I could have picked an apartment that was at least big enough to fit the couch. Instead, it sat at a strange angle across one corner of the room. Either that or block the doorway.

I would have gotten a place that allowed pets, too, but I just didn't have the luxury of time to browse through rental listings. Once that Were had discovered my last apartment, I was out of there in four days flat.

What was the point of unpacking when it didn't feel like home?

Life hadn't been exactly all new-pumps-and-Oreos since my soul mate Marek and I split more than a year ago. Well, more precisely, he split. Demivamps pushed to the brink of evolution tended to do that, since their own society generally wants nothing more to do with them. Evolution is a one-way street, more or less. Nothing can bring a brinking DV back from that terrible edge.

Nothing, except maybe for me. Still, it didn't make me immune to being dumped. Marek had made it crystal clear he didn't want to see me anymore when I tracked him down after the Crap That Almost Killed Me. I was an old fashioned girl, you know? If a guy made love to you one night then tore out your throat and exsanguinated you the next, he should at least call you in the morning.

I sighed and pulled out a stack of mail I'd brought home from the office. Before meeting Marek and the rest of the DV, writing my column was barely enough to justify my gainful employment at *The Mag*; I usually contributed to other features in order to claim a regular paycheck and benefits. (It shames me to admit the lengths to which I'd go for health insurance.)

Unfortunately, being Sophia for the American Demivampire also made writing my advice column a full-time job, since the DV decided it was the perfect way to petition me. Every once in a while, a letter would contain an emotional signature so strong it evoked the Sophia. I couldn't risk having my eyes change color in front of the mail clerk again.

It was almost like face-on petitioning, really. I could simply sort the petitions from the human letters and get on a roll. Once the Sophia responded, the answers flowed smoothly. First drafts were last drafts and, when I included select petitions for print in the column, they were the ones that impressed my editor most. I would then mail the remaining responses off to their respective petitioners.

Sometimes the petition was doubled with a pushy compulsion, a "read mine first" or some other obnoxious request. That sort of thing really bunched up my boyshorts. Of course, I couldn't complain about it at work because no one knew about the Demivampire, much less that I was their spiritual guardian. Hence, all the off-the-clock work.

Give Until It Hurts Sophie, that's me.

Flipping through the mail, I breathed a tiny sigh of relief. None of the envelopes triggered a compulsion so I figured there was probably nothing I couldn't handle today.

I sliced open the envelopes and began to sort the letters into piles.

Column, column, petition.

The petitions were easy to spot even to someone who couldn't sense DV power; each was addressed *Dear Sophia* and signed with a real name, not a witty pseudonym. I had a growing number of regulars who made me think I ought to start charging them.

Column, petition, column, Rodrian.

I blinked, trying to focus my eyes and dispel my surprise, recognizing the handwriting on the envelope at once. Rodrian Thurzo preferred writing to typing and he had a real thing for fountain pens.

Yep, *that* Rodrian. Marek's brother.

When I pulled out the letter, the power signature tripped a switch in my brain, triggering my Sophia. My eyes changed so fast I swore I could feel them flow from brown to oracular blue. I had to sit down before I fell over and felt behind me for an afghan to wrap around my shoulders. The chills were so intense I thought my teeth would chatter.

Damn that Rodrian.

Once my Sophia settled, I unfolded the letter and read it. The letter contained a brief request to meet him at his Tenth Street office. Some sort of business proposition. I couldn't imagine what business he could possibly have with me.

I especially couldn't imagine what was so important that he'd send enough power to turn my intestines into balloon animals. I came *this close* to throwing up on Fraidy. I'm sure the cat would have loved that.

So. Business with Rodrian. Now the question remained: would I go?

I arrived at the Tenth Street offices ten minutes early.

Not that I was in any particular hurry. It had been almost a year and a half since I'd ridden this elevator or stood in this reception area or looked at the broad door that led to the interior of Rodrian's office. Fifteen months was a long time—time enough to change wall art and hire new receptionists and make strangers out of two people who had once been as close as family.

I arrived ten minutes early only because I was nervous. I walked quickly when I was nervous.

At the receptionist's polite nod I took a seat near the windows. The sparse waiting area had not been designed for comfort. People waiting to see Rodrian Thurzo needed no distractions or trivial ways to pass time. I longed for a stack of well-worn magazines, something to occupy my hands and my mind.

Instead, I curled my hands together in a quiet semblance of patience and dreaded the moment the door would open.

I never had to sit out here before, waiting to be granted an audience.

My composure slipped and I squirmed. Technically I hadn't asked for an audience with Rodrian. I'd been summoned.

Bossy jerk that he was, Rodrian probably wouldn't have thought twice about commanding me but he hadn't. His letter had been politely written, a carefully worded request.

However, the moment my skin touched the paper I knew this was no ordinary letter. Mental actions spoke louder than words. Request or not, I really had no choice. He had laden it with emotion and was clever enough to use the one particular emotion I couldn't ignore.

*Need.*

I wrinkled my nose and grimaced at the mahogany door, promising to come up with new descriptions for the type of jerk he was. *Conniving, opportunistic,* and *manipulative* seemed a good way to start the list.

Eventually, I gave up and sighed. Someone else would have to come up with the right word because Rodrian wasn't my jerk anymore. As far as I was trying to be concerned, I was here on official Sophia business. I sat still and stared impassively at the door and tried to look professional.

I was sure I failed. Par for the course these days.

"Ms. Galen?" The receptionist's inquiry broke through the nervous buzz of my thoughts and I sprang to my feet as if she'd pressed an ejection seat button. "He'll see you now. Do you need a guide?"

I quickly shook my head. I knew it wouldn't be an escort who guided me to his office but rather a compulsion. "No, that's all right. Left wing, at the end?"

She beamed a Stepford Wives smile at me and turned to answer the phone. The door slowly swung open and I walked through as if it was something I did every day. No big deal, right? Just official Sophia business.

I paused in the bend of the V-shaped hallway as a hum of power enveloped me, making the air feel sandpapery. The subtle wards buzzed like dull electricity and I recognized Rodrian's "signature" upon each one. They were a new addition; I hadn't known he could set wards like these. They seemed alert, like guardians. Watching. Waiting.

Nonetheless, they were easy to disregard. My control over the Sophia had improved a bit since it first emerged and now I wasn't so simple-minded that I could be swayed by suggestive spells. In fact, I'd come to attribute the foolish antics of my youth to influence by spiteful Demivampires. I didn't make those mistakes anymore.

Now, mistakes wouldn't leave me humiliated. They'd leave me dead. A real motivator if ever there was one.

Tugging a strand of hair out of my eyes, I turned to the left and headed down the hall. Time to take care of business and get home before the daylight died.

Rodrian leaned in a doorway across from his own office and I took in the entire sight of him at once. His dark hair was shorter; his bangs used to fall chin-length when he didn't gel them back. Now, despite the gel, stubborn strands broke loose to fall around his eyes, making him look younger. As usual, he wore dress pants and a tailored shirt, wide cuffs closed by glinting cuff links, but he slouched against the door as if wearing a t-shirt and jeans.

I heard his voice as he made some light comment, saw the smile playing on his mouth and in his eyes. My approach made him look up. His smile didn't fade but it changed.

His power reached me a moment later. It was only a brief touch before he pulled it back but it was enough. More than enough. I had been sitting on empathic pins and needles anticipating this moment. That little bit of Rodrian that leaked out at me blasted like a radio with the volume turned all the way up.

I faltered in my steps and gave him a tiny frown that said *it's not polite to knock the Sophia down with one's power.* His businessman veneer slid all the way up and he went into full-out professional mode.

"Miss Galen." His voice was low, smooth, controlled. The familiar sound curled itself around my insides and squeezed.

"Mr. Thurzo." I responded as dryly as I could. Not difficult, considering I was completely cotton-mouthed.

He gestured toward his office door. "Please, go in and be comfortable. I'll be in momentarily."

Rodrian was a lazy decorator. Like many bachelors, he was content to live in unchanging surroundings until someone else decided he needed to change.

His office hadn't benefited from someone else's intervention. Everything was the same as I remembered— the broad oak desk, the stacks of leather-bound ledgers, the antique ink pot of cobalt glass. Even the comfy couch, cushions so soft and accommodating I used to slip off my shoes and curl my legs beneath me, listening to Marek lecture his younger brother.

I ignored the couch's silent invitation and perched instead on one of two straight-backed chairs facing the desk, which reminded me of the hot seats in a junior high school principal's office. I was here on business. I had to be.

He closed the door behind him and the air moved as he took his seat. A single file folder lay on the blotter before him. He thumbed the edge, hesitating before opening it, and sat back in his chair. "I'm surprised you came."

"I'm pretty surprised myself." I lay my hands gracefully

upon my lap. My pro smile popped on, the one that didn't show teeth. It was my *Go on, dear, I'm listening* smile. It was my equivalent of assuming the Sophia position.

According to his request, Rodrian needed me. It meant I had the upper hand. The notion made me level my shoulders and I donned what I hoped was a patient, expectant expression.

"You've been busy," he said.

The pro smile slipped. I couldn't help the eye-roll. "Understatement. My second job really cuts into my free time."

Rodrian looked puzzled. "What second job?"

Instead of answering, I closed my eyes and concentrated on the thread of power drifting from him, wrapping my mental fingers around it, as if it were a rope, and pulling. The part of my mind that was the Sophia roused and stretched before unfurling into awareness.

Chills having nothing to do with the autumn weather brushed down my arms, leaving gentle swirls of tingles in their wake. Opening my eyes I gazed back at him, knowing they shone a bright and startling shade of blue.

My gaze locked onto his, and I gave his essence a little tug before releasing my hold. The Sophia slipped back into hiding, my eyes darkening once more to their usual brown. The DV weren't the only ones around here with nifty eye tricks.

Rodrian stared back, his own eyes glowing like hot amber. He'd seen my blue eyes, felt my empathic touch. Surprise had loosened his control, and he was unable to keep the light in his eyes from answering.

Most DV couldn't when I touched them that way.

"Ah." His voice was rough as if I'd given him a lap dance. "The Sophia."

His hungry look made me uncomfortable. I twisted my

ring and avoided looking at him. "Yep."

"How can you consider that work?"

I wrinkled my nose. "What, saving the world from vampires isn't work?"

I expected him to laugh but he only tilted his head. "You're not a slayer."

"No, but an ounce of prevention is worth a megaton of cure."

Rodrian was quiet for a few long moments. "You stopped attending the Conclave sessions."

"Yes," I said quietly. "It became too difficult."

"Difficult?"

"Emotionally. My own personal issues kept interfering." I didn't want this to turn into a conversation about Marek, even though he may as well have been standing right here next to us. I was never truly free of his presence, thanks to my obsession with him. "It's just easier to do the Sophia stuff through the column."

"So I've heard."

That would explain the stack of *Mag* issues sitting on the windowsill but I was too modest to point them out. "Yeah? Did you hear I got syndication? The column's been picked up by six other markets and management let slip a West Coast rumor this week. *The Mag*'s making loads of money."

"Then why—"

"*The Mag* is making money," I said. "Apart from a raise and some extra bonus in my Christmas stocking, I'm still a columnist who does her best work for free."

"That doesn't sound fair." He frowned at me. I figured he would—his first love was profits. Things like *volunteer work* and *charity* probably gave him a rash.

"I'm glad we agree. But who argues with destiny and wins? I can't stop being the Sophia. I just have to do it my way. And anyways..." I jerked my shoulders in an uncomfortable shrug and slid my purse across my lap to a new position before gripping it tightly, urging my fingers to be still. "This is just as good as any other way. It's not like I'm going to slip on Grecian robes and move into a drafty old temple anytime soon."

"Funny you should say that." He flipped open the folder. "That's why I asked you to meet with me today."

As suspicious as I was, I couldn't help but perk up. "I'm getting a temple?"

"No," he said. "But there's a mansion lying around if you want it."

"I think I missed the joke."

"I'm serious, Sophie." He glanced down at a neat stack of pages. "I'm referring to the country estate you've visited with my brother. We are offering it to you."

"And, why?" I was baffled. A thousand things had crossed my mind as the possible reason why I'd been summoned. Getting a house was not one of them.

"Do you remember the wards on his private quarters?"

I nodded. Marek had explained they were a security measure. Those wards were much stronger than the ones Rodrian had set down the hall but Marek had "tuned" them to me so I would not feel them, despite my empathic sensitivity.

"The wards don't recognize him anymore so they can't be removed. He told me you... seemed to enjoy your stay there and asked me to arrange its transfer to you."

"So, what, he doesn't like his mansion anymore and figured I'd want a hand-me-down?"

"A hand-me-down?" Rodrian's eyebrows almost disappeared under his loose bangs. Money wasn't something he joked about. "The place is worth seven figures!"

I gulped, suspecting all seven were in front of the

decimal place. "Then I definitely have to refuse. I'd never be able to afford the taxes."

Rodrian shook his head. "That's all arranged. A trust will be set up for that, as well as maintenance, staffing, utilities..." He looked down at the paper in front of him. "An income, too."

"An income?" I narrowed my eyes in suspicion. "Oh. I get it. I'm the maid, aren't I?"

"No, goof. The babysitter."

I gaped. I've seen fish on ice at the market with more composure than I had at the moment.

"I'm sorry," he said. "I shouldn't have called you that."

"Yeah." I waved it away. "Babysitter, Rode?"

His power pulsed warmly at the sound of his diminutive. "Yeah. Sort of. I'd like Shiloh to move in with you for a while. Would you object to it?"

"No, I...I just..." I stammered as if I had a clothespin on my tongue. This unexpected request left me reeling. "What's up with Shiloh? I haven't seen her in a long time."

"She, um...has a medical condition, something you can help her with. It's complicated."

Ah. That explained the sense of need I felt attached to his letter. "Details?"

The corner of his mouth twitched and he dipped his head. "Not today. I'd like to meet with you another time to discuss all that. It's—Shiloh. My baby girl. I can't talk about her and business at the same time. It wouldn't feel right. Does that make any sense?"

I nodded when he looked at me for a response. Family was separate from business. I found both comfort and disappointment in his idealism. "You've been thinking about this for a while, haven't you?"

"Look, Soph." Rodrian abandoned his corporate act and pushed his chair back. "I haven't been the most considerate of friends, I know. I've been busy and things have been...hard. Just hard."

"I know," I said softly. "Don't explain."

"But I need to." He leaned against his desk, trying to close the distance between us. "I never forgot about you and I need to tell you—"

"Nothing. You need to tell me nothing. I don't hold anything against you, or..." I waved my hand and avoided saying a certain name. "Any of your people. Would've been nice to get a little help now and then, considering what's expected of me, but I'm not keeping score. Much."

"Sophie—"

"No, Rodrian. Don't explain. Don't apologize. Don't talk about things you can't change. It'll only hurt."

He lowered his eyes, seemingly chastised. I wasn't sure if that had been my intention. These days I didn't mean to do a lot of the things I did.

When he again looked up, the business facade was back in place. "Do you think we can work together on this, Sophie?"

"Of course." I gave him a sincere smile. I was nothing if not sincere; it was part of my job description. "I need to hear the details first but I'd never turn my back on you, Rode."

"And why is that?"

"Knowing you, the moment I did you'd snap my bra. Or are you too mature for that now?" I asked when his eyebrows shot up in protest.

"You haven't changed, Sophie." Relief relaxed his expression and he laughed.

"Oh, but see, that's where you're wrong, Rodrian. I've changed plenty." I pressed my lips together and kept from elaborating. "But let's not talk about it. Let's hear more about why you called me here so I can decide whether I leave laughing or screaming."

"Fair enough," was all he said before he got down to business.

After a twenty-minute demonstration of Rodrian's exceedingly suave vocabulary, I figured I understood enough of his offer to contribute. "So, basically, I've inherited a fortune."

Rodrian only shrugged in reply. That little dismissive gesture told me there were great discrepancies between our definitions of *fortune*.

"It's not right, Rode. I've always taken care of myself. Money wise," I added firmly, when he shot me a look of disagreement. It was the same look his brother used to give me. Marek had never believed I was capable of taking care of myself, either. He still didn't, apparently. "It's a lot to take in."

"I know it's a lot but I need to know. About Shiloh, I mean. The house isn't going anywhere." A tiny flare of anxiety broke through the demeanor of his power when he said her name.

"You really mean to guilt me into this, don't you?"

"Not at all. But I don't believe in serendipity. Marek's offer came to the table nearly the same time as Shiloh's condition became apparent. This isn't about guilt. This is about opportunity and—"

"Divine intervention?"

"If that's what you want to call it."

I chewed my lips and thought about it. This arrangement would solve any number of my current problems, decent housing and security topping the list. I wasn't stupid enough to pass up an opportunity, either.

However, I didn't have an overwhelming impulse to admit I'd been failing miserably at solving my own problems and needed help. I gave the help around here, darn it. "I need time. I can't just say yes to something this big. I mean, I'll do anything for Shiloh but the rest of it...I don't feel comfortable taking something from your brother."

"You can call me later if you want. Or I can stop by."

"No, that's all right." I hadn't had company at my new apartment yet—not even my Demivamp best friend Dahlia—and I didn't want to start. Being Sophia made me a big enough target without allowing the DV to taint my home with their power. Remembering what a flirt Rodrian was, I figured he'd spread it around like a tomcat. "I'll call you once I've had time to think about it."

Since we seemed to have concluded business, I stood to leave. Rodrian pushed away from his desk and hurried to escort me to the door. Something softened his expression and I worried he might embrace me.

Thankfully, however, he only offered a handshake. His skin wore a sheen of power that felt the way sunshine looked on water. The shake wasn't as efficient as it could have been but I didn't really mind. This business was personal. It could never be anything but.

"You'll call?"

"You bet," I said and smiled thinly.

When I walked out into the hall, he remained in the doorway. His eyes were almost a weight upon me as I left, and I tried to ignore the feeling that at any moment he might seize me and pull me back.

The next day, my editor called me into her office as soon as she got back from her morning meeting. As I shut the door behind me, Barbara Evans glanced up and gestured with a "help yourself" wave toward the coffee station. "We heard from St. Louis last night. They're on board."

I lifted my Styrofoam cup in response to her coffee offer. Once, Barbara's coffee station brought me a glimpse of paradise: the imported beans, the milk steamer, the little shaker tins of mysterious spices and flavors...

But my beverage of paradise disappeared into limbo after a near-death experience left me drained. A DV healer named Pontian banned me from drinking coffee, saying it would interfere with my blood loss treatment; I considered it a punishment for a crime I never committed. He never even told me when I was eligible for parole.

Being separated from the things I loved most had become a theme for me. At least it lent tremendous inspiration to my freelance writing.

Sinking into the big red chair by her desk, I set my cup down. "That's great, Barb."

She waved the air in front of her face. "Still drinking that stuff?"

Recently I had embarked on a chai kick. The creamy spiced tea was the closest I could get to recreating the mystical coffee experiences I'd once had at her coffee bar.

Barbara, however, didn't share my enthusiasm. She thought chai was disgusting and insisted I refrained from breathing on her while drinking it.

I sighed. "Did you call me in here to tease me?"

"Anyhoo. The column is spreading like wildfire. Tommy said he's gotten four unsolicited requests in the last week." Tom was Editor-in-Chief at *The Mag* and Barbara's supervisor. Anything that made Tom happy tended to make the entire office happy.

"Did you pitch him my idea about unique columns?"

"Yes," she said. "But I don't think he's sold on it. Tell me again why it's a good idea?"

"Well, the column has always been city specific. It was our own residents reading *The Mag*. People like seeing their own letters in print—makes for a strong connection and reader loyalty. If we branch out into new markets, the hope of seeing their letter diminishes. I think the response will diminish, too, and reader loyalty won't be as strong."

"But think of the work you're already putting into it. Are you going to write a column for every market every month? It defeats the purpose of syndication." She pulled out a drawer in her filing cabinet and flipped through some files. "Plus...I know you, kiddo. You love having free time. You've really bumped up your office hours over the last couple of months."

"Is my work suffering?"

"No, of course not. It's just that...you don't seem happy

anymore. I miss the old Sophie."

"I am happy," I insisted. "It's just that lately I've been a little tense." I hadn't told anyone about being chased, not even Barbara. Although she was my closest human confidant, she knew nothing of the supernatural double-life I led.

"I've been worried about you," she said. "You seem secluded. It's not healthy."

"I know. But the breakup...the funeral...I didn't bounce all the way back. I'd lost the people I could have counted on for support."

"You never lost me."

I would have hugged her if not for the desk between us. "I know. Thanks, Barb. If it wasn't for you, I don't know what I would have done." I raised my chai, eliciting Barbara's cheerful frown. "I'd toast you if you had a drink."

"Well, I'll be toasting you tonight after Tom gets through with me. You always made me look good, hon, and if you keep up your magic, I might not even recognize myself anymore."

Her phone rang and I used the distraction as an excuse to head back to my cube. I fervently hoped Tom would buy into the unique column idea. If I could swing that, it would cut my work in half. Instead of answering letters privately, I could use the DV petitions as column material, thereby satisfying work and the DV needs simultaneously. My obsession with answering each letter was largely responsible for my horrifically average-length work days.

Barbara worried about increasing my workload; she didn't realize my work load couldn't possibly get any worse. I was already doing the very work I proposed. Making it official would save me the effort of being my own secretary.

On my way into my cube, I snagged my mail from the

hanging basket on the outside of the partition. On Mondays the stack was so thick it didn't fit and the delivery person usually tossed the bundle onto the floor inside my cube. I had yet to catch them doing it but, when I did, they'd better be ready for an extremely dirty look. It wasn't right for anyone to go postal outside the post office. It was like people parking in handicap spots when they weren't handicapped.

I fished out the day's catch. Immediately, an envelope trimmed with red and blue stripes caught my eye. *Air mail.*

The address was handwritten with a purplish-blue ink that would have made Rodrian drool. The writer had used actual calligraphy, inscribing each letter with precise flourish. Simply looking at the envelope made me ashamed of my less-than-perfect penmanship. No return address. No surprise there. Most of my mail tended to be anonymous. The postmark was blurred but if I deciphered it correctly, it read "Budapest."

Just great, I thought. My free advice had gone international. Not that Canada didn't count but, anyways.

No compulsion on the envelope meant I had to open it if I wanted to know anything. The crisp page was carefully creased, ivory paper embellished with gold embossing and a faint fragrance. The letter had been written by the same hand as the address and the words swirled gracefully across the page, an elegant dance of the written word.

*Dear Sophia,*

*It is with great pleasure that I write to announce my intent to visit your city. News of your manifestation has traveled all the way to my country, and I cherish the opportunity to meet with you.*

*My journey will bring me to Philadelphia, Pennsylvania in October of this year. I have enclosed the information for the hotel as well as my itinerary. Please contact my representative so we may arrange to meet soon afterwards. I do not travel often and do hope we can make the most of my time in your land.*

*Warmest regards,*
*Sophia Eirene Biztos*

A Sophia!

I read the letter twice more before refolding the thin sheet of paper and sliding it back into its envelope. My heart thumped at the prospect of meeting another Sophia. Finally, I'd get to talk with someone about whatever the hell it was I should actually be doing.

The letter had been dated nearly two weeks earlier which meant she'd already be at the hotel. I picked up the business card she'd enclosed, intending to call immediately.

A twang of regret managed to strike its way through my happiness, however. I longed for a way to tell Marek about the letter. He'd searched for the Sophia for so long. It wouldn't be fair to keep such monumental information from him. I knew he avoided me out of guilt and remorse for what had happened the night we were taken by the Master but, by doing so, Marek estranged himself from whatever benefit my Sophia could be to him at a time when he needed it most.

He'd offered me the security of his country home. I still felt uncomfortable about accepting such a generous offer. At least now, I could introduce him to another Sophia. Sort of pay him back. Perhaps she could heal him and bring him back to his true self. It had to be torment for him, living on the precarious edge of evolution, knowing the slightest nudge would damn him forever.

I shouldn't get my hopes up. He might not even listen to me, let alone agree to see her.

Promising I wouldn't get my hopes up so high I couldn't retract them, I glanced at the hotel card and dialed the phone. About time I started doing my job.

A sparkle of inspiration struck at about four o'clock that afternoon and for the first time in weeks I enjoyed a quitting time free of dread. Although it involved considerably more effort than should have been necessary, it was well worth it.

God bless the parking garage next door.

I got off the elevator on the seventh floor and crossed the catwalk to the adjoining garage complex, following the ramp down to the elevator on the far side. I emerged on the opposite side of the block from my office building.

The Were-free side.

I would have done a congratulatory jump-and-heel click but those extra minutes meant I had to boogie to make it to my bus. Couldn't waste time bragging about my ability to outsmart a Were.

It should have been easy to ask Rodrian for help with my furry tracker. Why not? When he needed help with Shiloh, he had no problems calling me for a favor. However, offering a house in exchange was a huge pile of persuasion. I didn't quite have that kind of leverage.

But being Sophia should have counted for something, shouldn't it? I didn't take a paycheck or stock options or anything. Being Sophia meant I was destined to protect the DV. Shouldn't they protect me in return?

*But do I really do anything?* I scowled and sullenly stared out the dirty window, watching block after blurry block slide by. *Sure, I answer petitions all the time but am I really doing anything?*

Being a spiritual healer didn't provide the most quantifiable of data.

That was the big thing that kept me from asking for help with the Were who was tailing me. I didn't think I deserved the right to ask for anything when all I did was simply be myself.

And if I couldn't justify asking for help, I certainly couldn't justify taking a house. Not even one disguised as a gift, one that no one else on the planet could live in.

*My resourcefulness got me home without the Were seeing me.* I repeated it like a mantra until I convinced myself I'd be able to help Shiloh without taking Rodrian up on his offer. By the time I reached my apartment building, I'd made my decision. I would call Rodrian and tell him what I should save told him right then and there—no. Thank you but no.

The flight up to the second floor seemed longer than usual. Mrs. Petterson was on the phone again, her voice carrying like fifteen extra pounds in bikini weather, filling the narrow staircase. What she had against privacy, I'd never know. Who put their telephone right next to the door?

A thin gleam showed under Mrs. Petterson's door, sharp and bright in the dimly-lit hall. The gray square of window at the far end didn't offer much light. Stupid shorter days. Trying not to grumble and straining to see, I tipped my purse and felt inside for my keys. When I pulled them out, they dragged out half the contents of my bag, scattering them over the wooden floor.

Ninja Sophie, that's definitely not me.

As I stooped to collect my clutter, Mrs. Petterson's door jerked open.

"Do you mind?" Her hair rollers and cigarette and bright pink lipstick made her look like the Housewife from Hell. It must have been the angry curl of her lips that left me with such a distinct impression, despite serious doubt that she even really was a missus. Not that I was one to judge.

"I'm on the phone."

"I'm sorry, I dropped—"

Mrs. Petterson sneezed. And sneezed again. Five rapid *ketch*es before a wheezing *chew* with no room in between them for a *bless you*. I had to side-step her Marlboro when she sneezed it at me. Honestly. Pets weren't allowed but smoking was?

"How dare you bring a dog up here!" Her cigarette smoldered, forgotten on the floor. Eyes wide, she pointed a bony, heavy-ringed finger at me before sneezing again.

"But I—"

"Don't tell me!" *Ketchew!* "I told you I was—" *Ketchew!* "Allergic to dogs!"

"I don't have a dog." I knew she was nutty but this was raving madness. Would pepper-spraying her would do any good? I would be totally justified.

"Then he does!" She pointed behind me. "Get it and your friend out of here!"

"My fr—?" In the glare from Mrs. Petterson's open door I caught a glimpse of a shadowy figure sporting a ruffled head and a pair of orange eyes.

I screamed like a slasher flick vic. Mrs. Patterson echoed me with a phlegmy rendition of her own. The Were scrammed, stomping down the steps and banging the front door as he fled.

"My God, girl." Mrs. Petterson wheezed as she stooped to retrieve her cigarette. "What was that all about?"

I unlocked my door and lunged inside without answering. If she was offended, too bad. Jamming the lock across and twisting the deadbolt, I knew it wouldn't make the slightest difference.

That wasn't a burglar out there. That wasn't an ardent fan. That was something locks weren't designed to keep out.

I repeated a frustrated f-word litany and fought to calm myself, forcing slow corrugated breaths over the rapid bump of my heartbeat. Through the door, I could hear Mrs. Petterson, back on the phone, relaying the weird occurrence to her friend.

I didn't need to relive it. Retreating to the living room, I flopped onto the couch.

Another apartment down the drain. Maybe it had been foresight that kept me from unpacking. Foresight, or forewarning. Either way, I was out of here.

When I recovered enough to manage a casual tone, I dialed the phone. Rodrian picked up on the first ring.

"Hi, Rode." I smiled purposefully, trying to lighten my voice. "Ah. Saturday night sound good to you?"

*Dear Hopeful,*

*You have seized an important victory—you have held on to hope.*
*As long as we breathe, there is hope. As we press on through pain and loneliness, hope is our guide. It leads us out of the dark.*
*True love cannot die. It gets lost, sometimes. It may even be forgotten. But true love is an eternal spark that doesn't cease to exist simply because someone walks away. The spark dims with time and distance, yet may reignite if you are brave enough to press your wick closer.*
*You are blessed with a second chance to reclaim your love. You don't have anything to lose except solitude. If it was a true love you shared, there is always hope to share it again.*
*Be brave, and always be hopeful.*

*Sincerely, Sophie*

Saturday night I walked into Cordula's Bistro wearing a

little black dress and an overcoat of trepidation. (It went well with the faux pearls, actually.) I worried I might be overdressed but I was double-booked tonight—Sophia Eirene had invited me to her hotel later on so I wanted to make a good impression on her.

It didn't hurt to look nice for Rode, either. Never knew if he'd say something to Marek about what he was missing. Best to look spectacular in any case.

Rodrian wanted to discuss Shiloh's medical condition so I suspected this wouldn't be a light matter. This whole business with his family was as far from a light matter as it could get without imploding.

Guiltily, though, I'd still looked forward to it. Any subject would be worth dealing with if it meant I could be near them again. I missed Marek's family almost as much as I missed him.

You're getting carried away. I handed my wool coat to the check girl, thinking it might be best to keep the mental one. Fools rush in and all that.

The hostess escorted me to Rodrian's table. As she led me though the labyrinth of booths, I tried to ignore the pressing sensation of being an unmarked human amidst a roomful of hungry DV.

Rodrian rose and moved my chair for me. Even though I'd always considered it a silly gesture, it didn't look silly when he did it. He'd learned his gentlemanly affectations in a different era, and he used every one of his one hundred and twenty-plus years to his advantage. He liked being the focus of attention. It made for a worthwhile experience for anyone who cared to watch.

"You look terrific," he said.

I could have spent a good hour returning the compliment. Rodrian looked GQ perfect, as usual. If David Beckham ever gave up modeling—and knock on wood he wouldn't—Rodrian could step right in and womankind wouldn't spend a single moment in mourning.

"Thanks. I have a meeting afterwards. Sophia stuff," I added. I didn't want to elaborate, although I was positively itching to tell him about Sophia Eirene. This was about Shiloh tonight. I didn't want to distract him.

Taking his seat, he signaled to the wait staff, who filled my wine glass. I pushed my hair back behind one ear and rubbed my elbows as Rodrian began a casual conversation, seeming to ignore my fidgeting.

Eyes on me. Eyes and a sense of someone hovering right over my shoulder. Flickers of movement in my periphery kept jerking my gaze away from his face, making it hard to concentrate on him.

Sitting in a DV establishment, I felt like catch of the day. The sensation of being watched began the moment I walked in but I'd tried to disregard it. I've been around enough DV to learn to suppress my discomfort. In a restaurant, however, it became much harder to ignore. Appetites were sharper in places like this.

Didn't help that I kept catching glimpses of the manager, casting oily glares in my direction. Andre Caen wasn't my idea of a fun time. Or a nice time. Not even an okay time. I knew the difference between the Demivampire who cohabitated with humans and tried to remain un-detected among them, and the Demivamps who didn't care if we knew we were being hunted.

Andre Caen was of the latter group. He enjoyed being a bad time.

Eventually, I couldn't tolerate it any longer and interrupted Rodrian with a vague wave of my hands. "Can you fix this?"

"I'm sorry," he said softly. Stroking his jaw, he leaned over and stretched his fingers toward me, brushing my hair away from my throat and trailing them along the side of my neck. "I'd forgotten how sensitive you are."

Human patrons might have thought he was being affectionate or perhaps merely admiring my earrings. They missed the mystical caress of power that now surrounded me, effectively putting me off-limits to wandering fangs. By marking me, he'd taken me off the menu and made every DV in the place aware he'd placed me under his protection.

The discomfort lifted immediately. I closed my eyes for a fortifying breath and stretched a little in the mental breathing room.

"Thanks. That's much better."

Looking around, I took in the rest of the bistro. "We got take-out from here a couple times. Plus, I'd read a few reviews about Cordula's but this is the first time I came here. Nothing at all like Folletti's."

Rodrian, by profession, was a restaurateur. Folletti's was one of his previous establishments. Whereas Folletti's had been formal and elegant—the preferred destination for senators and royalty and men trying to impress the hell out of their dates—Cordula's was less stifling. This place specialized in pop rock music, boozy laughter, and finger food.

My worries that the little black dress would be overkill were quickly dispelled. Cordula's looked like a casual date place, an after work place, a night out with friends place all rolled into one. Little black dresses were the ultimate multitaskers. They were also the ultimate butt-savers, considering that Rodrian wore gray Armani. I supposed it was his idea of dressing down.

I tasted the contents of the wine glass and nodded my approval. The sangria was sweet and zippy like the perfect wine should be. I smiled. Rodrian remembered my preferences. "Have you owned this place long?"

He tilted his head and narrowed his eyes. "How did you know it was mine?"

"You mean you'd shop at your competition?"

Rodrian laughed. "Oh, gods, never. I acquired this last year and re-opened on Valentine's Day. Cordula means 'little heart'. Great tie-in for the marketing."

I glanced around, noting the full tables, the swarming wait staff. "You have a good thing here."

He looked steadily at me and said, "I know."

That wasn't a look meant for your brother's ex-soul mate. I picked up the menu to avoid looking back. "Is it okay if we order right away? I had an early lunch and a busy afternoon. I have a hunch you're going to talk more than you eat."

"Fine with me. I'm starved."

Starved was an understatement. Within ten minutes the table was covered with plates. No mystery where Shiloh got her hollow legs—she, too, had an admirable appetite, even for a teenager, and we'd spent most of our time together eating. It had been murder on my wardrobe. Thank goodness for stress and depression.

I watched him demolish the appetizer with college-boy zest before he moved onto a generous cut of Porterhouse, freshly cut and grilled medium rare. "Rode, how do you still fit in your pants?"

He titled his head, letting his bangs fall over one eye before pushing them back. "You want the serious answer or the other one?"

I blushed and he grinned. Just like old times.

"I do a lot of exercise." His undertone hinted at activities other than jogging and he grinned again before taking a drink from his glass.

"You haven't changed, either," I said.

"Nope. I'm too old to change."

"So I'd heard. How's Shiloh?"

"Funny you mention her. All this talk about not changing." The grin faded and his expression grew serious, emphasized by the tremor of concern in his power.

"She's all right?"

"Yeah, she's all right. She's just not...safe."

I shook my head a little to show I didn't follow.

"You know my girl's seventeen now."

"Yeah, how 'bout it?" I smiled. "She ready to take on the world yet?"

"No. That's the problem." He cleared his throat, looking acutely uncomfortable and I felt his power twinge with concern. This was the need that called me here—it curled around my core. "Shiloh has hypolution. She hasn't cusped yet."

"Cusp?" I vaguely remembered hearing the term used before.

"The change from human-like child to DV adult. You know our children grow exactly as human children—they're nearly indistinguishable. But the onset of puberty doesn't only bring physical adult characteristics. A DV teen goes through a cusp, an awakening of power and DV-specific physical changes."

It explained why I never "felt" Shiloh before—she'd always been just a regular person to me. "All along I thought she just had better manners than you."

"Shiloh? Manners?" His eyes sparkled with mirth a moment before growing serious again. "You've met her friends. Did you ever sense any of them?"

"Some, yeah. They didn't announce themselves the way adults do. Their power was weaker, diluted, unsteady." I searched for the right word in an attempt to describe a vague impression. Hard to describe what I didn't altogether understand.

I must have been close enough because he nodded. "Yes, exactly. But from Shiloh?"

"Nothing but sass." I sighed.

He pressed his lips together. "Well, I daresay that most of her friends would 'feel' like ordinary DV adult by now but you wouldn't feel Shiloh unless you used both hands."

"Why is that a problem?" I asked. "She sounds like a late-bloomer."

"It's more than that." Concern knitted his brows. "Her body is rapidly developing into adult, but without the cusp, her other attributes—her mind, her power—aren't keeping up with it."

Rodrian sighed and set down his fork. "I'll be blunt. Her body is beginning to require blood sustenance. Without her cusp, she doesn't have compulsion abilities. She can't obtain prey. The notion of consuming blood is as attractive to her as it is to you. She just doesn't have a taste for it."

Ugh. I wanted to push my plate away. "Is there a treatment?"

"Yeah, but it's dangerous. Pontian said the only way to overcome hypolution is to use blood rush to kick-start her cusp."

That was grim news. Rodrian had spoken to me about blood rush once before. Trouble-loving teens sometimes got their thrills doing it. It didn't involve death energy but, in young Demivamps, blood alone was enough to instigate evolution. It was a matter of being blood naïve and having zero tolerance.

I suddenly realized how difficult this was for Rodrian. When he'd first told me about blood rush, he'd been recounting the death of his son.

I steeled myself against pessimism. I had to be strong for Shiloh's sake. "Pontian knows what he's doing," I insisted. "He fixed me right proper, didn't he? I'm sure this treatment will be carefully controlled."

He nodded a little. "I have complete faith in him. Pontian is one of the oldest and wisest I know. It's the therapy I fear. She'll go through withdrawal and it will be painful. I hate knowing what I have to put her through. And seventeen—she's a typhoon of emotion. Do you remember seventeen?"

Did I ever. Grief laced its fingers around my heart for a moment as I remembered who I'd been at seventeen. I'd found and I'd lost so much at that age, events that defined the parameters of my deepest ideals and made me who I was today. Feeling a little guilty about placing so much value on events that happened half a lifetime ago, I allowed myself only a small private moment before I smoothed the crease in my brow and from around my soul.

"Yeah," I whispered. "I remember seventeen."

"So you can understand why I need you? Why Shiloh needs you? Not just as Sophia, but someone who knows her. Someone who cares for her."

"I do understand. Did you talk to her about us shacking up together?"

He gave me a sly I'll let that one go kind of look. "She says it'll be a never-ending slumber party, especially when Brianda comes to visit."

Brianda was Shiloh's older sister. "I don't really know her."

"I don't think you met her yet."

"Not officially. She carried me once." Brianda had rescued me the night of The Crap That Almost Killed Me; I'd have bled to death if she hadn't delivered me to the healers in time. We didn't exactly make conversation—it had been a rough night, with me almost dying and all.

Something moved behind his eyes, but the pulse of his power didn't give anything away. "Don't worry. The Stocks is so big you'll be more like neighbors than roommates when she's actually there."

"The stocks? That sounds ominous." As in rack and guillotine and iron maiden ominous.

"Does, doesn't it?" He grinned, giving me a flash of his eyeteeth. They weren't fangs by any stretch of the over-active imagination but their sharpness gave his smile a hungry, wild look nonetheless. "Black Oak Stocks is the name of the estate. It's been called that as long as I can remember. A lot of the trees on the property are old black oaks. It's where the name comes from."

"And the stocks part?"

Rodrian shrugged and sliced off a portion of steak, balancing the bite on the back of his upside-down fork. So Euro-cool. "Every old house has at least one skeleton in the closet."

"Well," I said, "as long as they're cleared out before I move in."

"Afraid of skeletons?"

"Hardly. I just need the closet space." I shifted in my seat and smoothed out my napkin. "When do you expect Brianda to show up?"

"Hard to say. She's busy with new projects. Doesn't talk details, really, and she's never needed a nanny to follow her around." He chewed, wearing a pensive look. "She's been her own person all her life—just sets a goal and pursues it into the ground. She's aggressive and focused but she has the benefit of good judgment."

"Family trait. She's a Thurzo, through and through."

"I don't know." He concentrated once more on his steak. "I look at her and only see her mother."

Rodrian had never discussed his wife before. He didn't wear a wedding band, and he definitely didn't act married. I ventured along the topic carefully. "You don't talk about her. Is she in the past?"

"In the past." He seemed to muse the phrase. "I suppose that's one way to put it. Most of the time, she's in the past."

"Are you still married?"

He lifted his shoulders in a shrug and reached for his glass. "Still mated."

"Same thing, right?"

"Depends on the DV. Less to some. More to others."

"I get the impression the relationship is a little one-sided."

"Good call." He pressed his mouth into a thin line and looked away, seemingly more interested in the walls than the conversation.

"I'm sorry. I didn't mean to pry."

"No, it's me. I should be honest."

"But if you don't like talking—"

"Not that. I never knew anyone who needed to know about her. She's—away. She works in acquisitions, an artifacts dealer. Always traveling. From time to time she pops in, reminds me why I can't live without her, and leaves again, usually after conceiving another child. It's her way."

I wrinkled my nose. "That's your relationship? You're just a stud?"

His eyes lit with mischief. "Not just any stud."

"Nice. Seriously. That's it?"

Rodrian sighed and set his fork down. "She's the only woman I ever loved. I guess my love is destined to be ninety-nine percent waiting and hoping. That one percent, when she finally comes home, is worth the wait."

That sounded melodramatic, even to me. "It's cruel. No one should repay devotion with separation."

"And yet, it's love. I can't not feel it. I can rage and argue against it but, in the end, it changes nothing." His irises

45

warmed, a reminder of the inconstant nature of hazel eyes. Sometimes brown, sometimes gold, sometimes green.

I remembered green eyes that glowed the same and softened my position. "I can relate."

"I know." Rodrian reached across the table and patted my hand. "It makes us kindred spirits, our misery."

As lovely as it sounded, these days I was too tense and bitter to appreciate the beauty of unrequited devotion. I steered the conversation back to the scheduled topic. "It'll be nice to see Shiloh again. I'm glad you think I can help. I'd hate for her to go through this alone."

"She'd never be alone," he said. "But knowing that you'll be there somehow makes it feel less lonely." He raised his glass solemnly. "Thank you, Soph."

Lifting my glass in reply, I sipped the wine. Unconsciously, I toyed with my necklace with my free hand.

The pendant was made of blood red jasper, an oblong cabochon that had been inscribed in tiny intricate detail. Egyptian hieroglyphs streamed across the stone spelled out a passage from the Book of the Dead.

A spell.

A prayer to Isis, begging her protection.

I'd worn it nearly non-stop since Marek gave it to me, calling it my "good luck charm." Maybe this spell was the reason I was still alive. There was only a brief time I hadn't worn it. Marek had torn it from my neck during The Crap That Almost Killed Me but one of the DV had found it and returned it to me, repaired. A tiny chink in the gold chain was the only sign it had ever been broken. The necklace was scarred, just like me.

I treasured scars. Scars were not open wounds—they were a sign that wounds eventually heal. They reminded me that, although something bad happened, something good had happened first.

Most days, I needed that proof.

Rubbing my thumb along the back of the pendant, I thought about the other set of hieroglyphs that decorated the back of the pendant. They were encircled by a magic cartouche, engraved into the stone as surely as they were scrawled across my heart.

His name.

Marek had asked that I never forget him, and I'd promised without hesitation, without a thought of how much it would hurt to remember him when he was gone.

Rodrian smiled at me, his power feeling a bit less burdened. He had complete and utter faith that I could help him and Shiloh get through this. And I wanted to— wanted to be near people I loved, people who understood what I myself had been going through since the Sophia decided to manifest itself in me.

I just wasn't sure I was ready for more reminders of what I'd lost. It was just a matter of time before someone would say his name, in that certain context with that certain implication and those scars would reopen all over again.

I soaked up Rodrian's power, basking in the hope he'd found, and did what I did best: I faked it, and hoped no one would notice, and prayed that I could somehow make everyone all better again.

With a smile that I'd practiced in front of a mirror, I set down my glass. "Everything will be just fine."

I gave my pendent one last squeeze in supplication. Heavens forgive me if I'm wrong.

By the time my ten o'clock appointment with the Sophia rolled around, my nerves were jangling like a box of metal hangers. It was probably the Lo-Carb Monsters I drank on the way to her hotel. My hands had developed a noticeable tremor, and I had to tuck them under my arms when I stopped at the reception desk for her room number. Hopefully, I wouldn't develop a kidney stone or be mistaken for a junkie.

Note to self: two energy drinks were pushing my upper tolerance.

A uniformed woman opened the door to the suite, showing me into an opulent sitting room. There wasn't anything presidential about this Presidential Suite, unless by *President* they meant *King of the World*.

The room was an exercise in elegance. Ivory walls, bone-colored carpet, tasteful accents of crystal and brass. Even the high ceiling was a sight to behold—a sculpted molding formed a rectangle that framed the room below. The wall to my left boasted a white marble fireplace, the mantle bearing twin crystal vases of white orchids and green tender shoots. A cheery fire cast its glow onto the arrangement of pristine white furniture arranged around a long glass coffee table.

Two couches faced each other across the low table, one high-backed and high-legged, the other lower and less imperious. It was the sort of arrangement that spoke more about politics than aesthetics. Behind the sofas, three tall windows spanned the far wall, their sumptuous beige drapes pulled completely open to invite the night inside.

The night sky provided more color than anything else in the room. Against the cream and ivory and crystal décor, the windows revealed long panels of purple-black, the color of moonless midnight. Stars hid themselves from city dwellers, replaced by the electric lights of surrounding buildings and far-off bridges. The view was breathtaking, although I usually found all heights a little on the breathtaking side.

I was afraid to sit down, feeling too much like a commoner. This Sophia certainly had expensive taste.

A door on the right opened and a regal woman made her entrance, pausing at the door and surveying the room as if to determine the extent of her audience. Her pale pink woolen suit, with its tasteful black pipe trim and delicate lace collar, only needed a hat to put every First Lady from the last century to utter shame.

She had an air of expectation around her and, when her gaze settled on me, her eyes measured me as if she could see right through me.

"Sophia," she said. More like announced, as if her declaration alone would make it so.

At this point, I didn't know if I should kneel or bow or melt backwards out of the suite altogether. I remembered my posture, tried to look as pleasant as possible, and hoped it would suffice.

"Welcome, Sophia. I am the Sophia Eirene." She pronounced her name *Irene*, her voice rich and cultivated, made velvety by the undercurrent of an Eastern European accent. If voices had color, hers would be jewel-toned: sapphire, garnet, and onyx.

The door opened once more and another woman entered, carrying a silver coffee service. She was the opposite of Eirene; her hair, an indistinct shade of brown, was pulled back in a severe bun and her expression revealed a sturdy sense of gravity. A single glance at her convinced me she knew little of cheer. Although her clothing was functional and unadorned, she, too, had a sense of quiet elegance. Something told me Eirene would not tolerate to be near anything unbefitting of a court.

"Ah, Dorcas. The table there will be fine." Eirene folded her hands before her, looking every bit like the headmistress of a charm school. Dorcas set the tray upon a coffee table. "It is cold and late, Sophia. Coffee will please you?"

"Actually, I can't drink coffee." The meekness in my tone wasn't faked and I glanced apologetically at the silver pot. At her stern glance for my refusal of her gracious hospitality, I added an explanation. "Doctor's orders."

Eirene raised a hand but never moved her eyes from mine.

"A tea service, Dorcas," she said, her tone slightly cooler. The maid disappeared with the offending coffee, and Eirene took a seat on the higher of the two couches, indicating I should sit across from her. "So. Sophia. I am glad we are able to meet. My time in this country is short but I did so want to meet the newest Sophia."

I sat down and smoothed my dress, which now seemed

more flighty than functional, given the ambiance. "Have you been Sophia very long, Eirene?"

"Longer than you can guess." Frankly, I would have guessed she'd manifested in grade school because she looked much younger than I. Her grace and eloquence practically moaned maturity, though. I supposed it was a cultural affectation. Or Clinique. "What is important, however, is not my control over the Sophia Oracle but rather this opportunity to share information and experience."

I gulped and tried to keep from looking crestfallen. Information and experience? I had almost zilch. The only thing she'd learn from me was how to play Sudoku and how to avoid uncomfortable public confrontations with DV on the first day of the month. Somehow, I had the feeling she'd be disappointed in my share.

"My Sophia, em...manifested a little over a year ago," I said. "So my experience is somewhat limited. None of the local DV know enough about the oracle to share information with me."

"DV...Demivampire?" At my nod, she continued. "Not even the Thurzo Clan?"

I felt as though I swallowed a glob of Play-Doh. "Thurzo Clan?"

She stiffened, lifting her chin and narrowing her eyes. "We'll not play games, Sophia. I've looked into you before making contact. You are acquainted with one Marek Thurzo. He is well-known in some circles for having done extensive Sophia research, and he was the Demivampire who discovered you. Is this not true?"

"It is," I said. My suddenly-thumping heart was wrecking my phony composure. I uncrossed my legs and planted both feet to stop my tell-tale foot jiggle. "It's just that he didn't tell me much and I don't see him anymore."

"He has mentioned nothing of the Canons?" She sounded shocked.

I shook my head, feeling quite inadequate, even though I could hardly be blamed for anything Marek failed to disclose. Leave it to me to look villainous when feeling victimized. Briefly I thought about the big book Marek had dumped onto my lap the day he first mentioned the Sophia. Why hadn't I looked at the title page?

Oh, wait. He'd just told me I was an oracle and I was a little flabbergasted, that's why.

"Odd. For someone who has traveled so extensively to my country in search of the Sacred Oracle, one would think he'd have shared it with his pet Sophia."

"I am not his pet." All thoughts of Marek's dusty old book went poof, gone, bye-bye. I couldn't keep the indignation from my tone.

Thankfully, she didn't seem to take offense; rather, she smiled as Dorcas re-entered the room with a fresh tray.

Eirene poured the tea herself and offered me a cup. "That is a relief to hear. I have met other Sophias who had been deceived into believing they owed allegiance to one particular group of Demivampire. I hope you have not been lured into thinking along such lines."

I took the cup gratefully, warming my hands against the porcelain. "No, of course not."

"Excellent." Eirene smiled. "So, will I have the honor of visiting your temple?"

"I'm sorry, I don't go to Temple. I'm Catholic."

She blinked twice. "Your court. Your place of honor, where you grant audience to the Demivampire and offer them counsel."

I was way out of my league. My court? Was that what I was supposed to have? I did just about all things Sophia through the advice column. I had pen-pals, for crying out loud. How could I tell this Sophia my court was nothing more than a five-by-seven cubicle?

"Well," I said, thinking fast. "At one time we held sessions at a private courtroom downtown. However, lately I've been holding fewer face-to-face sessions and participating in more private dealings. Through... correspondence."

She issued a pleased sound. "Ah! I, too, engage in much written correspondence. My land is vast and steeped in tradition. Writing is a personal effort, very desirable for counsel."

I rallied a bit and sat up straighter, sipping at the tea. Not Lipton. Of course not.

"What about your magic?" she asked.

I almost choked on a swallow. This time, I couldn't fake it. My blank stare gave me away.

"Your magic," she repeated. "Your empathy. How many recoveries have you accomplished?"

"I don't understand, Eirene. I know about the empathy part, but...*recoveries?*"

She dropped her hands into her lap and looked away. "How can it be a Sophia doesn't know such basic trivia? It is the premise of the Oracle, straight from the Canons them-selves."

"But I didn't know about the Canons until—"

"Are you sure you are Sophia?" Her shrewd look nearly peeled my skin. "Thurzo may have been mistaken."

"He wasn't wrong." I kept my voice level. "I simply have had no guidance. I've been left to myself to figure this thing out and don't think I'm happy about it."

Eirene sat quietly for a few moments and sipped at her cup.

"You are completely untrained," she said at last.

"Yes, I am." I set my cup down on its saucer, missing its

warmth immediately. "Can you help me? These Canons—can I see them?"

"There is but one known collection of the books and they are incomplete, at that. I've seen them only a scant number of times, as the Circlet travels constantly."

"The who?"

She sighed and clearly fought to maintain a civil expression. "The Circlet of Sophia is a group which services the Sophias. They travel from land to land, since Sophias do not travel well themselves. I put great strain upon my comfort to leave my own lands in order to meet you, even though I console myself that there will at least be some small worth in it."

"Oh." I felt small and utterly incapable. If I hadn't pinned all hope of Marek's redemption on this one woman, I would have made an excuse to use the bathroom and slinked out the door. "The DV never mentioned—"

"They cannot mention that which they do not know. The Circlet is a Sophia matter, unknown to the general masses. They are the keepers of tradition, the enforcers of our order. They have not yet sought you?"

Seeing my head shake in negation, she sighed. "Not promising at all. They know where every Sophia is at all times. Surely, you should have been indoctrinated by now. But never mind. I have a great memory for such matters. I can share what I know with you until we find them."

My spirit soared. "Really? Thanks, I—"

She cut me off with an imperious lift of her hand. "Keep in mind that I am here in your lands for a short time only. I, too, am reluctant to spend time away from my people. I do not wish for any of my moments here to be wasted."

"Of course not."

"Good." She smiled once more, like the sun breaking free of the clouds. She seemed to swing back and forth between royal stiffness and gracious helpfulness. I wasn't sure which face she favored but I fervently hoped it would be the latter. "I have primary business to attend and my correspondence takes precedence to your tutoring. You will accommodate me, of course."

I nodded. I had a distinct impression she would be a royal pain in the ass but I always said beggars couldn't be choosers. Unfortunately, in this case, I felt more like a beggar than ever. "Let me know what works best for you. I really appreciate your time."

"You are most welcome," she purred. "I am sure our meetings will be mutually beneficial."

Rodrian picked me up in his silver Audi TTS the next morning and took me out to The Stocks for a walk-through.

What a harrowing ride. He zipped in and around traffic like a kid playing Pole Position. Sports cars made me nervous, especially ones that weren't designed to do well in high speed crashes.

But his driving wasn't really what was bothering me. All of the weaving in and out of traffic simply added to my apprehension about returning to the last place Marek and I had spent time together as a couple.

Today's venture wasn't intended to be a trip down memory lane. I was supposed to view the property, look at the suites, and get an idea of what I'd do with the place. Rodrian knew I'd only had a limited tour during my brief stay there. I didn't clarify that I'd only seen the gym, the pool, and Marek's bedroom. That sounded trashy no matter the circumstances.

The porch seemed wider than I remembered, the double doors more massive and intimidating, the foyer ceiling higher and colder. I'd half-feared that ghosts of those memories would attack me at the door but, in the late morning light, everything looked different. Younger. Sharper.

Amazing what a different slant of the sun could do. It was like Oil of Olay married Mr. Clean.

I'd also half-expected to see the place full of white-sheeted furniture ghosts but there weren't any of those, either. Rodrian explained the staff kept the house ready so it never had lain completely empty. The thought of mysterious staff living in the same house with me wasn't encouraging, so I settled for pretending I'd be moving into a hotel.

He disarmed the alarm while I glanced around. The only new thing I noticed was a bunch of lilies in a vase upon the side table. Crossing the foyer, he beckoned me to follow him to a set of two enormous pocket doors, which he slid open to reveal a den. A grand fireplace occupied the far wall and an impressive bar had been set up in the front corner. Two couches and a huge armchair made a very casual and inviting group, implying the room had been designed for the enjoyment of company.

The first thing that struck me was the color: red.

Not sultry lipstick red, or Santa suit red, or even Coke bottle red. Earthy red, baked clay red, inside-of-my-eyelids-on-a-spring-morning red. Grounded and substantial.

Thick carpet of short burgundy plush cushioned my feet without sucking them in, and stretched wall to wall in a subtle pattern of dark and light diamonds. Here was a cozy closeness the cold foyer lacked.

Walls of dark paneling stretched toward an unadorned beige ceiling. Wine drapes over sheer ivory curtains matched the chocolate-cherry upholstering of the furniture. Warmth. Comfort. And strangely, food. Appetites would be awakened in here.

Red and lots of it. I'd never been in a red room before but I guessed I couldn't say that anymore.

Back out in the foyer, he pointed to the open archway leading to the dining room and kitchen beyond. "The housekeeper wanted to know if you had any...culinary persuasions."

I tried not to snort. "Ah, not really. Why? I don't have to do KP, do I?"

"No." He sounded relieved. "Bethany likes to be in charge and hoped you didn't have any thoughts about trying to take over."

"You mean she won't let me in there at all? Not even to do dishes?"

Rodrian shoved his hands into his pockets. "Will you be angry if I said no?"

"No. I mean, it's her kitchen, right?" Secretly, I rejoiced. My idea of a three-course meal was a Hot Pocket, Ritz crackers, and Edy's for dessert. "I wouldn't want to cramp her style. I'm sure whatever she does will be fine. If she ever needs anything, of course I'll be glad to help."

"I'll let her know. Now, the lower west wing houses the garage and guest suite..." He opened the deadbolt and swung open the double doors. "You can keep the doors open if you like. It's just habit I keep them locked."

I shrugged my indifference and rubbed my fingers together, glancing over my shoulder at the twin staircases sweeping up toward the second floor, where the living quarters were located. Rodrian cleared his throat, reclaiming my attention. "You can see them later, if you'd like. Why don't we head upstairs?"

The right side of the second floor housed Marek's

private rooms, which took up the majority of the east side of the house. Rodrian tactfully only pointed out the left as he led me upstairs.

The upper wings were separated in the center by a lush private office, similar in shape and size to the den directly below it. Here, too, was a fireplace, clean and dark with disuse but the bar had been replaced by an office nook and the carpeting with gleaming hardwood. A staunch antique desk set sat facing the room while full bookcases lined the walls, forming a picture perfect backdrop for a lawyer's ad.

The desk was in current use, covered with a familiar spread of leather folders and fountain pens. Rodrian confirmed my suspicions with a grin. "You must have me all figured out. I've run the estate affairs from here. My brother didn't come here often in recent years and never used this office, anyway."

I walked to the windows and pushed aside the white curtains, revealing French doors that opened out to a balcony. Pressing my face to the glass and turning my head, I realized the balcony wrapped around behind the fireplace to another French door on the other side.

The balcony overlooked the grounds behind the house. A large stone patio and gazebo took up a large amount of space down to my left, and the rest of the grounds sprawled out into empty field. Beyond the field, some distance off, stood a tall forest, deep with stark trees, presumably black oaks. No other house was in sight.

Having lived in the city for so long, the view amazed me, and I warmed to the prospect of seeing that splendid piece of God every day. It was hard to look away. "I'm kind of partial to my old desk. I could just set it over here by the windows and you could keep yours where it is."

"This is your place now, Soph. You can do whatever you'd like. These records can go back to my office."

"No, really. Just keep it. You'll be here often enough, I imagine, to check on Shiloh and stuff."

"Whatever suits." He shrugged. "It's nice of you to offer. I appreciate it." His voice sounded non-committal but his power was positively glowing.

"Hey," I joked. "*Mi casa es su casa.*"

"No." He rubbed his mouth, expression difficult to read. "It's definitely not my *casa*. So, want to go see the suites now? You can pick any one you want."

He gave me a sidelong glance. "Maybe even decide today?"

"What's the hurry?"

"Shiloh. She's waiting for you to pick your room."

I laughed. "Little eager, huh?"

"There's that." He paused to flip through a few papers on the desk. "Brianda got a call earlier. Her obligations are...pressing. The sooner we get you girls settled, the better."

His tour revealed six separate suites the size of mini-apartments in the left wing. Each suite was decorated in a different shade and had its own sitting room and bath; three of them shared a common area made up of an open den and a kitchenette. I couldn't imagine why Marek, the ultimate loner, would have built a house filled with spare bedrooms.

*Perhaps he built it with dreams of a large family in mind.* I guessed, in Marek's current condition, a family of his own was firmly past consideration. At least with Rodrian's girls moving in, it would seem like part of that dream could be reality.

I'd been determined not to think of him while I was here, trying to reduce his presence to an objective, factual minimum. One simple sympathetic thought was all it took for his essence to take hold. Marek's memory lingered as we concluded the tour of the wing and returned to the top of the staircase.

Catching the briefest scent of leather and sandalwood near the open office door, I peered down the hallway leading to Marek's quarters. The scent was like an invisible touch on my shoulder, holding my attention.

If I had to stay here, I had to face it all now.

Great windows lined the front of the house, designed to let light stream into the hallways of each of the upper wings. On Marek's side the drapes had been drawn, causing the long hall to disappear into uninviting shadows. It seemed like even the light was forbidden access to the abandoned quarters. Determined to stare down my past, I confronted the shadows and headed down the hallway. Rodrian quietly followed behind.

The air felt different in this part of the house and, as I neared the massive door that led to Marek's former chambers, I sensed something else. A stir of air, as if air itself was a living thing. I passed through a spot that felt like a radio between stations. The air buzzed along my skin, bathing me, submerging me, pressing into me with unseen fingers.

The wards. They sizzled along my skin, raising goose bumps all the way up into my scalp, and I held my breath.

Then, just as quickly, the sensation faded. The wards had recognized me and sighed away, granting me permission to continue.

I twisted the heavy latch, an old-fashioned handle high up on the door. The room was dark. Stale air rushed out, a dusty taste with it. I stepped in cautiously, feeling for the light switch.

Everything looked exactly as I had remembered it. I could have been here yesterday. If what Rodrian had implied was true, I was the last person to have been inside this room.

The bar glinted with glass and crystal bottles, empty decorations. It was all for show. It was pretty, though, and I remembered how they sparkled when the colored lights shone behind them. A wide L-shaped couch faced the windows, its matching armchair pushed to the wall.

A thick layer of dust coated the end table. I dragged my finger through it, leaving a streak. The staff didn't come in here to clean.

I walked over to the windows and dragged open the heavy drapes and solid blinds, letting the light spill in. Immediately the room changed, taking on new life. Sunlight had a way of reviving things that had grown stale.

It was a pleasant improvement. In the nonjudgmental sunlight, it was once more a hotel room, a rented space, a borrowed lodging. Shadows of the world made shadows of the heart much deeper. If I had my way, these curtains would never be shut again.

Turning around, I noticed a dusty paper on the bar and picked it up. It bore my handwriting, a note penned on the back of an office memo regarding the Citywide Expo I had attended last year.

I'd spent a long time trying to forget that event. The whole thing was supposed to be a lousy waste of a weekend spent dealing with work. Over the weeks leading up to it, I'd built up a healthy supply of dread and disgust and resentment for the office manager, Donna, who'd hosed me into doing it. The expo was a PR event, and I'm just not a PR person.

Little did I know that stupid expo was the beginning of The Crap That Almost Killed Me. I'd been ambushed by vamps in the parking garage, part of a set-up organized by that jealous vamp slut Donna. They had actually shackled me to a wall. Really. Shackles. In Balaton. It's not like they sell them at Pier 1 Imports.

Closing my eyes, I took a steadying breath. I'd worked desperately to create this sardonic bubble of disdain for the whole thing in order to forget it but once I start thinking about it, I can't stop. I balled my fists, clenched my teeth, willed myself to stop, just stop. *Don't go there.*

But this memory was a landslide. Once I slipped, it was all downhill, swept along with everything I'd felt or known or wished. I remembered Donna, getting her just but cruel desserts. I remembered the Master, the beauty, the voice, the touch inside my head. I remembered Jared, my best friend, my last sight of him a lifeless pile on the floor.

*Don't. Please.*

I remembered Marek, reduced to a seething predator. His eyes a violent emerald fire, his teeth fully bared, his DV power a roil of hate and desire and destruction. When the Master unleashed Marek, he grabbed me. There was nothing of my lover in him. He was cold, alien. He ripped my throat and devoured me. I should have died.

Why didn't I die? I did, I did. Just not all the way.

And I have lived with it every single day since.

So much for not remembering. I brushed the page off to read it.

*Honey, if you get back before me, this is where I'm at. I know you want me to stay here, but if I don't show up, Donna will kill me. I won't be long, I promise. Love, S.*

I stared at it, the letters swelling and blurring, caught between one thought and the dreaded next. He was gone. The Crap That Almost Killed Me pretty much killed Marek, too, because he wasn't Marek anymore. He was a DV on the Brink of Falling. And I wasn't doing anything about it.

"Sophie?" Rodrian's muffled voice startled me out of my reverie. "Are you okay?"

"Yeah," I lied. Crumpling the note, I tossed it into the

trash can behind the bar. "Why are you still out there?"

After a slight hesitation, he cleared his throat. "I didn't want to try the wards."

"Oh." Hmmm. A ponderous thing. "I'll just look around a bit more, if it's okay."

"It's fine. I'll wait downstairs for you." The sound of footsteps retreated down the hall.

Three doors led from the parlor. One opened into a guest half bath, which looked as if it'd never been used. Another revealed a personal library I'd never be able to ignore, no matter how hard I'd try. The third...well, it was Marek's bedroom quarters.

Not his, I reminded myself. These weren't his rooms anymore.

I stood in the doorway, taking it in and facing my ghosts. A four-post king-size bed loomed against the far wall, curtains closed and quiet. The furniture reflected the styles of antiquity Marek had always seemed to prefer. All in all, I have to say I took it quite well, despite having glimpsed my old overnight bag moldering on the bureau.

By the time I made my way back out to the staircase where Rodrian waited, I wore a painted-on smile and had made two decisions.

First, I'd picked my rooms and second, that bed would have to go.

Once Rodrian accepted my decision, it didn't take long for Shiloh to settle in. By the time the movers pulled up to the doors with my belongings a week later, Shiloh had already made herself at home and was putting the kitchen staff to rigorous use. She met me at the door in a whirlwind of hugs and chatter and swept me up the stairs toward the tri-suites where she and her sister had settled.

The tri-suites reminded me of the dorm I'd lived in during college. Okay, so maybe we didn't have a thirty six-inch widescreen plasma television or a Bose sound system. Still, close enough. If someone hung up a poster proclaiming that everything I needed to know I'd learned on *Star Trek*, it would be sophomore year all over again.

Shiloh must have unpacked like the Furies hounded her because it looked as if she'd been here for years instead of days.

"How'd you get it all moved in so fast?" I plucked a throw pillow off the futon and fluffed it. "You haven't been skipping school, have you?"

"I tried," she said. "But Dad's a truant officer. He really believes in the existence of the Permanent Record." She rolled the inner bag shut in a box of Cheez-Its and tucked the lid flap closed. "He's the one who took care of getting it all done."

"Wow. He does have a sense for design, after all."

"Hardly. He just did what he always does when there's real work to be done. He cheats."

Figured. He was such a brat. "Cheats? You mean...uses his talents?"

"No," Rodrian said from the doorway. "I delegate the work."

I almost jumped. The way the DV could just sneak up on you drove me nuts.

"Lazy," I said.

"Resourceful." He wiped his upper lip with the back of his hand. "Sophie, when you're done, come downstairs, please?"

"Okay." Neither his expression nor his power gave me a hint. "I'll be down soon."

As I turned back to Shiloh, I glanced into the open bedrooms. Only Shiloh seemed to have unpacked—one bedroom was still empty and the middle was full of sealed boxes. "Is Brianda here?"

"Not yet," Shiloh said. "Her stuff is here but I don't know when she'll actually show up. She's busy with Uncle Marek again. She'll come home sooner or later." Shiloh grabbed my hand and tugged me into the efficiency kitchen just beyond the common room, dropping the cracker box on the counter. "And look! Bethany said if I promise to stay out of the big kitchen downstairs, she'd keep the fridge stocked up here. Oh..."

She sighed blissfully and stroked the microwave with a

tender touch. "I love this microwave. It's got two popcorn settings and there's a bacon tray up here and..."

Eventually I extracted myself from her jubilation and headed downstairs to see what Rodrian wanted. I paused to watch two men bringing my desk upstairs. Sobering to realize I'd been able to pack my entire life into a U-Haul.

When they reached the top of the stairs, I recognized Greco, one of Rodrian's security guards. *Security guard* might be too timid a term. Rodrian's force was more like a SWAT team. I called them his "muscle" and other various terms of endearment. They were good guys.

For the most part, anyway. Andre Caen, Cordula's manager and all-around Mr. Bad Time, was definitely not one of the guys. Could be why I didn't see Caen getting his hands dirty carrying in my boxes. I still couldn't figure out why Rodrian gave him so much authority, why he made Caen his right-hand man. Maybe their shared history made up for Caen's lousy personality.

Gian Greco was head of security and he took his job very seriously. On the job, he was prepared for anything. He was fond of saying something bad happening was a matter of when, not if. I found his lack of optimism annoying but always felt safer when he was around.

Off the job, I almost didn't recognize him. Today he wasn't wearing his holster or thick black vest, deceivingly tailored to look more like Old Navy than Navy Seal. Clad in a long sleeved Ed Hardy t-shirt and jeans with a pair of metallic-glazed wraparound sunglasses on the back of his neck, he looked like just about any other shaved head in Balaton.

Until he turned around. His five foot ten stature might not look overpowering but the wit and intelligence of his eyes let everyone know exactly what they were up against. No matter the situation, he'd already considered each possibility ten steps in every direction. He was never surprised. As a result, he was never bested.

Greco's eyes lit with a flash of dark gray recognition when he saw me, more or less the DV equivalent of "hey" and a wave.

"Oh, no." I grinned. "You've been demoted."

"Not really. I consider it weight training. You really made the most of every box." He said something to the other mover and they set down the desk. Slapping his hands against his thighs, he leaned on the rail and took a breather, although he looked anything but winded.

His hands rested on his hips, a stance he favored when he wore his Kevlar vest. Body armor had a way of changing simple habits, like how to position one's arms comfortably. "How've you been?"

"Better, now," I said. "It's a relief to be here."

His eyes went on-duty; Greco looked at me with the intensity of a hawk, dark-eyed and piercing. "Relief? Why? What's been going on?"

I realized I said the wrong thing to a security man. This probably wasn't the time to discuss the wolf that had been chasing me so I thought fast. "I just meant the packing and waiting. You know. The whole temporarily homeless thing."

His intensity dropped a notch as he grinned. "I've moved around myself. I know what you mean. Living out of boxes for the first week is a real pain."

"The first week? Try the last three months." I scanned the foyer but didn't see Rodrian. "Are they all done?"

"There's still furniture on the truck. I better get this inside."

I thanked him and headed down. It was turning out to be a family reunion, of sorts. Well, almost. I didn't suppose the head of the family would be playing guest of honor anytime soon.

Rodrian stood outside, talking with one of the movers. They wore discouraged expressions and did a lot of head-shaking.

"What's wrong?" Squinting in the bright sun, I lingered in the doorway and peered into to the open bay of the truck. As far as I could see, only my bedroom things remained.

Rodrian excused himself and the mover headed back onto to the truck. He placed his hand on my back and urged me back inside, away from the chilly wind. I hadn't removed my coat yet but Rodrian only wore a sweatshirt and jeans. I didn't know he did manual labor.

I also didn't know it was possible to make a sweatshirt look like it belonged in a Calvin Klein ad but Rodrian's body had a certain talent in making everything he wore look bedroom-eyed sexy. "There's a little problem. The wards upstairs...they're pretty strong."

I blinked and focused on his face, trying to pay attention. "Yeah?"

"The movers can't cross them."

"Oh." Good to know the wards were picky. I felt safer knowing they actually worked. "Is that a problem?"

"They can't get your bed inside...or take the old one out."

"Oh." I hadn't expected that. "Are they sure?"

I glanced out at the men, who looked like they'd recently experienced something ugly. Maybe one of them tried to move Euphrates' pet carrier. I shuddered before remembering the cat was locked safely in the bathroom upstairs.

"Yeah," Rodrian said. "What do you want them to do? Do you want to pick another room?"

"No," I said. "I'll figure something out. For now, can we

put my bed downstairs in the guest suite?"

He nodded. "The boxes, too?"

"No, upstairs in the hall, if they don't mind."

"Okay." Rodrian nodded before turning back to the movers. "Joe, can you come in here?"

He strode to the door, leaving me alone in the bright foyer to contemplate both this unwelcome development and the expression he'd worn as he turned away from me.

By suppertime, Greco and the moving crew had gone and Bethany, the housekeeper, called us into the dining room for a feast—baked ham, real mashed potatoes, even yams with cinnamon and brown sugar. I got the impression it was more to establish herself as rightful owner of the kitchen than to feed us poor waifs, but who cared? The woman cooked like my grandma.

Shiloh alternately devoured dinner and chattered like an eight-year-old on Tang. I hadn't seen very much of her over the past year and, as usual, there was a world full of news to catch up on. I finished eating before she'd come close to finishing speaking.

"The move went well," Rodrian said when Shiloh finally paused for breath.

I agreed and reached for another roll. "I didn't think it would happen so fast. The last few times I moved, it was a nightmare. A recurring one."

I briefly thought about the Were who'd been pursuing me. Every time I moved, he managed to find me. No matter how safe I thought I'd be in a new place, I'd spot him on a corner or near a doorway or walking down the other side of the street and *poof!* So long security.

Well, the nightmare was over. He'd never find me out here and, if he did, he wouldn't last long. Maybe the house guard kept Dobermans. If I yelled "release the hounds" would they go after one of their own?

"Perhaps you're done for a while," Rodrian said.

"Hope so. I'm getting too old for this." I used my napkin and pushed from the table, gathering up my dishes. "I've got a couple boxes of necessities to go through. I'll give you some daddy-daughter time."

Bethany sailed in and shooed me away, claiming all rights to anything of the kitchen domain, messes included. She did, however, nod toward the foyer, where my kitchen boxes (all two of them) still sat, looking like the last puppies at the pound and reassured me the staff had the place under control. I got the point.

Fine by me, I thought. I was more demand than supply, anyway. Now I was comfortably full of the proof that Bethany had meant every word she'd said. Harboring not the slightest grudge, I lugged the boxes upstairs to Shiloh's suite, thinking the kitchenette was more my speed.

"Let me." Rodrian caught up to me on the stairs and tugged them out of my arms, Shiloh following close behind. "You should have left these for me to bring up."

I frowned but didn't put much effort into it. I was never a tremendous fan of lugging boxes around. "I'm not helpless."

"I know. But it's okay to delegate."

Once in the suite, Shiloh flipped open the top box. "What's this?"

"Stuff from my old apartment."

She pulled out a ceramic wall plaque, a pale blue tea pot bearing the letters *WWMD?* that was a throw-back to my single and long-abandoned attempt at playing happy homemaker. "Do we have to use all of it?"

"No." I slipped it out of her hand and cradled it to my chest while Rodrian set the boxes on the snack bar. "If you don't need any of this, leave it in the box and I'll take it to the garage."

"Okay." She grinned, toothy and bright. "You should move into the third room so we can be real roommates."

I laughed at her eagerness. "How about I just sleep over on late nights?"

"Deal." Her cell rang, a sudden blast of hip-hop remix, and she peered at the screen. "Ooh, it's Luke. Later."

She disappeared into her room, closing the door with a subtle variation of her signature teeth-rattling *bang*. Luke was her big crush and almost-boyfriend. I remembered seventeen so I couldn't take her abrupt dismissal personally. He was the priority, not family or me or anyone else she could count on as solid parts of her life.

"The wards giving you any trouble?" Rodrian pushed one of the boxes away from the edge and leaned against the counter.

"No," I said. "Honestly, I don't even feel them."

"They're old. Really old. Still as powerful as they ever were."

"I meant to say something earlier," I said. "Nice wards at your office."

He didn't outwardly register the compliment, although his power did a small manly kind of grunt. "I've been practicing. I hadn't really needed those skills before."

"Is business getting dangerous?"

"No, not that. I never had to do them myself before. Marek did all the warding." It was my turn not to register a reaction at the sound of his brother's name but it was a lot harder than concealing pride. "I decided it was time to renew my skills. Could you tell they were mine?"

I nodded.

"Damn." He flashed an irritated grin and scratched at his temple, tousling his hair. "I still can't get the knack of removing my essence at the end."

"Do you have to?"

"It helps, especially with security wards. If someone's looking for me, they more or less point the way."

"I guess it's a DV thing, huh? The ability, I mean."

"I don't know," he said. "I don't have a human perspective. I'm not sure what you can or can't do in the first place." He cocked his head at me and flashed a grin. "Well, you, I have a pretty good idea. Still. Warding is an extension of compelling. Humans don't seem able to compel, so I assume they can't ward, either."

Skunked again. How did I keep ending up on the short end of the evolutionary stick? First fair skin, now this. "Maybe the Sophia can help out. Can you set a ward and explain it while you're doing it? I'll watch and see if I can offer a suggestion."

"Why not?" He glanced around, expression set in concentration. "Let's go downstairs. I know just the room."

Once inside the den, Rodrian started the fireplace and made sure a fast fire was blazing before moving to the center of the room. "The process of setting a ward is pretty straightforward. First I choose a target. We can ward the entire room, or just a part of it. I guess as far as lessons go, bigger would be better."

I moved a pillow and flopped onto the couch. Now, this one was comfy. The fluffy back felt like I was snuggled against a pile of pillows. "That's what I've always said."

"I was hoping you would." He dropped the academic veneer and leered at me. "I'll try not to disappoint."

"Just try to get the job done, buddy."

"Right. Second, we need an intent. One of the main uses of a ward is to add a layer of security. Since the home is secure, we can try a simple confidentiality ward."

"That sounds like a lawyer thing."

"Not really, although you won't find many DV attorney offices without them. A confidentiality ward keeps things private. No one can hear through a closed door."

"Hmm," I said. "Good for secrets."

Rodrian looked down at me, eyes piercing and copper bright. Wow, that caught his interest, even though it had been completely unintentional.

I shrugged to defuse him. "Not that I have any. Maybe one day I'll want one, so it would be good to have a room to keep it in."

Seeming satisfied, he resumed his lecture. "So. We have a target and an intent. Now we set the intensity. It screens people, more or less. We'll tune it to you, since it's your house, and to me, since I'm setting it. Hence, the ward will keep anything you or I say or do to ourselves."

I thought it over. "I wouldn't mind having someplace to speak with you in private. It's not like I can take you upstairs."

"You know..." His eyebrows lifted with mischief. "It takes much restraint not to run with that."

Oh, my God, he was relentless. "Please try."

"No fun. Shall we begin the ward?"

"Good a time as ever. Let me get ready." I closed my eyes and sank into myself, giving the Sophia a little nudge. Using mental fingers, I traced the edges of Rodrian's power, enticing the Sophia to respond. It did, albeit in a sleepy, offhanded manner.

I was a little disappointed by the lackluster response. Maybe the Sophia needed real reason to come out and play. Eyes still closed, I pushed farther into his power, past the outermost announcing layer to the personal core beneath.

He felt my touch and slipped a stream of eager surprise, his quicksilver spurt of emotion giving me the jolt I needed for a Sophia supercharge. The oracle shuddered through me as she took hold. Connection established, I opened my eyes and gave him a glimpse of Oracle blue.

He saw it. Had to tear his eyes away from it. Voice quiet, he sounded determined to focus on the task ahead. "Let's do it."

Rodrian circled the room, spiraling toward the walls as he paced. "A ward is only an extension of the common compulsion. See, compulsions affect living beings. Wards, on the other hand, only affect inanimate objects."

I wiggled to a more comfortable position, enjoying the rare treat of an actual info-share. Rodrian's main talents were acting bossy and making money—until now, I hadn't realized he could give such good oration. Guess it only seemed natural he'd pick up the skill after listening to Marek for so long.

"A compulsion is no more than a touch of power with the force of my will behind it," he continued. "It works only as long as the power stream is maintained, since a living being has a life force and a will of its own. Without constant contact, the target's will can break the suggestion and resume thinking for itself."

I cleared my throat delicately.

"Herself," he amended. His expanding path brought him to the edges of the walls, and he slowed his pace, lifting his arm, hand parallel to the wall. "An object, on the other hand, has no memory and no will of its own. A touch of power leaves a residue that continues to exert a force after contact is broken. Are you following any of this?"

"I think so. Your power is like slime and you sling it around the place."

"That's—disgusting."

"You said it."

He stopped his circuit and crossed his arms at me. "This is serious."

"Look, pal. You drink blood, okay, and you know where I stand on that. Now you tell me you fling your power around and leave residues. It doesn't paint a pretty picture."

All of a sudden, Mr. Flirty McJokesalot was all business. He leveled a no-nonsense look at me that made me want to duck. "Can you be a little more clinical? You're supposed to be using the Sophia to figure out what I'm doing wrong."

"Oops." I hung my head, trying not to laugh. "Forgot, sorry. Okay. The residue continues to work after you separate from it."

"Yes. I place the power like this." He resumed his walk, lifting his hands and spreading his fingers. "I don't need to use my hands but I want to show you how I mentally direct my power over the surface of the target."

He circled the room, paying careful attention to windows and air vents and, finally, the closed doors. "I send my power up along the ceiling and down over the floor. The fire is energy, too, and it disperses the power up the chimney. This way, the room will be encapsulated."

Honestly, it only looked like he was waving his hands. I couldn't "see" anything.

But his power—I felt it in every pore of my skin. The Sophia perked up while Rodrian spread himself around the room, sensing the steady flow of DV power. I felt it swell inside my head, shifting my vision, dripping its cool manifestation down over me, chills and fog together. The Sophia filled my head, my body, my entire being, hungry for the touch of Demivampire power unleashed.

The Oracle took over.

All I could feel was Rodrian. Never before had I felt so much of him, all at once. The Sophia was submerged, my senses swelling, engorging themselves on his essence. Unaccustomed to such a vehement reaction, I grew alarmed.

I tried to draw my empathy back but it wouldn't be reined in. Alarm turned to panic. I breathed Rodrian's power. I tasted it. I drifted and spun and swam through it. Everything turned blue, the blue eyes of the Sophia, and I was lost in the slurry of his demivampiric power.

Rodrian's voice faded.

I couldn't breathe.

Trapped.

Terror.

The slurry solidified, pressing down like a violent change in air pressure. Blurry whiteness crept around the edges of my vision and the ceiling lifted, walls stretched impossibly long. Muffled pounding in my ears, like a cotton-wrapped clock. Breath wouldn't come. I grew light-headed, the white spreading.

Rodrian's face peered through the peephole at the end of my vision.

Gone.

My head thumped a thick rhythm as the room faded back in.

"Gods, Sophie. You scared hell out of me."

I cracked my eyelids, feeling couch beneath me and seeing Rodrian hovering like a nervous bird. No more passing-out white. No Sophia blue. No power. Just room and a concerned face.

"What happened?" I tried to sit up, but a silver streak of headache anchored me to the cushion. I sank back and closed my eyes, groaning. "What did you do?"

"I set the ward. You collapsed as I finished. What were you doing?"

"Dunno." When I rolled my head, it swam like a concussion. "I let the Sophia out and it went ape-shit. So much power. Where did it all go?"

"Into a new form." He sighed and reached to smooth my hair back. "I guess you missed it. Ah, well. I won't risk setting another ward like that around you."

"So the ward is there?"

"You can't feel it, can you?"

I pushed up, swallowing the ebb of nausea that bobbed behind the tide of looming migraine. He steadied me, helping me sit up against the back of the couch. "I can't feel anything but, then again, it hurts to try. I'll have to check it later."

"But you don't feel me anymore, do you?" He sounded hopeful.

"Not even with you standing a foot away." I groaned. "You broke my Sophia."

"That sounds so dirty." He grinned, full of adolescent appreciation at my ability to say something so provocative.

I wanted to hit him. "Ugh. Not now."

He squatted in front of me, peering up into my face while I shielded my eyes, holding my forehead in place. Slowly the pain receded, dull booms like noisy upstairs neighbors fading. Stomach settling. Breathing easier. I stretched a wan smile at his distressed expression.

"You okay?" He reached up and stroked the side of my face, concern and amber glints deep in his eyes.

I nodded and didn't barf. Good sign. "I'm fine."

"Okay." He breathed deeply and stood. "Look, I'm going to say goodnight to Shiloh. It's after eight and I wanted to stop in at Cordula's tonight. Need to sign off on a few things."

I didn't quite believe the last part. He seemed uneasy, and I suspected he wanted to find one of his blood dates. But, I didn't call him on the fib because it really wasn't my business.

Didn't have much time to dwell on how he spent his free time, anyway. I still had to unpack my closet. Testing my feet and finding my headache had faded to bearable levels,

I leaned and pulled him in a friendly one-armed hug, careful to press more shoulder to him than frontage. The smell of cherry and cologne still lingered and I inhaled his scent—not meaning to do so but unable to help it.

"Thanks, Rode." I'd sleep like the dead tonight, without the worry of actually getting dead. "Don't worry about the ward thing. We'll figure out a way to work together without blowing my head off."

He patted my arm. "You're a trooper, Soph. I'll call you."

Before I went upstairs, I stopped in the dining room, where Bethany was gathering up the tablecloth. An extra *thank you for the wonderful meal* earned me an invitation to sit and have a slice of cake. With mocha fudge frosting. I felt like a kid on her birthday.

I licked a finger and smiled. "I think I adore you, Bethany."

"Don't you worry, young miss," Bethany said. She flipped the tablecloth with an imperious snap and folded the square over her arm. "I've got all things covered down here. You've no need to worry. You'll see I'm more than capable of handling this house."

She looked around the room and sighed a contented sigh. "It's been my little kingdom for a long time. I pride myself in taking care of the ones who live here. It's nice to have charges again."

I smiled, feeling uncomfortably shy around the stern-faced woman, now that the lines of authority were softened and her maternal side shone through. I could handle iron-handed *hausfrau*. Softer was, somehow, harder.

A gentle Bethany reminded me of my Aunt Marie, whom I hadn't seen in a long time. My Aunt Marie was all the family I had left. Somewhere. I hoped so, anyway, and left it at that. I didn't need to deal with old issues with so many new ones piling up in the inbox.

"Thanks, Bethany. I like...being taken care of. It's a nice feeling. One I haven't felt in a long time."

"Well." She gathered the stack of napkins and hooked the napkin rings onto her index finger. "You'll never find any shortage of it here. No matter what walks through that door, if it's trouble, old Bethany will see to it. Good night."

She left me in the dining room, alone with the now-bare table and empty chairs, puzzled by her words and the sense of foreboding they stirred inside me.

I decided to head up to Shiloh's room to shake off the weird feeling. If anyone could provide a distraction, it'd be my new housemate. I hadn't had a chance to visit with her in a long time and I'd missed the girl.

I remembered her shoe and handbag fetish, too, so hopefully I could visit her closet. I needed a good closet tour to set me back to rights.

She was busy in the kitchenette when I got to the tri-suites. A pot bubbled on the stove and I sniffed the air. "Whatcha making?"

"Ramen." She yanked open the fridge and pulled out a bottle of ginger sauce. "Want some? I made extra."

"No, thanks. I'm okay. Still a big eater, huh?" She was taller, now, but still slender. "I don't know where you put it all."

"Meh. I have a fast metabolism." She shut off the stove and drained the noodles, shaking a liberal amount of sauce into the bowl. Grabbing a pair of chopsticks, she took her things over to the snack bar. "Hit the Keurig, will you? Dad said you don't drink coffee so there's tea in the cupboard. Earl Gray and junk."

I turned on the machine before sitting down next to her at the bar. "So, how have you been?"

She shrugged and finished chewing. "Okay, I guess.

School is stupid. I have a boyfriend, though, so at least that gives me something to do while I'm there." She grinned.

I knew better that to believe she was slacking off. Shiloh was a dedicated student who kept a four point zero with seemingly little effort.

"And...?"

"And...I got a new Coach for my birthday. It's pink. You'd love it."

I shook my head. "I mean, how are you? I mean how have you been feeling?"

She wrinkled her nose. "Fine, I guess. Oh, no. You didn't go back to nursing, did you? I don't want to be your guinea pig."

"No, Shy, not that. I'm just...concerned. You look tired."

"Duh. We moved today." She picked up several long noodles and held them over her upturned mouth, dropping them in like curly worms to a baby bird.

I huffed out a breath. "Fine, I'll just spit it out. What's going on with you? Your dad said you were feeling a little off."

"Oh. That. Yeah, well. I'm a cripple, apparently. Dad says I have to get hypolution treatments. Big deal. I don't see what the rush is."

I sagged my shoulders, relieved. "So you're not deathly ill? Your dad had me worried."

"Well, stop worrying." She downed the last of the ramen and carried her dishes to the sink. "Tea?"

When I nodded, she popped a K-Cup into the brewer and placed a big mug under it. The smell of Earl Gray instantly filled the little kitchen. Not bad. If it tasted as good as it smelled, I might be in good shape.

I really had grown sick of tea bags. They tasted like trips to my Aunt Marie's house—plenty of cream and sugar never quite improved the astringency of her tea. It tasted like proper old lady stuff. As a result, I'd declared myself allergic to Lipton's. "So, what's the deal with these treatments?"

"Beats me," she said. "I don't even know why I have to get them. I feel fine."

"But your dad—"

"That man overreacts to everything." She groaned and started another cup at the Keurig. "Honestly, he is so over-protective. I was just fine living with Brianda. She took perfect care of me. But now dad took over because Bree had to go off somewhere and all of a sudden he's mother henning me to death. So, I didn't cusp yet. Big deal."

"He made it sound like you're going to get sick if you don't cusp—"

She smacked her hands down on the countertop, her back still toward me. "I'm not ready for this particular conversation right now."

I chewed my lip. Her tone was taking on an edge I wasn't familiar with. Teenage cocky, I guess. I didn't have much experience with something like that. Better play it safe and not say anything that might set that tone off again. "Well, whatever. At least we get to see each other more. It'll be fun."

She brought her cup over to the snack bar and squeezed my hand. "I missed you, Sophie. Dad should never have kept us away from you."

I smiled back, caught off guard by the gentleness of her voice. It caught something in the back of my throat. I nodded. "Well. Things can be made right now."

"Except for Uncle Marek." She sipped her hot chocolate. "I wish he could be here, too. I miss him, and I miss you and him together. I wish there was a way to bring him back here, so we could be a family again. I just want him to come back."

I didn't know how to respond. I wanted what she wanted. Difference was, I had a secret. Maybe Eirene could bring him back. It just wasn't fair to get the poor kid's hopes up.

Her phone rang, rattling upon the counter top. She tapped the screen and leaned toward it. "Hang on."

Looking at me, she hung her head. "Can I talk to you later?"

I took my tea back to my rooms. Thank goodness for cell phone interruptions. I didn't need to be an empath to understand her frustration. I wasn't ready to have that particular conversation, myself.

My first night in Marek's room was a complete nightmare.

I tried to give it a chance. I changed the sheets, I opened the bed curtains all the way, and I emptied an entire bottle of fabric deodorizer into the room, turning the ceiling fan on high to get everything to dry. The bureau and wardrobe were empty, so I put my favorite sachets into every space. Remembering my teasing conversation with Rodrian regarding skeletons in the closet, I didn't open the one in the bedroom.

That closet could stay shut for now. I figured, one surprise at a time.

Even though the bed smelled like a lavender cloud, I could still detect Marek's scent. Leather and sandalwood. It was there beneath the fragrances in which I'd drowned the room, lurking like a constant reminder. I didn't know if it was just my mind insisting it was there, exaggerating a tiny wisp of scent. Didn't matter.

I lay awake all night long, restless upon the unfamiliar mattress, feeling contained by the big four poster bed. Memories of our last night haunted me and I replayed the events over and over in my mind. The motorcycle ride. The dunk in the pool. The love we'd made in this very bed. The thoughts kept tumbling around my head like socks in a dryer.

Exhausted as I was, I couldn't fall all the way to sleep until early in the morning. When I slept, I dreamed.

Marek, here, next to me, a presence, at first. A voice. A sensation of heat lying beside me. He spoke to me, nonsense words of comfort and love. I didn't know I was dreaming—I was too exhausted for lucidity. Caught up in the dream, I reached for him. It was our last night together, all over again.

He slid his hand over my bare stomach, wrapping around my side, tugging me, pulling me against him. I melted against his skin, the heat and the muscle so familiar. Lost in his scent. His breath against my neck, he murmured my name, a rumble of bass notes.

"Love me," I whispered.

And he did.

For the length of one precious dream, I was in the arms of the man I loved, allowing him to strip away all my doubts and my grief and he loved me the way he had before. I cried out, I nearly wept. Every emotion I'd swallowed and denied for the last year surged up and out, freeing me. I was loved.

Marek loved me and he consumed me and we reached completion. Every muscle in my body throbbed with longing to stay in that moment forever.

But then, the dream changed. Marek grew chilled, cold to the touch, and I realized he'd become a stranger. He drew back and lay facing away from me, at the edge of the bed. His breathing was low and ragged. Marek sounded like he was in pain.

I reached out a hand to stroke his skin. The coldness of his shoulder made me snatch my hand away. Fingers of fear crept along my spine and I shivered.

He rolled unto his stomach and propped himself up on his elbows, hair hanging over his face like a shroud. I pushed his heavy silken mane back over his shoulder, peering through the shadow at his profile: his proud nose, his sculpted mouth, his high cheekbones, his closed eyes spreading lush black lashes against his pale cheeks.

Marek turned his head toward me and opened his eyes. They glowed pale green, like icy mint, not at all the warm emerald they used to be. The color in his eyes had started to fade, just as his grip on his soul was slipping. He was Brinking.

He would Fall if I didn't do something. What could I do? Would love be enough? Would the Sophia be enough?

"Love me," I whispered, my heart splitting with grief and the desperate desire to bring him back.

"Oh, I will." He leered, sharp canines slipping free of his smile. "But you are not going to enjoy it."

He opened his mouth and grabbed me, dragging me beneath him. His mouth, his snarl, his teeth descended and he took my throat. All of my grief and longing and despair, all of those awful things from which I thought I'd been freed—all of it came rushing back, filling me, drowning me, suffocating me.

I was finished.

I woke up, a scream in my throat, too scared to release it, afraid he'd hear me and come back. I couldn't escape the memory of the glow of pale eyes. They burned on my eyelids whenever I blinked, like a retinal afterimage.

Grabbing my blanket and pillow, I slid off the bed and plodded out to the couch. It was a lot easier to sleep out in the parlor.

Dreamless sleep graced me the rest of the morning, making me think I might have to buy a sleeper sofa.

Marek's spectre could sleep in there by himself until he learned to behave.

It didn't take very long for me to adapt to my new surroundings. I didn't even mind living outside the downtown area, where I took the bus or walked when the weather was pleasant. However, living outside the metro area meant I had to drive to work every day. The driving part was a mixed bag, though. The last twenty minutes of my new commute home were pleasant and usually made up for the first thirty.

But the city driving—ugh. I hated driving in rush hour traffic. People did stupid things with their cars.

At least I arrived home in a good mood. On the flip side, I usually walked into work ready to breathe fire, fighting to unclench my teeth and to stop reliving all the flashes of what I wanted to do to some particular driver had there been no laws against dismemberment.

Technically, I could probably have solved the whole morning drive issue by getting up a lot earlier and leaving for work before traffic got heavy. But that would have been ridiculous. Me, give up sleep? Hell to the no.

The commute did have a redeeming quality, however: parking in the garage adjacent to *The Mag*'s building. I'd called the office about leasing a spot after I had my meeting with Rodrian but the gruff manager told me that not only were the spots *extremely* expensive but there was also an *extremely* long waiting list.

Stupid adverbs and the mean way people emphasized them.

One little phone call to Rodrian took care of everything, though, because for some unknown reason I soon got whisked to the top of the list. The same manager delivered my parking pass personally and told me that I was only twenty feet from the elevator on *The Mag*'s side. The Pope couldn't park any closer and not just because the Pope Mobile was too big for a compact spot.

The whole thing made me furious; I wouldn't have gotten it without Rodrian's help. However, my indignation completely dissolved the first day I drove out of the garage to go home. For the first time in months I didn't have to run away from that wolf-eyed bastard, and I sang along to my favorite CD all the way home.

Dropping my keys on the narrow table inside the foyer, I hollered. "Anybody home?"

"In here." Rodrian's voice called from the den. The doors were wide open and I could see the fireplace blazing.

I could get used to this, I thought. Feels like coming home already.

Maybe not, I amended as I came in. Rodrian sat on the couch, wearing a concerned face as Shiloh hunched sullenly next to him. Mascara made grey streaks under her reddened eyes, her pink nose hinting at recent crying.

I sat down next to her and patted her leg. "What's the matter? You okay, honey?"

"Just spiffy." Her stuffy nose made her voice sound thick. "If I was any better, I'd be twins."

"Shiloh had trouble after school today." Rodrian slid his arm around her shoulder and gave her a bolstering hug.

"What kind of trouble?" I searched Shiloh's face for a hint but she wouldn't look at me.

"Oh, you know," she said. "The usual *hey-look-a-wimpy-DV-chick* kind of trouble. I couldn't be normal, could I? Oh, no. I have to be a completely helpless dork whose uncle is the most hated guy in the world."

"What?" I shook my head at Rodrian, hoping for an explanation.

"Shiloh was followed after school. She thinks they might have been Weres."

"And they said that about Marek?"

"No," she said. "That's what the people who pretend to be my friends say. He betrayed all of us by throwing in with the vampires. They say I'm not DV either and God punished me for what Uncle Marek did."

I stifled an angry F bomb, not wanting to curse in front of her. "Jerks! Tell them to go float."

"Oh yeah," she sneered. "Me tell them. They're all cusped already. My whole class and half the juniors, too. All they do is tease me and use compulsions to make a jerk out of me, because they know I can't fight back."

Bullying made my blood boil, especially when the target was a sweet kid like Shiloh. "Brass knuckles ought to help."

"Sure. Me with brass knuckles. Know what Luke said? I'm the most non-threatening person he knows. He said that if I ran at him with a knife, he'd just say, 'Aw, that's cute, Shy, now give me that before you hurt yourself.'" Her voice wavered towards tears and she pressed her face into Rodrian's chest.

"This has been going on for a while, then, huh?"

"Since..." She sniffed, her nose stubbornly refusing to cooperate. "Since Spring. Tess cusped in February and every-one else did before school let out."

"You're not that far behind then, sweetie. Is she?" I looked over her head at Rodrian.

"It's, ah...a gradual process. Most of them started showing signs when Shy was fifteen. She hasn't even started yet."

"I'm right here!" Shiloh punched the pillow on her lap. "Don't talk about me like I'm not here. Maybe I'm not much but I'm still a person!"

"Oh, no," I said. "Honey, we didn't mean—"

"No one ever does. That's the problem!" Shiloh pushed to her feet and ran out, pounding up the stairs to her room. The door slammed and echoed like a boom of winter thunder.

"Okay," I said slowly. "What was that all about?"

"She's really upset. Her friends have been rather insensitive for a while now but being followed today really brought things to a head."

After school, he explained, she'd gone to the mall downtown, where she noticed a group of guys lurking nearby. They followed outside when she left. They never said anything or tried to touch her but by the time she'd gotten to Cordula's she was terrified.

"Were they Were?" My skin crawled as I sympathized, all too familiar with the dread.

Rodrian shook his head. "She can't tell the difference yet. It's an instinct that comes with the cusp."

"Crap, that's awful. Poor kid. I know what she's going through."

He raised his eyebrows. "You do?"

I decided now would be the best time to tell him, now that the problem was solved.

"Didn't I tell you?" I lightened my voice. "Before I moved out here, I got chased after work on a regular basis. I think I shook him now, though. I don't come out through the foyer anymore since I started parking next door."

Rodrian looked as if my news had pushed him over the line between concerned father and protective barbarian. "Why didn't you say something sooner? I'd have given you a guard! We could have gotten him!"

"Rode..." I shook my head. "It went on for weeks, long before I got your letter."

His anger faded into a puzzled look. "But why didn't you call me?"

I shrugged and looked away. "Same reason why you didn't call me, I guess."

"Aw, Sophie..." His voice was a strained combination of worry and frustration. "All that time... you were in trouble and I was too self-consumed to notice."

He scooted closer and wrapped me in a hug. "I'll always take care of you, Sophie, I promise. And you must promise to tell me everything. Are you being followed now?"

I shook my head and made a small negative sound. I'd closed my eyes and rested my chin on his shoulder. The simple touch made me feel valuable again, reaffirmed, validated.

"Okay. The first sign of trouble, you call me." He released me, stroking my shoulders as he pulled away. His eyes gently warmed with his hazel glow. "You mean too much to me. I don't want anything to happen to you."

"Thanks, Rode," I whispered. A small tear moistened the laugh lines I'd managed to develop, despite not having laughed much lately. "It means a lot."

"It's not nearly what you deserve. Not even close." He rose hastily and rubbed his palms down over his pant legs. "I'm going to check in on her before I go. Caen is pulling up the bistro's surveillance and I told him I'd be back to review it. Can you handle her tonight?"

"We'll be fine," I assured him. Dahlia planned on coming over to watch a movie. She'd provide the perfect distraction. "Kisses to Caen."

"How about, *no*? He'd only take it the wrong way."

"He should, the bastard."

"There you go, getting all sentimental again." He stooped to kiss me on the cheek. "I'll see you tomorrow."

I heard his dress shoes tapping on the tiled stairs and listened as his steps faded down the hall. After a few moments, I got up and headed upstairs to change. No one saw me lay my hand over my cheek, hiding the blush that warmed it.

Dahlia arrived soon after Rodrian went back to town and I got the obligatory tour out of the way. She was like me—more accustomed to simple living but not above admiring splendor.

I could tally up the people whom I consider dear friends on one hand. I had a best friend from high school with whom I traded occasional notes on Facebook; I had Barb who, despite being my supervisor, had become my closest confidant on every aspect of my life except the supernatural; I once had Jared, whom I count even though he's gone, because I still talk to him in my head when I'm lonely; and I had Dahlia, the DV who took care of me even when I didn't realize I needed the care.

Maybe two hands, now that I had Rodrian and Shiloh back.

Dahlia would never be what I'd consider typical DV, if there could ever be such a thing. For one thing, she's a vegetarian. Strange but hilariously true. I kind of assumed that someone who needs to consume blood to survive would be all into the meat experience but, no. She won't even eat fish. Eating with her can be a challenge sometimes but I always took a little comfort in her vow to eat nothing with eyes.

I have eyes. I like the security of our relationship.

Dahlia also has a cute little flip of an accent when she speaks English. It's like she curls around every word she says. She told me she was born in Puerto Rico but left when she was still a child. One day, I'll ask her when she was born. However, she's dropped so many casual references to historic events that I'm worried I won't be comfortable with the answer.

Despite my suspicions that she was old enough to have seen the Civil War, Dahlia appeared to be a young Latina, late-twenties at the most, with long curly hair that made me drool with jealousy, and brown eyes that would glow bluish-purple when her DV power surged. She worked as a social worker and loved violent movies. I admit I didn't get her, but I adored her and valued our friendship. She was everything I wasn't but she liked me in spite of it.

Halfway down the hallway toward my rooms she declared herself "not nosy enough" to gawk at my bedroom. I noticed she did a little shiver-and-chills shake of her head when she said it. Good manners prevented me from pressing further although I really wanted to know more about those wards.

By the time we worked our way to the tri-suite, Shiloh had regained most of her composure and agreed to tag along with us to the movie rental store for some nostalgia, located in a strip mall fifteen minutes away. Mini-mart, gas station, movie rental, cell phone dealer, and frozen yogurt/bagel shop. All the necessities of modern life, minus The Shoe Department.

"I don't get it. Where do they come up with this crap?" Looking up at a poster in the window, Dahlia wrinkled her nose. It was a promo for a vampire series that was soon to be released on video. "It's completely ridiculous."

"I don't know," said Shiloh. "He's pretty hot if you ask me."

"Not the guy, the whole vampire thing. Who came up with it? Don't people have better things to do than to romanticize death?" Dahlia looked at me, seeming to expect an answer.

I shrugged and made a *yeah, stupid people, what do they know* kind of face. Who was I to talk, anyway? Up until fairly recently, I thought mainstream vampire lore was pretty much as romantic as romantic got, what with the Victorian-style clothing and the eternal love/undying passion themes. Hanging out with the DV came as close to going through the looking glass as a girl could get without bleeding to death. My ideas concerning vampires were drastically different these days, thanks to my lovely experiences with them.

"I don't know why you get so bent out of shape, anyway." Shiloh held the door open for us. "My dad said that we're the ones that keep the farce going, to keep us a secret. You know." She deepened her voice to mimic Rodrian's. "Protecting our interests and all."

"As long as it seems made up, it may as well be, right? It's just stupid. If people really knew what vampires were, they'd stop with the love stories."

"Been going to DAVE again, Dally?" Shiloh said.

"Who's Dave?" I asked.

"Not who, what. D-A-V-E," Dahlia spelled out. "It's an organization. Demivampires Against Vampire Evolution."

"It's PETA for the undead," Shiloh clarified.

"As if." Dahlia sniffed and tugged her fluffy vest down

with an indignant snap. "We're an advocacy group that promotes the maintenance of DV values and lifestyle through education and awareness. We, as Demivampire, are a privileged society and as such we have certain responsibilities."

I thought it sounded snobby but I didn't say as much. "Awareness? Like, anti-vampire pep rallies? Movie boycotts and book burnings?"

Shiloh snorted. "That's good. I have to remember that."

"No," Dahlia said patiently. "Although there are different target audiences, our biggest focus group is the adolescent demographic. If we can instill the proper frame of mind in our young, they'll continue growing with the right values."

"Yep, brainwash 'em early on," said Shiloh.

"I don't get you, either." Dahlia wheeled around to face her. "You're Marek's niece!"

The sound of his name made me flinch. I stiffened as if I'd been pinched on the ass by an old man. Shiloh, completely unfazed, stared her down. "So? I didn't plan that."

"No, but don't you think that you've got a duty to promote what you know is right?"

"What does Marek have to do with this?" I said.

"He's the founder," said Dahlia.

"Yeah, and he's also, like, a gazillion years old." Shiloh rolled her eyes with the practiced ease of the under 18. "What does he know about kids? Look, Dally, I totally agree with the whole *Vampire Is Bad* campaign, okay? My family had its share of turners and, trust me, I hear about it all the time. But you guys are like Nazis. You won't stop until every DV teen on the planet goosesteps to your drumbeat. Educate the kids, that's fine. But you can't make choices for them."

"We do educate," Dahlia shot back. "Kids don't listen. You guys think you know everything, but you're still just kids. You need an older, wiser person telling you the truth. Someone who's been through it."

I slipped away to look over the new releases, since I didn't want to be associated with the "older, wiser" reference. I suppose it was silly, since Dahlia'd probably been in Girl Scouts with my grandma.

"Well then, start by giving us someone who's actually been through it, instead of some old guy who read a self-help book about it."

Yikes! Definitely wanted distance from the old reference now. I spied a historical romance on Queen Elizabeth that I'd seen advertised and picked up the DVD case before continuing down the wall.

"Shiloh, you're awful defensive," Dahlia said warily. "Is there something you want to talk about?"

"Great gods, no." She pushed the movie case she'd been holding into a vacant space on the shelf. "I don't use. I know kids who do but I don't. But you know, stuff like this makes me think maybe I should, just so I'd deserve the lecture for once."

She turned on her heel and stormed out, letting the door bang shut behind her.

"Holy crap," I said. "I hope she didn't take off. She had a rough day, and I'm supposed to keep an eye on her."

"Don't worry." Dahlia flicked through the cases in the "three for twenty" bin. "She's sitting in your car, sulking."

Typical teenager. "So, you do drug abuse education, too? That's a good thing. Why'd she get mad?"

"Because it's not exactly anti-drug. It's anti-blood. Teens don't need blood until they reach their cusp. But like cigarettes and drugs, blood poses a temptation. The forbidden apple. Blood in the uncusped DV can accidentally trigger evolution reactions, even without death energy. Mostly it just hyperactivates their powers, like a power surge, but some kids get addicted to the surge. They're called 'lution junkies. They even coined the nickname *'lution* for blood used illicitly."

Now I realized what made Shiloh so upset; the topic hit too close to home. I didn't think Dahlia knew about Shiloh's condition or about her brother Boxer, who'd been an evolution junkie. Boxer had turned vamp and had to be exterminated. I shuddered, remembering the day Rodrian told me, the pain he'd carried with him for decades.

"The world is becoming so violent, Sophie. Is it wrong for us to keep kids from accidentally killing them-selves? DV are lucky to be what we are. We just want to preserve our kind. Is that such a bad thing?"

"No," I said. "It's not wrong. But remember, kids don't make sense because nothing makes sense to them. Keep giving your message but don't stop looking for better ways to communicate it. Their language seems to change weekly. I think it's so that adults can never figure out what they are up to."

My phone buzzed as it alerted me to an incoming text. Slipping it from my pocket, I read Shiloh's message: R U CMING OUT HERE OR DID SHE BRAINWSH U 2?

Sighing, I smiled at Dahlia. "Got one?"

Dahlia grinned and held up a military action film. The girl loved violence. Her idea of a stuffed animal would probably be a war hammer. I couldn't figure her out some-times. She was so cute, yet harbored wicked tendencies when it came to her guilty pleasures.

I'd once asked her about her savage streak; all she'd say was that she used to be an *enforcer of peace*. It sounded so militant that I figured she'd have to kill me if she told me anything.

I countered with my Elizabethan film. Dahlia wrinkled her nose. "Tights? Again?"

"What? I like tights. And they're called *hose*."

"Great," she said. "Hose and bum rolls and big dresses. What do you see in that stuff?"

I waved it enticingly. "There's a beheading in this one..."

"Okay, you win." She grinned as if I'd promised ice cream. "But we watch mine first."

I handed my card to the cashier, waving through the window at Shiloh, who slumped in the front seat. I got an exasperated *are you coming?* look for my troubles, and she tapped at her wrist watch. Someone was wearing her pissy pants tonight. "Promise not to talk about DAVE on the way back? She's going through a bad time and lately she's been touchy. Rode would kill me if she threw herself from the car to get away from your rhetoric."

"DAVE?" Her eyes glittered with innocence and she picked up the movies from the exit counter. "Who's Dave?"

Once we got home, Dahlia tried another approach with Shiloh. She was a counselor, after all, so I didn't try changing the subject.

"Cusping isn't all that bad, Shiloh." Dahlia closed the door of the microwave and hit the popcorn button while I pulled a big orange bowl out of the bottom cabinet.

Shiloh crossed her arms. "Name one thing that I shouldn't hate about it."

"You'll manifest your gifts, for one thing."

Shiloh chewed her bottom lip and I could almost hear the wheels grinding as she thought about it. "Well, I have been wondering what that would be like. My dad is always showing off with his."

"Showing off, eh?" I wiped out the bowl with a paper

towel before opening the fridge to look for the spray butter. Sure, the box said *butterlicious*, but I had higher standards than Mr. Reddenbacher. That man had never endured the throes of PMS. If he had, his product would have been banned by the FDA.

"You've seen him, Sophie. Gods forbid he actually uses a key to unlock anything. He never looks where he's driving. I'll bet he doesn't even get out of bed to pee at night. He probably just compels—"

"Enough," I said. "I get the picture. The big, gross, peeing-in-bed picture."

"What's your family good at, Dally?" Shiloh asked.

"You mean my gift? Well, I'm a fabricator."

"Of..." Shiloh rolled her hand, trying to prompt Dahlia for more information.

Dahlia, looking sheepish, toyed with the hem of her shirt. "Of...whatever I need, I guess. I can...create...stuff. I don't know how to explain it."

"You mean, make stuff appear out of thin air," I said. It sounded too good to be true.

"No, it's a little more complicated than that. It's more like I can...rearrange matter to assume a form that is more convenient."

"Ooh!" Shiloh looked like she was ready to spring. "Can you make me a Vera?"

"Sure, if you don't mind a knock-off." Dahlia picked up a sheet of notebook paper from the snack bar and crumpled it. When she twisted her hands over each other, I caught a glimpse of blue and green cloth expanding between her fingers, growing into a flash of familiar paisley.

Shiloh's expression twisted in revulsion and she grabbed Dahlia's hands to stop her. "Ew! Never mind then. I'll keep working on Dad for another purse. What's the point of getting talents if you only make cheap imitations?"

Dahlia winked at me and pressed the cloth first into a ball, then flat as she unfabricated the despicable faux purse into a sheet of paper again. "Sometimes, a cheap imitation is better than nothing at all."

"You keep telling yourself that." Shiloh tossed her hair back. "But you buy cheap, you get cheap. And people know cheap when they see it." She ducked behind the fridge door to rummage through the shelves. After a moment she lifted her head and peered over the door. "Not that you look cheap, Sophie. I mean, it looks good on you. Not cheap. Much."

I smirked. "Thanks, smart ass."

She didn't find the popcorn I'd tossed into her hair until halfway through the movie.

"Now there's a familiar expression," Barb said, glancing up as she hung up the phone. "You look on edge enough to strangle someone but happy enough to do it smiling. I haven't seen that look on your face since the week Starbucks opened across the street."

I'd popped into Barb's office to hand over some column work for the new market. So far, so great—I had a file full of mail from across the country that I'd tried to hold off on sending since I'd be soon going local in their area. I would take advantage of the timing as long as possible. Two-Birds-With-One-Stone Sophie, that's me.

I stifled a forlorn sigh. "Yeah. Free mocha lattes. I almost got caffeine poisoning."

"You didn't fall off the coffee wagon, did you?"

"No."

"Then why the look?"

"Stupid people in the parking garage again."

"Ah. Explains the bared teeth. Now the happy part?"

"I'm digging my new crib. House." I hurried to correct my unintentional Shiloh-ism but I wasn't fast enough.

The sounds of slang made Barb's forehead wrinkle. "So, you did it. You moved again. You know, maybe you have an addiction to moving, kind of like those women who get addicted to plastic surgery."

"My neighborhood and I weren't getting along. And my neighbor—" I stuck out my tongue and pretended to retch. If I thought about Mrs. Petterson's bare legs long enough I wouldn't have to fake puking. "Things are different now that I'm house-sitting in the 'burbs. The change of scenery is doing me wonders."

"House-sitting? For who?"

"An old friend."

She eyed me, making me feel like a child awaiting approval from a parent. Part of me really needed her approval right now.

After a moment she dipped her chin and rocked back in her chair. Approval granted. "About time you have something to smile about."

I relaxed a little and flopped into the red chair by her desk. "And Shiloh talks non-stop, so I don't have the excuse to remain secluded anymore."

"Roommate? You?"

"She came with the house. She's great, although I don't understand half the things she says."

"Wait—you're living with a foreigner?"

"No," I said with a laugh. "Although, when you think about it, aren't all teenagers a little foreign?"

"Teenager?" Barbara looked at me over the tops of her glasses, the scrutiny making me squirm. "Whose house did you say it was?"

"My friend." I uncrossed my legs. Crossed my ankles. Crossed my legs again. Why was I afraid to say it?

"Rodrian."

"Your ex's brother."

Uh, oh. She used The Tone.

"Sophie. Are you sure this is a good idea? I know you're hung up—"

"I'm not hung up!" Okay, a little loud. Protesting too much.

She drummed her fingers. "You are. I'm not blind. Who was your last date?"

I didn't answer. How could I explain? *I lost my soul mate, who was DV and wrapped me in an unexplainable sensation of power, so there's no way I can go back to plain old human dating?*

"Right," she said. "You haven't moved on. Which means, you're doing this because you think you have a shot to get him back."

"No, I don't." Another thing I couldn't explain: *My ex is more vampire than Demivamp these days.*

"Then why? Why would you get involved with them again? They ditched you."

"Give me some credit. Can't I help someone out?"

"That's what you do. But most people don't move in with someone to do it. You're going to get your hopes up and you're going to fall down, hard."

I dug my fingers under my leg, trying to keep from shrieking with frustration. I couldn't use the end-all argument: *I'm the freaking Sophia!*

"What do you get out of it?"

"A cool place to live and a parking spot next door."

"And what's the catch?"

"No catch. Shiloh lives there. I drive her to school on my way to work."

"But why you? Why did his brother call you?"

"Shy asked him to." Okay. Maybe not truth but definitely conjecture.

"And so out of the blue you said yes?"

Funny she said *blue*. That was the color that usually got me into trouble these days. "Yeah."

"But that's not like you."

"I know. But like you said: I've only been existing. Buried myself in work. I needed a change. Plus, I hated my apartment. Hated it. This plan seemed like a good idea. If it doesn't work out, I leave. No strings."

"Famous last words. Just remember." She pointed her red pen at me as if she handed down a judgment. "It only takes one string to hang you."

I left the office for lunch, and regretted not packing a lunch the moment the wind hit me. Waiting for the crossing signal to change, I dug my cell out of my purse, and took a steadying breath before lifting it to my ear.

"Hello, Marek. I know it's been awhile but I had to call. I met someone. No, not like that. There's been no one since—" I abandoned the line and kept going. *Don't lose it now, Sophie.* "I met another Sophia. She came all the way from Europe and she can help you. She can—"

I stalled. "She can bring you back. Please. Just let her try."

I wanted to say so much more, to finally just say it. *I miss you. My life has a big jagged hole in it because you are not here. I think of you and it hurts to breathe. I drive by your house in Chaucer's Square, hoping to see you, even if you're just a shadow in the window and I get so excited when I see a light on but then I remember you have a timer set in the dining room and I miss you, damn it. I miss you because I can never love anyone the way I love you.*

I sighed and lowered the phone. Another failed trial run. If I didn't soon get it right, I'd never work up the courage to actually dial the phone.

If I could just get him to listen, maybe I could finally fix all the damage the Master had done. Could I rewind the evolution that had been forced upon him? Could I pull him back from the edge, the thrall of Brinking? Could I do anything to heal his soul?

I didn't know. All I knew was I had to try. I loved him with every single breath I took, every single moment that dragged by in my solitude. I had to try.

I had to dial the phone.

And I probably only had fifteen seconds to convince him to hear me out.

I had to keep my emotions out of it. I had to be all business. I had to approach this from a logical stand-point so that he could see this was the right thing to do. He'd searched for the Sophia for so very long—a lot longer than I'd been around. He couldn't have for-gotten that, not like he'd tried so effectively to forget me.

That was the key to my success in this call. I had to be the Sophia, the oracle for which he'd searched for so long. I couldn't remind him that I loved him, because he might remember he once loved me. He didn't want to remember.

I stowed the phone in my coat pocket with a frown. I wasn't ready to call him yet. But I knew—without a sliver of doubt—I was running out of time.

Crossing the street, I headed uptown to the Euro-style deli. I hadn't gone a block before I noticed that footsteps echoed a few paces behind me, and a casual turn of my head gave me a glimpse of my orange-eyed pursuer.

Wolf-boy was back and seemed more determined than ever before.

My frustration found a new outlet. This stalking crap was going to stop. Now.

I gripped my keys, threading them through my clenched fingers to form a spiky fist. They were the most weaponish thing I had in my purse.

I was tired of running out of work. Tired of looking over my shoulder. Tired of being hunted. Life had already thrown enough crap my way, what with the vampires and the Sophia and the bullshit of having to drive in rush hour traffic every day.

A narrow service alley veered off to the right between the closely packed buildings. I turned suddenly and struck off along the littered curb.

The alley was deserted except for myself and my soon-to-be ex-shadow. Our footsteps clacked in time, echoing off the walls, until he slapped through a puddle I'd purposefully missed. Slowing my pace, I took out my cell and pretended to dial it in my left hand. I steeled my nerve, put on a mean face and, when I heard him come up behind me, spun and jumped into him with a scream.

My sudden move caught him completely off guard and I knocked him over. I clambered onto his chest and pressed my pointy key-fist into the tender skin under his chin.

"Holy shit, Red!" His voice was tight with alarm, despite the softness of a light Southern drag. "Don't kill me!"

"You're lucky I didn't!" I bared my teeth and snarled into his face. "What do you want from me?"

"I'll tell you everything. Just..." He struggled a little before lying still. "Please, get off. Or at least move your knee. You're squashing my..."

"All right, all right." I got off him before he could finish. I knew exactly where my knee had been; I'd strategically placed it in case he had any rapey inclinations.

He pushed himself up on his hands but remained on the ground. I stood over him like some kind of conqueror, what with the keys and the pissed-off stance. The stance, however, relaxed a little when I saw how young he was.

It disappeared altogether when I looked at him closely

enough to recognize him.

All this time I'd been followed by the funny kid from Dark Gardens. This was the guy who'd known Tanner, the Were assassin who'd attacked me last summer. The only reason I survived was because I'd bit the guy.

"Are there others?" I'd known my pursuer was Were but knowing he was related to Tanner made the threat worse. I scanned the area, but the alley was empty except for us. I'd never noticed anyone else following me but Weres tended to move in packs.

"No, just me. Can I get up without you jumping on me again? It's filthy down here." He wrinkled his nose against the odor of city street and alley refuse.

"Filthy? Good. That's what you get." I backed away out of reach while he got to his feet. "You've been following me for months. What's the deal?"

With a shrug he lost the swagger. He shoved his hands into his pockets, his shoulders hunched up as if he guarded himself. I recognized it as the stance of someone who was used to getting knocked around. "I just wanted to talk."

Eight different valid protests flashed through my head but as usual, my heart cut through the logical nonsense and said the exact opposite. "Fine. Just—not here; it's nasty. We'll go around the corner to the deli."

He looked relieved. "Really?"

"Yeah. Just no funny business. I don't like Weres."

He grinned impishly. "You'll like me."

I raised my eyebrows at him.

"Ok. How about you just don't *not* like me and we'll go from there?" He flashed a devilish grin reminiscent of the one I'd seen him wearing before all the badness happened that night.

I remembered his antics, and I remembered the desperate glance he had thrown my way when the DV had hauled his buddy off.

How could I say no?

Ten minutes later we sat at a window booth in my favorite sandwich shop. He couldn't try anything in plain view.

"What made you brave enough to finally talk to me?" His mouth was full of roast beef on rye, which he devoured in bites big enough to choke a normal person.

He'd eaten half of the sandwich in three chomps before even saying anything other than his name was Toby. Poor kid was hungry. I'd already taken in his worn clothes and knew he'd been living lean.

Great, another stray.

"Simple," I said. "This was the first time you followed me at lunchtime. Every other time it'd been sundown or later." I paused to take a small bite of my own sandwich. "Today I was convinced you weren't fronting a vamp. Anything else, I can handle."

"Werewolves are something you can 'handle'?" His voice had that borrowed bravado again.

"Skinny ones like you, apparently."

He grinned wide enough to show all his front teeth. They looked human enough but the grin was phony. A bluff. "You just caught me off guard."

"Sure, whatever you say. Enough bullshit. Who was Tanner?"

His face darkened but he didn't avoid the question. "My brother."

I groaned. "Your brother?"

"As much as I ever had one. He was the only one who ever looked out for me. That's why I've been following you."

Swell. Tanner was his brother and hero. I didn't have a particularly good feeling about what would come next.

"Why, so you could finish his mission?"

"No! I'd never. I want to make it up to you. What he did. He wasn't all bad. I feel like I gotta do something to prove that."

I watched his face carefully, wondering if I'd be able to detect some sign of deception. With a carefully neutral shrug, I feigned disinterest and picked up my Diet Coke. "No need. It's done."

"It's his honor," Toby insisted. "He was good to me, and I have a debt to repay. I'll pay it by helping you."

"I don't need any help."

"Then I'll hang around until you need me."

Oh brother, I thought. Just what I needed, a werewolf tagging along like some furry Boy Scout waiting to do a good turn. I had enough problems already. "Can I have a napkin?"

He dug one out of the canister and held it out to me.

"Thanks," I said. "You helped me out. You're free to go."

"Oh no." He shook a finger at me. "You don't get off that easy. This is serious stuff, Red."

I sighed. Couldn't blame me for trying. "Why is it so important to you? I have to be honest, I wasn't fond of your brother when he cornered me in the club that night. He wanted to do seriously bad things to me, and I had night-mares for weeks about the whole thing. I don't need this kind of baggage."

"It's a—" He lowered his voice and leaned closer. "Wolf thing. Tanner's wolf is stuck here. It didn't die with him."

Toby dropped his head and stared at his sandwich. "I know what happened to him after those Demivamps took him away. He was my blood brother so...when he died, I felt it. But his wolf is still here. I know you don't understand what I mean but—do you believe in a soul?"

I nodded. Didn't think he needed to know exactly how much I was involved in the whole soul thing.

"Well, suicide is a crime for...a person like me. If the Were doesn't die honorably then the wolf can't join the Great Pack until it has fulfilled its debt. Trouble is, Tanner's wolf is just like him. It doesn't know a darned thing about making up for anything. So that's why I have to do it for him."

"And how will you know when you've accomplished it?"

"I don't know," he said. "But I'll know it when it happens."

The waitress dropped our checks on the table, and his expression clouded over. I didn't want him to embarrass himself so I reached for both slips.

"Hey." He slapped his hand down on them.

"Lunch was my idea." I tried to tug them free. "I got it."

"You can't pay for me." Toby sounded offended. "You're a girl."

"A girl who clobbered your ass," I reminded him. "Don't make me fight you for the check."

I pulled out my keys and jingled them in a mock threat.

He held up his hands. "Ok, but next time—"

"If there's a next time." I pulled out my wallet and thumbed through the bills. I hated when people made promises they couldn't keep.

Dahlia got tickets through one of her DAVE contacts for a multi-band concert at the old Majestic Theatre in Philly and asked if Shiloh and I wanted to go. I'd heard of a few of the performers, although I hadn't gone to a show for quite some time. The ticket listed three local bands opening for a newer rock quintet who'd recently released their first album.

The headliner, Strokkur, only brought up disturbing links when I Googled it. Hard rock had been a lot different when I was a teen. Music seemed to be getting a little extreme. I wasn't sure I could claim rights to being a part of the culture anymore.

When I was younger and less averse to fighting my way through general admission crowds, I'd been a sucker for live music. I could never get Barbara to go to a show; she preferred to listen to studio recordings in all their produced perfection. Not me, though. My creative edge recognized the spark of a muse in others, and I felt beholden to pay it my respects.

Now that career and adulthood had derailed my pursuit of concert hall happiness, all I had was a pile of treasured ticket stubs and concert tees. Those, and memories of music's up-close-and-personal pounding sensation in my lungs from the excessive amplifier volumes. Good times.

Since Shiloh didn't have her license yet and Dahlia drove a tiny import with a back seat so small Shiloh refused to get into it for fear of wrinkling her pants, I drove. I even managed to find a parking spot close to the theatre.

I called it luck, but I knew the DV would say luck had nothing to do with it. Marek had never had problems finding a parking spot; he probably just compelled people out of the way. Dahlia's gift was more creative than causative so I suspected tonight was a matter of simple human timing. Either way, we were fortunate. The night was freezing. East coast Novembers were wintery, especially in a harbor city.

The posters outside announced the event would be an all-ages show. We waded through the mobs of teenagers crowding the sidewalk toward the main entrance. Shiloh recognized several people and alternatively chatted and scowled as we pushed in through the doors.

The Majestic had once been a single screen movie theatre before the current DV owners remodeled it into an open area concert hall/bar. I'd been here only once before and spent the entire time upstairs in the mezzanine, which was off limits to the under-aged because of the bar and therefore much less crowded.

Plus, there were actual seats. I liked seats. Usually the boots I wore to concerts were more for admiring and less for actual walking around in.

I glanced at the staircase leading up to the mezzanine and saw the bouncer check an ID and shake his head at a slightly-built blond boy. Shiloh must have recognized him because she busted his chops when he sulked past us toward the all-ages auditorium. "Nice try, Jackson. You really look twenty-one tonight, too. Your lack of win shocks me."

Crap. I guessed Shiloh wouldn't get past, either. We passed the ticket booth and entered the auditorium. I cringed and almost swallowed my gum. The place was packed. I could feel loads of DV. A handful of intensely emoting humans. And—others.

I couldn't feel them but I knew they were there, the way astronomers looked at the night sky and surmised the presence of a black hole simply because they saw nothing at all. Those people were like spots of empty. It didn't concern me as much as the sudden rush of oppression that caught me and made me feel as if everyone had turned to stare at me.

"Dally..." I leaned toward her and grabbed her hand. "Can you mark me?"

She shrugged and reached up to fix my coat collar before running a finger along her jaw. It looked like a baseball signal more than anything else—not at all sexy—but then again, I'd only been marked by guys in the past. The sensation stopped immediately, and I surveyed the room with more confidence.

Until I saw the crowd. Gah. I definitely had outgrown general admission crowds. Especially metal crowds. I hadn't realized people pierced so many body parts.

Shiloh swung back to face us, wearing a scowl. "Ugh. There're tons of Were here."

"Is that normal for a place like this?" Being a DV oracle, I couldn't sense Were. They were as blank as humans.

Shiloh frowned. "I wouldn't call it normal."

"It's normal," Dahlia said, wearing an expression that

more or less said Accept Peace Willingly or I Shall Beat It Into Thee. "Most public places are. But I agree, there are a lot of Were here tonight. I heard one of the bands is Werekind. Maybe they brought them in."

Shiloh persisted. "Can we go upstairs, Dahlia?"

"You don't have ID," I reminded her.

"That's okay. This is a DV-run place." Dahlia moved to the side as a group of rowdy college boys pushed their way to the gated bar area. "Let me see if my friend is working."

Dahlia disappeared in the crowd. Shiloh and I stood like an island as concert goers streamed around us. The intro music cut off as someone came on stage, much to the pleasure of the roaring crowd. A *wang* of feedback accompanied a man's rowdy voice when he introduced the opening band. It wasn't the most eloquent speech I've ever heard but the multiple references to alcohol and fluent f-bombing seemed to provide substantial motivation to the super-charged crowd.

As the crowd surged forward to pack closer to the stage, the people rushing through the doors jostled us. Dahlia reappeared before we were sucked into the undertow of the audience, gesturing for us to follow her back out into the foyer.

We showed IDs to the bouncer who merely nodded. Instead of heading up the mezzanine staircase we passed through the door beyond him. The door shut behind us quickly and I made out the shape of another staircase in the dimly-lit side chamber.

"Up here." Dahlia spoke into the shadowy muffledness and began climbing. I grimaced, dreading the long hike in boots up several staircases. It had to be better than trying to keep my balance out in the sea of crazy that had flooded the auditorium.

The exertion was worth it. The balcony was unlit since

guests were not permitted on this level. Flashes of color blinked in the darkness; when the stage exploded into bright light, I could make out figures wearing headsets and operating spotlight equipment.

Further back along the walls stood other men, apparently standing guard; their eyes flashed and a few bowed in our direction. Polite touches of power announced themselves. I realized they recognized me as Sophia. I waved back, feeling familiar with them although they were complete strangers.

We made our way to the edge of the balcony and perched in the front seats. It was very warm up here, partly due to the lighting rigs hanging less than a foot below us, and I shrugged off my heavy coat. The music pounded but, far away from the amplifiers, I had no need for earplugs.

Shiloh and Dahlia chatted behind me as I leaned on the rail and watched the show, extremely content. I was spoiled now, I knew; I'd never be able to stand general admission after being up here. It was like having box seats. Totally worth the unsettling thrill of extreme heights.

I squinted down through the glare of the lighting rigs at the crowd below and spied a familiar face and shock of hair. "Hey, there's Toby."

"Who?"

I forgot that I hadn't told them about him and pointed down at the crowd. "Green shirt, blond spikes. The Were."

"You recognize a Were, huh." Dahlia sounded skeptical as she leaned her arms on the rail, scanning the crowd. "How'd you meet him?"

"Well, I danced with him at Folletti's one night, right before his best friend threatened to bite me."

Dahlia's eyes took up their violet glow. "Wasn't that the night I met you?"

"The same."

"I remember him now." Dahlia's eyes simmered as her facial features appeared to sharpen with her displeasure. She narrowed her eyes and pinched her lips tightly together, her power taking on an aggressive edge.

I tried to disarm her by keeping my tone light. "Yeah, him. I bumped into him a little while back. He seems like a good kid."

Shiloh appeared uninterested and put her feet up on the railing. "Weres are stupid. Ugh. There should be leash laws here."

"Sounds like you have them all figured out, *chica*," Dahlia said.

"I do. The rest of my life might be in shambles, but at least I know Weres suck ass."

"You're Marek's niece, all right." Dahlia spoke without taking her eyes from the crowd, missing the looks Shiloh and I exchanged.

"What are the guards for?" Shiloh tossed her hair over her shoulder and indicated one of the guards with a nod of her head.

"I guess they're always here," Dahlia said. "See the insignia on their jackets? There're special ops."

"Special ops at a rock show? I know those guys are scary, but..." I glanced around the balcony, scanning for any-one other than the guards. "What do they think will happen, a terrorist attack?"

"Not terrorists." Dahlia shrugged off her jacket and settled into her seat. "There's been some outbreaks of Underground activity over the last few months."

"That's why Brianda has been away so much," Shiloh said. Reaching into her bag, she pulled her MP3 player free. Either she'd grown tired of the band or the conversation itself. Shiloh knew plenty about vampire and DV dealings but usually avoided the subject. "She's been helping Uncle

Marek keep order. I guess the vampires don't like him being Master so they cause trouble."

Dahlia nodded. "The special ops are slayer patrols. Every guy who doesn't have a power signature or a human vibe is scrutinized. In fact, the ticket takers and bouncers are special ops too. They scan everybody coming in."

I didn't know if I should be relieved or worried that they were so close. "Do they work for Marek?"

"They used to."

I didn't persist. I suspected I knew when they stopped being his. "So, what do they do, frisk everyone? I don't remember feeling like I was under any special scrutiny, except for the not being marked part."

"Not everyone. Only the guys."

"Isn't that a little sexist?"

Dahlia looked at me as if I had spoken in Klingon. "How do you figure?"

"The Master's a guy, the armies are guys, the lawyers are guys, the toadies are guys. Any and every vamp I've had the horrible misfortune to meet or hear about is a guy. Where're all the women? Home spinning thread for the men's Renaissance faire outfits?"

Dahlia turned her big creamy eyes on me, which glowed like electric violets. "Oh, Sophie, don't even joke about that. That's not funny."

What really wasn't funny, I thought, was this mysterious hush-hush way that DVs tended to dance around subjects.

I didn't like being out of the loop and I didn't like having to admit I didn't know something. I'd much rather fake it and play along.

However, I found myself in more and more situations that I couldn't bullshit my way through. There was simply too much unknown when it came to DV issues. I'd clarify one thing only to realize there were fifty more unanswered questions. My education regarding the Demivampire seemed to be going as smoothly as stacking dry sand.

Now apparently there was a hang-up with girls that I had to sort out. Breathing a quiet huff of tried patience, I smiled. Sarcastically. I couldn't help it. "Can you just explain it, or do I have to look it up online?"

Dahlia's eyes still simmered—obviously not a good sign—and she kept her voice low. Did she forget we were at a concert? "Sophie...there are no female vampires. None."

"Why? Are women too weak to evolve?" I looked back and forth between them waiting for an answer. Shiloh applied herself to a box of Nutter Butters that she'd produced from her backpack and feigned deafness secondary to ear buds. Dahlia looked like she'd rather leap from the balcony than tell me. "Out with it, Dally."

"No, women are not too weak to evolve," she admitted. "It's just the opposite. Females turn as easily as men. They just don't survive as vamps."

"Does the process kill them?"

"No. They are hunted. Exterminated." She looked at me for a long second. "By vamps."

"The boy vamps kill off the girl vamps?" That didn't make sense, even for things like vampires. "Why the hell would they do that?"

"Fear. Females are naturally aggressive. You know what I mean. Look down there." She pointed over the balcony to the audience, where in the midst of the crowd a turbulent mosh pit had opened up.

Gah. I hated that sort of thing. It was the main reason I looked for bar seating at concerts.

"It's girls doing it," she said. "Most of them are humans, too. Not that blonde though; she's definitely DV. See how pushy she is?"

I watched the roiling sea of bobbing bodies, a couple thrashing sharks smashing into everyone within reach. I shuddered, even more grateful for my seat high above the teeming crowd. I hated heights but hated general admission of the thrash age more.

Dahlia echoed my shudder. "Can you imagine how vicious a female vamp would be? I've heard tales about Brianda, and it frightens me to think how she'd be if she Fell. Female vamps would destroy everything in their path in their quest to own and control and consume. That's why the vamps destroy them as soon as they rise. They're afraid."

My thoughts turned toward home where I'd soon be living with the apparently legendary Brianda. She'd only stopped in once before to drop off a few boxes and to cuddle up with her baby sister before going back to work.

Brianda was striking, a blonde version of Rodrian, tall but balanced. She didn't have Shiloh's buoyancy, but when she smiled it was warm and sincere. Watching her with Shiloh convinced me that even though she wasn't her mother, she could double in a second. The love she had for her was undeniable and complete.

I looked over at Shiloh, who found feathers on the floor and dropped them over the balcony. I felt my good ole gut sense make the connection. "Ah, I see."

Dahlia looked confused. "See what?"

"You know, what makes them so fierce. It's love."

She looked down over the edge at the crowd. "You mean jealousy. Competition."

"Not at first. In the beginning, there is only love."

"Love? Love makes a female vamp evil?"

"Not evil. Fierce. It's a mother's instinct, to protect and fight for her offspring. But when children grow up and start taking care of themselves, the instincts and fierceness remain. In some people, it gets misdirected. When someone like that evolves, the fierceness becomes twisted. The lack of a soul begets evil, turning fierceness into something much worse."

I thought about the females in my life, the DV who lived their lives threatened by this awful destiny. "Brianda has something to fight for. She's DV enforcer, like Marek was. She has a purpose, an outlet for her strength and ferocity. You do too, if you stay the course you are on. Sadly, not everyone has a purpose. They are the ones who get lost."

Shiloh spoke up suddenly. She pulled the plugs out of her ears and peered at me. "Your eyes are blue, Sophie. What did I miss? What were you talking about?"

I reached out and patted her hand, feeling the tingle in my brain diminish. My eyes must have bled back to their usual brown, judging by the disappointment in Shiloh's face. "We were talking about you, in a way."

"And I missed it," she groaned. "I bet you were about to fix the mess my life turned out to be, and I missed it."

"You missed nothing you still cannot discover for yourself."

Dahlia had turned back to look down to the stage. I could almost hear her hashing out her plans for DAVE and a whole new onslaught of teen outreach events.

"In English?" Shiloh persisted.

"You need a purpose in life."

"A purpose? Like a crusade? Woo-hoo!" She did a little victory dance with her knees and pointed fingers. "I'm gonna find me a purpose!"

I only smiled. I didn't understand again, but sometimes it was just easier to play along.

After the set ended, we crept down the back steps to the foyer where the merchandise booths and food vendors were set up. Shiloh wanted a soft pretzel, and I wanted to stretch my legs. Not that walking was any more comfortable than sitting—I had to walk down the steps backwards because my boots were so jacked. Damn you and your peer pressure, Colin Stuart. These boots weren't made for walking, especially not down steps.

A familiar voice sounded behind me. "Hiya, Sophie."

I turned to see Toby, who wore a boyish grin. "Hey, Toby. How are you?"

"Okay, I guess." He shrugged and glanced over his shoulder. "I didn't know you came here."

"Dally's idea." I stepped to the side and nodded at the girls. "I'm a little old for this scene."

"Ah, you're never too old for a good time."

"We're back," Shiloh said from behind me. Her voice was louder than it needed to be, considering there was no one on stage and the foyer was relatively quiet.

I gave her a *be nice* kind of look. "Toby, these are my friends, Shiloh and Dahlia."

"Nice to meet you," said Dahlia. I could still feel she had her guard up, simmering beneath her pleasant mask.

"Pleasure's all mine, ladies."

Shiloh huffed derisively. "Sure is."

I stepped on her foot. "Everything okay with you, Toby?"

"Oh. Everything's great. Just great." I noticed his smile grew whenever he glanced at Dahlia.

Her own expression didn't change but the pulse of her power quickened when she smiled back, her aggression fading. I had to look twice at her. Did she just flutter her lashes?

"You staying for the next band, Sophie?" He seemed to have difficulty concentrating on me as he spoke.

"Actually, we're heading back to Balaton." Dahlia volunteered. "Need a ride?"

Shiloh interrupted. "I'm sure his friends are looking for him. Aren't they?"

Toby scratched his head. "I don't know where they got to, anyway."

"I don't suppose you wanted to come along?" Dahlia stepped a bit closer, her smile a bit wider. "Dangerous streets for girls to walk alone at night."

"What?" Shiloh whacked Dahlia on the arm. "Since when is the street dangerous for you?"

"I can't ignore a damsel in distress," Toby said hurriedly. "That's if it's okay with you, of course, Sophie."

"It's fine." I ignored Shiloh as she crossed her arms in disgust. "Let's go. Grab your coat."

"I didn't wear one," he said.

"Hot-blooded?" Dahlia blinked after she said it, as if shocked she'd be so bold. She shocked the hell out of me, anyways.

"Dense is more like it," Shiloh said. "It's freezing outside."

"I agree," I said, before Shiloh could continue. I had a nagging suspicion that he didn't have one to wear. "Let's go before it gets any colder."

"The sign said *Noodle Shop*, didn't it?" Shiloh gave Toby a little extra grief as he looked over the menu wearing a dismayed expression.

He tugged at the neck of the hooded sweatshirt Dahlia had procured for him before leaving the club. It was dark red, almost brown, with a pattern of shiny metallic lightning streaks flowing down the hood and along the sleeves.

She swore it wasn't stolen but I still couldn't figure out how she made stuff appear out of thin air. I knew Shiloh thought it was a neat trick; I'd caught the envious look she gave Dahlia as she'd tossed the sweatshirt to him. She probably just hated to admit it since it benefited the young werewolf.

Dahlia reached over and adjusted the neckline, tugging on it; the fabric obeyed her touch and assumed a more comfortable fit.

Toby's expression lightened at her touch and the looser fit of the previously too tight collar.

"Sure," he said. "I just thought they had other stuff."

"Like?"

"Meat," he said, matter-of-factly.

"Not this place." I grinned and pointed to words on the menu cover. "They only serve veg dishes here."

"Veg?"

"Vegetarian."

"Why'd they do something like that?"

"Well," Dahlia said. "Some people don't eat meat, and they prefer to dine in an establishment that shares their beliefs."

"That's crazy!" Toby was loud and looked too shocked to care, even when several heads turned in our direction.

"Ain't gonna make friends that way." Shiloh grinned happily, pouring a second sugar packet into her teacup.

Shock melted into confusion and Toby gaped at her. "How do you figure?"

"Because I am a vegetarian." Dahlia showed a composed *one wrong word and you die* smile. Enforcer of peace, I reminded myself, and hoped I didn't have to remind her, too.

He threw me a look that clearly displayed his trepidation and carefully selected his words. "Well...you must...have tremendous will power. I admire a person who sticks to her convictions."

Dahlia glowed. Shiloh rolled her eyes in one part disgust

and two parts defeat. She slouched in her chair, groaning and disappearing behind the menu again. I flagged down a speeding waiter so I wouldn't have to watch budding romance. I hated cheap soaps these days.

Shiloh's mood lightened considerably once the food arrived, and she amused us all by doing inappropriate things with her chopsticks when the waiter wasn't watching. I personally wouldn't have eaten with them after she let them hang from her nostrils but, since teenagers had little patience for lectures on germs and manners, I only laughed. Rude, germs, or no, it was still funny.

Dahlia had talked Toby into ordering a spicy tofu dish, explaining the finer points of protein and texture and other probable lies. I'd eaten tofu before. Meat substitute, my Aunt Fanny. Flavorless squish was more like it.

Toby probably would have eaten the tablecloth had Dahlia suggested it, so of course he agreed.

"Not used to spicy food?" I pushed my water glass across the table to him as he gulped down the last of his own. Dahlia wore a *you're doing just fine, honey* kind of look and smiled down at her bowl.

"No, I'm not," he gasped. "What did you say this was again?"

"So, Toby." Shiloh pointed her chopsticks at him. "Are you going to convert?"

His eyes watered and he cleared his throat several times. "Convert what?"

"You know, go veg, like Dahlia. I mean, you guys were getting all Lady and the Tramp over that chow fun. It was so cute."

Dahlia flushed. "Knock it off, Shy, or I'll knock it off for you."

"Sheesh. Touchy, touchy."

"Lady and the Tramp? That's funny. It is," I insisted,

when Dahlia turned her glare on me.

"I'm not a dog," Dahlia said.

"But he is, hence, the funny."

"I hope ya'll are going to clue me in," Toby said.

"It's a cartoon. Forget it." Dahlia picked up the check and pulled out singles for a tip, but Toby stopped her, smoothing out a fistful of ones he'd pulled from his pocket.

The ride back to Balaton was awkward, to say the least. Dahlia and Toby crammed themselves into the back seat and suddenly ran out of things to say. Maybe it was a case of two-minutes-in-the-closet—it's one thing to notice an attraction to someone but another thing altogether to be so close, so soon. The Cavalier didn't offer much in the way of healthy personal space.

Then there was Shiloh, who exhaled noisily every time one of the kids in back would make an attempt at conversation. Most of the time, they were reduced to gazing longingly at each other when the other wasn't looking.

Swinging onto the exit for downtown, I interrupted the two love birds' fledgling attempt at getting to know each other better.

"Where to, Toby?" I asked him.

"Oh, anywhere. I can walk."

"It's freezing out." Dahlia cast a stern look at him. "We'll drive you so you can be out of the wind."

"Well, if you insist, Miss Dahlia."

He gave me vague directions to an intersection about ten blocks away. I felt like the mom whose turn it was to pick the kids up at the mall. Shiloh slumped in the front seat, earbuds firmly in her ears, looking out the window and excluding herself from the conversation.

I pulled over to the curb when I reached the intersection Toby had given. He leaned forward between the seats. "Something wrong, Soph?"

"No. But this is the corner, right?"

He looked blankly at me a moment before it sank in. "Yep. I wasn't paying attention. Thanks for the ride, Sophie. Nice to meet you, Dahlia. You too, Shy."

"Yes," Shiloh said, and I pinched her leg.

"See you around." When Toby climbed out the cold air rushed inside and devoured all the heat. Shiloh turned up the heater full blast.

I honked the horn and drove off, watching in the rear-view mirror. Dahlia settled back in her seat with a pleased smile, waving through the window at Toby, who lingered on the corner. Her power pulsed with rosy tingles, a warm happy glow; the girl was definitely *in like* with him.

As I headed uptown to drop her off at her apartment, I kept a mental finger on the thread of her power, remembering a time long ago when I'd once felt that bright and optimistic feeling, hoping that her luck would be better than mine had been.

"What a night." Shiloh rested her head against the window once we dropped Dahlia off. "I'm pooped."

I circled the block and headed back downtown so I could get back on the parkway. "You look it, honey. Why don't you close your eyes?"

"I'm okay." She blinked drowsily. "I just get so tired these days. I guess school is catching up with me."

I suspected it was more than school that sapped her energy. "How do you feel?"

"I dunno. Tired, mostly. But sometimes my stomach hurts. I can't eat the way I used to."

"I can't eat the way you used to." I laughed, remembering her hollow legs.

She chuckled weakly but there was no humor in it. "Yeah, well, I can't eat sometimes, period. Even normal stuff, like tomato sauce or cheese. It makes me throw up and I'm always in the bathroom. And it just hurts, all the time."

"Maybe you need to see a doctor. Where's the pain? High up by your ribs? Down lower?"

She shook her head. "It's everywhere. And anyway, I told my dad a long time ago, when it first started. I had to go to his family doctor, and he was the one who said I was sick in the first place. He's the one that said I had hypolution."

"Oh. Rodrian told me about your therapy coming up." I glanced over at her as I slowed for a red light. We were near the intersection where we'd dropped Toby earlier. "Are you worried?"

She slumped down further in her seat. "Doesn't matter. It hurts so much sometimes that I think that maybe it'll be a good thing to go through with it. What can hurt more than it already does?"

She finally closed her eyes so I didn't say anything else. Waiting for the light to turn, I looked through the window and noticed a figure huddling against the glass of a storefront, taking shelter from the wind. It was another thing I hated about the winter; the nights were crowded with homeless who sought shelter in corners and on stoops and near steaming subway grates. I lived in a palace, for the love of God. How was any of that fair?

The cross traffic streaked past and headlights briefly illuminated the person squatting in the shadows. A glint of shiny caught my attention as light gleamed on the metallic print of the person's hood. As the light changed, I realized I recognized the shirt.

Dark red that blended with the cold bricks behind him, except for shiny streaks of jagged metallic paint that streaked down the hood and sleeves. I hesitated and the car behind me tapped its horn, causing the hooded figure to raise his head from the spot of warmth he'd created between his chest and knees. We looked at each other through the glass as the driver hit his horn in a longer, irritated-sounding blast.

Toby.

I swung the first turn I could but, by the time I managed to find my way through the one-way streets and much-too-long traffic lights, he was gone. I circled the adjacent blocks and scanned the streets. I didn't see him again.

Shiloh had fallen asleep and missed the whole episode. The ride home was long, quiet, and full of troubled thoughts of the young Were and whether he found a warmer place to sleep.

My dreams that night were only more of the same. Hard to rest easy in a mansion when all you could think about is a kid sleeping in a doorway.

Monday came and brought with it a fresh influx of petitions. I never thought I'd ever have wished for it but, just once, I longed to get a petty letter about choosing colors for bridesmaids dresses or how do I tell my friend to leave my boyfriend alone or something—anything—that didn't turn my eyes blue at work. I knew I'd get caught sooner or later and the hell if I knew how I'd explain it to Barbara. She was big on eye contact.

I sorted the envelopes into their usual piles of *column* and *petition*, noticing that the petition pile was three times the size of the column. How did Sophias manage to help everyone who needed it? I was only skimming the DV by taking mail requests. There had to be even more out there that needed their burdens relieved.

How could I even begin to be what they needed?

First of all, I had no idea what to do about Shiloh. She looked worse every day and I knew the stress was eating her. Rodrian would be unnaturally quiet when he stopped by, preferring to sit in the den and read. I'd taken to splitting the couch with him, enjoying the blaze of the fire and the comfort of his presence. Although we chatted, he still remained distant. I'd even gone so far as to tell him about Eirene, the visiting Sophia, hoping this momentous news would liven him up.

He didn't show any interest in the subject whatsoever. If I didn't know better, I'd swear he didn't believe me that Eirene even existed. Eventually, he'd call one of his blood dates and leave to meet her, leaving me alone in a big house full of silence.

What kind of Sophia did that make me? I lived under the same roof as people who really needed me, and I read books with them. Wow. Pass the Sophia trophy on over.

And why the hell was I avoiding talking to Marek? If I were any kind of Sophia, I'd march right over to his townhouse, bust open the door, and drain him of every icy miserable feeling inside him. I'd Mr. Clean his soul until it shined like daylight on a mirror. I'd bring him back to rights, and this whole mess would be solved.

So why didn't I?

There was only one reason: I was inadequate. A charlatan, a snake-oil simile, a cheap knock-off of a real Sophia. Couldn't ask Barb for advice, could I? Nope. Not only would I lose my job—because who wants to pay an advice columnist who couldn't advise herself—but I'd lose my friend when she found out I'd kept my oracular secret from her all this time. She'd also probably get a restraining order on me once she saw my eyes go crazy blue.

I couldn't ask Dahlia because what would happen to me if the DV found out I sucked at being a Sophia? Would they run me out of town with pitchforks and jeers? Would I be turned away from restaurants and shoe boutiques because their DV owners banned me?

God, what a mess. And, great. I couldn't even ask God what to do because I lost my VIP voucher for Heavenly advice when vampires killed my priest and best friend.

What a train wreck.

Slicing open the column envelopes, I pulled the letters free and began skimming them for potential column topics. As hard as I tried to get into my work, I couldn't stop my inner diatribe.

At least I got to see Eirene tonight, I thought. She was the only person I knew with whom I could commiserate. Only thing was, Eirene wasn't the most compassionate of people I'd met. Maybe I was short-changing her—we'd only met once, after all, so I hadn't exactly taken a lot of time to know her. Maybe it was simply her country's custom to behave so sternly with strangers.

The thought didn't do much to put me at ease. Prickly was still prickly and prickly made for an uncomfortable time, especially for a hugger like me. I just had to give her another chance. The main thing was that Eirene was a Sophia and she had offered to teach me what I need to know. She was my Obi Wan. My only hope.

I grimaced. She'd be the crabbiest Jedi ever. Still, it would be better than trying to figure out the Force on my own.

"I want to know your life, Sophia." Eirene and I sat in the parlor of her hotel suite, where a spread of bread and cheeses and spicy crab dip covered the coffee table. Cheesy crabs equals amazing. "What makes you who you are?"

It wasn't worth a memoir, but I told her anyway. "Okay. I've lived in this area all my life. Grew up a little north of Allentown and went to college in Philly. I practiced nursing for a while before taking a job at *The Mag*, where I work now. I write an advice column, which is either coincidental or destined, considering that I'm Sophia."

"You make it sound like a list, dear."

"What else could it be?"

"I want to know who you are. The Sophia doesn't choose someone simply because they have a fitting occupation. What is within the woman matters."

"I don't know. I mean, I don't think I am anything special."

"Marek Thurzo thought you were special. Did he not?

Wasn't he the one to discover you?"

Marek thought I was special, all right. So much so that he dumped me, despite me being his potential salvation. "I guess. He said there was a spark in me, a willingness to champion a lost cause. I've always been compassionate, to the point of self-sacrifice. It's not something to brag about."

"But it is something." She leaned to dunk a piece of bread into the creamy dip and set it on her plate. "Compassion, true concern for the plight of another, is rare today. Your description of self-sacrifice, however, confuses me."

Big shocker, I thought. "I'm too nice, or so I've been sneered at."

"Rightfully so."

I almost gasped. "Excuse me?"

"*Too nice* is not complimentary. It is a sign of epic weakness."

"Or maybe I'm just trying to be the change I want to see in the world."

"You are a Sophia who is only rudimentarily aware of her abilities and her duties." She sipped at her wine. "Focus on improving yourself. When you know yourself better, you will be better able to serve the world."

I really did not like this woman. I liked the idea that she might help me improve my oracular self, I liked her generosity with food, but I did not like her. How long would I sit here and tolerate her attitude before working up the courage to flip her off and walk out? Taking a big mouthful of dip only kept me from making a smart comment. It didn't give me a backbone.

Eirene didn't appear to realize I was coming to a boil beneath my skin. Or, if she did, she didn't give a turd. Some empath.

"Tell me about your family, your friends," she said. "The DV to whom you have grown close."

Lucky for me, the answers were the same for all three. I briefly told her about Rodrian and Shiloh, and our life together at the Stocks. She appeared keenly interested, sitting forward without wrecking her posture. I congratulated myself on picking the right topic.

"So," she said. "The child has hypolution. It is a concern, indeed. I have known many who did not survive."

"Lack of treatment?" I guessed.

"The treatment itself." She set her glass down and patted her fingers together. "It needs to be handled by a professional. Of course, in earlier times, there was no treatment. The strong survived, the weak did not. It is nature. Today we have advancements in technology and medicine and the DV have a greater understanding of their biological systems. Still. Blood in an uncusped DV can have drastic effects."

"Drastic?" I didn't like the sound of it. "How drastic?"

"The DV who is forced to cusp comes into an unnatural power. Their power lies dormant and forcing it to awaken often strips the Demivampire of the ability to control their power."

"Is it painful?"

She nodded. "And it is dangerous. Not only to the patient but also to others unfortunate to get in the way of their unleashed energy. Who is this family?"

I didn't want to blurt out Rodrian's business. He confided in me, for one thing, and I knew enough about patient privacy to respect it. Still, she knew about Marek and that I'd been involved with him. She was a Sophia, after all. If she knew, she could help.

Isn't that what I wanted? For a Sophia to help Marek? This was one of those times to err on the side of helpfulness. And if I wasn't enough to help Shiloh, it was my duty to find someone who could. "It's Thurzo."

"Marek's family," she confirmed.

"Yes." I prepared to duck her criticism.

It never surfaced. "Good. It is proper that you are shown your due. You deserve a nice home. Of course, in my land, where the Sophia is venerated, this is the very least of tribute but it is a start. Remember. It is one thing to provide guidance. But to directly assist in treatment of hypolution?" She clucked her tongue. "That is asking much, even from one who is so selfless and giving."

She made it sound so sissy. I almost hackled. Well, I goose-bumped. Same thing. "I wouldn't call it directly assisting. I'm more emotional support."

"Result is the same."

Feeling I'd lose no matter what I said, I changed the topic. "Is it only the DV that recognize the Sophia?"

"Who else would?"

"Weres, perhaps?"

"Weres." Her upper lip curled as if she tasted something bad. "Surely you do not mean lycanthropes?"

"I do."

"What would possess you to even consider them? Animals! They are beneath the regard of the Demivampire, and should be beneath yours, as well."

"But, they're people—"

"Once, perhaps, but no longer. Their blood is tainted. Poisoned. They lure the unsuspecting Demivampire into taking their blood, cursing them to wretched animal form. The world would be better if it were purged of the filthy lot of them."

Marek would have enjoyed this particular conversation. I could imagine him leaning back, crossing his fingers over his chest, and wearing a smirk that said *See? I told you so.*

"Did you just refer to the Horus Bird Phenomenon?"

"Do not romanticize it with elevated titles."

"I'm not." Lifting my chin, I tried to look smug and well-informed. "Marek owns a laboratory that researches it. That's the terminology they use."

"Research? What is there to know? It's a curse. It steals everything from a Demivampire—their memories, their power. Their destinies. The Curse of Horus is a tale to be told to young Demivampires, to warn them of what will befall those who stray too far from their own kind. If bloods mix, the curse takes hold. The Demivampire becomes an abomination."

She glanced around, as if worried someone could overhear. In a more subdued voice, she continued. "And so. What has his research yielded?"

"They are looking for a way to reverse the process."

"Prevention is key. Kill the shape shifters, eliminate their poisoned blood, and the problem ceases to exists."

I studied my lap for a moment, my lips pinched shut so I didn't get myself kicked out of Sophia class. Conversations with Eirene, I found, were strenuous exercises in diplomacy. I didn't realize the society of Sophia would be so bipartisan. "Killing is wrong."

"Is it not wrong to cause destruction? Is it wrong to eradicate a disease?"

"People, Eirene. They are people."

"Your concern should only be the welfare of Demivampire." She waved to Dorcas and the maid cleared the table. "Is your heart in the vocation?"

"How can you even ask that?"

"It is my duty to ask. We are a small but vital resource to the Demivampire. A faulty Sophia will do more damage than good."

Yeah. Faulty. A good word for a nagging suspicion. "I

know I haven't been nominated for Sophia of the Year, but...how bad am I? Am I hopeless?"

"Oh, no." She left her seat to sit next to me, patting my hand and doing this polite hug-thing with a light touch on my shoulder. "Not hopeless, dear. Just untrained. We can discuss your technique. You primarily practice through correspondence, yes?"

At my nod, she continued. "Then we will explore opportunities to expand your practice. Most of your...deficiency, I suspect, is theoretical. You must establish your station. Learn to take what you deserve. We will also approach the subject of understanding the importance of selection."

I shrugged. "Which is?"

She pressed me again with her polite half-hug. "Knowing who to save and who to let go."

Maybe Eirene was right, I thought, as I drove back to the Stocks. Tired as I was, I was grateful for the light traffic. I liked having the road to myself. It gave me the opportunity to drive lazy.

I also liked a chance to use my high beams. I could actually see the road that way. The Cavalier was getting a little old and could benefit from new headlights, as well as a long list of upgrades. Oh well, it was owned. Not having a car payment was a wonderful thing.

Eirene's words were stuck on repeat: I needed to establish my station. As much as I hated agreeing with her, she'd made a point worth considering. If I established my station, perhaps I would grow into the role a bit better. I needed to stop acting like a Sophia and actually be a Sophia.

It was time I got a promotion. But how?

I thought about what I did as a Sophia: I wrote letters.

That was pretty much it. However, didn't Eirene say that correspondence was a good thing? Okay, then. I did most of my Sophia work at, well, work. However, it wasn't like I could apply for a Sophia-related position at *The Mag*.

I could, however, use a little leverage. Didn't my column bring in extra income for the company? Wasn't I working harder than ever to get more columns out to more markets? Sophia or no, I was an asset to *The Mag* now. I deserved a little something, I'd say.

Such as a real office.

I'd been in the same cubicle for almost seven years. Seven years of no privacy. Seven years of overheard conversations. Seven years of other people's aftershave and perfume and sneezes wafting in and contaminating everything in my cube. Once, I erected a beach umbrella roof over my cube but the nasty office manager made me take it down. I'd been considering plastic wrapping the top ever since.

Recently an office had opened up when an editor retired. Although it was being used for storage at the moment, I couldn't see why I couldn't ask for it. An office would give me the privacy I needed to get the petition letters read and copied into the column. Imagine that—doing work at work instead of at home. What a novel concept.

If I could convince Barb to give me the office, it would definitely help make it feel as if I'd earned some type of station—and this was as close as it was going to get to ranking up as an actual Sophia. After all, less distraction meant better Sophia action for my Demivamps. The two jobs were really closer to being one and the same.

Now, I thought as I pulled up my driveway, if only I could work up the nerve to go along with such a ballsy plan. I'd never asked Barb for anything and I had no idea how it would go.

Oh, well. Sometimes you had to take a leap of faith. If only I didn't have such a huge fear of falling.

The next morning, I paused outside Barb's door to gird my mental loins. It was go time.

"Hey, Barb," I said, as I marched into her office. "I was wondering if I could move my desk."

"Is Tiffany driving you crazy? I figured she would. That laugh of hers can be like a mosquito in the ear."

"Yeah, I guess, but it's just noise in general. Getting hard to concentrate in the open office."

"I don't think there's an open cube."

"But there is an office."

She looked taken aback. Private rooms in our department were at a covetous premium. "Office?"

"When Ben retired, nobody took his office. I was thinking maybe I could."

"You know that offices go to the seniors by pool—"

"And I've been the first topic of business at the last several editorial meetings. The column is generating real income for *The Mag*. No one else on my level can claim that."

"But you still don't have seniority. I can't justify—"

"Sure you can." I exuded a bit of Sophia persuasion, even though she was human and not as sensitive to my empathic touch. "I spent the morning evaluating the staff. I know I'm not taking what is due someone else."

Barbara chewed her lip, twin furrows dissecting the line of her brow. She was on the fence. All she needed was a nudge in the right direction.

I amped up another Sophia push. Not like I was using hypnotic powers to brainwash her so this could hardly be an ethics violation, right? "My productivity benefits your department. You'll be ensuring that the success of the syndication continues."

"I'll run it by Tom."

"Tom doesn't care who sits where, Barb."

"There's a good reason no one took that office before. I can get a lot of flak for this."

"From who?"

There it was. We were at an impasse. This was the point where, time after time, I gave in. Backed down. Slinked away. If I even made it this far.

And that had always been my problem.

It was difficult—physically difficult—to face off like this, to keep determined eye contact, a solid square of posture, a hard line of mouth. This wasn't me.

Barbara's gaze dropped to her desk. I wondered if she had trouble seeing me this way. "I'll...see what I can do."

I smiled with both cheeks and all my teeth. "Thanks! That's all I hoped for."

She didn't smile back and, when I left, she didn't say goodbye.

A little more than an hour later, an email from Barb came in.

I read the first line of the message and experienced a fat wave of satisfaction. So long, hive. Guess who'd be leaving the office collective to dwell in an office with a real door? Sophie the Conqueror, that's who. I spent a few seconds on fist pumps and congratulated myself. For the first time I wanted something, I went after it, and I got it.

But at what price? The rest of the email was cut and paste from an actual job description. Offices were reserved for full-time salaried staff. I wasn't salaried but, if I interpreted correctly, I had to start acting like I was. Top of the list was the weekly minimum hourly requirement and the skeleton schedule of editorial meetings. I noticed there was no weekly maximum and no overtime. Seriously? Over-time was a *contribution to the company*? I got my office, all right, and they threw in the prison bars for free.

So this was what getting my due felt like. Had to be honest—it was overrated.

Shortly before noon, the intercom buzzed and I heard Barbara's signature greeting. "Hello, hello?"

I sighed. I'd inferred a lot of tone from her email earlier, despite knowing the rules of office etiquette, and I had convinced myself that Barbara would hate me forever for being so pushy. I'd even decided that if I had to cave and relinquish the office, I'd do it. That *hello, hello* meant all my worries were one hundred percent my own neuroticism.

I saved my work and picked up. "Hi, Barb."

"Want to do lunch here today? There's a boxed lunch conference upstairs at noon."

"Thanks, but I planned on going out. Got an errand over lunch."

"Sounds like more work. Enjoy."

Truthfully, her suggestion was a lot more appealing than what I had in mind. The temperature seemed deter-mined to remain below fifty; I'd actually worn an undershirt under my blouse. Today was a day for indoors and hot drinks and a space heater under my desk. My lunch hour was going to rot.

The image of Toby sitting in that doorway the other night had haunted me. I knew it wasn't up to me to make sure he was okay—the kid was old enough to take care of himself. At his age, I'd had two jobs and managed to put myself through school. Maybe I'd had a negative net worth thanks to my student loans, but I had survived.

Toby wasn't me, though; the young Were seemed to have absolutely no anchor. I knew Dahlia had taken a shine to him, and I trusted her shrewdness would compensate for my lack of ability to make good character assessments. Compassion for his less-than-admirable plight had gnawed at me all weekend, and by Sunday evening I'd made up my mind. God help me, but it was time for an intervention.

I usually took my lunch break around two. The rest of the office usually went out between eleven and one but I often got into the zone doing column work, losing track of the time. I obeyed the muse, not the other way around. Since I'd made it a habit of leaving the office at nearly the same time every day, I set an alarm so I wouldn't get off schedule.

The alarm paid off. Toby was in the foyer and slid next to me as I walked out. I noticed he wore the sweatshirt that Dahlia had given him. "Hi, Soph. What's going on?"

"Lunch and an errand. Want to join me?"

He shrugged. "I guess. I don't have to be anywhere for a while yet. I got time."

I'd counted on that. I didn't have to be a Sophia to see the lie play behind his eyes, the little shift when he glanced away. He played it smooth, though. I had to give him that. "What have you been up to?"

"Aw, you know. Same old. Looking for work. No experience means no one wants to give you any. I guess I need to network a little more."

I nodded. That, I believed. Thankfully, Dahlia had been using her social worker mojo to fill me in on Were social structure. "Can't your den help out?"

"Den?" Toby belatedly pulled up a smile, much like a kid who got caught lying but was determined to lie his way out of it. "Well, you see, I don't see them all that much."

I decided to be blunt. "Do you belong to one?"

"Not really. No."

"Then they can't help you." I pointed across the street at the convenience store and we stepped up to the crosswalk. "Where are you staying?"

"Downtown. You know, you dropped me off there the other night."

"But I didn't see you going in anywhere." I was starting to sound like my mother. If I wasn't careful, I'd end up grounding us both.

"I saw some friends and stopped to talk to them, and ended up walking around for a while."

I reached for his elbow, pulling him to a stop. "Toby, tell me the truth. Are you okay?"

He shrugged away, distancing himself from me. "I'm fine. I don't know why you're asking. I can take care of myself. You too, if you'd quit being so stubborn and let me do it."

"Sorry." I looked away and softened my tone. Funny he should say something like that and odd he should seem to be sincere about it. "I guess I get carried away. It comes with the job."

"It's all right. Just don't hound me about it. You said you have an errand. What is it?"

"I, em, need help out at my new house. I just moved in

and the place is way bigger than I can handle. I hoped to find a private security firm, someone off the books. No one in the phonebook says they hire out experienced Weres."

He snorted. "You really think they'd put something like that in the Yellow Pages?"

"What do I know? You're the only Were I know. I thought maybe you could give me an idea."

"Well, what kind of work is it?"

"Not too complex, really. I mean, the house has a kitchen staff and a grounds crew and a security system. I was looking for someone who'd be part body-guard, part assistant." I figured official-sounding titles would be enough of a smokescreen to disguise my lame attempt to provide help without appearing to do so. "You know. A hood would be cool. I always wanted my own hired thug, maybe one with an eye-patch or a chainsaw arm. But I probably should go with someone a little less obvious."

"Why Were?"

"My staff are all DV, but the world has more than just DV in it. I'm just covering my bases."

"Any requirements?"

"Just one."

"Which is...?"

I looked him dead in the eye and sighed. "I have to trust them."

He chewed a fingernail and seemed to take it in.

I still didn't know him, even though I already felt responsible for him. Something about his ruffled hair re-minded me of one of my brothers, who'd had a cowlick that took up the entire crown of his head. His hair had been untamable. I remember getting it to lay down, just once—but that was because I'd slathered his hair with petroleum jelly. Mom wasn't pleased, although my father had just shrugged and nodded.

It was a long time since I had a brother. I couldn't let a memory dictate how I felt about this kid. However, I knew my gut, and I trusted my gut. My gut told me this kid was an orphan and that resonated with me.

When we reached the door, he pulled it open for me and we headed for the hot food counter. I selected a foil-wrapped bundle and elbowed him. "Don't make me eat alone."

"I wasn't going to. Lunch is on me." As he picked up a burger, he cleared his throat. "Is it something I could do?"

"I don't know. I mean, you'd have to move in and I don't know if that's something you're willing to do." I motioned to him to put it on the tray, and I slid our order down to the beverage station. He filled his cup with root beer. Not my favorite, but I took some anyway, hoping to convince him we were on the same team.

"Sounds like charity," he said. "I don't like that."

"Then don't look at it that way. I have a big place. You have none. There's nothing wrong with staying there until you get your feet on the ground. You can't get a real job unless you have an address and a social security number. Stay at my place until you can establish both."

"I do have a social security number. I just haven't needed it."

"Well, soon you'll have an address, too."

"I'm only going to keep owing you. At this rate, you'll own me."

"I told you, I need help. I don't know what kind yet, but I know I'll need it."

He handed the cashier a beat up-looking ten and asked her for two bags. "Can I think about it?"

"Sure. I didn't think you'd move in immediately."

"I'll, ah, meet you when you go to lunch Wednesday. I'll let you know what I decide to do."

Once I got back to *The Mag*, I called Rodrian's cell.

"Hey, there." His voice was warm, and I could almost hear him smiling. "You at work?"

"Yeah. I just came in from lunch. I was wondering if you were doing anything tonight."

"Nothing that can't be put off. Are you asking me out?" His teasing tone made me duck my head, as if I'd worried someone could overhear him. I wished he wouldn't go out of his way to be so damned luscious. Then again, he probably wasn't trying.

"Nothing so promising. Would you drive me to my meeting with Eirene tonight?"

"Sure. Can I ask why?"

"Couple reasons. Seven okay?"

"Can do. See you then."

I hung up the phone, and, feeling like my ducks were nicely lined up, I went back to solving other people's problems. Well, the ones I got paid to solve, anyway.

The front door slammed at ten to seven.

I shut down my computer and trotted over to the door of the office where I'd been working. "Hey."

Rodrian slid off his black raincoat and ruffled his bangs back as he looked up at me. "Shiloh home?"

"She's up here. Come on up." I retreated to my desk as I heard the clink of his keys hitting the side table in the foyer. Shiloh had been sitting on a futon we'd dragged over from the tri-suites. The office had been too officey for her comfort.

"Well," Rodrian said. Shiloh patted the cushion next to her and Rodrian leaned to kiss her head before sitting down, stretching his arm out along the top of the couch behind her. "How was your day, sweetheart?"

"Okay. I have a feeling Sophie's going to ruin it, though."

Rodrian regarded me intently. "She is, is she?"

Shiloh's voice dropped to a loud whisper. "She's been

pacing for an hour. Looks like she's rehearsing for an argument."

I stopped pacing. Dang it. "Hello? Not deaf."

"And she's touchy, too."

"Sophie, what's on your mind?" Rodrian pushed up from the couch with a sigh and crossed the room. He sat on the edge of his desk and crossed his arms. Uh, oh. His power held a taint of suspicion.

"Well." I faked a relaxed smile. "I wanted to run the idea of a house guest by you both."

"Dahlia?" Rodrian asked.

I shook my head. "No."

"How about that hottie from the movie store?" Shiloh smirked. "The one who tries to impress you with his almost vast knowledge of foreign films?"

Rodrian looked peeved. "What hottie?"

"Not a hottie. And no. Not him."

"Who, already?" I could tell Shiloh was reaching the end of her patience, which ran shorter than normal these days.

"My friend, Toby."

"Who's Toby?" Rodrian maintained the peeved expression. "That sounds like a pet's name."

Shiloh guffawed. Really. "Good one, Dad. Fitting too, don't you think, Soph?"

"That's not nice, Shy." I frowned at her in what I hope was a parental manner.

She shrugged it off. "That's the way the ball bounces. Incidentally, does he fetch?"

"Can we be serious?"

"Serious, as in *not funny*? Or Sirius, the Dog Star?"

I used my no-nonsense voice, which was as effective as a kiss on the cheek. "Shiloh."

"Who is Toby?" Rodrian raised his voice, cutting us off.

"My friend." When he tightened his lips, I knew a

compulsion would follow if I didn't come out and say it. "He's Were."

"Absolutely not," Rodrian said.

"Why not?"

"Wait," said Shiloh. "Even I know the answer to this one. He's Were."

"He's a person," I insisted. "He's not a criminal."

"You know this for a fact?"

"Depends on your definition of *know*." I tried to look anything but inept, as if he wouldn't sense it.

"What's he do for a living?"

My stammering blew any chance of convincing Rodrian that Toby wasn't a bum.

"Right," he said. "No. Not a chance."

"I thought I had autonomy here."

"Of course you do."

"Then, I want him to stay."

"And I strongly urge you to reconsider." Rodrian smoothed all expression from his face.

Wow, here I thought we were past the Bossy Jerk phase of our relationship. Wrong Again Sophie, that's me. "Rode, it's almost winter. He doesn't have any place to go. Dahlia will vouch for him. "

"Dahlia knows him?"

"Mmm hmm. So does Shiloh."

"She does?" He craned his neck to look at her. "You do?"

Shiloh wouldn't look up. "Yeah, and he's annoying. But...Sophie's right. He doesn't even have a coat. I feel a little bad for him."

"See?" I edged closer to Rodrian and did my best to look plaintive. "I need to help him, Rode."

"Oh, sure. Play my sympathy." He rested his brow upon his raised fist. "It's up to Shy."

She stared at me so hard I could almost see the wheels turning in her brain. "Keep him out of my rooms. Especially my kitchen."

"Deal."

"No shedding in the house or clogging up the pool filter with fur."

I laughed. "Deal."

"And no barking or dog noises. Especially no howling. What's with the howling, anyway? Shut up! It's the moon, loser. Get over it."

"Finished?"

"Almost. Is he housebroken?"

"Now you're just being a smart ass."

"You bet." She grinned. "Weres are stupid."

I sighed. "Deal?"

"Deal."

I turned to Rodrian, technically not needing his approval but hoping for it anyway. His resigned expression was good enough.

"Okay," he said. "But, I'm warning you—one wrong move and I'll skin him alive." He meant it; if his power ever gave an impression of rock-solid conviction, it was then. He might not be as forbidding as Marek had been but he meant every word.

"He'll be on his best behavior. I promise." I was cut off when Shiloh's cell phone rang.

She flicked it open as she got up to leave. "Oh, hi, Lori. Guess what? We're getting a dog."

"Who's Lori?" Rodrian tugged on Shiloh's sleeve. "I don't remember that name."

Shiloh pulled out of his reach and hurried for the door. "Overprotective much, Dad? Jeez."

Rodrian watched her leave, a look of disappointment upon his face. It didn't brighten when he turned back toward me. I sank a little inside.

He glanced at his watch. "You want to grab your coat? It's nearly seven."

"Sure. I'll meet you downstairs."

I went to my room to get my woolen coat, crossing my fingers that my little request wouldn't make for a cold ride in to the city. I'd hate for a little thing like Toby moving in to get between me and Rodrian, especially when things were going so well.

He got us to the hotel in record time, despite the heavy influx of cars. Maybe it was luck the way spots opened between the lanes, allowing him to zig-zag the entire way. Maybe he was really annoyed with me for pushing for something I knew he hated. Either way.

I struggled to find something to talk about but couldn't get past small talk. I glanced at him a few times but he seemed intent on the road.

Rodrian's curiosity pressed down on me the entire ride over, even though he'd never actually said anything about wanting to meet Eirene. I broke the silence once more as we neared the hotel. "You want to come in?"

He flipped on the turn signal and merged into traffic without even looking, a habit that made me cringe. It was as if the turn signal was enough to make everyone give him the room he wanted. Bossy driver.

"Nah." He wasn't being cold, exactly, but I could tell he was still irritated with the whole Toby thing. That didn't stop him from being curious.

"Come on. I know you don't believe she exists. See for yourself."

"I guess I could stop in just a moment." His voice was neutral but I detected a quick blip of *oh, goody*. I rolled my eyes. No wonder he only dated human women. We must all seem like bubbleheads to him.

He flicked on his flashers and pulled up in front of the hotel. Rodrian waved off the advances of the doorman who had hurried toward the curb, holding his cap to his head with a gloved hand. Rodrian opened my door himself and sheltered me with his arm. Together we hurried inside, grateful to escape the bite of wind.

The lobby swarmed with guests arriving and departing. After a moment I spied Eirene and her assistant sitting apart from the busier part of the lobby. I refused to refer to Dorcas as a servant, even though Eirene treated her like one.

Eirene seemed to watch everyone at once, her black eyes darting from one to another like a cat. Dorcas sat nearby, stern-faced and uninterested, as if waiting for a command to reanimate her.

Dorcas spotted us before Eirene did. A luggage trolley slid between us and by the time it had passed, they were on their feet and heading our way.

The Sophia wore a sly smile, a cat-like smirk to match her wary glance, and made no effort to hide her interest in Rodrian.

His hair was loose tonight, his bangs flopping down around his eyes like a cologne model in a *Cosmo* ad. I didn't understand how he refrained from flaunting his appeal. I supposed that although he was excruciatingly handsome, Rodrian just considered it his face and never thought twice about it. Except when he could play it to his advantage, that is.

Tonight, he seemed aware she was checking him out. He fell back a step, brushing his hand against my waist and hovering behind my shoulder.

"Sophie..." Eirene's voice was a purr of smooth charm. "So glad to see you again."

Although she looked only at me, the expected introduction loomed. I sure as hell didn't want to introduce them. She'd already openly appraised him and I suddenly felt protective of Rodrian. I nearly stepped in front of him to block him from view.

It would have been rude. Thankfully my manners prevailed. It was abundantly clear to me that a woman like Eirene took manners and protocol very seriously and I couldn't afford to offend her.

"Hello, Eirene. Dorcas," I added. I nodded to the ubiquitous woman. She didn't acknowledge me but Eirene's eyes did a sideways slide, a hint of almost-disapproval. Oh well, err on the side of kindness, I always said.

I half-turned to Rodrian but, between that moment and the next, he began to broadcast, releasing an emotional current so powerful I almost buckled beneath it. It wasn't power, per se, the calling card DV used to announce themselves; it was just emotion. Raw, unrestrained emotion.

Startled, I looked up at him, wondering what could have happened. His bedroom eyes and charming smile revealed nothing of the pain and worry in which he drowned me. *Shiloh. Vague fear for Shiloh's safety. Shiloh's delicate condition.*

A slight touch of his hand, a small pressure on my lower back, told me not to react. It was followed by a compulsion that forced a calm expression onto my face, a smile for Eirene. All the while, Rodrian streamed anxiety so intense that I caught images. *Shiloh, weak. Shiloh collapsing. Shiloh in a hospital bed, bruised eyes, thin breaths. Shiloh screaming in pain.* He clamped down harder with his compulsion, forcing me to drink in his pain while appearing to be perfectly fine.

*Do not react,* his compulsion said. It took every ounce of strength I had to obey, even with the force of his compulsion.

Behind my serene mask, I swallowed hard and focused on his hand. "Eirene, this is Rodrian Thurzo. Rodrian, this is Sophia Eirene, who has been gracious enough to offer me her tutelage."

Her eyes flashed briefly, a spark of Sophia blue, as she offered up her delicate hand, palm down. He hesitated a moment before grasping her fingers and bowing over her hand, all the while pouring out anxiety and commanding me to be still. I closed my eyes, nauseous from the strain and hoped his compulsion would prevent me from being sick on Eirene's shoes.

"A pleasure," she murmured. If she felt his emotion, she certainly didn't show it. Of course she had control and grace under pressure. I resented her for it. "Our newest Sophia is fortunate to have such handsome acquaintances. It makes the work more enjoyable, does it not?"

"Not as fortunate as are the DV," he replied smoothly. "Who knew salvation could be wrapped in such exquisite packaging?"

Laughter, the sound of crystal chimes, tinkled as she basked in his charm. "Mr. Thurzo is too kind."

"And running late." He sighed as he allowed his emotional storm to subside. "I'm saddened to part company so abruptly. Call me when you are ready to leave, Sophie. All right?"

I nodded, confused and concerned over his display. He sent a discreet wave of assurance.

"Ladies." With the slight nod he'd perfected as a restaurant host, he left.

"Is everything well with you?" Eirene tilted her head toward me once Rodrian had disappeared from view. "You seem troubled."

Slowly, my stomach untied its knots. "I—am. For a moment I thought—something was wrong."

"How so?"

Hadn't she felt him? I'd have fallen to my knees if not for his compulsion keeping me upright. "He's distraught. Family problems. Something must have set him off. I could have wept for his pain."

"Oh." Her voice was even. "Yes. His emotions were painful, were they not?"

I nodded, looking back over my shoulder toward the doors, still concerned and wondering if I should have followed him.

"Yes. It is evident, the work you have ahead of you."

I turned back toward her sharply, not believing my ears. "What?"

"You are troubled by his pain. You do not know how to shield yourself, do you?" Her mouth pressed into a thin frown. "Small wonder you seem to have such a weak constitution, battered about by every little emotion. You expend too much energy, caring for every little hurt."

I protested. "A Sophia is meant to care—"

"Yes, yes. To care. Not to drown in every emotional river that is cried. Honestly. How do you expect to be of service to the Demivampire race if you exhaust yourself over one single person? Tch." She shook her head slowly, dark eyes boring into mine. "Control. If you do not learn a semblance of control, you will only be a puppet."

I narrowed my eyes. "You mean you didn't have the least bit of compassion for him? You didn't want to help him?"

She frowned in superiority. "Of course I felt him. Of course I wanted to reach out to him. I chose not to react, to loosen what little hold you have over your Demivampire. If I had offered my gift to him, you would have lost him."

Humility flushed my cheeks, chasing the last of my chill away. Nothing like a good reprimand to warm those cold November evenings.

Eirene, apparently, was as adept at ignoring my discomfort as she was Rodrian's. She assumed her audience-receiving smile and took up my hand as if we were lifelong friends. "Come, Sophie. We will dine in my rooms. I fear we have no time to waste with you. Your lessons must begin at once. Or else—"

She looked at the empty space where Rodrian had stood only moments before. "Or else you lose them, one by one."

Eirene settled onto the couch directly across from me, skirt smoothed across her lap under still hands. "Imagine... imagine a circle on the ground around you. Lift it up."

"What do you mean?"

"We are raising a barrier."

"A wall."

"More than wall. It encloses you on all sides."

"How high does it have to go?"

Her eyes flicked away and back as she blinked twice. "That is not important. First you must raise it."

"A circle."

"Circle, yes."

"But a circle isn't a wall."

"Not a wall. An—enclosure."

"So, a tube. What if they come over the top?"

She dropped her shoulder and exhaled through her nose, looking very much like she wanted to rap my fingers with a ruler. "You are making this harder than it needs to be."

"Fine." Honestly, I wasn't trying to be aggravating. "A circle. What's it made of?"

"Yourself, of course."

I stared blankly. She wanted me to build a meat circle?

"Your magic." Eirene leaned forward, as if by doing so she could push comprehension into my brain.

"You keep saying magic. I don't have magic."

"Your empathy."

"My empathy isn't a solid thing."

"Neither are your barriers. They are power, same as what you feel from the DV."

"How can I make a circle with that?"

She closed her eyes in utter frustration. "Just try. Think of something physical to which you can relate. Close your eyes. See the circle on the ground. Lift it up. Let your magic form a curtain, which hangs from it. That is your barrier."

Well, that did give me a bit more to go on. I closed my eyes and imagined I stood inside a hula hoop. Slowly I lifted it, trying to imagine the curtain hanging and eventually focused on the image of standing inside a shower curtain. It was close and clingy and I hated it, but if it was what she wanted... "Okay. Then what?"

"I will test it."

A sharp mental jab hit me in the side, hard enough to register physical pain. I yelped and dropped the hula hoop. The shower curtain barrier crumpled and vanished. "WTF, Eirene?"

Eirene barked her displeasure. "That was no barrier!"

I rubbed my side. "No kidding. I didn't know it was supposed to be an iron curtain."

"You are not concentrating."

"I am! I just have no idea what I'm supposed to be doing."

She pressed her lips together in a grim smile. "Then I will have to show you."

She rose and circled the table, stopping in front of me. She placed her hands on the side of my head, thumbs making an uncomfortable pressure on my temples, and closed her eyes.

I felt a tremendous twist, like a pulled muscle deep inside my head. For a moment, I saw a double image—myself from her standing perspective and her from mine—and panicked.

"Close your eyes," she said. "Focus. Go to the place where the Sophia sleeps."

I closed my eyes, sinking into the place where the Sophia coiled itself. I was inside the Sophia.

A gentle almost-color, warmly lit, the only sound being the windy pulse of blood in my ears. It was the visual equivalent of the feeling of curling in a warm bed, knowing the alarm wouldn't go off. Comfort and security.

*Now, watch.* Eirene's voice sounded around me. *Your circle.*

A hazy glow appeared where I'd imagine my feet to be, if I had a body here. Enchanted, I reached for it.

*Yes. Lift it.*

It rose around me with the slightest mental effort. It wasn't a curtain, exactly; it was a sheen of power, like a film of bubble solution. It swirled with color, cobalt and gold, a stretch of breezy summer sky. I reached out to caress it, and it flowed around me like water, like sand. Everywhere, the scent of apples and smoking wood and clean wind.

It was me. My personality, my wonder, my delight. It ran through the colors, making them dance. Everything my DV friends had ever said about me, my scent, it was here. I touched the barrier and recognized it. It recognized me.

Eirene made a pleased sound. *Your magic. That is you. If you know what you are, you can keep others out. Look through it. Look for Dorcas.*

I noticed a concentration of reddish-black haze hovering nearby. I tried not to think how it suited her less-than-sparkling personality while I reached out my hand in its direction. *That?*

*Yes.*

*Do all people look like—that?*

*There are similarities, I would say. You will eventually learn to recognize specific Demivampires by the appearance of their power.*

"But I didn't think you were DV, Dorcas." I wasn't sure she could hear inside my head. This whole experience was so strange I wasn't sure what was real.

Eirene laughed, a tinkle of brittle crystal. *She isn't. She is...unique. Now. We will test your barriers again. I fear that Dorcas is not as restrained as I am. You will do your best.*

I gulped, watching the barrier waver. Summoning my resolve, I focused on the strength of the barrier around me. The sheen of power responded, color pulsing thicker, brighter. The strength of the shield was controlled by my will.

Distracted by the discovery, I nearly missed the ball of red-black haze hurtling toward me. Steeling myself against the blow, I focused on my blue and gold swirl and resisted the intruder. I kept my colors and my pattern intact, untouched, and they deflected the ball.

The ball retreated, and Eirene's voice sounded. *Good. Now tell me what you did.*

*I'm—not sure. I saw color coming at me and reacted.*

*Reacted how?*

*I didn't want the color to ruin mine. I—kept mine pure.*

*Yes.* Her mind voice lifted with approval. *Now. Again.*

Another ball of dark streaked toward me, this time with enough force to jar.

*Good. Again.*

Time and again, different color patterns, different shapes, different levels of power came at me. Some struck with trembling force, while others melted against my barrier, seeking a way to insinuate itself through. Time and again I held my power, my curtain of protection around me.

*Yes. Yes. Well-done, Sophia. Now, I will show you how to reach through your barriers without compromising them. Reach for me.*

The reddish-brown blob of Dorcas' light hovered just outside my periphery. On my guard, I kept it in sight, expecting a sneak attack. *I don't see you.*

*I am here.* The Dorcas-haze stretched and multiplied. I hadn't expected her to be the same shade of ick.

Did all humans look like that? Did I look like that? Because, I had to admit—it was a pretty gross color.

*Let me inside your shield.*

I let the circle fall around me and felt her move closer to me. Once she was "in", I raised the veil once more.

*And so we start...*Taking my mental hand in hers, she reached through and the barrier yielded, stretching easily. *You can touch the power of others in this way, adjusting the thickness of the barrier to control how much you allow though. It is always yours to control.*

*Mine?* I reached out again, without her assistance, and felt my power hum along my skin, covering it like a tight glove. I couldn't believe it. I had the control?

Her throaty chuckled filled the confines of my barrier. *You always had the control. You just needed to learn how to use it. Now.*

She turned our attention back outside the barrier, where the reddish-black mist congealed into a ball. *You defend yourself, while reaching out to the other power, as I watch.*

Dorcas reared and charged as the assaults began anew.

I thought they'd never end.

It was well past two when the Audi pulled up outside. By that time, I stood against the front window, resting my head against the glass. Eirene and Dorcas had remained behind in their suite so there were no awkward goodbyes. I didn't waste a moment running out to the car.

As I pulled the door closed, he leaned over the steering wheel and watched me buckle in. "I thought you might end up having a slumber party with your new girlfriend."

Too weary to even make a proper *ugh* face, I winced and settled back in the seat, aiming the heater vents at me. "I'm gonna be crap for work tomorrow. I spent the last hour looking for a way to leave and couldn't think of one that wouldn't offend her."

"She seems high-strung."

"Not even close to the right word." I loosened my scarf as I warmed to the heater. "She's so experienced. And, apparently, there is some set of books that talk all about what I'm supposed to have already figured out. Canons, she calls them."

I looked over at him to see if the name registered. He shrugged.

"Yeah, well, anyways. The Sophia Canons are conveniently guarded by some mysterious group, who tuck them away in a tiny church in Hungary when they aren't traveling."

"Hungary?" Rodrian's interest seemed to pique. "Marek spent a lot of time there."

"I figured as much. I found a bunch of travel books upstairs about Hungary. Frank once mentioned they'd been there, as well." Frank was Marek's foster son who'd spent his childhood with the Thurzos. I didn't like thinking about Frank. When he was killed by vampires, a part of me died with him.

"Marek told you about our family, didn't he? Our father's line came from that area."

Of course, he hadn't. Marek and I hadn't shared enough time together. I didn't waste time mourning our relationship, though; I was too tired.

"Get out," I said instead. "Marek never told me about your ethnic background. He made allusions to some ancient culture but all this time it was just Hungarian? What an ethno-snob."

"Not Hungarian," he said. "Older than that. Our line began long before Hungary drew borders around itself."

"Figures. Can't be ordinary. Do I get a clue?"

"Thrace. He traced our lineage back to Thrace. Beyond that, it gets murky."

"Thrace. You mean, *Spartacus* Thrace?"

"The same." He smiled. "I should have known, your love for ancient culture includes Thracians."

"Not exactly. Apart from reading *National Geo-graphic*, I don't know much."

"Nor do I. Marek's the historian, not I. The only books I like are the ones that tell me how much money I have."

Practical Rodrian.

"I suppose that will have to change, now," he said. "Somebody needs to carry our history. I always thought it would be Marek." The expressway was nearly empty, and he left the speed limit far behind. Even if he were to get pulled over, I was sure he wouldn't be above compelling his way out of a ticket.

"He's the strong one, the smart one, the one with worlds of research and knowledge in his head. I never prepared to be head of our family. Marek's supposed to be here, damn it."

So much came pouring out in a flood. I had no idea he'd been feeling this way. Pitiful, actually, considering who I was supposed to be.

"Rode, easy. Come here." I reached out for his hand but he pulled away as far as the seat would allow.

"No. Don't touch me."

"What did I do?"

"It's not you, it's the Sophia. Don't make this easier. I have to do it on my own."

"Why?"

He clenched the steering wheel, his knuckles paling under the effort. "Marek did."

"Marek didn't have a Sophia to help him."

"Exactly. He managed just fine."

"Did he now? I'll say. He managed himself right to the brink of evolution. That's something to admire."

"Don't talk about him like that." His anger turned defensive.

"I'll talk about him any way I choose. I believe I earned the right. You're messed up, Rode. Your emotions are warring and you're not at balance. I can't stand by and watch you beat yourself to pieces." I reached out and grabbed his arm; at first he jerked away, recoiling as if he'd push back. The muscles bunched tightly under my hand but he remained still and didn't shake me off. Gently I woke the Sophia and allowed his anguish to drain.

"I can't tell you how to fix Shy. I can't tell you how to become your brother. But I am the Sophia, Rode, and I can ease your journey. Would you deny me the only thing I can offer?"

"It's not the only thing you can offer." His power reared and settled, taking my notice, making me aware of the predator within. It was a subtle shift; Rodrian's power always had an aggressive undertow to it but it was the rough desire to acquire, to accumulate. Not greed—just the want for more. It suited the business man.

Now it was as if his power lost the Armani shell. Aggression in a less refined form isn't classy. It's just aggression.

And a predator is still a predator.

"It's the only thing that I'm offering right now," I said firmly. I was too tired for gentle redirection, and I thickened my shield. Controlling it was still a skill I had yet to perfect, so I more or less threw everything I had into it. "It's up to you to do the right thing."

"Why me?"

"Because I can't stop you from doing anything."

"You make it sound like you're at my mercy."

"I am."

He opened his mouth to protest, but seemed to have second thoughts. "I suppose you are. So why do you stay?"

"You're worth the risk. All of you are."

He took his left hand off the wheel long enough to slide my hand down to his other hand and held my in his solid grip. "I'd never betray your trust in me. Do you believe me?"

"I believe you're sincere when you say it but I also know the rules now."

"Rules such as..."

"Your free will isn't the same as mine, Rode. Just as you have the ability to compel humans to go against their will, evolution holds the same sway over you. It's nature. You'd never betray me on purpose but, one day, evolution might push you to do something you normally wouldn't."

"You really believe that, don't you?"

I nodded. "How else would anything make sense? Marek wouldn't have done what he did if it hadn't been for a force beyond his control."

Guilt and sorrow streaked through Rodrian's power. I felt him ebb away as he tightened his control, pushed his barriers up, and locked me out. "I guess."

"At any rate, Eirene has my work cut out for me. There are plenty of rules she said I'll have to learn. Apparently I'm lucky I haven't bubbed everything up to hell with my ineptitude. Thank God she's here."

"Why?"

"Because she knows how to be an actual Sophia. Don't you see? She can help Marek. She can help all of you. Me?" I snorted. "I'm a lousy Sophia. Maybe now I have a chance to actually do some real good."

"Lousy? Compared to what?"

He had a point. "I'm not sure exactly but I'm pretty confident that I'm not operating on a goddess level."

"You're not a goddess, that's why. You're an oracle. Oracles interpret things. Make cloudy things clearer. Not even close to being a goddess."

"Eirene seems to think otherwise."

"Maybe because she's a snotty bitch."

My mouth dropped open in shock and I stared at him.

Never mind that I secretly agreed with him. "She's a Sophia, Rode. I think she deserves a little more credit than snotty bitch."

"When she acts like it, I'll take it back."

"But she's a real Sophia. She's read the Canons. She knows how to do her job."

He sniffed, a disdainful sound. "Does she now?"

"Sure." I shrugged. "I watched her."

"Too bad she wasn't willing to prove it to me."

"Is that why you forbade me to tap you before? You put on a show? To test her?"

"Yeah." He ignored my glare. "I couldn't help it. I had to see if she was any good."

What a slut. Did Rodrian need to test-drive every woman he met? I huffed out a breath, feeling much crankier. "Well?"

"Well, what?"

"Was she any good?"

"No."

"No?" My mouth hung open. Good thing there were no flies around.

"No. I practically had to sit on you to keep you from reacting, even after I compelled you. You almost broke free of it. She never batted an eye."

"I know. She said she ignored you."

"Ignored it?" His voice was incredulous.

"On purpose," I insisted. "She said she didn't want to interfere with my DV." I didn't add that she'd implied that one taste of her and my puppy would run away from home. Frigging Pied Piper bitch.

Rodrian shook his head and cast me a dubious glance. "Yeah, well, anyone who could ignore feelings like that, on purpose or not, isn't my idea of a Sophia. I wouldn't want her. As far as I'm concerned, you're fine the way you are.

You don't need to take pointers from someone like her."

"I'm afraid I don't have a choice. I'm going to see her again. I have to," I added when he groaned. "I'm missing something, Rode. If she's the only Sophia I'll ever meet, then I have to keep seeing her. I promise I won't learn her bad manners."

"It's not bad manners I worry about, Soph. It's just bad, period."

"I'll be okay. Everything will be okay."

"Hope that's a premonition," he said as he pulled up the driveway. "Because, so far, all the omens have been pretty bleak."

A few days later, Toby met me up in the parking garage after work. All he had was a duffle bag, which he stuck in the trunk. While we drove out to the Stocks, I remembered how inadequate I'd felt when I moved in, lamenting that all I owned fit in a U-Haul.

All Toby owned fit in the gym bag in my trunk.

He cracked the window, despite the cold sting of winter. He just wanted to smell the wind, he said.

Sometimes, I forgot the kid was a werewolf. I only saw the ruffled hair, the charming grin, the subtle vulnerability in the way he held himself. Then he'd go ahead and do something like press his nose to the open window.

He chatted all the way out but fell silent when I pulled up the driveway. I remembered the first time I'd come here; I'd been stunned, too. It was a gorgeous driveway flanked by green trees and flowering bushes in the summer. In November, all that remained were bare branches with a few stubborn dead leaves attached. Not exactly a warm welcome.

He shouldered his bag and followed me up the porch steps without speaking a word, gazing around at the lights and the columns and the high roof.

"So this is where you live?" Toby was incapable of disguising his amazement.

"Yeah, quaint, huh?" It slipped out. Marek's choice of words. Funny how I adopted them. I unlocked the door and showed him inside.

His eyes grew round when he took in the foyer. I guess the chandelier was a bit daunting.

"Depends. Does *quaint* mean *hoo-wee, shi*—"

"I was joking, Toby." I shrugged and looked at him as he paused in the doorway, holding his duffle bag on his shoulder. "You want to come in all the way? You're letting the bought air out."

Toby managed to take his eyes off the ceiling and hurried inside, closing the door carefully as if he were afraid to get fingerprints on anything.

"Well," I said, "you get the abbreviated tour. Upstairs are the bedrooms, no need for you to worry about those. Office there, den there." I pointed to each door. "Kitchen down that way, enter at your own peril. I have to tell Bethany you'll be staying here. Basement through that side door there. The basement is neat, so feel free to explore. I guess the guest room is yours."

We headed down the hall toward the guest suite. "If you keep going you'll hit the garage and back patio door but your room is through here. Those other doors stay locked since the guest suite has its own patio entrance. You can come and go if you need to."

I pushed open the door to the guest suite and showed him in. It was like walking into a little house; the Stocks had originally been a simple farm cottage that had grown a mansion attached to it. It had been Marek's idea of "adding on."

The suite had kept its rustic trappings, looking authentically decorated in what I figured was probably post-Revolutionary Americana and was completely out of character with the rest of the property.

Living at the Stocks had often made me feel out of place and sometimes the *you-break-it-you-buy-it* feelings ran a little high. I'd often escaped the oppression of luxury by coming down here to read, enjoying the simple feel of country and flannel and comfortable imperfection. Euphrates usually stayed down here when I was gone. Rodrian even had the grounds man install a pet door so Fraidy could go outside whenever he wanted.

He was a very happy cat here. I wondered how he'd react to a werewolf moving in with him.

Toby crossed the sitting room to the windows and peered through the curtains. "Wow! That's some big yard, Red."

"You mean you didn't notice it from the driveway?"

"Not really. The house was in the way. These woods yours?"

"Yeah. Hey, if you need woods, there you go. Just don't leave presents on the door mat."

"Oh," he said. "I expect I'll be gone by full moon. This is just temporary."

"Sure," I said, although I didn't believe him. "Anyway, that's your bedroom around the corner, there."

He bounded through the door but came to an abrupt stop.

"Gee," he said, sounding less than enthusiastic. "Bed's so...well, I can smell you. Not that it's bad, or anything," he added hurriedly.

"I know and I'm sorry. It's my old bed. I stay down here

sometimes." I hadn't really thought it all the way through that someone would be sleeping in my bed. It kind of struck a discord. I had it broken in, just the way I liked it, and now some goofy kid was going to wolf it all up. "Sometimes I can't sleep and I come down to read. I'd offer you one of the rooms upstairs but Shiloh is up there and I just don't think that would go over well."

The house phone rang. "I got to get that. Make yourself at home."

I sprinted out to the foyer and up to the office. If I didn't soon get a phone put in the den, I thought, my heart will explode. I wasn't built for such strenuous exercise. Maybe I needed the Rocky theme for the ringtone.

Caller ID showed it was *The Mag*. Who could still be there at this time? "Hello?"

"Hello, hello," came Barb's voice. "Emergency editorial meeting at seven tonight."

"Seven? I just walked in. You mean I have to come all the way back into town?"

"Happens. Marketing lost a full-page ad and we need to fill the gap. It can't wait until tomorrow."

I shouldered the phone and shuffled through clips and piles on my desk. "Do I need to bring anything to offer?"

"Nope. You'll pretty much just sit there, listen to everyone else, and agree that what they want is right. This is a seniors meeting. You're too junior to contribute."

"Then why do I need to come in?"

"Appearances. That office of yours comes with a lot of baggage, kiddo."

No kidding. I was starting to regret my choices. Still. I had to maintain my station. I couldn't stop being a Sophia, and it wasn't like I could give back my office. I really liked it. It was a huge sneeze guard. I sighed.

"Sophie? Are you there?"

"Yeah, okay. I'm just thinking about the drive. There's construction in the eastbound lane. Traffic was backed up for miles."

"Make sure you give yourself enough time to get in. You know, it wouldn't have been a problem when you lived in the city."

I considered that. Of course, I left my last apartment because I was being chased by a werewolf. Who, incidentally, turned out to be a friend and, also incidentally, was some-where downstairs getting ready to move into my house. Damn and blast. My compassionate choices were already biting me in the ass.

Well, at least it was only figuratively. I wasn't the biggest fan of teeth marks.

I ran down to the tri-suites and checked the fridge, hungry and hating to run out on Toby so soon after bringing him here. Finding a bowl of leftover rice and beans from Dahlia's last visit, I stuck it into the microwave and hit the leftovers button.

Might be a good idea to find a hot dog or two to add to it, I thought, remembering Toby's dismay at the noodle-and-nothing-else shop, as he called it.

By the time I had everything heated, it was almost time for me to head back to town. I stopped in the office to pick up my purse, which I'd dropped on the desk when I had answered the phone.

Toby was in the office when I walked in. He was perusing my music collection with amusement. Why was my taste in music funny to these kids? Hard rock was a perfectly enjoyable form of music. An art form, if you will.

He lifted his chin in the direction of my rooms. "What's down the creepy hallway?"

"Oh." I was pretty sure I knew which one he meant. "That's my bedroom down there."

"How can you stand it? I get itchy just looking at the door."

I shrugged and held out the covered bowl. "I don't know. It doesn't bother me."

"Well." He took the bowl, sniffing it and smiling his appreciation. "I don't think you're like anybody else. You must be a heck of a lot more if you can stand that pit of pricklies. Feels like a booby trap or something. No wonder you've been sleeping in my bed."

I smirked. "Just stay out of trouble. I need to go back to work for a while so maybe you want to hang out in your room until I get back."

I didn't even point out how much I disliked hearing him say "my bed" and mean "his bed". Oh well, I made the bed, no matter whose it was now, so I supposed I'd have to lie in it.

Sad thing was I didn't know what bothered me more: him sleeping in my bed or me going back to sleeping in Marek's.

Just—ugh.


Three hours later, my patience for evening driving depleted, and my brows lowered in stubborn disgust at having to waste an entire evening at a useless appearance at a stupid editorial board, I arrived home feeling slightly punished. Curse you, day job. I was too tired to shake my fist in anger.

Once upstairs, I faced down the mammoth bed, glaring at it. It was time for a change.

I set upon the task of removing the thick bed curtains. Perhaps it would help alleviate the dreams and the fear of confinement. That's how I felt when I woke up from one of those dreams. Trapped.

The poles were tight and took a little elbow grease (and

more than a little swearing) but eventually I got the curtains off. I dragged the dusty things out to the hallway and heaved them over the banister, intending to take them downstairs to the industrial washer I'd seen in the boiler room. Returning to my quarters, I gave one last inspection of the room.

The only thing left to do was to get rid of the cruddy old sword hanging over the bed. I hadn't really noticed it before when the bed clothes were in the way but now it stuck out like the anti-Martha Stewart had taken a go at decorating. I didn't relish the thought of falling asleep with a monstrous-looking blade dangling over my head.

Euphrates had wandered in and investigated the room, pausing to rub his back on the bureau and against the leg of the bed. Eventually he hopped up on the bed and sprawled across my pillow, stretching and rubbing his chin against the blanket. He blinked lazily at me, giving me his best glare. Hopefully we'd both be sleeping good tonight.

Feeling pretty much defeated as far as my bed went, I grabbed a stack of sheets from the linen closet in the hallway before heading down to check on my newest orphan. Downstairs Toby was fooling with the pet door. He appeared to be pretty fascinated by the little gate.

I lifted the stack of sheets in explanation before I walked toward the bedroom and peered through the door. He'd rearranged the room completely, positioning the bed under the now-open window.

He glanced up when I rapped on the doorway.

"I met your cat," he said.

"I saw. You didn't scare him, did you?"

"Nah. He came in through the pet door, I guess. He's pretty smart. I asked him where he came from and he led me to that little door. He's a cool little guy."

"So. You made friends with my cat? I figured he would

have fallen down dead when he saw you."

"Aw, he don't like strangers?"

"He doesn't see many, no, but I'm sure you're the first Were he's met."

Toby just lifted his shoulders in a shrug. "It's not the moon yet. He thinks I'm just a guy who knows how to pet a cat the right way. Don't tell him, okay? About me, I mean. I don't want to upset him."

Were we still talking about my cat? Toby spoke of him as if Euphrates was a person, not an animal, even though Euphrates considered himself the smartest beast in the room. "No problem. And here—I brought you fresh sheets."

He looked contrite. "Thanks. I just don't want to cause problems by wearing your scent like that. People might get the wrong idea about us."

Oh, boy. That was another thing I hadn't thought all the way through. What if cohabitating with a werewolf caused problems for him? I was fine taking a dirty look from Rodrian but I hadn't given any consideration to Toby's position.

"I have some fabric freshener upstairs," I said. "I'll grab you some. Like, right now."

By the time I got back downstairs, the curtains—and Toby—were nowhere to be seen. I took the fabric freshener to his room, calling for him. Not there, either. Maybe he'd tried out the pet door. As I checked out the dimensions, wondering if he'd wolfed up or whatever we would call it, I heard the basement door clack shut. His footsteps sounded in the hallway a moment later.

"Where'd you go?" I asked.

He shrugged. "I took your stuff down to the wash. Wasn't sure what soap you wanted so I just used the all-purpose stuff."

I blinked. I figured I'd end up grabbing a corner and dragging them down, step by step. Getting them over the rail to drop them into the foyer had been strenuous enough.

"It's just that—whatever was on them, I could smell them all the way down to my room." He looked apologetic. "I have territory issues. That smell was telling me to get out and I just didn't think. Please don't be mad."

I could just about hug him. "Oh—I didn't mean for you—you did me a huge favor."

He gave me a dirty look. "If you think this favor is enough to get rid of me, Red, you got another thing coming."

"What's with that, anyway? You keep calling me Red. Hello, brunette with highlights!"

"Yeah." He shrugged, attempting that cocky smooth act once more. "But when you're the Big Bad Wolf, every chick looks like Little Red Riding Hood."

I launched a fitted sheet at him but he ducked the missile with a short laugh. The second time he wasn't so lucky. "You're goofy, you know that?"

"Another famous dog, by the way. Where you going?"

I headed for the door. "Got work to do. Shy will be home soon, so try not to set her off. Later."

"See ya, Soph." I laughed in the hall as his falsetto voice sang: "Whose bed, Grandma? It's Red's bed. Say what?"

Goofy. Perfect name for him if ever I thought of one. At least he was good for a laugh. Gawrsh.

I practiced barriers until well after eleven, waiting for Shiloh to come home. By then I couldn't wait any longer. Shiloh hadn't returned any of my texts so I had no idea where she was, who she was with, when she'd come home. I called Rodrian, crossing my fingers and chewing my lip, praying he would answer the phone himself. Thankfully, he did.

"Do you have Shiloh?" I asked. "I haven't seen her since this morning."

"What? No. Hang on—"

I heard the phone click. He must have been trying to get her on another line because after a moment he picked up. "She's not answering. I'm on my way. She knows she's supposed to let you know where she is. That's it. I'm taking her keys."

He ranted several minutes longer before hanging up. Good. I wasn't overreacting, then.

He continued his tirade upon arrival. I waited in the den

while he called everyone short of the National Guard. He even called Brianda.

Rode had to pull the phone away from his ear when Brianda yelled. Shy would be grounded for the rest of her life and, considering how long a life she had ahead of her, she was screwed.

Eventually he settled down and joined me in the den. I had a feeling he was more worried than angry so maybe a little Sophia time would help him rest. Rodrian held a legal pad in his right hand, evaluating notes from his meeting and sounding ominously quiet about it. I huddled next to him, curled up in the hollow formed under his left arm where it rested along the top of the couch. The den was cozy and comfortable when the fireplace burned.

Cradling my glass of wine, I stared absently at the fire, listening to it pop and sear its way through the heavy log he'd thrown on earlier. It had been so long since I'd been this close to anyone. I'd missed it.

I'd missed him.

Rodrian hadn't seemed the same since the night we argued on the way back from Eirene's. He had been acting different, more cautious around me. Maybe stomping around and yelling about Shiloh earlier had helped tenderize him because he didn't seem so guarded now.

I'd grown fond of Rodrian when Marek and I were together. He and Shiloh had become family to me. His presence and his mental touch were familiar, a comforting reminder of happier times.

I'd spent the last year completely alone and utterly abandoned but had been determined to survive. I didn't want to admit my deepest feelings. I didn't want anyone near me. I didn't want anyone to get close enough to touch. I feared only pain would follow.

I'd been wrong. Now, at least, I had a little of my former

happiness back again. Rodrian's presence seemed to banish a bit of the hollowness I felt living here. We'd experienced too much together in the past to be mere friends now. It was that bond that permitted our closeness now, this intimate friendship.

I brushed against Rodrian's power. Uncertainty, wavering confidence. Time to squash those feelings before they ruined the whole night.

"So, who answered the phone the other day?" I hadn't recognized the woman's voice. Usually whenever I called his place he let the machine screen it or, if one of the Brute Squad was there, they'd answer. It was ultra-rare that a woman ever answered, even though Rodrian was practically a chick farmer.

"Hmm?" He dropped the file as if I'd startled him by speaking. "Oh. Mindy. That was Mindy."

The name wasn't familiar. "DV?"

"No. She's...a friend."

I'd heard the slight hesitation. "Girlfriend?"

"Not really. We see each other occasionally. Lunch. That sort of thing."

"Oh." I laughed and nudged him with my elbow. "Why didn't you just say so? She's a blood date."

He shrugged and hid behind his file again. "I don't like to bring it up."

"It's not like I don't know."

"No, but..." He rested the file on the arm of the couch. "Marek said he'd never discussed it with you. I wasn't going to, either."

"True," I said softly. "He didn't. Maybe he would have, if there had been time."

"Doesn't it scare you? I mean, after all that happened. I thought it'd be a bad subject around you."

"It happened. It was a long time ago. It's hazy." Teensy

white lie. No use in giving him something else to worry about. And anyways, I figured if I said it often enough, it'd eventually become the truth.

"It was Marek," he insisted.

"Yeah. It was." The sharpness of my voice was almost unintentional. I took a deep breath, letting it out slowly. I didn't want to ruin the night, either. "It wasn't Marek's fault. It wasn't mine. And I'm good as new, now."

Only a small bit of sarcasm in that last part.

Rodrian slid his arm down from the top of the couch, hugging me closer. He pressed his cheek to the top of my head and inhaled deeply. "Yeah, pretty much."

The gesture made me remember something Dahlia had said when I'd been recovering from The Crap That Almost Killed Me. She'd said that before I lost most of my blood, I'd smelled nice—and explained my blood had a pleasant scent to it, like smoked apples. Squirming in my seat, I looked up at him. "Do I smell nice again?"

A faint smile crossed his lips. "Yes."

"What's it like?"

"Sophie..." He sat straighter and dislodged me from my nest. "I really don't think this is a good conversation for us to be having."

"Why? Did I say something wrong?"

"No. But I can't do this. I can't sit and talk about something like this, not with you. Not when I'm trying so hard to be what you need me to be."

"And that is?"

"Anything but vampire."

I frowned. "You're not vampire, Rode."

"No, but I am DV. I'm covered in your scent but you're forbidden fruit. How can I talk about it? It just makes it harder."

"I'm sorry." Sighing, I pushed up to my feet. I hadn't

meant to do it, but I had ruined the night anyway. Kill Joy Sophie, that's me. "I didn't know. I'll go."

"Don't." He stopped me with a touch on my arm. "Don't go. It's the absolute last thing I want."

His eyes simmered as he searched my face. Suddenly I was afraid to know the first thing he wanted. I wanted to know, despite the faint alarm I felt.

"I've never asked you to be someone that you're not." I looked him squarely in the eye, hoping he'd get every shade of meaning in my words.

He stood and picked up his folder, busying his hands with it. "I know. But I don't want to hurt you."

"Do you hurt Mindy?"

"What?" Rodrian blinked, seeming startled by the question, and backed away. He dropped the notes he'd been perusing onto the bar. "No."

"What does she smell like?"

He shrugged, still avoiding direct eye-contact. "Warmth. Spice. It's vague. Depends on what she's eaten recently."

"And me?"

Rodrian sighed, a small defeated sound, and crossed back over to where I stood. He wore an expression that I was sure I wore whenever he nagged me with one of his bossy compulsions. *Don't make me do this,* the expression said. *I wouldn't do this if I had a choice.*

Eyes half-closed, he leaned and breathed me in, his long bangs sliding across my cheek and his lips brushing my ear.

"You make me think of the fall," he murmured. "Crisp. Harvest. Bounty. You wrap me in Autumn. Bright sun, cool wind. Apples. I don't understand the imagery, but that's where your scent takes me. You're full of promise and generosity. It makes my head spin, my heart ache, and my mouth water."

Rodrian pulled away slightly and circled behind me

where I couldn't see him. I held my breath, afraid to move.

"It's not just blood, Sophie. I'd swear your soul runs through your veins. It must be the Sophia that does it. I know I should feel awed and humbled."

Emotion tightened his voice, as if it had become painful to speak. "But I'm not. It just makes me desperate to think of ever not being able to be near you."

I turned to him. His eyes spilled amber light as he confronted me, the glow brightening as he looked down into my face with a haughty *you-wanted-to-know* look. "This is what your blood does to me. I am DV. I can't hide the truth."

He seemed to be daring me to cry, to pull away, to run.

I wouldn't fold that easily. I'd let Marek pull away because he didn't want to hurt me. I'd let him go because I didn't want to face what he'd become. Well, I wasn't that person anymore. I was the Sophia. I was plain old Sophie. I had to be all of me so I wouldn't lose any of them ever again. "You...don't hurt Mindy?"

"No, I don't." He blinked a few times and looked away. "She enjoys how I make her feel. I have...ways to distract her from the pain."

"Would you hurt me?"

"Oh, Sophie." His voice was little more than a groan. "Please, stop. You're killing me."

"Rode, I want to know."

He fell back onto the couch, sprawled out with exasperation as if it weighed him down. "What do you want? Believe me when I tell you you're wrong. It's not good for you."

"I haven't asked for anything but information."

"How strong do you think I am? Marek couldn't resist you. Why do you insist on testing me?"

"I'm not testing. I...I just have this feeling that..." Words evaded me, and I wrung my fingers together like a wistful child. "Shit. I don't know. I don't feel wanted any-more. Everyone needs me these days. But who wants me? If you didn't need me, would you even have me around?"

"Soph..." He looked up at me. "How can you doubt yourself?"

"I used to feel the exact opposite. I'd been engaged, once. I could have been married with children by now, but no. He only wanted me. He didn't need me. I couldn't be satisfied with something so shallow as *love* or *desire*." I paced to burn off some of the angst that was beginning to take over. "Now, it's need, need, need. I'm so damned useful. I have a big world to save now. But it'd be nice, you know, to be wanted. Even if only for a little blood."

Rodrian wore a sympathetic expression but his voice was firm. "Sophie, I'm the last one you should be doing this with."

Rodrian was the only guy I trusted. There was no one else. "Why?"

"The question is who."

"He's gone. Marek is gone." I spat the words. Couldn't he get it through his head? "I am not going to live my life waiting for him to come back."

"He is my brother."

"And I'm your sister, right." It sounded meaner than I'd intended but I couldn't take it back. "I get it."

I stalked toward the fireplace and hunkered down on the ottoman, hugging my knees to my chest. The velvet of the cushion, warm from being so close to the blaze, mimicked my hot frustration. There was nobody else I could talk to about this and yet he insisted on keeping this distance between us. Maybe I acted petty but I'd gotten tired of begging for information.

"Sophie..."

I didn't look at him, focusing instead on the wavering flames. "No, Rode, I'm sorry. I went too far. We have a lot to worry about. I don't want to lose you now over something like this."

His breath suddenly stirred against the back on my neck. I never heard him get off the couch.

"Honey, you will never lose me. And..." He trailed his fingers through my hair, pushing it forward over my shoulder. His breath poured hotly onto my skin, matching the heat of the fire. "You're not my sister."

I shivered. It was the way he'd said it. "What am I?"

"More. Everything. I don't know."

"Would you hurt me?"

"Never." He whispered, his voice reverberating with his power as it rubbed against me. Light touches, teasing, tentative. Testing me.

"Would it hurt you?"

"Oh, no." His mouth brushed the hairs on the back of my neck and he inhaled, drinking me in again, before wrapping me in sensation.

It began as a trickle, a warm thread of amber glow that dripped down through me. A tiny corner of my mind insisted this was wrong—morally wrong—but it was surprisingly easy to ignore. Subtle pleasure melted my insides, softening me and awakening me, making me gasp.

Rodrian chuckled, a soft and deep melody. "Just imagine what it's like for me."

"Don't have to imagine it." I twisted to face him. He'd been kneeling behind me and now sat back on his heels, looking up at me as if I had been dancing. I used his shoulder to boost myself to my feet and tugged on his arm, pulling him up to his feet. "I'm empathic, remember? I can feel you."

I raised my hand, stroking his face, the silk of his clean-shaven jaw. He brushed his fingers up my arm and pressed his hand over mine. So easy to stand this close to him, so comfortable. I could feel his hunger. "Taste me."

He closed his eyes and made a low desperate sound. "I can't hold onto my control when you do this."

"Taste me," I insisted. "I need to know."

Holding my hand still, he turned his head and pressed his lips to my open palm. When his eyes opened they glowed like bronze coals. A sharp look, one meant to urge me to change my mind.

His tongue slid along the delicate skin of my palm, a tickle that struck chords lower and deeper. Teeth scraped against the fleshy pad below my thumb.

Rodrian bit down, his gaze a wild fire, a desperate light that sought fuel and fury and threatened to consume itself.

No pain. The pressure of his mouth, of his hand holding mine, but no pain.

His eyes fell closed, mouth working as he drew my blood into his mouth. Heat and pleasure washed over me. Heat and pleasure dripped from the velvet of his lips, the silk of his tongue. Heat and pleasure poured into me, drenching me like slow, thick lava.

I watched him swallow and forgot to breathe. I closed my eyes, feeling my center of gravity roll out from under me. I grabbed his shirt to keep from swaying when something in my head dipped lower, as if dropping. Vertigo.

His tongue swept across my skin quickly before he pulled his mouth away.

"Sophie!" He slid his free arm around my waist to support me. "Are you all right?"

"Rode." My voice was husky and I swallowed hard, recovering from the brief yet intense experience. My balance had returned but the memory of the internal swooning swirl still shook me. I released my clutch on his collar. "You've been holding out on me, buddy."

He licked his lips slowly and pulled my hand to his chest and pressed it flat over his heart. It thumped madly. Rodrian chuckled, mouth curling with a small but decidedly proud leer. "Have I?"

"Hoo, yeah." I blew out a tight breath, feeling my pulse slow, return to normal. And—was that afterglow?

Rodrian laughed and pulled me closer, snuggling me against his chest. "You've been holding back, too. I always knew you were something special, but...wow. That was hot."

"Hot, huh?" I grinned into his shoulder, glad he couldn't see my face. It shouldn't have meant that much to hear him say something like that.

A muffled thump sounded from the foyer as the front door slammed. The clatter and the racket that drifted in under the doors announced Shiloh's arrival. Brianda's voice, too, as she continued a lecture in true Thurzo style.

I pulled back, suddenly self-conscious. The tiny voice of protest suddenly seemed loud enough to listen to again. "Kids are home, dear."

"Yeah." He laughed softly. "Um, Soph..."

"Sophie?" Shiloh's voice echoed in the foyer, growing louder as she approached the den. "You in here?"

"Yeah, Shy." I shook my head at him apologetically. Whatever he wanted to say would have to wait.

"She can't hear you, Soph."

"Why not?" Before I could press further, the door clicked open. "We're in here, Shy."

"Who's we? Oh. Hey, Dad. Thanks for treating me like a lost cat. Did you really have to send her looking for me?" She jerked a thumb at her sister, who now stood silently in the doorway, arms crossed, blocking any attempt of

Shiloh's escape. "Why not send patrol cars with flashing lights and ninjas dropping out of the sky? It'd be a lot more subtle and maybe I'd still have friends by the time your goons haul me off."

"Maybe next time don't disappear like that. Sophie called when you didn't show up or answer your phone. Do you have any idea how worried she was? Hand over your keys." Rodrian went into full-out Mad Dad Mode and bossed a blue streak at her. He gave Shiloh a leveling look which took the buoyancy out of her expression. "You broke curfew again."

"But..."

"But nothing. Be glad I don't restrict you to the grounds. Now, get. I'll see you both tomorrow. I've got more work to do."

Shiloh left mumbling but I caught every other word as she headed up the stairs to her room. They weren't happy words.

Brianda followed her out, making sure she made it upstairs. I heard the clacks of her boot heels on the tiles of the foyer. I'd only taken a quick admiring glance at her boots when she'd come in; they were made of brown, worn leather with spat-like wraps and antiqued buckles. Kind of bad-ass military style, which matched her canvas pants and leather blazer.

Brianda's outfit alone should have made an impression on Shiloh's friends. Did she also have a bandolier or a low-slung belt with a laser blaster? One thing was for sure—if I were off being truant with my miscreant friends and someone like Brianda came for me, I wouldn't have to worry about those kids hanging out with me anymore.

Satisfied, Brianda came back into the den a few moments later. "Who are her friends these days? They aren't the same kids I used to see her with. I don't recognize any of them."

"No idea," I said. I tucked my thumb into my back pocket, suddenly worried she'd see my hand and know what had just happened between me and Rodrian. "She doesn't bring anyone over and she doesn't talk about them."

"Keep a watch on her. I'm concerned. I can't always get away to go after her." She hugged Rodrian. "I'm sorry. I wish I could be here."

"Sophie has everything under control." Rodrian smoothed Brianda's hair and kissed her on the forehead. "Thanks for bringing your sister home."

Brianda nodded at me before she left. If Rodrian thought I had everything under control, he was delusional. I'd never felt more out of my element in my life.

Rodrian wordlessly gathered his things to leave and I retrieved my wine glass. As he put on his coat and grabbed his satchel, I touched his power again. He was all business once more, our brief interlude gone from the front of his mind.

*Strange, that's not the only thing that's gone.* The uncertainty and the lack of confidence had disappeared, too. Only determination and focus remained. Purpose. Rodrian seemed to have sorted something out along the way.

At least one of us did. I seemed to have accumulated yet another problem.

I wanted more of him.

Crap.

Shiloh spent the next morning being snarky and rude, evidently pissed at me for calling her father on her. I'd hoped to work things out in the car when I drove her to school but she got a ride. I heard the front door slam as I came out of the office with my purse and keys and barely reached the window in time to see the car speeding down the driveway.

I had no idea what to do with an angry teenager. All day long I endured horrific imaginings of flash mobs and viral videos and being strangled in my sleep. Weren't there books on this sort of thing? And were any of them actually helpful?

Rodrian drove her home shortly after I'd returned, as though he'd meant to time it perfectly. She stomped past me without a word and slammed the door to the tri-suites behind her. Okay. Guess we wouldn't be talking tonight, either.

Rodrian stayed only long enough to tell me that he'd be

back to pick me up later for my meeting with Eirene. Something big loomed in him. I could feel his anticipation, his eagerness to set something in motion. I didn't pry; I merely wished him luck.

He looked surprised by my intuitive words but thanked me with a hug me before he turned to leave.

It was not a sexy hug. Thank goodness.

Toby wandered out of his rooms and met me in the foyer where I still stood, wondering if I should go up after her. "Everything okay, Red?"

I rubbed my brows. "Do you understand teenagers, Toby?"

"Naw," he said. "I sure don't. I was never a normal teenager myself."

"Not normal? I didn't think there was such a thing."

"I was a kid when I turned," Toby said. "It was three days before my fifteenth birthday. Hell of a present. At least I got one."

My stomach sank. Even when I didn't try, I always managed to say the wrong thing. "I'm sorry, Toby. I didn't mean—"

"It's okay, Soph, it's just what happened. I don't talk about it much, is all."

Toby stuffed his hands deep into his front pockets and hunched his shoulders, ducking his head. I knew a burden when I saw one. If I couldn't get close enough to help Shiloh, maybe I could reach out to Toby. The Sophia didn't respond to Weres but I was still an advice columnist. I was still wired to reach out and help people.

I couldn't ignore Toby's need for a friend, not when he lived under my roof. He was my responsibility.

"Come on. I'll ask Bethany to bring something to the den and we can talk about it."

Toby's eyebrows lifted. "You don't like to talk about

Were stuff."

"But I want to know about you, Toby. As a person. You're my friend."

"Your friend?"

I considered it and nodded. "Yes."

He straightened a bit while he walked past me into the den. Good. Maybe I could help him out, after all.

He settled on one of the couches, sprawling sideways and testing the cushions with a bounce. "Fancy couch. I never sat on anything like this."

Curling my leg beneath me, I tucked myself into the corner of the other sofa and drew up my knee. "Do you have any family left?"

His expression darkened but he answered me. "My momma'd run off when I was just little and my daddy worked nights, slept days. Me and my big sister were pretty much left to ourselves. She made sure I washed and ate and went to school. I didn't make it easier on her, though.

"She didn't like me, I don't think. She hated Momma for what she'd done, and she hated having to take her place. But she tried. I guess when that boyfriend asked her to go with him, though, she figured it'd be more fun than staying home with a rock like me."

"What happened to her?" I asked. "Did she run away?"

"I don't know where she'd gone off to." Toby scratched his head. "Doesn't matter."

I glanced up at Bethany when she came into the den, carrying a covered dish. She set it on the bar but lingered, listening to Toby. I don't think he realized she'd even come in.

"She left, and I ran wild," he said. "Cut school right away. I'd just come home at the usual time in the afternoon in case Daddy woke up.

"Then I started taking off at night. I met a new crowd.

They hung out at Pally's Pool Hall, near the Industrial Park. It was on the rough side of town."

I sighed. "That's what I worry about with Shiloh."

Toby stared at me. "You should worry. It was there it'd happened. I don't remember much, other than I was shooting a good game and was thirty dollars up. I had on a blue shirt, my favorite one. It was worn thin and soft like a baby's cheek and just tight enough to make it look like I had some muscle. I loved that t-shirt. When the fight broke out in the parking lot, we all went out to watch.

"People stood around watching these two guys fight, drinking and yelling. Fights were fun. I'd been in a couple of scraps myself, but watching was just as much fun, and hurt less the next day.

"Me and my buddies kept to the back of the lot, near some bushes. Didn't want to get dragged into the fight, you know? I heard a noise and, when I looked behind me, I saw a big dog in the bushes, like it was watching the fight. Another one ran right out, right up to the two guys that were fighting. It just ran right out and, next thing you knew, it bit one of them.

"Darndest thing I ever did see. Never saw an animal do that. I backed away from the fight, a little afraid of the big dog that was tearing into the one dude. I forgot all about the dog that was behind me. I must have kicked it or stepped on it, because it yelped and bit me too."

Bethany cleared her throat, capturing Toby's attention.

"Were bites are not gentle," she said.

Toby laughed ruefully. "No, they sure ain't. Took a good chunk out of my arm. My friends ran, the sumbitches. I ran after them. Back inside Pally's I could see my arm was bleeding pretty fast and it burned like hell. There was a lot of blood on my blue shirt and it looked like grape jelly.

"It was all I could think about. Grape jelly. I made a

sandwich when I got home and fell asleep on the couch. By morning, I was burning up sick and Daddy was standing over the couch, calling my name. I just wouldn't shake.

"He yelled about the bite and took me to the hospital. The thing that seemed funny to me was how much like a father he was acting for once. He was finally being a father and I was too sick to care.

"He called off work the whole week. I got fourteen stitches and two shots and got told to stay in bed. Daddy actually cooked and tried to take care of me. He even switched onto day shift so he could be home when I was home. I never got to tell him it was too late. He never got a chance to be my father again."

"What happened, Toby?" I said.

"One night, about two weeks later, he was watching TV. I never knew he could use the remote. He was in there, laughing and drinking a beer. TV was loud. He didn't hear what was happening to me in my room.

"The moon had risen and it was nearly full. It gleamed right through my bedroom window and hit me like a punch in the nose.

"I changed. I didn't understand what was going on. It happened so fast and hurt so bad that I don't think I even hollered. I don't remember my first night at all. Maybe you're not supposed to.

"The next morning, waking up and looking like me again—that I remember.

"I was naked in the backyard and the sky was light purple, like the sun was going to come up soon. I could hear Tam Jenkins next door banging his lunch pail around, getting ready to leave for work. I didn't need him to call the police on me for streaking."

Bethany had taken a seat on one of the stools near the bar. "It is a terrible thing to endure alone," she said. "Small wonder the Werekind tend to be a savage lot."

She tilted her head and looked at Toby. "You, boy, seem to be an exception."

Toby stole a glance at her and nodded once, her assessment causing him a moment of shyness.

"I snuck inside and got dressed and stuffed a backpack with whatever I could fit in it, and I took what money I could find in Daddy's top drawer. He was still asleep on the couch. I didn't wake him up. No point in hearing him tell me to get out and never come back. Then I ran. I never stopped."

"Didn't you ever—" I whispered.

"No." His voice was like a stone. The word just fell out of his mouth. "You know, it's ironic. Me getting bit reminded him how to be a dad. But it also taught me I wasn't his son anymore. I met Tanner before the year was out, up in North Carolina."

Here was the part I dreaded, the mention of his best friend. He'd been only an enemy to me and I steeled myself, waiting for the story I knew I'd have to face one day. I couldn't be any use to Toby if I shut down every time he said the guy's name.

"When I felt the moon coming on, I'd find woods. I learned to steal extra clothes and hide them before the moon took me. Gradually I got to keep my brains while I was wolfed up. Didn't mean I always used them, but..."

He paused and glanced up. Bethany had uncovered the plate and I could smell the savory aroma of steak. She carried a plate over to him, offering him a steak sandwich. He looked up at her, unsure, then took it with a shy nod. She held out a plate to me, too, but I wasn't sure I had an appetite yet.

"One moon I was in a nice patch of wood," he continued. "Trees were so thick the moon couldn't find me.

It was just a game I played. She always knew where I was. I got to like the moon. She was the only one who loved me.

"I was full of rabbits and nowhere close to being tired of chasing them. So, when I caught a smell of fur—of wolf—I ran to find it.

"When I ran into the clearing, I saw them. Two big brutes, fighting like they meant to kill each other. I watched quietly and stayed back in the scrub. I sure didn't want to get jumped.

"When finally one lay still and didn't get up, the other looked at me. I was afraid. I smelled my own fear, so I knew he could too. I lay down as small as I could.

"He came over for a look at me, growling. Then he sniffed at me, hit me with his nose, and walked away a couple of feet before he stopped to look back at me. He called me, told me to follow him. So I did. We ran out the rest of the moon together.

"When I woke up he was close by putting on his shoes. He saw me looking at him and said 'my name's Tanner.'

"'Toby,' I said.

"'Got a pack?' he said.

"I shook my head and looked down, 'cause I sure as hell didn't.

"He tied his boots, stood up and tossed my clothes at me.

"'You do now,' he said. 'Let's go, brother.' And he took care of me ever since."

Toby took a bite, chewing and watching me, waiting for my judgment. I could tell he really needed me to say something honest.

"He was good to you," I said.

Toby nodded. "I know he wasn't always a good guy. He made money doing the stuff nobody else wanted to do. He kept other wolves from hurting me and we made our own pack. He kept me safe and gave me a home and didn't turn his back on me, even though I was good for just about nothing.

"I can't judge him by the mean stuff he did because it was just work. I should have been road kill or froze to death when winter came. But I didn't, because Tanner saved me."

A hundred things had gone through my mind as he told me his story. *This likeable, goofy kid—this is the back story? Who lives through stuff like that and emerges sane? Or alive?* I didn't need the Sophia's compassion to sympathize and he became dearer to me in that instant, just for telling me these details that anyone else would have kept locked inside.

Perhaps Toby was stronger than anyone gave him credit for being; admitting your ugly past and your thread-bare circumstances took courage. He didn't run away from a challenge. I vowed to not run away from him just because I thought he was one, too.

Maybe he mistook my silence for horror, because he got up and crossed the room to sit next to me. Taking both my hands, he urged me to meet his eyes. I saw no shame in them. Instead, I saw a determination to do what he thought was right, even if it meant it facing an added challenge in making me believe in him.

"Sophie," he said. "I know that what he did hurt you. It wasn't personal. You were just a job. I'm sorry he scared you. And I'm going to make it up, I swear it. I have to do it. His wolf is always with me and I can't outrun it. His ghost will follow me forever if I don't."

He didn't need to say another word. If there was one thing I understood, it was being haunted.

He sighed and stood, wiping his hands on his jeans. "Thank you for supper, Miss Bethany. It was delicious.

And if you'll excuse me, I need to go out for a while. I feel like running."

"Not running away?" Bethany collected his plate and set it on the bar.

"Nope." Toby smiled while heading out the door. "People only run away from bad things."

Bethany chuckled as she finished cleaning up. "I think you have a champion in him. Good. You need one."

"Am I that bad off?" I almost whined.

"No." She paused in the doorway. "But there is badness coming."

I made a mental note to ask Rodrian what Bethany's talent was and hoped it sure as hell wasn't foresight. Then again, I did have a meeting with Eirene tonight.

Maybe Bethany was spot-on with the badness. Oh, the joy.

Eirene sat in the hotel lobby and, as usual, wore a look of unabashed distaste as she surveyed her surroundings. It made me wonder what kind of luxury she was used to living in. I mean, this had to be one of the most prominent hotels in the city. She barely refrained from curling her lips at the decor.

I knew I was in trouble because I was late. Driving me into town, Rodrian drove me into town but he wasn't his usual zippy self. The drive was leisurely, his mood chatty.

I hadn't anticipated leisurely and chatty.

When she spied me, she rose quickly as if relieved to break contact with the settee. Dorcas stood a second later, clinging to her side like a shadow. "I thought you weren't going to come this evening. I wondered if I'd be dining alone."

Her voice was reproachful and she arched her perfect eyebrow at me.

"Traffic held me up. That's all. I'm sorry." I didn't think

details were necessary. They'd make my apology sound more like a justification.

She relaxed her brow. My lucky day.

"We dine at *L'Orcus Tavolo* tonight. We will walk. It is a most beautiful night. These taxis, they are utterly revolting."

The restaurant was several blocks away and it was freezing outside. I sighed to myself, and heartily agreed with her choice. If I didn't become an ice cube by the time I got there, it'd be my lucky day. Again.

We were seated in a quiet corner. Dorcas stood at the wall, her shapeless brown dress allowing her to blend with the tapestry. It was kind of creepy, actually. Lately she'd become kind of a chameleon, disappearing in my periphery. I had to remind myself she was there. God help me if I learned to dismiss her the same way Eirene did. I don't want to be that kind of person.

Lifting my glass of water, I sipped and tried to avoid drinking the lemon wedge. "Eirene, what do the Canons say about the blood of a Sophia?"

"Well." She seemed taken aback. "A direct question on an extremely discomfiting subject. Sophias do not share blood. It is forbidden."

Oh, dear. Not a good thing. "But why?"

"What have you been doing?" Her voice lowered in warning. "I must warn you—"

"Look. It's no real secret what happened to me. I lost blood to a DV who in turn overthrew a master vampire. Nothing could have been done about it. Since that night, a lot of people made comments about my blood without really telling me anything useful. What can you tell me?"

Eirene pursed her lips, a look of harsh concentration on her delicate face. "There is more to this. Be completely honest or I will not help."

"It was Marek." I licked my lips, rolling them between my teeth as I sought the best words. Eyes on the table, I made my confession. "After Marek took my blood, a DV healer named Pontian..."

"Ah, Pontian," she interrupted. "He is very old. Very close to the edge. He has not fallen, yes?"

"Well, not then, but he did have a freaky way of reading my mind."

"A sign of how close he is." She paused, reflecting and drumming her nails on her water glass. The rhythmic tinkling made an odd accompaniment for such doom-stricken words. "Soon. Soon he will fall. Even a great heart such as his cannot resist forever."

"Eirene? That's harsh."

She shrugged and squared her shoulders. "It is nature. You, too, are a part of nature, part of the Balance. You cannot take sides. You belong to all."

She drank from her glass and Dorcas stepped forward to refresh it. I can't figure out why we bothered to go out to eat because she never ordered anything. She'd scour the menu and ask countless questions of the waiter, reminding me of a parent whose child had food allergies. In the end, she always settled for only bread and fruit, which she barely touched.

But she always insisted on paying the check and insisted I enjoy my meals. So I did.

The waiter arrived with our orders and I smiled at the plate in anticipation. Fillet of pork with Anjou pear glaze. Garlic and roasted red pepper potatoes. If I wasn't worried about her reaction, I might have Tweeted a picture of the food. Meals like this made my evenings with her bearable.

"So." Her voice sounded thoughtful. "Marek has taken your blood. Small wonder it is, he keeps a territory of vampire under his command. Your blood must have made him powerful, indeed. I wonder, what more would he have gained if he had taken your death, as well?"

I shuddered and swallowed hard. "That's not really something I care to ponder."

"Oh, but we must."

"Not tonight, we don't."

Eirene reached across the table and took my hand in hers. The night was seasonably frigid, and her hands were still cold from the walk. "I see the pain in your eyes, Sophie. We will wait to discuss it another night."

She turned my hand over in hers, rubbing it to warm it. I didn't bother to pull away since friendly overtures were rare for her but, when she rubbed my thumb a little too firmly, I winced.

She caught my reaction and tipped her head to look at my hand. The ambient lighting revealed the faint mark of Rodrian's teeth and a streak of pink healing flesh.

"And this," she announced, "is not an old scar. There is a story forthcoming, I presume." Her dark eyes glittered with condemnation.

I sighed, embarrassed. I felt very much as if I'd been caught with a hickey. "It's hard to explain. I can't put a label on the relationship."

"The relationship is unimportant. All that matters is that someone takes your blood. Do not trivialize it by attempting to make some 'relationship' seem so much more important."

I hung my head, chastised, and used a fork to chase an artichoke tip around my plate.

"Was it DV or vampire?"

"What?" I looked up, shocked to hear the words emerge from her mouth. "Why would I let a vamp do this?"

"I am not making accusations. I am accumulating facts. You could make this easier by simply telling me."

"He's DV." The name wasn't important, especially not after her little tirade. Anyone who knew me would be able to narrow down the list of suspects rather quickly.

"He? Not they?"

What did I look like, a slut? "Only one."

"How much blood?"

"I don't know. It's not like I bled into a measuring cup."

"From where did he take it? The palm..." She turned my hand over in hers again. "...is a juicy bit to be sure, but there is not enough blood flow to slake a thirst. A main vessel or a site on the torso would give a lot more."

"All right, already." Her graphic description nauseated me and I pulled my hand away from her. "I get the picture. Not much blood, then."

She evaluated me through narrow eyes. "It is a stupid thing you do. You waste it. You do not even know what you are. You have no idea what makes you special. What if the secret lies in your blood? You do not know what you lose. You cannot be sure what you do to the poor fool you feed."

*Aw, crap.* Thirty years of Catholic guilt just about sprang up and out at that. Now it wasn't only being caught with a hickey—I might have given him Sophia herpes, too.

"Shit." I swore under my breath. "What if you're right? Pontian said my gift was tied to my blood."

"He did?" She regarded me intently, seeming to consider it. "He would know. That one keeps many secrets. So. You knew your gift was in your blood and yet you continued to squander it. You are blessed with the Sophia Oracle, yet you refuse to allow it to have its fullest potential. Any other serious failings you would care to share with me, before I decide you are a hopeless waste of my time?"

"Oh, Eirene. Don't say that." I needed her. I might not like her much but damn it, I needed her. She was probably the only other Sophia I'd ever get to meet. If I pissed her off I'd be even worse off. "What I did was in ignorance. No one else but you can teach me. Please, Eirene, don't give up on me. I need you."

She smiled indulgently, mollified by my pleading. I got the impression she really got off on it. Someone else with an ego fetish. Yay. "My dear, you are a Sophia. You should not beg. It is beneath you. It is for them to beg, to plead before you. I will stay, even if only for a short time. But you must be ready to unlearn many things. The Sophia shapes you, not the other way around."

I let out a big sigh of relief. "Thanks, Eirene. You won't regret this."

"I am sure. I have yet to do something I regret." She surveyed the remains of our meals. "We are finished, for tonight. I shall retire. Dorcas, my rooms are ready?"

"Ma'am. Everything is as you require."

"Good. Sophie, I will meet you again the night after tomorrow, as we did this evening."

"Eirene," I hesitated. "Any way we can meet earlier? These late nights are hard on me. I work day shift."

"As do I," she answered coldly. "Do you think I do nothing all day? I am Sophia. My time is not my own. I scarcely have time to properly enjoy meals in this city. You are fortunate I have this time to offer to you."

I cringed. "I'm sorry, I didn't mean..."

"And stop apologizing. When you are properly trained, you will realize your life is not your own, either. So. The evening after next. Same time."

"Right. Thanks, Eirene." I resigned myself to continued unpleasantness for the sake of improving myself. It had better turn out to be a fair trade.

On the way home, Rodrian wanted to stop by the office. The elevator ride itself was a trip and a half—at this time of night, there was very little activity on the office floors and he bewizarded the car to move at Holy Moley Express speed. My stomach puddled into my shoes and I had to hold the rail to keep upright. He just laughed and, once I was able to breathe again, I did, too.

I had to admit, he was fun sometimes. I wondered if Marek had shared his sense of humor when he was younger and less burdened.

Once in his office, I got comfortable while he shuffled through some drawers and muttered under his breath.

"Hmm?" I looked up from my tablet where I was editing some column work.

"It's not here," he huffed. "I have to run upstairs to Records to pull some files. Want to come with?"

Needing a break, I stood and stretched before walking over to the mini-refrigerator he kept in the corner of his office. It looked like a filing cabinet but was actually a Maytag with a false front. He usually kept bottles of Bela Lugosi Light (or whatever he called his blood supply) inside, but at my request he'd added a few cans of iced tea. The cans were on the door so I didn't have to dig through his blood bank to find them. What a prince.

"I'll just stay down here. More comfortable." I tugged out a can of sweet tea and wiped the rim with the bottom of my shirt. "Besides, I've got catchup of my own to do."

"You can do that upstairs."

"No, I can't."

Rodrian's power tasted different tonight and I didn't think it was due to the filtering of my newly constructed barriers. The new confidence was still there, firmly rooted and entirely his own.

Something else was there, too, and it had nothing to do with self-esteem. It had everything to do with me. I wasn't ready to explore it. "I'll just distract you."

"Is that a bad thing?" When he sat down behind his desk, I heard the click of a lock. He removed a set of keys from a bottom drawer, palming them.

I looked away, flicking only a side glance toward him. I didn't feel comfortable enough to face up on the topic. "It might be, yeah."

"Are you worried about what happened last night?"

"Ah..." I studied the pop-top of the iced tea can, wondering how to crack it open without breaking a nail. "Not so much what had happened as what might happen."

Rodrian sat back, expressionless, as if waiting for my response to dictate his. "What's that?"

"I don't know. I—" Pacing to the couch, I dropped down and pushed my purse out of the way. Walking barefoot on broken glass would be easier than talking about this. "I don't want to complicate things between us. Not this soon."

"Complicate things. That's a nice way to put it."

"Is that sarcastic?" I met his eyes, looking for a sign of smart-ass.

"No. Really." No smart-ass, only honest agreement. "*Complicated* is just the tip of it. I thought about it a lot last night. And today. And on the way to pick you up at work. And all though dinner..."

"So, it's a heavy topic." I chuckled, lightening the load of the admission, but quickly returned to the weight of the matter. "And?"

"And I think there is room for us in all of this. Room for you and me to stand on our own. Last night emphasized how our relationship has always hinged on my brother."

"Kind of hard to banish his presence."

"Yeah. And it's not right. You're valuable to me, not just because of your past relationship with Marek. You are important to me. And not because of someone else's perception of you. Does that make sense?"

"I don't want to lose what I felt last night before... that." I looked down at my hand, where the faint imprint of Rodrian's teeth still made a rosy curve on my flesh, a slight tenderness of a fading bruise.

"Why would we lose it?"

"Touching and feeling are two different things."

He quietly considered it, his power churning in concentration. "So...you worry that anything physical might damage the spiritual."

"Maybe." Some of my trepidation eased and the tension in my neck and scalp melted a bit. Still there, just not squeezing-down distracting. Perhaps he did understand.

"I won't try to fill you with words. I only promise to prove we've nothing to fear."

"Except Marek finding out."

"Do you really worry about that?"

"Yes. No...yes," I decided. I hated simple questions with complicated answers. "I don't want to strain your relationship with him."

"And yours?"

"I don't have one." Pushing against the couch in a hasty effort to stand, I got up to look for a napkin. I hadn't klutzed anything up yet but there was still time. He'd kill me if I made a mess on his burgundy suede cushions. I busied myself searching the room for a tissue box, a paper towel, a chamois. Anything. Anything to keep from investing myself in the question.

"You sure?"

"Why wouldn't I be?" I sounded distracted, masking the truth perfectly. No tissues. Damn DV and their immunity to drippy noses. "You know we don't speak."

"Maybe not. But that doesn't mean there isn't a relationship."

"A relationship isn't one-sided. It's more than kissing on a mirror, pretending it kisses back." I gave up on the tissues and faced him.

He pushed his chair back and stood, sliding the keys into his pants pocket and walking around the desk so nothing stood between us. "Maybe you're both relating, just not to each other."

"Hence, no relationship."

"Wrong. Maybe there's just a barricade separating you. I know you want to try. Maybe he does, too."

I lifted my shoulders and hands, frustration adding a different heat to the discussion. In this light the window dressings behind him looked more red than brown. It wasn't a soothing shade. "Why would you say that? Why would you say things that could give me hope?"

"I...don't know." He crossed an arm over his chest,

resting the elbow of the other upon his hand, and rubbed his temple. "You're right. I'm sorry. I can't speak for him. He won't even speak for himself."

Rodrian raised his index fingers, palms out, emphasizing his delicate point. "But I get the impression that you still have a relationship. It might not be going anywhere but you are still holding on to something. You're afraid to disturb the remains of what you had."

How could I argue with that? Sidestepping might work. I was good at that. "He needs the Sophia. I have to preserve some kind of trust so I can reach him. Eirene can help him, I know it, and if I anger him, he won't give the Sophia a chance."

"You *are* the Sophia," he insisted. "You're one and the same. No separation. Don't deny yourself because of a misconception."

Self-denial was the whole point. There were reasons why I'd become a gun-shy adult, especially when it came to the big guns like relationships and trust. My false confidence folded like an empty balloon and I sank back onto the couch. "I'm sorry, Rode. This is tougher than I expected. Can we adjourn until later? You gave me a lot to consider."

"All right, sure." He opened the door but paused in the doorway. A mischievous glint brightened his eyes and he tilted his head, letting his hair tumble down. He wouldn't be Rodrian if he didn't make one final play. "You're sure you don't want to come up? It's warmer upstairs."

"I bet it is. Down here is fine."

He took a moment to come back over and mark me, his fingertips sending a line of tingles down my back. If I didn't know better, I'd swear he tried to tickle me. "All right," he said. "Call me if you need me. The extension is marked on the phone."

"Okay." I took a sip of tea, but it was like drinking a t-shirt. Dry and solid, unrefreshing. Something to strangle on as if the conversation hadn't been enough.

"Sure you'll be okay?"

I winkled my nose, thinking *Go, already.* "What's the worst that could happen?"

Lost in concentration, I felt around on the cushion for my phone when it chimed an annoying gong noise—my incoming text alert.

From Rodrian's phone: *Where are you?*

*In UR office, duh,* I texted back.

*Lock the door*

*Y?*

*WARDS! LOCK IT!*

I dropped the phone and lunged for the door, a dozen simultaneous images flashing through my mind. Too late! The doorknob rattled and the door swung open, bringing me face to face with unknown danger.

Vampire. Were. Mugger. The Blob.

Not—

Marek.

We froze in each other's sights. My heart pounded, the alarm maintaining its intensity even after I realized who it was.

Marek looked every bit as perfect as my heart remembered him. His eyes glinted briefly, like sunlight on ivy, before solidifying into a polite and impersonal green. My heart threatened to stop in mid-beat.

Marek wore a dark green button down shirt, one of my favorites; the cotton was slept-in soft and the collar always stood just right when left open. His sleeves were unbuttoned but not rolled up to his elbows as had been his custom when I'd known him. Even unbuttoned, it looked more formal, restrained. His black boots, pointed-toe cowboy boots with a sturdy heel, were new to me. I'd never seen him in cowboy boots. They weren't his style.

I took in every detail at once, then dropped my gaze, feeling like I'd taken something that didn't belong to me.

"Sophie." He greeted me brusquely, as if I were no more

than a receptionist. "I'm looking for Rodrian."

Not exactly the tone of voice I'd daydreamed he would use. The shock reminded me: this was not a drill. And, as usual, when all other senses failed me, the smart ass took over. "I'm fine, Marek, thanks for asking. And you?"

He exhaled through his nose. "Yes. Of course. Sophie. Are you truly fine? You look...weary."

"Forget it, Marek," I said softly. "I'll go. Rodrian ran upstairs to Records but he'll be back soon. I'll wait down-stairs in the lounge for him."

I'd spent a long time half-wishing for a chance to see Marek, just once. The lines were rehearsed, rewritten, and perfected over eighteen months of daydreaming. Now that the curtains had finally gone up, what did I do?

I got stage fright, that's what.

What a coward I was. All I could think of was getting out, going somewhere, anywhere he wasn't. I grabbed my tablet, fumbling to get it into my bag. Stupid fingers weren't working right. It was like trying to shove a brick into a change purse. Leaving my bag hang open, I snatched my coat up and cut a straight path for the door where he still stood.

Swallowing down the buzz of my heartbeat, I tried to ignore the chill radiating from him. In my daydreams, I never considered the cold barrier he wore around himself, the emotional wall of ice. Pulling my awareness in tighter to avoid brushing against his power, I kept my eyes down and avoided looking at him, knowing that, if I did, I'd be entranced by his terrible, cold beauty.

Dahlia had told me about vampiric powers. I didn't want to find out if he actually had them.

He'd stepped aside to allow me to pass but as I tried to slip through the doorway, he said my name and stopped me.

Literally.

The compulsion wasn't rude; it was simply a whopping dose of *Obey Me* that glued my feet to the floor. With deceiving nonchalance, he reached out his hand.

I braced for the shock, dreading the contact. Would his touch feel cold, like his power, or room temperature, like a vampire? I didn't want to discover what he'd become.

His fingers pressed gently on my arm. Neither. Marek's skin was warm, alive, like it always had been. Some-how, that was worse.

Marek inhaled sharply and narrowed his eyes. Our physical contact perforated his chilly barrier and I felt his true power. He was angry.

"You are marked," he announced and pressed his lips into a tight, pale line.

"Well, yeah." I screwed my brows together and glared up at him. "Human in a building full of DV, remember?"

He smiled. It was humorless, an animal's false smile. The truth showed in his eyes. "So. Now my brother is your protector?"

I shrugged, feeling my throat tighten. "Someone needs to be."

"And you think that is all a marking entails? He's marked you. As his own."

A wave of heat and something else washed down me, head to toe. I was getting pissy. Supposed it was my survival instinct: mouth off when you can't fight back. "Why not? Nobody else will."

"Nobody else should. He's touched you." Marek frowned and leaned closer, breathing through nose and mouth. His voice held an edge of menace. "I can smell him on your skin."

"It happens," I snapped.

He wasn't deterred by my rebuke. "And—something

else. A different smell. You are trying to hide something from me."

I couldn't bear this confrontation, this closeness. Remembering I was no longer immune to his threat, I balled my fist, hiding the mark of Rodrian's teeth, and shuddered. "Is this really necessary? I'd rather you let me leave."

His expression didn't change but he dropped the compulsion. I owned my feet again. I stepped away, broke contact, felt him fade. The chill returned.

My chance to run. I should have been out of there. So why wasn't I? I hugged my purse and coat closer to me, covering my chest, and backed away only a step.

"Rode said..." I pretended to be on professional duty, summoning courage I didn't possess. I'd forgotten how to be Sophie and couldn't remember how to be Sophia. "You didn't leave the family business completely. You run both now."

By both I'd meant DV business and the vamp stuff he'd more or less inherited when he'd slain the Master. I didn't know too much about the latter, nor did I want to. The DV business, however, had ethical and honorable intentions behind it; not only did Rodrian own several businesses in and around Balaton but Marek also ran the private biotech research company just outside Philadelphia.

"True. I do." Marek seemed to expect an explanation as to why my nose was in his business.

"Well, I...just mean that I do a lot more Sophia work now." Since the day I received Eirene's letter, I'd been hashing out a way to tell Marek about her. She was my big excuse to reconnect with him. Now, when he finally stood right in front of me, all my rehearsed scenarios flopped. Marek's penetrating stare scoured me, scraping away the thin film of delusion that had been responsible for my boldness, and I lost the courage to say her name. "I wondered if..."

"If I needed you?" Marek finished for me, using a tone that laid bare my foolishness.

"As Sophia." My face glowed and I fought to freeze my expression.

"Thank you for the generous offer. However, I can manage on my own." His jaw was set in a stony impassive line and he looked down the smooth line of his nose at me. Cold. So cold.

I left before I could embarrass myself any further.

Marek shut the door behind him, stranding me in the dim and silent hall.


I'd plowed halfway through my second Cosmo by the time Rodrian found me. Normally I didn't go for the high octane stuff but it was as close to anesthesia as I could get without a prescription.

Despite the buzz, my brain still scolded me, feeding the fires of my humiliation. Stupid me forgot alcohol made fire worse.

Being drunk was bad. All the brain cells officially belonging to me turned mushy and clumsy and the only ones that still functioned were either my autonomic nervous system or that chunk of brain where the Sophia lived. I couldn't walk a straight line but I could still blink and feel every DV in the room.

At first it was a welcome distraction; I could concentrate on what others felt and ignore my own painful thoughts. Although I kept my eyes front and forward, I could almost see certain people around me by the emotions they oozed, kind of like infrared vision.

The small bar wasn't very crowded and I detected only a slight tinge of human. The humanity emotions were mainly a hazy kind of yuck, mostly guys looking at girls and thinking the usual scummy thoughts that most guys did in a bar. Physical inventories of *tits, ass,* and *mouth,* as well as more in-depth evaluations such as *is she with someone* or *would she pay her own cab fare home.* That sort of thing. Ah, to be single again.

Oh, wait. I was.

The few DV present were, by contrast, loud and clear feelers, and it didn't take long for me to realize I was on the radar of every single one. At least they were more polite. I caught several sidelong wishes, hesitant wonderings if I were approachable.

Well, I was off the clock. I applied myself to my cocktail and kept my eyes on the glass in front of me. Body language was universal, no matter the species. Eventually I clamped down and blocked everyone out and focused on the blanketing buzz in my brain.

I didn't know Rodrian stood behind me until he put his hand on my back. I waved a weary wrist and continued shredding the coaster. Quietly, I was relieved. Marked or not, I was tired of being alone.

"Come on." He lifted my purse off the bar and held out a hand to help me off the stool. I hopped down, testing my feet through the remoteness of insobriety, and wobbled. High octane, indeed.

He wrapped his arm protectively around my shoulders. With a familiar despair settling over my soul, I let him take me home.

Dear Lonely,

Love is a difficult thing to relinquish.

Sometimes, love is denied us, yet we cling stubbornly to belief in higher entities like hope and destiny. We believe what we'd felt as lovers is too noble and too blessed a thing to simply disappear. We try to believe separation is temporary and reunion is ordained by gods and muses.

We fool ourselves.

As hard as it is to accept, people change. Something in the workings of their souls is altered, redirecting the course of their emotion, stranding us on a barren strip of wasteland where previously had been an ocean of adoration. We get left behind. We get forgotten. We have to accept that people do change.

You suffered a painful ending of your relationship. Time doesn't always heal wounds; time causes new tissue to form over them, sealing off sensitive layers that once recognized us, separating us further. We can't go back to that happy place when the other has already moved *on.*

*Be realistic, and protect your already devastated heart.*

*Sincerely, Sophie*

I'd been trying to tackle this letter for weeks but, since having run into Marek, my answer has taken a completely different tone. The last week and a half had been a quagmire for me.

"Moon's up." Toby walked into the den and hopped onto a bar stool, swinging it back and forth and banging his feet into the stools on either side. Little habits like that made me feel like he was a boy to be protected, regardless of his enhanced genetics. Never mind those orange eyes, which made him look years older.

I sprawled on the couch, frowning at my tablet. The column work had me feeling rather sour. Tough material to deal with. At least my newest response sounded sincere, if overly desolate. Oh well, that's what made it so realistic. I frowned deeper, not caring if my face stayed that way.

It took a second to break my trance. "Huh?"

"The moon. She's up."

I glanced through the windows but I couldn't see anything but black night. "How do you know?"

"I can hear her."

"You can? Oh." Hey, one more nifty factoid about werewolves: their hearing was so keen, they could hear the moon. A couple jokes immediately lined up for delivery but I held them back. It wouldn't be safe to tease him so close to his change.

The difference between trust and belief in a person largely depended on how well you thought that person knew himself. I wasn't a hundred percent confident that Toby knew himself all that well. This wasn't a good time to explore the boundaries of his self-control.

"I never heard the moon before," I said instead. "What's it sound like?"

"She," he corrected. "It's definitely a she."

"I'm sorry." For what, I didn't know. "What's she sound like?"

"Music. She sings. It's soft but I know her voice."

"I never thought hearing voices is a good sign."

"Not always, no." He swung the chair again and rooted in his back pocket, pulling out a bag of beef jerky. "Especially when it's the moon. You can't ignore a voice like that."

Curiosity nibbled at me, despite my firm dislike for Were-y things. Before I knew Toby, I had a clear (albeit biased) opinion on the Werekind; spending time with him had gradually reshaped it, given it a more human impression. While there was no danger of me running to embrace all things furry, I would be willing to admit that maybe Tanner had been just a crappy representation of the rest of the species.

Plus, the moon was a pretty cool thing. I was a devoutly lapsed Catholic, but the cool religions worshiped it and Shakespeare wrote about it in, like, every other play. I couldn't become a moon-hater just because werewolves had such a crush on it. "What does she say?"

"See, that's the thing. She talks different to everyone. Tanner, he once told me..." He cut himself off. "I guess you wouldn't care to know."

"No, it's okay. You can say it." I shrugged to show him I didn't mind. With Toby being around and talking about him all the time, his stories had put a layer of bubble wrap around the yucky memory of the Tanner I'd encountered. A little cushion, some translucency. It softened the badness of what that criminal had done. "What did he tell you?"

Ripping a strip of meat with his teeth, he chewed with a crowded, open mouth.

"Well," he said, when he could speak around the lump, "one night, it was a couple days before full. The moon was just starting to rise. I could hear her. She comes out with a whisper, saying hello. When I'm alone, sometimes I say hello back."

He grinned around the leathery meat, the sheep in wolf's clothing peeking out.

"But not when Tanner was around. He'd just tease me, I bet. So anyway, this one time we were in the car on our way out to his running place. He didn't like changing in the city, either. We'd just turned on to the highway and, as we went over a mountain, the moon was completely up. We were talking but it just kind of died off when she came out. It was hard not to listen to her and it got real quiet in the car. Then out of nowhere, he started to laugh, real hard.

"'You bitch, you,' he said.

"'What did you call me?' I said.

"'Not you,' he laughed, 'her!'

"I didn't understand why he'd say something so nasty about her. She was the most beautiful thing in my life. When it was time to change, she tried to make it easy on me and she always sounded sorry and happy at the same time. Bitch was never a word I'd use on her.

"'Why's she a bitch?' I said.

"Tanner said, 'You'd call her a bitch too, if she talked to you like that.'

"'Oh,' I said. 'She talks to you, too, huh?'

"'Dumb ass,' he said. 'She talks to all of us!'" Toby leaned toward me. "By us he meant Weres."

I raised my hand, resisting the unnecessary explanation. "I figured."

"Oh," Toby said. "Well, 'She never said anything bitchy

to me before,' I said.

"'She's not bitchy,' Tanner said. 'She's a troublemaker. She knows what kind of fun I like and she was just egging me on. There's a town off the next exit. Lots of things to chase!' And he smiled with all his teeth so that I knew he wasn't talking just rabbits.

"I never told him what the moon said to me. He probably wouldn't-a thought I was much of a man. The way he talked, the moon was like a kinky ex-girlfriend. She wasn't like that to me. She was more like..." Toby's voice trailed off as he chewed, expression pensive.

He seemed to have gotten lost in his thoughts.

"A mother?" I guessed.

He twitched his shoulders and pulled out another chip of jerky. Chewing slowly, he rewrapped the small package and turned it over in his hands.

"Yeah, maybe." He slid off the stool and stuffed the plastic bag of jerky into his back pocket. "I never really thought about it. I just always thought it was strange how she could be saying different things to different people at the same time."

"Maybe the moon is different to each of you. Maybe she's what you need her to be. Some women are like that."

Toby thunked his feet from side to side.

"Maybe," he said. "I mean, that's what you are, anyway."

I wrinkled my nose. "I guess so, especially if you need a wrinkly-eyed hag hanging around, telling you what to do."

"Don't put yourself down like that, Red. You can ask anyone to describe you and they'd all say something different and none of them would be lying. But I guarantee if you'd ask them, they'd all agree on one thing: they couldn't live without you."

Hopping to his feet, Toby waved and casually strolled out as if he hadn't just said the most staggering thing I'd heard in a very, very long time.

Euphrates woke me up when he thumped onto my chest with a sullen *mroaw*.

It took me a second to rouse enough to hear a car crunching on the gravel. I spied Rodrian's silver Audi through the upstairs windows and couldn't imagine what would make him show up at such a late hour. Grabbing my robe, I struggled to get my arms into it while I hurried downstairs, tying it shut just as I opened the front door.

Mr. Wrinkle-free Oxford trudged up the last steps looking like he'd just gone five rounds with a pack of preschoolers. His tie hung untied around his neck, top three buttons undone, shirt untucked. Even his hair was tousled, as if he'd just gotten out of bed. In short, Rodrian looked an absolute wreck.

*My God, he's been mugged.*

Before I could ask him what happened, he staggered through the door. "Hey, Soph, c'n I come in?"

I blinked. "Rode. Are you...drunk?"

"Mmm." He wobbled a little and gestured toward me, staring unashamedly at my chest. "Cold out here for that, isn't it?"

Goose bumps of thermostat proportion announced themselves from beneath my robe, and I crossed my arms to hide them. "Welcome to Sophie's Home for Wayward Souls."

He grinned and swayed into the foyer. I almost laughed as he slowly veered toward the den as if there were more than one door. Pushing the door shut, I locked it and reset the alarm. "I never saw you drunk before."

"Yeah. Sucks. My blood date was high. I didn't find out until it was too late."

"Nice," I scoffed. "I didn't know you dated junkies."

"I don't. She's a lawyer. I guess she was burning her candle at both ends tonight." He sank onto the couch and groaned with relief. "Mind if I stay the night? I have to burn this garbage out of my veins. I'm compromised."

"That's fine. You need one of your bottles?" He kept bagged blood in the house. Maybe it would dilute whatever was making his head spin.

"Nah," he said. "I'm full, thanks."

Ugh. What a mental image. "Well, if you're okay, I'll go back upstairs."

"Please, don't," he said. "I'm not tired and if you go upstairs I can't go with you." I glanced over my shoulder at him. "I just feel like talking. Stay with me?"

"Sure," I agreed. "But if you're drunk, I might as well have a glass of wine myself. That way maybe you'll make sense when you blabber."

"Oh, I never blab—abber."

Did he just hiccup? Good Lord. "Whatever. Just keep your voice down so you don't wake up Shiloh."

"Shhh," he stage-whispered. "Don't wake the baby."

I sighed as I got down a glass. It was going to be a long night.

Rodrian was a complete motor-mouth. He went on about work and women and his date in particular. He ranted about Eirene for some time before telling me how wonderful I was and how wonderful Sophias were in general.

We played Chinese Checkers for a while but gave up because he kept bumping the board, making the marbles move. Funny thing was that the marbles always ended up in more strategic places for him. I quit once I realized he was using his talent to cheat.

When I yelled, he protested so charmingly I didn't throw the marbles at him. Very hard, anyway. It sure was funny watching him try to duck them, though, and even funnier when he picked them up. As much as I hated to admit it, Rodrian was a fun drinking partner. At one point I considered asking for a good electronic dart board, the kind bars installed for darts league, but reconsidered. I'd never stand a chance against a cheater like him.

The wine loosened my tongue more than I should have allowed but I figured, since he was loaded himself, he'd forgive me. This would probably be the best time to broach subjects that were normally off-limits. Something had been bothering me long before I'd moved into the Stocks, long before Rodrian approached me.

As I slid the game box back under the couch, I attempted a nonchalant tone. "Rode, you ever wonder how Marek could have gotten taken by the Master?"

"I don't think about it." He sprawled bonelessly in the corner of the sofa, head back against the cushions, staring at the fire with drooping lids.

"I'm sure he was betrayed." I scooted around on the

couch to face him. "Do you remember Donna, my old office manager?"

"Mmm hmm."

"She was involved with Chal and, that night when everything happened, she said he was the one who gave her to the master. Chal must have been a mole."

Actually, saying Donna was "involved with Chal" was somewhat understating it. It was like saying hookers were involved with their clients. She'd been his skank before she'd become the master's whore. Not that I was biased against the dead bitch but, anyways. Bygones.

Rodrian rolled his head from side to side and closed his eyes. "No, I don't think so."

"It's got to be. And Chal was Caen's toadie. It fits together. The motive is there. I know Caen hated Marek."

"Look, Sophie." Rodrian sat up as if he'd suddenly remembered he had a bone structure. "Caen can be an ass, okay? But he's loyal. He had a personal thing against my brother, but he didn't betray him and he didn't get Chal to do it for him."

"Are you sure? It's so convenient that Caen banished Chal before he could say a word to defend himself." The night Rodrian's men captured Tanner after his failed hit on me, the Were managed a suicide before the guards got him to talk. As a result, the DV never found out who had hired him.

Caen had put Chal in charge of detaining the Were and had been the one to discipline him for the suicide. I personally thought Caen rushed the proceedings a bit, and suspected he knew something he wasn't telling. "A hit on Marek's girl would have been a major blow. With Chal having a major connection to the Master, it only seems logical that—"

"No. Whatever Chal was, he wasn't a link between Caen

and the old master. Caen has no vampire allegiance. Period." His power matched his tone, a warning that I better not push the issue.

"Then who did, Rode?" I crossed my arms and glared at him, angry that he'd get so bossy-meanie with me. Warning, indeed. "If there's a traitor out there then we're still not safe."

"There is no traitor, Soph." He blew out a big breath and slapped his legs. "Haven't you figured it out yet? Marek got caught because he wanted to get caught."

"That's the stupidest thing I ever heard. Why would he—?"

"Because." He balled his hands into fists. "It was the plan right from the beginning."

I mustn't have heard it right. "He planned it? You mean..."

Rodrian avoided my eyes. "You weren't supposed to be there. You were supposed to stay here until he came back but you didn't. You went to that stupid Expo thing, you got nicked, and you nearly got yourself killed."

I was suddenly standing without remembering doing it. Disbelief made me numb. All I could think was *What's wrong with Rodrian? He needs to shut up.*

"Did you ever wonder how we managed to rush the place and wipe out the vamps? How was it possible we were all there at that precise moment? It was planned, Sophie."

Why was he still talking? My insides trembled and my foundation threatened to crumble beneath me. Rodrian kept right on as if he weren't destroying me, my foundation, brick by brick.

"You just...got in the way. You weren't supposed to be there. Marek didn't know it was going to happen that way."

Some dark hot molten thing had replaced the air in my

lungs. "What way? The way he almost killed me?"

"No, Soph. How could he have known at the exact moment he was pushed past reason, you'd be the blood waiting for him? Vamps don't make distinctions when they feed. It's only heat and blood. It's like trying to single out one chicken in a full coop. You were only blood and heat to him."

Tears scalded my cheeks in a sheet, bitter and angry.

Rodrian lifted his head, his face twisted with guilt as he spilled his secrets and watched the effect they had on me. "It's the worst thing that could have ever gone wrong. He figured you were smart enough to figure it out on your own, eventually."

I held my breath, trying to suppress the sobs that were knotting my chest. It didn't work. "So nice to know he had such a high opinion of me."

"Sophie, he told me...it was after you tracked us down at the new club. He was relieved it was you. He was prepared for a terrible risk but he wouldn't have survived if it hadn't been your blood. He took in a part of your essence and it gave him unimaginable strength. It kept him from being destroyed. Does that make you feel any better?"

"No." I looked at him as if he'd sprouted horns. I remembered the pain and the grief and the loss. I remembered being abandoned and the taste of the revitalizer Pontian forced me to drink so I wouldn't die from hypovolemic shock. "It doesn't. It only makes me angry."

"Angry? How?"

And then it took over—a dark hot emotion that dwarfed me. Anger. True anger.

Everything that had happened wasn't some unfortunate turn of events. Marek had planned it. This was betrayal, defined past any lingering doubt. The anger erupted and spurted out, seeking a target.

It found Rodrian.

"Because! We were supposed to have a life! We were supposed to live happily ever after! It was perfect and we had hope and all my pain was finally gone and he left. On purpose! Knowing that whatever paradise we had, he'd end it. And now I have nothing." I sucked air through gritted teeth, sounding like an animal, my hands clawed and fisted to keep from pummeling the truth into him. "I have been an empty shell that, for the last year and a half, held nothing but loss. I didn't even have my best friend anymore because he killed him, too, and that makes me angry."

Rodrian sprang to his feet, the tipsiness completely vanished from his copper eyes. "Oh no, Soph. It wasn't like that."

"It was. I lived it. You don't know what it was because you weren't there either." I pressed my hands into my eyes. Hating myself for drinking, for remembering, for being vulnerable. I hated Rodrian for making me trust him and love him so much I couldn't blame him.

I should be blaming him. He, of all people, could have been honest with me. All this time I poured out my heart and prayed for events to reverse their unfortunate selves. All this time he knew the truth and he lied to me.

I whirled but he got in my face, grabbing my arms and twisting me so I couldn't look away. I resisted, squirming until he issued a frustrated sigh and seized me with a ruder-than-usual compulsion.

Oh, no. He did not just do that.

I pulled up my shields, sliding a layer between us, using it to chip away at his compulsion.

He held onto me, narrow-eyed with determination.

Leaning into my barriers, I poured a shitload of HOW DARE YOU into them. I got close to breaking free of him, and smiled viciously, feeling him pull back.

Suddenly he released a pulse of power so tremendous it banged my barriers back at me, rocking me with a physical blow that left me gasping for breath, still pinioned under his mental grasp.

Defiantly I glared up at him, choking back the sobs. "Give me one good reason why you ditched me, too."

"I couldn't be there," he said. "I didn't trust myself."

"You didn't trust yourself?" Eyes wide and mouth agape, I bunched everything I had and shoved at my barriers, striking his own power and breaking his compulsion. "It destroyed me, Rode. My life nearly ended in more ways than one and you were having self-doubt issues?"

"Sophie, you don't know the whole story and you're drunk. Don't jump to conclusions until you can think about it."

"About what!" I thumped my fists onto his chest, hard enough to make him back up half a step. "I lost everything I wanted!"

"And you don't think about anything except what you want!" He paced away and threw his hands up in disgust.

"Oh, I've been so self-centered." I sneered at him. "Tell me, Rodrian, did you lose everything?"

He gave me the dirtiest of looks out of the corners of his bright eyes. I saw the glint of teeth.

I'd pushed him to a bad place. I knew it. I couldn't stop. "Haven't I paid enough attention to you, Rodrian?"

"No." He shook his head, his hair tumbling from behind his ear, spilling over his eyes. "You haven't."

"Poor baby! Why was I so neglectful? Oh, that's right, you abandoned me. Keeps coming back to that, doesn't it?"

"You want to know why?" He turned fully toward me, his head lowered so he had to look up at me. His eyes were completely alight, the brightness so sharp against the locks of hair that hung down. "You weren't safe from me."

I should have been alarmed at the predator seething back at me, but I was surging with anger and getting reckless. "Well, sorry to inform you, but Marek didn't leave enough for seconds."

"Yes, he did."

He grabbed my shoulders again and descended. Too fast. I didn't even have time to worry. His face was so close. His mouth was so close. His teeth—

My throat wasn't the target.

He kissed me with a desperation I'd never felt before and that kiss demanded a response. I reached up and pulled him down against me, tasting his mouth and feeling his power and his desire lace around me, through me. It was a jolt of electricity that left a trail of heat behind.

Abruptly he broke away, breathing heavily, eyes wide with some unnamable emotion. Our bodies were still close together and his power seeped into me. Disbelief, righteousness, fear. He seemed to wait for me to give a sign, any sign, of what he could do next. One signal from me and he'd run with it. I knew what he wanted. It would be so easy to say *yes*.

I swallowed. Hard. Twice. His eyes begged for any excuse to take me. My breath shallowed into panting and I swayed on my feet.

What did a girl do when she was drunk, heartbroken, and incredibly aroused by a beautiful man? Certainly not what I did. All the wine I'd swallowed had decided that enough was enough and it wanted out.

Rodrian sped me toward the sink before I ruined the rug and even held my hair back, handing me a wet rag when I finished embarrassing myself. He chuckled softly as he got me upstairs and carefully aimed me toward my rooms from the hall.

Although I couldn't feel him once I passed through the wards, I suspected he tarried in the hallway, listening to make sure I'd gotten in okay. I think I'd mumbled *thank you*, but I wasn't sure the words actually made any sound.

His power, however, remained a living memory, sharp and clear as I fell into dreamless sleep. I just wished I'd been sober enough to remember what it'd tried to tell me.

Hangovers sucked, especially when accompanied by the lingering fog that traps your thoughts inside your smoggy brain, preventing you from getting any real peace. All the water in the world couldn't rehydrate me because my soul was leaking. I'd betrayed myself.

I couldn't have prevented that kiss but that wasn't why I beat myself up. It was because I failed to act. I didn't tell him to stop. I didn't take it farther. I barfed, which is a definitely involuntary response. What a coward. I couldn't even act upon my convictions, whatever the hell they might have been at that point.

Hangovers sucked, especially when accompanied by senior staff meetings where Tom Butchman singled you out and asked you for your input and you provided the room with a working definition of the word "agape."

Hangovers especially sucked when all you could think about was how much unfun a meeting with Eirene would be, when all you wanted to do was collapse in bed with a bottle of migraine reliever and a box of tissues and an unsympathetic cat.

The night air was brittle, the kind of cold that made fingertips split and nails break. Not that I worried about a manicure or anything. I just hated new reasons to bleed.

Eirene didn't seem to mind the cold; I guessed it suited her personality. It also gave her an excuse to wear expensive fur. I already knew Eirene's definition of saving the world didn't extend to Weres, but apparently it also excluded baby seals.

I wasn't as sumptuously garbed. My flannel-lined peacoat only reached halfway to my knees; my denim jeans weren't quite thick enough to keep out the winter bite. I hadn't thought to add a layer of Under Armour when getting dressed for tonight's meeting.

The light of a near full moon slid down through the artificial forest of cityscape as we crossed the parkway. After the night's intense barrier exercise, Eirene had suggested a walk to refresh ourselves. Personally, I wanted to crawl under my bed and die for just a little while but I guessed I owed her that much.

Chester Memorial Grove wasn't Central Park by a long shot but it could have passed for a piece of it. It covered a four city block square just outside of downtown, where the buildings weren't as tall or struck as close together, acting as a buffer to the parkway and I-95, which stretched past Balaton on the far side. Naked trees stretched skinny arms and crooked bony fingers into the cold night, basking in moon glow and streetlight, a strange shade of silver and gold.

The expression Eirene wore was inappropriate for walking through the cold, dark, and spooky. She looked as pleased as a genteel lady strolling through a summer garden. I wore a frozen determined smile over jaws clamped down to keep from chattering.

I was beginning to suspect she was a little nutty.

Dorcas plodded dutifully behind us. A few backward glances revealed she wore the same look she always did: unassuming, invisible, unremarkable. I guess Eirene was enough personality for both of them. What a depressing thought.

"Ah," Eirene said. "Beautiful night."

I shrugged and set off another chilly shudder. "At least it's not snowing."

"You don't like snow?" Her voice warmed and lifted with surprise. "Hmm. I like snow. It reminds me of home. The winters are very good there. Long nights, black skies. Lots of reasons to stay indoors. Lots of reasons to be outside. The snow would fall for weeks, piling up, covering roads and blocking doors. I like the snow."

"I guess snow is nice," I admitted. "The whole 'no two snowflakes are alike' thing."

"A silly myth. Of course they are alike. If you hold out your hand and catch only ten of them, you cannot make assumptions about the countless ones falling around you." She waved a knowing finger at me, and the streetlights glittered off her black eyes. "Never be fooled by what you see. It's what you do not see that will kill you."

The park was deserted except for the three of us. Not surprising, since it was past last call. Even the bars were closed by now. Our footsteps clacking sharply on the cement walkway, we headed along the diagonal path toward the center square. A World War II monument had been erected there, a great wall of black marble graced by evergreens. It was bright and optimistically solemn in the afternoon but I had no idea what it might look like in midnight shadows. Unfortunately, it seemed I'd find out.

"You are progressing well in your control," Eirene said.

"How do you feel?"

Besides exhausted and numb? "Better," I said. "People are starting to feel like people again. I'm not walking around in a sea of others' intrusions."

"Very good!" She clapped her hands, the leather gloves muting the sound. "That is exactly how you should come to think of it—intrusion. You are not an open target, waiting for the barrage of every passing emotion. You have a station, an elevation above the masses. You will allow what you choose. No one should make you accept them."

I appreciated her praise—a rare thing for her to validate me in such a way, considering how abysmal I'd felt when first meeting her. Despite my progress, I burned to know more about the rest of the Sophia world. "Do you think we can begin discussing the Canons or the Circlet? You only mention them in passing and I know there is so much more to learn."

"In time, in time. Tonight is for enjoyment. We have several nights remaining until I must depart."

"Depart? So soon?" Wow. Never thought I'd utter the words. "But we haven't really—"

Suddenly, she put her gloved hand upon my arm, her other hand up in a gesture to be silent. She looked around. "We are being followed."

Swell. Three women alone in a deserted park at night. Unless Eirene or Dorcas knew *Jiu Jitsu*, we were in trouble. Her eyes fixed upon something in the darkness under the trees and I dug into my pocket for my cell phone. The cold had long numbed my fingers and I could barely get them to work. "What is it? Do you see someone?"

Dorcas pulled up to stand alongside Eirene, her expression utterly unreadable. Eirene looked tense. Great. Miss Non-Emoting Ice Queen showed a genuine response and it was worry, of all things. I peered through the darkness toward where they were staring. Nothing except shadows.

And a flash of white eyes. And another.

I backed away and pulled at Eirene's arm. "Eirene," I hissed. "Vamps! We gotta run!"

"Run," she echoed. "They are here to kill you. They do not recognize me. Go. Run. I'll delay them."

"What? No! We all go!"

"Go," said Dorcas. Her voice seemed to take on actual sound. "My mistress knows what she is doing. Go before it's too late for you."

Fine by me. I had no death wish. I ran.

I took off across the park, running on pure adrenaline, following the northbound path that would come out near the underpass.

The path led me away from downtown, toward less densely packed city where help might be harder to come by. But I was running away from vampires. It would have to be a fair trade.

I burst out of the park onto the city sidewalk and ran north. The underpass was a quarter block away and separated from the park by a narrow dirty path that had been trampled into the snow. I plowed through a muddy puddle, the water sending up an icy spray that soaked my leg and made me curse.

The underpass was dark, lit only by the fleeting headlights of speeding cars. Each flash of light illuminated lumpy shapes against the far walls. Homeless, I realized, huddled desperately against the cold, insulated by walls of stuffed plastic bags and precious dry cardboard. I hoped they'd forgive my rude intrusion but, since I was running for my life, I wouldn't let it chew me up too badly. I focused only on reaching the brightly lit distant gas station.

Once out of sight of the park, I slowed. My pant leg was

soaked through and cold water had dripped into my boot, leaving a sharp ache of sensation. I paused to catch my breath and glanced behind me, looking for Eirene. No one. The lumpy outlines of the homeless remained silent and still, more like scenery than humanity. Nothing. No one.

Voices made me look toward to the far end of the underpass. Three young guys, perhaps coming from the club that was a few blocks away. They loped along with a bouncy walk that reminded me of my burnout friends from 1989. Barks of sporadic laughter, sound of someone spitting. Classy.

I resumed my walk toward the gas station, head nonchalantly up, walk brisk and purposeful without looking panicked. All I could think of was digging out my cell phone but I didn't want to advertise that I had things in my pocket in case one of the guys was a mugger. I hated the city for making me afraid of being alone at night. There had been vamps back there, for crying out loud, doing God knew what to Eirene, and I was worried about a couple of guys?

Indignantly, I raised my head a little higher and marched.

As I neared the group, one of the boys stopped laughing and shook back his choppy blond hair. "You okay, lady?"

"I'm fine." I smiled and didn't slow down.

"Your pants are wet."

I kept walking.

He passed me but suddenly shot out a hand and grabbed my arm. "Didn't you hear me? Your pants are wet."

I swallowed panic and tried to gently twist out of his hand. "Yes," I said. "There's a puddle back there. Look out for it."

He didn't let go. "Maybe you been running. You sure got soaked."

I finally succeeded in pulling free but, as I backed away,

one of the guys slid behind me. Where was a car when you wanted one to go by? He poked my back with a finger, not hard enough to hurt. Panic zipped through me. "She ain't running anywhere now, is she?"

*Like hell, I'm not.* Deciding to take my chances with the traffic, I threw myself away toward the street. A car blasted its horn and swerved to miss me.

The one behind me grabbed my arms and wrenched me back. He jerked my head around to face the other two, who stared me down with bright eyes, shades of brown and green. DV, I realized when one leaked his power. They'd been working hard at locking it down before.

"Leave me go," I said. "I'm marked."

The blond laughed, his voice sounding mean and oily. "We ain't looking for a snack. We're just retrieving you. Those nice people you ran from want you to come back."

*Oh crap, they're with the vamps!* The realization hit me at nearly the exact moment that his compulsion did. It slammed into me, stunning me and sagging me nearly to the ground.

Blondie grabbed a fistful of my hair and yanked my face up to his. His chin-scrape stubble caught the light like frost. "Now walk," he said. "And stay quiet."

My feet obeyed.

I meekly marched toward my doom.

Blood hummed in my ears as my heart sought to beat somewhere outside my chest. A car passed us and all I could do was roll my eyes at it, listening to the sound of fading hope as it hummed away down the street.

Soon we were out from under the bridge and rounding the curve leading back to the park. I strained my ears to hear any sound at all—from Eirene, from Dorcas, from anything—but the night was silent and expectant, waiting for me to fill it with my screams.

As we strode through the park, I desperately looked for a sign of Eirene. Seeing no dead bodies, I tried to take heart. My feet splashed through dark puddles, so much darker than muddy water. I refused to think of them.

The DV marched me to the darkest of shadows, a thickness of trees near the monument wall. The blond called out: "We brought you the Sophia, as you commanded."

A flash of light, too quick for me to follow. Vamps eyes.

I couldn't curse. I couldn't pray. I could barely breathe.

"Thank you," came a smooth voice from the dark. Wait. I knew that voice. Disbelief kept me from making the connection until she stepped out into the glow of the street-lights.

Eirene. Her white fur coat was slashed and bloodied.

"You save me the trouble of chasing her through these filthy streets. Release her." Eirene's eyes flashed icy blue and her face was alight with haughty rage.

"Who are you?" The blond snarled and wrapped his arm around my throat, choking me. I pulled feebly at his arm but the hold was like iron.

"I am your punishment. The Demivampire who align themselves to the vampire are lovers of death. Come, lover, touch me. Welcome my embrace."

I felt the DV compulsion drop as he stiffened and pushed me away. I felt a different horror as I watched the blond kid obediently slide toward her enticingly opened arms. "What are you doing, Eirene?"

"Giving this one what he wants," she answered coyly. Her red mouth and black eyes beckoned seductively to the young man, whose expression was twisted by conflicting emotions. "He courts death with his allegiance to the vampire. I'll give him death. Will you die for me, my handsome one?"

"What?" He sounded so young. "Die? I don't want to die."

"And yet you make contracts with vampires. They are walking death."

"I don't want to die," he insisted.

"I don't care what you want." Her hand flashed, whipping a wide arc toward him, a streak of moonlight on silver and a dark mist that shadowed the air. Suddenly the silent night roared with terrible sound: a cry of pain, a thud as the boy dropped, a wail from the other DV as they watched and waited.

I fled, desperately running and hoping none would catch me this time.

I felt them as they died. There had been no time for me to concentrate on the circle and the barrier and so the Sophia was bared, the explosion of emotion scalding me with its intensity.

I felt them clearly as if I thrust the blade myself. Their cock-sure brutality and their lust to do harm melted into fear and remorse as she condemned them. I felt their pleas for mercy, and the nakedness of their desperation cut me like shards of glass.

How could she destroy them, feeling what I felt?

Despite their anguish, they kept a measure of defiance; the evolution they'd tasted still gripped them. The lure of immortality would not have diminished with a near-death encounter. It wouldn't have changed them. Their souls weren't tainted, they'd been putrefied with twisted desire.

Maybe they couldn't be saved. Maybe Eirene was right.

My tears froze upon my eyelashes, absorbing the chill of the air. The city streaked by as I raced to my car. I shook with terror and cold, trying to steady my hand enough to get the key into the door. The freezing night had left my hands painfully useless, my fingers tight and brittle enough to snap. Adrenaline sizzled through me, but my hands remained numb.

"Damn it!" I hissed when the keys dropped from my senseless fingers. Crouching against the side of the car, I tried to stay out of traffic while feeling for the key ring.

They were grimy and wet with melted snow and I hurriedly wiped them on my leg as I stood up. Just as I did, Eirene and Dorcas appeared on the sidewalk, staring at me over the car.

"Open the doors for us, Sophie."

"I'm not in for this!"

"I said, open the doors. We cannot be seen like this. In the car we will talk."

"Those were people!"

"Open the door!" Her voice sounded desperate. "I don't know if there are others!"

Frantically I popped the doors and we slid inside. I pulled out with a lurch, swerving into the thin traffic and rounding the corner at a reckless speed.

"You are upset," she said.

Upset? A little bit, yeah. "You killed those boys."

"I eliminated the vampire threat."

"The DV, damn it!"

"They were part of the threat," she said calmly.

I couldn't believe what she said. "You're a killer."

"I am not a killer." She wiped at a thick smear of blood on her coat, running her fingers through the ruined fur. I hated to tell her she'd need more than spit on a hanky to get it clean. "Those vampires were killers. Those DV were killers."

"You don't kill. It's not right."

"And what should I have done? Should I have saved them? Should I have shown them the folly of their allegiances? Should I have redeemed them?" She leaned toward me. "They are lost. They chose their life's paths. They had forsaken the lives they had and chosen instead a damnable existence. There is no cure for that! No Sophia can fix that! Such a small symptom of the disease. It was no crime to cut it out, to remove it from tainting the whole. Their deaths are for the greater good."

"Every life is precious," I insisted.

"Even the ones that would hand you over to the vampire for slaughter?"

I didn't answer.

"Sophie." She spoke in a gentler voice, reaching over to lay her hand on my arm. "Sophie, our lives were in danger. If the Sophia dies, then all DV are lost. Can you imagine the value upon your life? Is it not worth protecting? Is that not for the greater good? You must be strong enough to do the right thing, even if it's the hard thing. I must teach you that the hard thing is the right thing. You are too soft, too forgiving. Not everyone can be saved."

She tilted her head up. "Isn't that right, Dorcas?"

"Yes, ma'am. Truly as you say."

"See? Now. I think my appetite has rallied. Such good a brisk walk will do for one's constitution. Will you dine with me?"

I forced a non-disgusted look onto my face. Did she really think I could eat after watching her exterminate those DV or staring at the blood on her coat, her fingers? "No, it's late. I'm not hungry."

"Hmm," Eirene assented. "I understand. Dorcas, arrange for my needs in my quarters upon our arrival."

"Yes, ma'am." Dutiful, like always.

I dropped them at the hotel. Eirene had taken off her coat and carried it, carefully folded on her arm. She couldn't possibly have worn it without attracting attention. I'd been seen with her often enough that a call to the cops would have eventually pointed them in my direction.

I began to shake as I drove away. I didn't remember the ride home. All I could think about was the way she had decided those DV had been too far gone to save.

I prayed urgently for God's help. I never wanted to make that kind of choice. I knew if it were all left up to me, I'd never make the right one.

I needed a break.

Every part of my life had definitely reached the over-whelming stage. Every measure of achievement or progress was canceled out with something undesirable.

I was closer to Rodrian but now I had a mountain of drama to sort through. I had an office, a much-needed spot of sanctuary, but it came with the aggravating bundle of corporate bull. Toby seemed to be finding his feet and any day I hoped he'd tell me his quest was over; however, the moon was coming close to full and his wolf was becoming apparent. Euphrates hadn't come out of my bedroom in a week. I got to see Marek but he shattered my hope of getting close enough to tell him about Eirene.

And Eirene? Oh, hell. Don't even get me started on that hot mess. I might be good at barriers but if she thought I'd start executing people who didn't fit her standards of worthiness, well, forget it. I'm done.

After work, I grabbed a burger and a caramel frappe

and, once home, retreated to my haven: the small library in my quarters.

My computer and desk were in the office so, by default, I spent a lot of time in there. However, sitting at my little desk in that wide open room didn't feel as comfortable as it had back in my apartment by the harbor. Even with it backed up into the corner, I still felt like an interloper, a stone in the middle of the path. At one point I thought about getting a single partition wall to close off the space but I put the sprags to that plan. I couldn't believe I wanted to make a cube at home. The notion alone should have given me hives.

Whereas the office had been barely lived in, Marek's personal library had a comfortable broken-in feeling that suited me like second skin.

The room was furnished with two old, stuffed, and well-worn armchairs, one the color of the Atlantic Ocean on a July afternoon and the other such a wretched color—Burnt Sienna, no doubt the ugliest crayon in the box—that it must have been more comfortable than anything else on the planet if Marek had reason to keep it (turned out it was.) A long slender lamp, hanging its shade from a curved brass neck, peered over the brown chair as it sat closest to the door, across from a wall of knick knacks and books that, truthfully, seemed to cry *Dust me!* before *Read me!*

A small rectangular table, high-legged yet stout, had a gray marbled glass top, its edges rounded to follow the clover-leaf-cut corners of the table top itself; it fell away in long geometric lines to its scallop-shelled feet. Very Frank Lloyd Wright. Very nice and, surprisingly, very well-used, like the comfy old chairs.

Everything else in the house seemed new or at least barely used, straight from the catalog; these few pieces were cherished and personal. Funny how a scratched wooden table or a frayed cushion showed personality, added character to an otherwise magazine-perfect decor. These pieces might be the ugly sisters compared to the rest of the house's furnishings, but these were the sisters that were the most fun to hang out with.

Books, real books with worn spines and signs of diligent use lined the shelves. It was a breathtaking collection, spanning ages and cultures on countless subjects in an array of languages: German, Greek, Latin, Hungarian...not like I could do more than admire the pages. I was language-handicapped; my only talents for second languages extended to the Spanish I learned in high school and my penchant for learning for foreign curse words.

Whenever I needed space, I came up here. It was like a little museum in its own right. The only thing that pricked along the edges of comfort was the certain knowledge that, of all the rooms in the house, this one had the most Marek in it.

The books, the statuettes, the tall lamp—I could almost see him sprawled in the blue-green chair near the window, legs straight out and crossed at the ankle, chin resting on chest and book balanced on belt buckle. Almost, but not quite. I always looked away before he could manifest and felt shamed at the thought of coming in here just because of him.

Then again, most days the *almost* sense nagged at me no matter where I looked. I never felt true comfort. Always that prickling along the edges of my comfort, that worry/hope that I'd turn a corner and see him again.

I had to work harder at facing my reality. For all that this room had the most Marek, it was still just another empty room.

If only I could escape Marek's scent.

It lingered, tiny traces that never seemed to be in the

same place twice. Leather and sandalwood—not an easy scent; too unfamiliar and foreign, an acquired taste. The scent caught the throat like a curry, a dry heat that lingered and flavored everything after it and was uneasily chased away by refreshment. The leather was unlike the leather of the sofas Rodrian favored; it was the leather of old harness and oil coat, empty but for the invisible scent of steel.

Leather and sandalwood. Not a common or modern combination but, then again, Marek's best qualities were neither common nor modern. The scents suited him well.

Rodrian's scent was easier on the palate. Brut cologne and cherries, a smell I breathed in through my mouth because smelling wasn't enough. The scent wanted to be devoured.

It was the scent that had overwhelmed me the day we set the ward on the den. Up until then, I'd never really noticed it. Afterwards, I asked him why he wore Brut, that seven dollar bottle from the drug store, when he certainly could afford anything he wanted.

He asked me, "What does it make you think of?"

I told him the truth: my first boyfriend.

Even a high school kid could shell out the bucks for it. It smelled like summer and wife-beater t-shirts and menthol cigarettes before they were lit, tucked behind an ear beneath a sandy brown curl. It smelled like something I'd always want but knew I could never have again.

But all I said out loud was: *my first boyfriend.*

He'd given me a long lingering look and said, "That's what they always say."

At least Rodrian's scent didn't crowd me here in Marek's room. I couldn't handle both of them at once.

Scents could be powerful ties to our memories. For once, I'd like one to bring up memories that weren't painful—or conflicting.

I settled into the ugly brown armchair and stared at my phone. This was it. I couldn't stall anymore. I scrolled down the list of contacts until I got to his number and hit call. The phone rang. My heart pounded. Oh, crap. My voice would shake and I'd sound like a dorky teen and the ringing stopped—

Oh, God. This was it—

"Leave a message."

I crumpled. Voice mail.

Another failed attempt. I knew those three words like I knew the sound of my own name. The quick breath and pause right before he spoke. The bass rumbles of his voice, the dark tone he inflicted upon the words because he hates checking voice mail and he's really hoping no one actually leaves a message. If it was important, he'd once said to me, they'd get a hold of him another way.

I didn't have another way.

Or did I?

Rodrian was an everyday part of my life now. Why couldn't I get him to say something to Marek? Better question: why didn't he tell Marek about Eirene himself?

What if he already had?

I hated these questions, these doubts and anxieties and I knew, beyond all doubt, that I wouldn't be stuck here, battered around like a cat toy, if it wasn't for that damned voice mail I knew he'd never check.

*Marek,* I silently begged while I redialed the call. *Just pick up the phone. Both of our lives depend on it.*

"Can I hang out with you, Soph?"

Shiloh's voice sounded from the echoey hallway just as Marek's voicemail greeting came on. I dropped the phone onto the table and walked out to the entrance of my suite. Peering out, I saw her leaning against the wall, dressed for bed.

"Are you sure you want to try coming in, Shy? We never tried to get you pass the wards."

She slid toward me, still holding up the wall. One arm hugged her waist. "I don't care if it hurts. I just want to come in."

I didn't like the word *hurts*, especially when it looked like she was already suffering. I went to her, putting my arm around her shoulder. "We can go to your room. I'll stay with you if you want to try to sleep."

She shook her head, tousling her hair. "Please? Just take me in there with you. It feels too empty out here."

I took a deep breath and looked back at my door. The wards weren't visible—I didn't even really remember where they began. What would they do to her?

Closing my eyes, I urged my Sophia sight to feel out the ward. I couldn't see anything that way, either. All I could see was my barrier, my self, drawn in and thinned down, unnecessary at the moment.

Then I had an idea.

I pulled Shiloh to me, tighter against my side.

"We're going to try walking in together, Shiloh." I tentatively took a step. "If you get uncomfortable, tell me and we'll abandon ship."

Head against my shoulder, she nodded.

I exhaled loudly. "Here goes."

If the wards recognized me, perhaps there was a way to cloak her somehow, to sneak her inside. I closed my eyes again, pushing my barrier out. It ballooned against Shiloh, flowing around here. Using a mental hand, I tugged what I thought was Shiloh's aura closer to me. My barrier resisted.

Leaning into it, I reached around her on all sides, encompassing her, drawing her into my circle.

My barrier stretched where she pressed against it. Carefully, I thinned that section while putting more behind her.

With a soft pop, she broke through my shield, coming to rest within my safe zone.

Guess that was as good as it would get. I opened my eyes. "Now, we walk."

Step by step, we approached the doors. I felt the wards buzz against me, halting me. They pressed against my barrier but it wasn't discomfort. It was...rather like a tickle.

After a moment, they sighed away, leaving us free to continue. I supposed I'd just gotten frisked by my own wards.

Once inside my parlor, I paused. "Okay so far, Shy?"

"Uh huh."

Slowly I drew my barriers back in to me, noting the thin glow that still clung to her. It sparkled and faded as I watched.

Suddenly, Shiloh's eyes widened and she rubbed her arms, patted her cheeks, looking wildly around.

"What's wrong?" I grasped her shoulders.

"Nothing. I—" She pushed her hair back, looking wary. "That was weird. Something just—I don't know—like feathers, all over me. Electric feathers."

I laughed, covering my mouth. "That sounds crazy."

She managed to chuckle. "I guess magic is a little crazy. Anyway." She pointed to the minibar. "What's in there?"

Good to know her hollow legs hadn't suffered the strain of hypolution. Maybe there was hope, after all.

Once full of hot chocolate and pistachios—really, she ate the strangest things—Shiloh wandered into the small library where I'd already sat down to read. She perused the shelves, fingering the knick-knacks and making faces at the photographs. Thus distracted, she didn't notice my assessment of her.

The freckles that she usually kept hidden under cosmetics announced themselves, making her appear so much younger than seventeen. Her complexion was pale and tired; shadows under her eyes from lack of sleep.

I hadn't seen much of her since she'd gotten mad at me for sending Brianda after her. She'd done a good job at not being around. "You want to try going back to bed?"

She shrugged and slipped into the armchair. "I just don't feel like sleeping."

"But you look tired."

She shrugged again. "I am."

The wind howled outside, a wind storm too fierce even for rain. It seemed to be attacking the house, punishing it for being in the way. I pitied Toby, out in the woods on a night like this. Fur or no fur, the weather was brutal.

"I don't like the storm," she admitted. "It sounds awful out there. It's like the wind is screaming."

Setting down the book I'd been reading, I stopped to listen.

"You're right," I said. "That does sound like screaming. Creepy, huh?"

"Yeah." She tucked her feet up and hugged her knees, a quiet ball of exhaustion. So un-kinetic, so unlike the Shiloh I knew.

Lowering my barriers, I sampled a mental current and grew concerned when I detected a distinct taste of muted terror. She really must have been spooked after all, if I could actually feel her. "You want to talk, Shy?"

"Not really," she said. "I just don't feel like being alone."

Outside the wind blew something loose and it thumped distantly. The groundskeeper would be very busy tomorrow.

Grateful for the coziness of the room and the sense of privacy it lent, I thought it might be a good time to talk. I'd seen so little of her since she changed crowds and I felt farther from her than I'd ever felt before. Seeing her huddled in the chair made my heart ache—she looked so fragile, so vulnerable.

The sense of urgency had grown stronger. "There is no reason to be afraid, Shy. We're safe here."

"I know."

I opened up and tried to feel again from her emotions. "Then why do you feel so frightened?"

She wrinkled her nose at me. "I don't."

"Someone is terrified." The wind picked up again, wailing. I tilted my head toward the window, feeling for the thread of power the way I'd often strained to hear a faint sound. It led me out of my seat and I circled the library before heading out into the parlor. The terror was stronger.

In the hallway, it was stronger still. "Shit!"

"What?" she called as she followed me out into the hall.

"That's not the wind!" I thinned my barriers as I raced toward the foyer. I could hear someone banging at the door, screaming. The terror was broadcasting clearly: Dahlia.

I took the stairs two at a time.

"Hang on!" I punched the alarm code and jerked open the deadbolt. The door flew open under the combined force of wind and Dahlia and she lunged inside, still screaming.

Throwing herself against the door, she howled. "Lock it! Lock it!"

"What's wrong?!" I shouted. "Dally! Stop it!"

She sobbed and gasped for breath. Sheer terror made white noise of her power. "Out...there..." she gasped.

"Out there?" I prompted.

"Were!"

"Where?" I repeated. "Oh! Were! Damn it! Toby!"

"Toby?" Shiloh yelled from the top of stairs. "You told me he left!"

"He did! He said he'd stay away for the moon. Damn it!"

Dahlia's shoulders shook, her eyes wide. If she didn't calm down I'd have to tap her. She never let me use my Sophia on her before and I half-worried she'd beat me down when I was done. "Come on, I'll get the fire going in the den."

I led her inside. Dahlia sank onto the couch, holding her cheeks.

"Sorry, Soph." Her voice trembled, but she wasn't scared anymore. "I lost my head. I'd just never—seen—you know. Toby. Like that."

"Neither have I," I admitted. "Why did he go after you?"

"He didn't, exactly. I just got out of the car and when I walked up to the door, I heard growling. I looked behind me and he was hunching there, at the edge of the porch lights. All I saw were his eyes and teeth and I knew he would hurt me."

"Toby? He wouldn't hurt you." I pressed her shoulder and looked into her eyes, which held violet fire. "Do you understand? Toby wouldn't hurt you. I just suppose when in wolf form, he acts wolfy. But he'd never hurt you. Not any of us."

"Whatever. I'm calling Dad," Shiloh announced from the doorway.

"No, Shy!" I tried to stop her but she sprinted up the stairs. I doubted Rodrian knew how to fight werewolves. Hopefully, he'd stay home. I didn't want either one of them to get hurt.

Outside, the wolf howled, a jagged sound of menace. Dahlia's control slipped and I felt the pulse of worry that flared her sparkling gaze.

"We're safe, Dally. All the doors are locked. He can't get

in."

The words had barely left my mouth when the screaming started again.

This time, it was Shiloh.

A matted-looking gray wolf had cornered Shiloh between the office and the hallway to her room. I could see her eyes, huge, white as she clutched her cell phone to her ear, begging her father to save her. The constant stream of her voice sounded like a ribbon of panic unfurling.

The wolf was about as big as a German Shepherd but thicker across the chest. It crouched, hackles up and growling, ready to spring upon Shiloh. And I knew it wasn't garden-variety wolf, either. A shimmer played around it, like a pearlescent aura. I never saw a Were in wolf form before but I knew without doubt this wolf was Were.

"Toby!" I screamed from the middle of the foyer. The wolf started at my voice and spun around, focusing on me through the rungs of the banister. "Dally! Lock those doors!"

Her pale face disappeared as the doors boomed shut and the noise drew the wolf away from Shiloh. Watching it pace a few steps closer to me, I jerked my head toward the office and I yelled. "Go, Shy!"

The wolf snapped angrily when I shouted, and it glared at me, muscles bunched. The shimmer of Were-power moved like a lazy fog over its fur. It didn't so much as growl as rumble, a ragged, mean sound. Rust-colored eyes slitted while they followed me. I carefully felt my way up the steps toward the wolf. All I could do was hope that Toby would recognize me.

So far, it only looked like a wolf that wanted to rip into something. Preferably a soft, meaty something.

Shiloh seemed plastered to the wall, cell phone

forgotten. She couldn't tear her eyes from the wolf. Frozen.

"Go, Shy." I tried to keep my voice gentle so as not to rile the wolf further. I stood at eye level with it, where it crouched on the second floor. Only the bars of the railing separated us. I knew better than to think the bars provided any safety. Just because something looked like a cage didn't mean it actually was a cage.

The wolf stalked forward, one menacing step at a time, until I could feel its breath. Saliva dripped from its jaws, gleaming beneath curled lip. Directly behind it, Shiloh inched her way toward the office, her progress excruciatingly slow. I wanted to scream at her to hurry.

I didn't dare scream. I didn't dare breathe.

Instead, I summoned the Sophia and stretched out toward Shiloh. I only got a muffled sense of terror; it was vague and directionless, even with the Sophia trying to draw it in. She was simply too human to respond. I strained to draw off some of her terror so she could snap out of her stupor, get into the office faster. I didn't know how long I could hold off the wolf.

This was the first time I'd seen Toby in his other form. I'd always expected Toby the wolf to resemble Toby the kid. Maybe the fact that I'd never encountered a werewolf before had something to do with the innocence of the assumption.

Once again, proof on what making assumptions did to you and umption. Thank you, Samuel Jackson.

Whatever had been Toby before the moon came out was swallowed by fur and claw and snarling rage. He once said he'd learned to "keep his brains" while he was in wolf form. Right now, all I could do was pray that it was true, because the situation sure as hell didn't seem very optimistic to me right now.

The only thing I recognized were its eyes—the dark

orange canine eyes that Toby had been wearing the last few days as the moon swelled. At least before, his lopsided grin and ruffled spikes had softened the animalistic effect of the eye change.

Now, they were wolf's eyes above muzzle and teeth and nothing human remained.

It sounded a low, menacing growl, a constant rumble of sound that went right through me. It didn't know me, didn't care. There was nothing goofy or sweet or laid-back about this wolf. It was Werewolf. It was wild.

I was prey. And I was in deep shit.

Shiloh slid her hand toward the open door and, just as I thought she'd make it into the office, she tripped and hit the floor flat out. The slap of impact made the wolf spin on its haunches and it whirled, snapping and advancing on her.

I sprinted the remaining steps and ran toward my wing, knowing it couldn't resist a chase. "Come on, furball! Show me how tough you are!"

My door stood open. If I could make it inside I might get it shut in time. I lunged down the hall. A door slammed behind me. Shiloh made it in to safety.

The movement behind told me I might not be so lucky.

Behind me the wolf pounded nearer, silent. Not even the click of nails on tile. The feet of space separating us dwindled to inches. I wouldn't make it. Hands out, I reached. I prayed—

The wolf yelped, a squeal of pain. I looked over my shoulder. The wolf had stopped halfway down the hall, snapping at the air. Toby once said the air felt "prickly". Would prickly be enough to stop a wolf?

A foot away from the door—almost there—

I landed badly on one foot, twisting my ankle, my full weight behind the impact. Stumbling, I hit my knees and palms first before rolling to a stop on my side.

A new target.

The wolf, seeming to forget its annoyance, narrowed its eyes and sprang.

Growl twisted into a howl of pain when the wards stopped the wolf in mid-air. It looked like the animal had slammed into a glass wall and slid down, hitting the floor heavily on its side.

The wolf scrambled to its feet and ran off, away from me. I emerged once I heard it on the steps, listening to it run down to the foyer and down the hall to the guest suite. A howl from the backyard, followed by another, farther away.

I ran downstairs and yanked the hall door shut and, with relief flooding the remnants of my adrenaline away, I twisted the lock. Sagging against the door, I caught my breath, refusing to think how ugly things could have gotten.

*Damn it, Toby.* I clenched my teeth and swore a silent oath. *How could you be so stupid?*

I took a moment to regain my composure before calling the girls.

"All clear." The doors opened, faces peering out in unison. Shiloh flinched when the wolf howled, distantly.

I knew what she was thinking: it would never be distant enough.

I couldn't think of any other way to get into the house, unless Toby was some sort of spider-wolf and had climbed through a bedroom window. We headed to the tri-suites and locked the doors shut behind us.

Finding some bean-and-cheese burritos in the freezer, I unwrapped a few and stuck them in the microwave. Dahlia sat at the snack bar, toying with the sugar bowl, looking very much like she'd lost her best friend. Unfortunately, I wasn't going to be good at consoling now that her sweetie had turned monster on her.

I could commiserate, I supposed, considering my sweetie had his own troubles. But misery doesn't always like company. That was what made my job so damned hard.

Even Shiloh seemed abnormally perceptive of the situation. She leaned against the counter, not looking at either one of us. As soon as the microwave beeped, she pulled out a burrito, wrapped it in a paper towel and bee-lined it to her room.

"Dad's on his way," she said. "Call me when he's done yelling."

My stomach tumbled. Sometimes a hard job was infinitely easier.

When Rodrian showed up, I had to invoke the Sophia to calm him down.

He didn't do a quiet angry like Marek—Rodrian was a yeller and a fist waver. Dahlia crouched against a bean bag chair in the corner and endured his interrogation, only speaking to answer questions and clamming up when he yelled over her. Eventually, I realized that he could probably go all night long and decided it was time to intervene.

Despite my empathic touch, he'd continued to seethe. He made plans to stay the night in the spare bedroom so I went to bed. No point in sticking around when I had work in the morning, especially with the looks he kept shooting at me.

I slept rather soundly considering I'd gotten chased by my first werewolf. Guessed the demonstration of my wards in action did wonders for my peace of mind.

"I'll kill him." Rodrian paced in the den. I watched him over my mug of insta-tea. Bright morning sunshine streamed in through the windows behind him but he seemed immune to the cheer. So much for thinking he'd be calmer after sleeping on it. "Get rid of him or I'll kill him with my bare hands."

"Rode, sit down already."

"Don't tell me to sit down. I've had it, Sophie. First he had his buddies follow Shiloh to scare her, now this. It's stupid, letting him stay here."

"I trust him."

"Really? That's a comfort. I asked you to keep Shiloh here so she'd be safe. This is not safe!"

"Shiloh's fine. He wouldn't have hurt her. Dally said that wolves don't go after DV blood."

"Shiloh isn't DV enough, Sophie. Remember? She's too human. You said so yourself."

*Shit. Maybe he's right.* "I know how bad it looks but I trust him, Rode."

"Well, I don't."

I angrily snatched at his power, trying to cut through the verbal bullshit and almost choked when I realized what he really felt. "I don't believe it! You're jealous."

"Not jealous. Concerned. What if he tries something when I'm not here?" He lowered his tone. "Just get rid of him. Please. Before someone gets hurt."

The doorknob to the guest suite rattled. I'd forgotten that I latched it the night before. Immediately I walked out to the foyer, intending to unlock it for Toby.

"Don't." Rodrian followed me to the foyer.

I whirled around and pointed at him. "I'm going to talk to him. You stay here."

He began to protest but caught himself, pressing his lips into spiteful lines. "Fine," he said. "Just yell when you're in trouble."

"Thanks for your undying confidence in me."

Toby's voice sounded on the other side of the door.

"I'm coming," I called. Flipping the lock, I cracked the

door.

He peered through. "Something wrong, Sophie?"

"Yeah." I looked back at Rodrian, who stood defiantly in the den's doorway, arms crossed in a perfect imitation of his uncompromising brother. "Can we talk in your room?"

"Sure." He retreated down the hall and I left the door wide open. I never kept secrets before and I wouldn't start now. If Rodrian wanted to listen, fine by me. It'd save me the trouble of repeating myself later, anyway.

"You left your outside door open last night," I said.

"Well, yeah. I didn't know what time I'd get back this morning and I didn't want to wake you up."

"Well, it's not like anyone slept much."

He looked clueless. "Why not?"

"Why not? Oh, I don't know. How's about you going after Shiloh last night? That's good for starters."

"Shy—what are you talking about?" Toby sank onto the small loveseat, confusion plain on his face. "I stayed in the woods last night. I told you I wouldn't be here."

"Come off it, Toby. Can't you just admit you were here? I thought you kept sense in wolf form."

"I do," he insisted. "And I wasn't here, I tell you."

"Oh, so what, you want to tell me it was some other wolf in here last night? I know your wolf eyes."

"I got plain old wolf eyes. They're nothing special."

"Toby, please." I lowered my voice to an urgent whisper. "You're in a lot of trouble. Rode wants to break your neck for going after Shiloh. If I don't convince him I can control you, I won't be able to stop him."

"Sophie...did you ever see me shift before?"

"No, but does it matter? A wolf went after Shiloh and Rodrian is gunning for you. Who else could it have been?"

Toby groaned and covered his face with his hands. "I knew it. I told you he'd never stop following me."

"Great!" I yelled. "You're having friends over? Couldn't wait until there wasn't a moon out?"

"It wasn't a friend. It was Tanner. I told you, Sophie."

"Really? You want me to believe that was a ghost?"

"You better, because it was Tanner. Except he's getting powerful. Someone is feeding it power and if it gets any stronger it's going to be real for good. And that would be very bad. For me and for you."

"Yeah, right. Tanner never tried to kill you."

"Well, he knows I took an oath to salvage his wolf. He wouldn't like knowing I tried to ensure his wolf met up with the Great Pack."

I sat down heavily, unable to stand up when my knees went to mush. "What are you saying, Toby? His ghost won't stay a ghost? Can't you get it to leave?"

"Told you. There's only one way."

"Rode will never buy that."

"If he's smart, he will. Tonight, I'm going to prove it wasn't me." Determination made him sound grim. He wasn't serious very often, but when he was, it was like he'd become someone else. "You're gonna watch me change."

"If you change in this house, it'll be right before Rode kills you."

"Then make sure he doesn't." His voice was hard. "I haven't done anything wrong. Don't let something happen that you'll regret."

My gut instinct knew he told the truth, and his forceful attitude convinced me to believe him. I couldn't live with myself if I didn't give him the chance to prove his innocence.

I didn't want Rodrian to hurt him if he was innocent, either. If I couldn't trust Toby, he couldn't stay—and being less than fond of kicking orphans out into the street, I didn't want to make that decision until there was no other choice.

Toby was right. This was the only way to prove it hadn't been him and solve all those problems.

"All right, I'll tell Rode. Just...stay out of sight today, okay? Don't give him an excuse." As I headed to the door, I remembered something else. "I thought you might be hungry today. Bethany made ham and loaded up your fridge."

"Ooh, ham?" His eyes lit up with delight. "Thanks, I owe you one."

"Not that crap again," I retorted and left.

That evening, Toby sat cross-legged inside a huge steel cage, trying to look nonchalant about sitting in his shorts in front of a room full of hostile strangers.

I didn't like the cage. The bars were a prison, humiliating and dehumanizing. However, it was the only way Rodrian would agree to Toby's request. He wouldn't take any chances, he'd said.

I glanced up at Dahlia and Shiloh, who were sequestered on the top of the stairs close to the safety of the office. They had a clear view of the cage down in the foyer but were well out of harm's way. Rodrian stood with them, staring imperiously down at the cage like an emperor waiting for a sacrifice.

The foyer itself had been closed off completely; even the pocket doors of the dining room had been drawn out. The white walls seemed endless and encapsulating, a cage of its own.

Seven of Rodrian's men surrounded the four sides of the

cage, standing against the walls. They stood as impassively immobile as the Buckingham Guard. Earlier, upon their arrival, Greco had lifted his chin at me in greeting. Caen had given him a harsh reprimanding glare, which I knew Greco must have privately blown off. He liked me more than he respected Caen.

Caen took up position in front of the door, facing Rodrian. He wore a sinister smile as if he'd been promised he'd get to hurt someone tonight. It only made me hope he'd end up in a friendly-fire accident.

I was torn between my loyalty to Rodrian and my concern for Toby. I'd glanced up at Rodrian several times but he wouldn't even look at me. He gave me the clear impression he was still angry that I'd go through this much trouble for a Were.

Well, screw him, I thought. Toby had never shown anything other than goodness since he'd followed me home. I wouldn't cut him out of my life until I had proof he needed cutting. He'd get the chance that Rodrian hadn't given me, when Marek dropped off the grid and decided that abandoning me was easier than dealing with his stupid "issues." Double-screw him with a wire brush.

I wandered back to the cage and crouched next to it, alongside Toby.

"You okay?" I said in a low voice, but it carried in the silence, amplified by the natural acoustics of the room. I didn't have to look at Rodrian's face to see his disgusted expression; he broadcast it at me, making sure I had no doubts about how he felt.

"Jerk," I muttered. Raising my mental barriers, I blocked Rodrian out. "Not you," I added when Toby looked at me questioningly.

"It's ok," he said. After a pause, he added: "Soon, it'll be soon."

"Is it going to hurt?"

He shook his head. "I've been doing this for too long for it to really hurt anymore. It's just how it is."

"Oh." I thought it sucked when someone had to accept pain as a normal part of life.

"It's ugly, though. You don't have to watch if you don't want. I promise I won't go no where." He reached over and poked at the cage before looking back over his shoulder at the faces staring down at him. "And you probably want to back up. It gets pretty messy."

"I'm not going anywhere." I was determined to conquer my fear of Weres once and for all. If I couldn't witness this, I'd be sunk. "We're going to show them all together."

Despite the cage and the impending change he man-aged a smile, but it wavered. "I guess we are, and how—"

The "how" trailed off into a sound of pain, soft and full. Slowly, he pushed to his feet but ran out of room. Hunched over, he glanced at me and shook his head. Tall kid in a cage too short for him. It wasn't right.

He stretched his arms, looking stiff as he hooked his fingers into the iron grid above him, and hung his head. "Are you ready?"

Before I could say "no" he dropped into a hunch again, curling into a tight ball and hugging his knees. Pain drew his brows down, and beads of perspiration began to glisten on his temples. Toby's breathing quickened and he rocked, trying to ride out the pain.

"Toby?" I whispered.

"I'm o—oh..." His voice melted into a moan. "Back up!"

Breathing became panting, labored gasps of pain.

Powerless to help him, I clung to the cage, unable to slip even a hand through to touch him. He rolled his eyes toward me, the look full of desperation and madness and agony.

He stopped breathing.

Stopped breathing, stopped rocking, just stopped. His eyes glazed over.

"Toby?" I tapped nervously on the cage. "Toby? Toby!"

"What are you doing?" called Rodrian.

"He's not breathing. Something's wrong with him." I banged at the cage, trying to make him move. "Toby!"

"Back away." Rodrian's voice was taut.

"No. Something's wrong!"

"Back away, Sophie. Do it now!"

Without warning, Toby exploded.

Really exploded.

His flesh cracked like thick wax, splitting down his arms, his back. It split and spread as something bigger struggled to free itself of its shell.

With a roar it erupted from the encasement that had once been Toby's body, fragments flying and splashing in all directions. I recoiled, pelted by chunks of wet congealed flesh as I stood two feet away from the emerging wolf.

Toby's neck cracked, his head separating from his shoulders, and he shook it free. It slid loose and fell, hitting the side of the cage like an empty hat. For a brief moment I could still see Toby's features on it. It looked like a latex mask, mouth open in a silent scream, before it began to melt into itself.

I ripped my eyes away from his discarded human face and looked up into his new one—wolf.

Free of the old skin, its features rapidly filled out. The snout pushed itself longer into a muzzle. He bit away the waxy flesh from his claws, claws that scraped away the huge chunks that still clung, glistening, to his slick new form.

The wolf, drenched in slick gel, looked matted and newborn. Stretching his hind legs, one at a time, he pointed his nose toward me, sniffing, scenting me, before turning to examine the others in the room.

And just like that, there he was. Full wolf, standing a few feet from me. No menace, no threat. I forgot the slime that dappled me and approached the cage, staring in wonder. "Toby?"

The wolf yawned once before shaking himself vigorously, spraying me with sticky globs of werewolf glue. I yelled and backed up, too late.

Toby barked softly, almost a chuckle.

"Laugh it up," I warned. "I can always have you fixed."

Rodrian shot me a bolt of power and a look of impatience as he descended the stairs. "Is it done?"

"Uh, yeah, I guess." I remembered why Toby was imprisoned and decided to get the trial over with. Toby paced around the cage, turning to face the girls for inspection.

Rodrian gestured to the girls, drawing them forward to the balcony railing. "Is this the wolf that attacked you last night?"

Dahlia still looked a little dumbstruck by Toby's transformation, her mouth open in a tiny O. Shiloh gave her a rude jab with her elbow.

"Quit staring like that, you freak," she hissed, before leaning over the rail. "Is he in there good? He can't get out, can he, Dad?"

"He's secure," he replied. "Even if he broke out of the cage, he wouldn't get far." On cue, the goon squad moved as one, and metal gleamed in each man's hand.

"What do you call that?" I put my hand on my hip and pointed at Caen's gun.

"A precaution," he replied. "Shiloh, can you see it?"

She shook her head. "I want to get closer."

"Don't show off," he warned.

"I can't see, Dad, and I'm not going to let you shoot

Sophie's friend just 'cause I can't see."

"Remember, Sophia." Caen's voice cut through the tension. He smiled at me with all his teeth. It was feral, not friendly. "Human shields are not very effective shields."

He followed it up with a touch of his power, a cold squeeze on my shoulders, a rub on the back of my neck. It was intimate, and it was terrifying. There was no way he'd miss at this distance. I knew there was no reason he'd want to.

I met Caen's eyes once and silently begged him to back off, just once. He returned my plea with an up-and-down glance. Appraising. Not caring.

I was just food to him. It's all I would ever be. I had to let it go and stop seeing change where I wanted to see it.

"Greco." I didn't take my eyes off Caen. "Can you keep him from shooting us?"

"Just get this over with, Soph." He sounded restrained. "The sooner we can leave, the better."

Shiloh drifted down the steps, once step at a time, chewing her lip.

I held out my hand to her as she hesitated on the steps. "It's okay, I swear, Shy."

Hand in hand we stepped back up to the cage and Shiloh scrutinized him. Toby sat on his haunches and waited for his judgment.

"Dad." Shiloh's grip would leave a bruise if she didn't relax. "I don't think he's the one I saw."

"You don't think?" Rodrian's tone sounded impatient.

"No, it's not. The other one was shiny, like sparkly. It kinda glowed."

I looked down at Toby. She was right. Toby didn't have the same sheen of power along his fur. He looked like a regular wolf. Why hadn't I noticed? Maybe I still had Were gunk in my eyes. Or, more likely, my brain was still chasing down my senses, which had fled screaming when Toby's body broke apart and a wolf spilled out.

"And it was way meaner," she said. "Toby looks like...a puppy."

The tip of Toby's tail twitched a little, and I narrowed my eyes at him. If he sat up and begged, I'd leave him kenneled all night.

"Sophie," said Rodrian. "Can you get him to act mean?"

I rolled my eyes. "Sure," I said. "Hey Toby, wanna know what Rode said about you? He said you were mangy."

Toby cocked his head at me as if I'd gone nuts.

"He said you were too poor for fleas. And," I added with a devilish smirk. "He said you were puny, pathetic, and probably a virgin."

The wolf gave me a narrow-eyed glare and stood up. Suddenly he dropped into a crouch, looking ready to spring, and snarled viciously at Rodrian. Toby had gone from zero to rabies in two seconds flat.

"That's great, Soph." Rodrian's voice sounded weary. "Really great."

"Hey, no problem." I could be a jerk, too, when I wanted to be.

Shiloh didn't seem afraid anymore, just curious. She hunched down, her hands on her knees, and scrutinized him. Toby's ears perked forward, the growl quieting and tail wagging just a moment, before he moved to the side so he could see around her. Glaring at Rodrian he snarled again.

Shiloh laughed. "It's not him, Dad."

"What?" He had to raise his voice over the racket the wolf made.

"Shh, Toby. I said, it's not him." She looked over her shoulder to her father. "The wolf that was here last night was different."

"Do you agree, Dahlia?"

"Yes, Rodrian. It wasn't Toby last night. The other one was bigger, darker, and sounded different."

"Fine. Tell him he's off the hook, then."

"You tell him," I said. "He can hear you just fine."

Rodrian spared me a look that said he'd rather not. "I'll be at my desk."

"Wait, I need the key." I held out my hand expectantly.

He paused mid-step and turned back to me. "For what?"

"Duh, to let him out," I said.

Shiloh's brave front dissipated, and she hot-footed it back upstairs with a squawk.

Rodrian cocked his head. "Why would you do that?"

"You can't leave him in there all night."

"Sure I can. Just because he wasn't the one to attack Shy last night isn't a reason to let him run loose in the house."

"So, put everyone upstairs and I'll let him outside."

"Not everyone. They stay." He jerked his head toward The Muscle. I glanced around at their faces to Caen, who smiled at me deliberately and cocked his weapon.

"It's not necessary," I insisted.

"Yes, it is," Rodrian said, and pressed his power forward to touch me.

He was a storm cloud of worry. This entire display wasn't because he wanted to make me miserable for sticking up for Toby. He was worried, for Shiloh and for me and for what could have happened last night when he wasn't here to protect us. Concern and guilt and some pathological need to appear tough in from of his men when all he wanted to do was carry us away in a safe hug.

I met his eyes, recognizing what he felt and understanding why he was doing this. Swallowing hard, I willed the sting of tears to melt back down. I hated knowing that I put this terrible strain on him in order to protect someone else.

He waved Shiloh and Dahlia away and they dis-appeared into the office. Once the door was closed, he signaled to Caen. Without as much as one of his classic glares, Caen simply led the guards out the front door.

Rodrian came downstairs to stand next to me in front of the cage. "You don't make it easy."

"Make what easy?"

He made a noise as he took the lock off the door. "Taking care of you."

"Huh," I said softly. "I guess I don't."

He gave Toby one last dirty look. "If you ever..."

The wolf sat motionless, meeting his gaze without wavering.

Rodrian pocketed the lock and opened the door, standing between us. I reached up to him, laying my hand on his shoulder, and brushed my mind against his to reassure him. For a brief moment, we connected.

"Okay." Rodrian followed his men outside and closed the door, leaving me alone with a werewolf in an open cage.

Toby padded out and sat at my feet, a plaintive look on his face as he licked his chops.

"What?" I asked him. "It's not like I have any treats."

His yip sounded like laughter as we headed for his rooms.

I didn't say anything as I let him out through the back door in his suite. Even though I knew that the wolf was Toby, even though he looked at me with complete comprehension, I still felt uncomfortable talking to him. What would I have said, anyway? It's not like he could have answered me back.

I let him out onto the patio and pulled the door shut against the wind. When I'd gotten back to the foyer, I slid the bolt shut. The thought of someone sneaking in again was not an appealing one.

Dahlia lingered in the foyer. "Is he okay?"

I shrugged. "Fine, I guess. He wagged his tail on the way out."

"Wagged his...oh. Gods." She hugged her arms around herself. "That was the strangest thing I have ever seen."

"Me, too, I think."

"I knew he was Were. I just never—"

"Put the face with the fur?"

She grinned. "Something like that. It just never seemed like an issue. Yeah, we're from different worlds, but that shouldn't mean we can't—" She broke off and cracked her fingers, one by one. "I mean, I know I just met him and I can't profess to know all there is to know about him but I sort of feel like I do. I know him. Something inside me recognizes something inside him and..."

Dahlia folded her hands over her heart and gazed at the door to his wing. "He makes me feel like I'm seventeen again. And I haven't been seventeen for a very, very long time."

I couldn't respond. One part of me wanted to make a tremendously smart-assed remark about just how long, indeed. But another part—a quiet, sad part—simply wanted to hold her because I remembered what seventeen felt like.

My own seventeen was spent in love with a boy from the wrong side of the tracks, a school-skipping, pot-smoking never-amount-to-anything delinquent who loved me better than I'd ever known. He taught me how to explore my deepest shadows so that I wouldn't be afraid of them and he taught me a great deal more in the shadows behind the mall where he'd hung out on weekends. In return, I taught him that pot was stupid, and skipping school only got you in trouble, and all in all my never-amount-to-anything Jared amounted to a huge amount, after all.

Was that how Dahlia felt about Toby? Could it be she'd discovered her unforgettable love?

I would do nothing to deter her from the thought, from the feeling of *seventeen again*. Every person who ever lived should have that blessing at least once in their life. Otherwise, we'd never be able to claim that we'd lived in the first place.

I looked carefully at her. "Are you going to be okay with him?"

She pursed her lips, reflecting. "I'll be okay with it, I think. It was just startling, the way he just came out of his body like that. I never saw anyone shape-shift before. But I think I can get used to that. It was almost...exciting." She wore a look completely unfitting for a vegan.

"And messy," I reminded her. The globs of werewolf juice had dried to itchy patches of crusty yuck, and I couldn't stand knowing I had Toby's bodily fluids all over me. "I'm heading up for a bath."

Truthfully, it wasn't only decontamination from Toby's biohazard that I wanted. I just needed a little time in the shower to hide the brewing, slow, hot tears, and to mourn the loss of my own seventeen, just one more time.

At least now, I was glad for someone else's seventeen. Hope for Dahlia's future kept me from dwelling in my past. It definitely made for a shorter shower.

Bonus right there.

Pontian had contacted Rodrian to arrange a consult. He wanted to evaluate Shiloh's condition.

She was extremely unhappy about it when she found out. I would be, too, but there was no alternative. She'd lost enough weight that her face looked gaunt. She'd even lost interest in her friends, opting instead to lay in front of the TV, falling asleep on the couch.

Shiloh was beginning to fail. We had no choice.

She, of course, saw things differently.

"Why do we even have to do this at all, Dad? I'm seventeen. I should be picking a college, and planning for prom, and making out in the back seat of a car. Instead I have to see weird old doctors who talk about blood and 'lution and forcing me to be something I'm not. Why can't I just be normal?"

"It's not that you're not normal, Shy..." Rodrian sat on the edge of his desk, hands in his pockets.

"What do you call it? Luke's already been accepted at

State. I haven't even filled out pre-apps." She paced toward the stereo and popped open the cabinet, stooping down to look through the stacks of CDs stored inside.

"There's time. We don't have to rush that."

"But this we have to rush? The gross stuff?"

"It's our way," Rodrian said firmly.

"Yeah, well, your way sucks. I'm glad it's not mine. I hope it never is. I just want to be normal."

"You're Demivampire. When Pontian's through treating you, you will be normal."

"No, I won't." She sagged into the high-backed chair next to my desk like a fragile toy. Even her fighting spirit drained quickly these days. "I'll never be the same."

"You'll be healthy, strong. You won't feel powerless."

"I'll be alone." Her voice was tiny.

I knew that feeling, that one that made voices sound tiny and confidence shrink and hearts feel crumpled.

Rodrian didn't seem to, though. He only sounded confused. "How do you figure?"

"Oh, I don't know. I'm guessing Luke will run screaming the first time my fangs pop out and he'll probably break up by a text message. That kind of alone."

"What about us?" I sat down my desk, switching on the monitor and loosening my towel-turban so that I could dry my hair.

Shiloh whipped a contemptuous teen look at me. "No offense, Sophie, but you're not my type. And anyways, you'll probably just die of old age long before Dad decides to show any gray. I'll still be trying to get into college when they have your funeral."

I dropped out of the conversation then. She'd tossed me too brutal a mental image to hold up an argument.

"Shiloh, you know what she meant. You're not losing your family."

"Oh?" The tears began to thicken her voice and she stomped over to my desk to snatch a tissue from the pop-up box on the edge. "What do you call what happened to Uncle Marek?"

"This isn't about him."

"No, it's about me. If I don't cusp, I don't ever have to worry about evolving. I won't end up shunned and hated by everyone on the planet."

"You'll just be dead." Rodrian seemed to finally lose patience. "Is that better?"

"It'll be easier than this." She grabbed a tissue from the box on my desk before turning away to blow her nose. "I don't care—"

She wavered, staring down at her tissue.

"Shy?" prompted Rodrian.

"Something's wrong," she said quietly. "Something bad."

She lifted the hand holding her tissue, turning to face us. Blood streamed from her nose.

"Daddy?" Her voice trailed off before she fainted.

Shiloh had revived and we got her into bed. Despite my years of Emergency Room experience, I'd never seen such a severe nosebleed. Shiloh choked on the blood and vomited a bright red puddle on her comforter.

Want to talk helpless? Try being me, knowing she needed to be cauterized, knowing I had no clue how much blood she could lose before she crashed. I ended up pinching her nose and putting a frozen burrito on the back of her neck. I knew she'd be okay when she stopped gagging and asked if I'd mind putting the burrito in the microwave when we were done. The laugh would have been a good one if there weren't so many blood-soaked towels on the floor.

Rodrian had called Pontian after carrying Shiloh into her

room. Pontian arrived within the half-hour, making me wonder how close he'd been or by what strange means he traveled. I didn't really want an answer to either question. The less I knew about the healer, the better.

It wasn't his lack of bedside manners that bothered me—I'd worked with plenty of people like that, and simply had made up for their deficiencies with kindness of my own. Pontian's healing abilities were more than evident to me, and I'll even go as far to admit I was curious about DV medicine.

There was one thing I didn't like—one thing that made me acutely uncomfortable about his presence, so much so that I had successfully avoided asking him when I would finally be off coffee quarantine. That should put it in complete perspective. I was willing to continue starve myself just so I didn't have to endure being near him, even if only to ask the million dollar question: was I cured yet?

That one tiny thing was that Pontian could read minds.

It was more than a DV talent. It was a sign of brinking. Pontian was old and he was close to the edge, where the line between DV and vampire was a hazy blur.

It wasn't that I was afraid he'd eavesdrop on my thoughts. I suspected he'd taken himself to that edge on purpose, because he wanted—no, craved—the power and the spike of strength the Brinkage would lend to his healing abilities.

That kind of play was dangerous. He flirted with damnation and didn't seem to mind the risk. It rubbed me the wrong way, on a deeper level than my being faithful or oracular. I just didn't trust someone who would be willing to die for the chance to grab more power.

I knew Caen was the same kind of man. Just because Pontian practiced healing arts didn't make him noble.

Pontian examined Shiloh, taking a blood sample and her

vital signs, before making her drink a small glass of remedy. It looked light years more appealing than the revitalizer he'd once made for me. Considering how the yucky revitalizer had kept me from dying of severe blood loss, I couldn't fault him. Still. Yuck. I knew looks were usually deceiving and I didn't envy Shiloh the experience of drinking Pontian's home brew.

I tucked her in and watched her drift off into a limp sleep. Stroking her hair away from her damp forehead, I sat on her bed and fought tears, knowing that she struggled in so many ways, knowing I couldn't take this burden from her. All I could do was stand by and try to absorb some of the overflow. Her battle was hers alone to fight.

Helpless. Damn near useless. As I pulled Shiloh's bedroom door closed behind me, the sounds of men's voices echoed down the hallway. Walking quietly toward the office, I stretched my awareness inside to determine who was there. Rodrian was clear, and if I didn't have ears, I'd swear he was alone. I couldn't feel Pontian at all.

I wondered if he'd ever be willing to examine my barriers since he had the ability to "get inside" people. Maybe after Shiloh got better I would be brave enough to ask him.

"We will begin in two weeks, when I return." Pontian's words sounded like granite. He'd never be able to play a doctor on TV, unless someone wrote in a storyline for McScary.

"Two weeks?" Rodrian said. "I thought we had more time."

"You don't. Her vascular system is losing integrity. That nosebleed wasn't the first. And did you think to tell me about the bruising?"

There was an uncomfortable pause.

"You didn't even know," Pontian continued. "I suspected as much. She is your child, Thurzo. Need I remind you how important she is? I would have started an hour ago, had my schedule been more accommodating. Two weeks. You have time to make arrangements. She can be treated here but I will require the amenities we discussed."

"Of course." Rodrian murmured his acquiescence.

The conversation sounded more or less over, so I walked into the office. Rodrian sat behind his desk, making notes on a legal pad. He didn't even look at me.

Settling his overcoat down upon his shoulders, Pontian flipped the collar straight before picking a satchel off the floor. "Ah, Sophia. You look much better."

"Yeah. I put the 'speedy' in speedy recovery," I replied. I supposed someone as old as Pontian had a loose grip on the idea of time. I refrained from reminding him it had been quite some time since my bout with anemia. "I'm relieved that you'll be helping Shiloh. She's got us worried."

Pontian ran a hand over his hair, a shocking mix of red and white. My grandmother once told me that true red hair never turned white; rather, it faded. Pontian's hair bore two distinct colors that mingled without blending. He had no faded red; the white was defiantly silver. "I'm surprised you didn't call me. You, of all people, Sophia."

Rodrian made no reply, but he stopped writing. His gaze remained on the desk, and I knew guilt ate at him, despite his attempt to keep his emotions concealed.

"I am glad you'll be here, Sophia. Blood rush is dangerous, even under controlled circumstances. She'll need you." Pontian shouldered his bag and walked to the door. "Two weeks. If you notice any dramatic change, call."

I waited until the front door slammed behind him before speaking. Not that it made any difference. "Amenities? What kind?"

"He'll create a clinic here for Shy," he said. "It needs a

separate entrance, since there will be a lot of people coming and going but it will be secure. The garage should be big enough."

"That much space?" I knew the garage was a pretty big place, even though I'd only opened the door and glanced in once or twice. The garage had four bays in front, two of which had draped vehicles parked in them; there was an equally spacious storage area behind them. Garage, smarage. Try warehouse.

"We'll have to build a recovery room, a storage room for the treatment, and a lounge."

"Oh?" I almost laughed. "A lounge? I didn't know clubbing was part of the therapy."

"It's not for Shiloh," he said flatly. "It's for the donors."

I struggled to find a response but failed.

"Treatment starts with stored blood. She'll be sedated, and Pontian will gastric tube it in. But once she begins to cusp, she'll need live sources. She'll have to be taught how to feed." He shrugged and flipped the pages over his notepad. "We have a good donor pool, and we want to keep them comfortable. They perform a tremendous service."

So Rodrian needed to build a DV feeding ground in my house. Yuck. "These donors. Are they your donors, too?"

Rodrian looked unsettled. "Gods, no. Not my type. Way too young. College aged, and mostly male. I don't do guys."

"Not even for blood?"

"Not a chance."

"Wow. You sound positively phobic."

"It's a preference. Chicks taste better, and they're nicer to hold. Not to mention they're usually good for a little fun on the side."

"All right. Enough already. I don't need to hear what a slut you are."

"I'm not a slut. I'm a chauvinist. I was only saying that I can usually get them to clean my apartment when we're done."

"Enough!" I turned to retreat to my rooms, leaving him alone to enjoy his sense of humor.

"Have you been practicing?" Eirene said.

I nodded. "I've actually improved. Thank you so much, Eirene. I can't think of a way to show you my gratitude."

She smiled indulgently. "Ah, Sophia. It is to our mutual benefit that you come to full strength. A Sophia can only be of use if she makes the best of her potential. There is no need to thank me. Shall I examine your barriers?"

I closed my eyes and raised my barriers, immediately sensing her white light on my periphery. It danced and flitted, tapping along my barriers, as it sought a breach. I kept it in sight, resisting the urge to bunch my barriers beneath her touch. I held them steady, concentrating on maintaining an even, impenetrable wall.

I lost track of her somewhere behind me and detected her only moments before she struck. I thickened my power to stand between us and deflected the blow, pushing her back.

Eirene clapped her hands. "Sophia! I am truly impressed.

You have been working diligently."

I didn't express that our little walk in the park had provided plenty of motivation. I was more determined than ever before to prove to myself I was nothing like her—that I could make a difference in this world without simply excising the broken parts. Increasing my defensive abilities was a bonus, especially since I knew even the good guys had killer instincts.

So I chose the more diplomatic route and displayed a mild smile. "I practice as often as I can. I admit that I feel... better now. Barriers help me keep separate from everyone else around me. I didn't realize how stressed-out I've become. I like being apart again. Since manifesting, it seemed like I constantly was in contact with everyone around me. At least now I have space."

"Yes," she agreed. "Space and sanity."

"Exactly. Thank you for that gift, Eirene."

"Do not mention it. It is easier to perform your sacred duties when you have control."

"Yes, it is. The barriers don't hold me back at all. If anything, I...think I've grown stronger."

Eirene leaned toward me, lifting her chin and peering at me intently, dark eyes glittering beneath her lush lashes. "How so?"

"I can't explain it, really," I said. "It's still so new. But, it seems like now that I have barriers, the Sophia has more space and has grown to fill it. Now it's braver, more confident."

"Interesting." She rolled her lips together as if freshening her lipstick and spread her hands. "Of course, always having been in control of my Sophia, I have no weaker state to which I can compare."

I refrained from making a face. Just had to be the superior, didn't she?

"But yes," she said. "I do recognize your description of the power filling you. I wonder if there is a way to judge your progress."

I had an idea, but it was one I wasn't willing to share. Rodrian could taste me again and compare. Knowing Eirene would have plenty of objections, I tried to forget the idea. It would only cause too many problems.

I'd spent enough nights, lying awake, thinking about him and the relationship we had. No matter what I aimed for, nothing fit because Marek always loomed. Despite all that happened to Marek—and all I had learned about what really happened—I still loved him and knew any other man would only come second.

And yet, the first thing that came to mind was sharing blood with Rodrian. How messed up was that?

Of course, I couldn't discuss any of this with Eirene. But part of me really wished she was different, just so I could.

"Well..." Her voice broke through my reverie. "I'm not sure what else I can teach you. You have strong barriers, and you exercise them. Your strength has improved because of it. I suppose it is all up to you, now, to be the best Sophia you can be."

She stood and smoothed her skirt into place. "Soon, I will return to my lands. My business here is nearly complete, and I grow longing for home once again."

"But we haven't—"

"We have done much more than I originally thought you could ever accomplish. You did seem to be such a hopeless case when first we met..."

Gee, thanks, I thought. "But the Canons and the Circlet. You've told me so little."

"We will write, Sophia." Eirene laughed and clasped my hands. "We will correspond. I am not leaving you forever."

Great. Another pen pal. Although I could live without

her condescending tone of voice, it wouldn't be the same as the one-on-one training she'd given me. Then again, no more slaughtered pre-vamps. For once, I'd like to not be conflicted.

Diplomacy must rule, I decided, since the Sophia society was too small to alienate one of them. "Will you have dinner at my home before you leave? At least let me show you my gratitude."

She nodded once, bending her head low with an elegant bow. "I would be delighted to dine at your home and look forward to it. You are most gracious. Dorcas, what day would be best for us to say farewell to our Sophia?"

"Thursday, madam."

Eirene lifted her eyebrows at me, waiting for my response.

I shrugged. "Thursday would be perfect. I'll arrange a car for you."

"That is most appreciated. Not a cab?"

"No, not a cab." I remembered her disdain for public transportation. "I'll send a driver."

She smiled. "That will suffice. Please, no sooner than eight o'clock. You know I take my meals late."

"Of course." Quietly, I rejoiced. It was hours earlier than I'd been going to dinner with her. Eight o'clock was practically teatime compared to our usual meetings.

As I waited for the elevator to arrive, I mused over which approach I should use to let Rodrian know I'd just volunteered his chauffeuring services.

The next evening, as I read over my column work in the den, I heard the growl of Rodrian's Audi outside.

"Has Pontian called?" Rodrian didn't even say hello; he barely paused to take off his coat before ducking behind the bar and rooting through the fridge.

I shook my head. "No, why?"

"I haven't heard from him since Monday, and there's a shipment of clinic supplies arriving tomorrow."

"Monday? You didn't mention that."

"Yeah, well, it was a strange call. He wanted me to consider changing the clinic site to some place up in Lackawanna County."

"That far? Why?"

"Better facility, I suppose. Doesn't matter. She wants to stay here. I just don't know why he hasn't shown up yet. Marek didn't mention anything."

"I didn't know Marek was involved."

"Neither did I." He looked perturbed and an uncomfortable ripple cut through the feel of his power. "But Pontian asked for his new number so I guess he is. I figured Pontian would be here to set up, at least."

"Well," I said. "I didn't see anything on the caller ID but I'll check again for odd numbers."

Rodrian didn't bother with a glass; he popped the lid off a chilled emergency unit and drank it straight. I'd never seen him so distraught that he'd do something so revolting right in front of me.

I reached out hesitantly, but he was locked down tight. "You don't think he's in trouble, do you?"

"No. I'm just worried about Shy. She's sick with anticipation. I hate to drag it out."

"I'll do what I can do to cheer her up. Maybe Dally will come over and keep Toby busy. He's still trying to make up for the whole wolf thing even though it wasn't him." Too late, I realized I'd never told him anything about Tanner's wolf. I didn't think now was a good idea to tell him about the whole ghost wolf thing. Quickly, I improvised. "I think he feels bad for leaving the pet door open."

"Not a problem, now. The pet door is gone, along with

some other unnecessary exits. I made a few security enhancements." He took another long draught, tipping the bottle as he did so. Blood coated the inside of the glass bottle like cough syrup. Big mouthfuls—he had to work his throat around them to swallow.

Really? Chugging? Ugh.

"You know I don't like him, right?"

"I know." I drummed my fingers against the tablet on my lap. Two men always meant a conflict, even when love wasn't involved. For once, I'd like to experience harmony. "But I can't turn him out."

"I wouldn't ask you to, even though I'd like to. It just seems so crowded here now. Too many people."

Funny, I hadn't heard a similar complaint when Brianda stopped by. How would he feel when she and her partner moved in? Totally different, I'd bet. "He's only one more than before."

"I know, but it seems like more."

Seeing it would be pointless to try to convince him otherwise, I didn't say a word. Looking down at the text I'd been working on, I realized I had lost interest in writing—column work of the non-Sophia variety, on a topic that seemed trite with Rodrian in the room. I flipped my tablet shut and slid my pen into the spiral.

"You're working." Rodrian sounded apologetic. "Don't let me interrupt but, mind if I stay awhile? I thought I'd go over the budget since I'll be too busy with Shy to do it next week."

I waved a hand. "You don't need to ask. You know you belong here as much as I do."

"I'm still not so sure about that."

"Of course you are. I hate it when you're not here."

He looked surprised. "Really?"

"Sure I do. I know I depend on you too much. I'm trying

not to rely on you, but I still look forward to seeing you."

"We're family," he reasoned.

"Yeah, I guess." He and Shiloh were as much family as I'd had in a very long time; Dahlia had stood by me when everyone else bailed, and Toby—well, he was more or less adopted. One big, happy family. Almost. "But it's different than that, too."

He leaned against the bar, arms crossed casually, and swirled the nearly-empty bottle from his fingertips. "Different, how?"

"I met you because of Marek, and we kind of fell into brother-sister roles. But I don't feel like that anymore."

I felt his power quicken with curiosity tinged with something else. "Easy, pal. All I mean is that I see you as an individual. Marek made us like family but I choose you, on my own, as someone special to me. What I feel comes from within me, not from any duty to your brother."

He nodded. "I feel the same, I think. Although, Marek kind of defined how close I could get to you. If it wasn't for him, I'd have jumped you long ago."

Laughing, I tossed a pen at him, and he ducked it with a grin. Sometimes, his flirting helped these difficult admissions. "Should I be flattered?"

"Maybe. Or relieved. Depends on how you look at it."

"You're not going to jump my bones now, are you?"

"Not with your watch dog sniffing around."

"Rode..."

He drained the last of the bottle and tossed it into the trash can behind the bar. "Don't be mad. I just feel like he's on my turf."

"Turf? Isn't that a Were thing?"

"No." He dropped onto the other couch. "It's a guy thing."

I drew a deep breath. I'd known things were going to

have to come to a head sometime. "If you're having guy issues, then we need to seriously talk about what's going on between us."

Rodrian didn't even try to duck the issue. "Then we have to talk."

"Okay," I said slowly. His directness put me on guard. "You go first."

He took a deep breath. "You know how I feel about you."

"I think I do. You don't always say what you mean."

"Finding the right words isn't easy."

"It's not easy because you have feelings that turn into issues and you try to cover them all up or explain them away as if you should feel guilty over them."

He chuffed out a held breath. "Do you have any idea how hard it is for me? I have no right to pursue you, but I can't deny I'm attracted to you. But it's deeper than skin or blood. You're not shallow. It'd be wrong to have superficial feelings for someone like you. So then I try to figure out how deep my feelings should be, and I hit one of two dead ends."

"Which are..."

"Marek, for one. I can't stop thinking of you as my brother's woman."

He made it sound like a title. Super. "Even though he stopped thinking about me as his woman."

"You were a significant part of his life. How can I forget that when I still see him?"

Frustrated, I looked away. "Dead end number two?"

"You're the Sophia."

"I should've seen that one coming. I'm not a national treasure."

"You're closer to one than you think. I'm getting a fair amount of flack, you know, for doing what I've done."

"What we've done," I corrected. This was the first time Rodrian had admitted our blood sampling was having repercussions. "I'm just as much a part of it as you are."

"People don't understand. Marek wanted you safe and secure, which is why he wanted you here. I asked you to take Shiloh in for the same reasons. But people talk. They say I'm coercing you and monopolizing the Sophia for my own gain."

"But it's not true!" Hearing those rumors made me angry. So did the realization that we weren't even worried about the same things. I thought he'd been agonizing over kissing me and tasting my blood, but he was worried about ownership of property. Men are from Mars, all right. "I do the same, if not more, for the DV since I moved here. You haven't monopolized me at all."

"I have." His brows were lowered, shadowing his eyes. No friendly spark, just dark mystery. Rodrian's usually tell-tale eyes were closed off, just like the rest of him. "They can see it. You don't."

"I guess not. So how have you?"

"I've taken advantage of you. I never should have tasted you."

Finally. We get to it. "It was my choice."

"Was it?" He raised his head. His eyes simmered, a hint of the fire they were capable of holding. "You mean, you weren't the least bit seduced?"

My face grew hot. I remembered exactly how seduced I'd been, and the memory left me with an uncomfortable mix of thrill and shame. "You never forced me."

"I don't have to." A faint fog of sensation crept toward me. I'd become extremely sensitive to his mental caress, craving it and straining to experience it. He didn't need to hold the flame very long before my wick would ignite. "Perhaps I've never lain with you but I know the taste of your skin, the feel of your flesh, the sound of your breath when we're close. I know what to do to you, and I know how to dissolve your defenses. I'm good at it."

He grasped my wrist, tugging it up to his mouth. I couldn't resist him. The reckless part of me didn't want to resist. He brushed his lips against my palm, tickling my skin, sending a shoot of thrill to spiral down through me. I felt his breath, the slip of his tongue. I wanted him to taste me. I wanted him to bite, to break my skin, to draw me into him. I wanted it with every quivering ounce of my body. I *wanted*—

With a jerk, I snapped free of the compulsion, snatching my hand out of his grip and pulling it tightly to me, out of his reach.

He just sneered. *See?* His eyes glinted with cruel playfulness. *I told you, I'm good at it.*

"Shut up." Suddenly, I didn't want him to say another word. It wasn't sexy. It was mean. A sense of self-loathing made me think that what we did was dirty and wrong, instead of an innocent extension of what we already had. It made me feel so bare, so used, even though I knew it wasn't true. "Stop saying that, like I'm just another blood date. I'm more than that and you know it."

"That's the problem. If it was only blood, or only sex, I'd have no problem taking what I want. But you're more to me than that." He pushed to his feet and paced to the fireplace and back. "I love you, Soph. I love you in so many ways. You're my mother, my sister, my lover, my best friend. You are my fucking goddess. But no matter how I love you, it feels wrong."

"Oh, Rode," I whispered. I looked up into his face, those beautiful amber-heated eyes, and pitied him for the distress I saw in them. "Love isn't supposed to be wrong."

"No, it's not. See? See why I have issues?"

"Yeah, I do." I nodded and took a deep breath. "You need therapy. That's one hell of an Oedipus Complex you got there. I can't believe you said I was your mother. You're, like, a hundred years older than I am."

Rodrian stared at me for the space of several heartbeats, eyes wide with frantic incomprehension, until the joke finally sank in. He chuckled, his voice shaky from the tension, and he slowly allowed his anxiety to break.

Gently I reached out Sophia's touch and drew away the worst of it, as if I stroked his worried brow with my fingertips. Rodrian closed his eyes, basking in the Sophia's touch, and responded, his power seeking and embracing me.

How wondrous, this connection—when everything else could disappear around us just because we sensed each other, felt the comfort and the familiarity. It didn't have to be blood—or hotness, for that matter. I needed the contact, the bridge to another person who really knew me and wanted the same things. We were entwined together, Rodrian and I, just for a single, splendid moment, before his power receded.

"See?" His face was drawn with regret when he gazed at me. His amber glow illuminated sudden tears. "It's all wrong. I'm sorry."

Rodrian left the room without another word, leaving me stunned. Shamed. I couldn't think of anything to say that might have stopped him, made him come back. I let him go.

Bethany stuck her head into the den.

"How many for dinner tonight?"

I shrugged. "Eirene and Dorcas, if Eirene lets her even sit down once. Rodrian is in the office but I don't know if he'll stay. Shiloh isn't home yet. And Toby—"

She raised her hand to interrupt. "I've already taken care of him."

"You like him, don't you?" I grinned at her.

She merely lifted her chin. "I have changed my opinion of him. He looks out for you. I will miss him."

"Miss him? Why?"

"He will soon be gone." She turned and left without embellishing.

It took all my restraint not to chase her down and ask her. First it was *Badness is coming* and now it was *Soon Toby will be gone*. What if Bethany had some kind of foresight?

I thought about that again. What if she did have foresight? Would I want to know? What if the next thing was about me?

Digging my cell phone out of my back pocket, I dialed Shiloh to ask if she'd be home for dinner. The call went straight to voice mail.

Figures. She was becoming more and more unreachable. Whenever she hung out with the new crowd, she pretended not to know me, let alone return a call. I heaved a sigh and sent a text instead. Couldn't give up just because she wanted to be difficult.

Was this what it was like to be a parent? I felt like I was always on the losing end. Rodrian had asked me to move in so that I could help with Shiloh during her treatment. What had I done, besides nothing? I was supposed to be her emotional support, her friend and companion, her Sophia. I hadn't been anything lately because I hadn't been able to even get her to stay home long enough to talk to me.

I missed our old relationship, back when we pretended I was her aunt, in love with her uncle. Now I was just someone who provided the bare minimum of adult supervision to prevent Children and Youth busting down the door and taking her away.

But Shiloh wasn't a child or a youth anymore, was she? She was seventeen, which, in her mind, was as adult as she was ever going to be. Part of me wanted to yell and lock her up in her room but then I remember my own seventeen.

Seventeen was the year I had met the boy who became the gold standard of love to me. No one in my life had ever come close to Jared, until Marek found me and taught me I could love again.

What if Shiloh had found her gold standard in Luke? I had to trust that she knew what she was doing because, at her age, I had known. Those feelings were real and life changing and they couldn't be dismissed.

Although I wasn't Shiloh's mom, I loved her. I cared for her. I wanted the best for her and for her future. The difference between me and Shiloh was that she wasn't completely whole. The hypolution was taking its toll on her body and her spirit. Her health was on the line.

I rubbed my eyes with the heels of my hands. This parenting thing was tough. No wonder Rodrian's mate was never around.

And no wonder he called me to help him.

My phone buzzed with an incoming text. I picked up the phone and unlocked the screen.

Shiloh? Will wonders never cease? Maybe I was emoting so strongly she could feel me. If that was the case, she was probably telling me to knock it off because her friends could "hear" me.

I wish that was what she had written.

In the next moment I was on my feet, charging up-stairs and yelling for Rodrian.

*Trbl tell dad find me help*

Brain churning, heartbeat a buzz, I paced the office, while Rodrian made call after call. First was Caen, whom he told to meet him at the Tenth Street office. Then he went down a contact list, calling each of Shiloh's regular friends to ask if they knew where she was, who she might be with. Each call ended in frustration and the same damned answer: no. No one knew anything, not even who her new friends were. They all assumed she had been staying home, sick.

His last call was the worst. I knew who it was even as he hit the name in the contact list because his power, for the first time, took on an edge of insurmountable worry and despair.

"Brianda," he said, his voice tight. "Shy's in trouble. I need you to try and pin her down."

I covered my mouth with my hands, dropping my shields lower and reaching out to Rodrian. The Sophia had been humming behind my shields, tasting but not drawing away Rodrian's pain. I couldn't bear it any longer. I knew how hard it was for him to tell Brianda her little sister was in trouble. He had lost his son long ago but decades had passed before he'd begun to heal. Now, he worried he'd lose his daughter. The pain threatened to return.

His agony swelled like a flood surge. I opened my gates and welcomed it all, despite the pain it caused me. I took it in, took it down, and sealed it away where it couldn't hurt anyone ever again. He turned to me, his relief evident. "I'll be okay, honey," he said into the phone. "I've got Sophie. She'll take care of me."

He said goodbye and hung up. "I've got to go. Caen is waiting for me."

I wanted to frown at the sound of my old pal's name, but if Caen could help bring back Shiloh, I'd hug him to death. It would be a win-win for me. "What should I do?"

"Stay here in case she calls or shows up. Call me if you hear anything." Rodrian tilted his head at the doorway and walked out. I trailed behind him to the den, where he went behind the bar. Stooping down in front of the fridge and pulled out two of his bottles. "I will keep you updated."

"I can't just sit here, Rode. Shouldn't I be doing more? Like, what if I sent out a Sophia SOS to all the DV?"

"Don't. You don't know who's involved. Just sit tight." He stood and walked back over to me, pulling me toward him and squeezing my shoulders. "I don't want you to worry."

"I can't do anything else but."

"Yes, you can." He let go of my arms and backed up a step. "I need a favor."

"Anything. You don't have to—"

I was interrupted by the shrill ring of his cell phone. He glanced at the number before picking up the phone to answer.

"Caen. I'll call back—" He listened. "Right. Wait for my

call."

I could hear Caen's voice protesting even as Rodrian slid the phone shut and dropped it on the bar. "Did he find out something?"

"This is more important. Listen to me. I need your blood. You probably understand already. Your blood gives me a boost. A power shot. I need that now. I have to get my girl back home safe, and I can't let anything keep me from doing it. Your blood can give me the edge I need."

"Do it, then." I would have done anything he asked. Just please, God, let Shiloh be okay. His need overrode my qualms about the issue itself: it was all so naked, now. I didn't want to believe I'd become a water fountain of power, so I concentrated on Shiloh, on Rodrian's desperation. On the Sophia and my ability to help.

I offered my upturned palm but he shook his head. His eyes were lit, searing bright. "Too slow. I don't have time to linger. I need it now, and I need it fast."

Dropping to his knees in front of me, he lifted my shirt, exposing my belly and the bottom edge of my bra before I could protest. Tilting his head back, he gazed up at me, lips parted, as if wanting to say something. Instead, he sent a sensual touch. It was gentle, at first.

Then it swelled. It was a constriction around my deep belly, and I reached back to the bar, holding myself up. I closed my eyes and swallowed. Slow, deep waves of pleasure. Building. His breath on my bare skin, lips brushing against the curve of my waist, fingers gripping tighter, digging into my hips.

He wasn't going to be gentle.

Thrill and worry thumped my heart, thumped in lower places, thickening my breath. He inhaled my scent, groaning softly. When he broke the skin, I came dangerously close to having a real good time.

My barriers fuzzed out as I drifted on the ebbing tide of sensation, and I followed the stream of my Sophia-laden blood that flowed into him, a tingle of out-of-body sensation. I cradled his head to my side and dug my fingers into his hair while he took three strong swallows. My center of gravity shifted, my knees dipped, and he pushed me against the bar for support. His tongue lapped firm lines along my side, rapid strokes to smooth the flesh closed. The bite was deep. It would bleed if he didn't fix the wound.

When he stood, he covered his mouth, closed his eyes. Flexed his power, let it expand. Rolled his shoulders and stared into my eyes. His DV glow was tiger-bright and dangerous. His half-smile was ragged, a cocky hint of reckless intentions, as he pulled my chin up and pressed a kiss onto my mouth. It wasn't as chaste as it could have been but, as I was backing down from a breathless edge, I couldn't resist him.

A whispered thank you and he was out the door, faster than I'd ever seen him move.

I slid a hand up my side, feeling twin arcs of raised flesh, still wet from his tongue. Couldn't resist looking at my fingers to make sure it wasn't blood. Of course, it wasn't. Rodrian wouldn't waste a drop.

I'd scar, I knew it. Even if no one would ever see the imprints of his teeth, this exchange was going to mark me forever.

As my heart rate slowed and my bones solidified, I leaned, elbows on the bar, remembering the rush and avoiding the thought of inevitable consequences. Spying something on the counter, I picked it up.

Oh, shit. Rodrian had forgotten his phone.

I gave it two hours before I decided it was okay to worry.

In the tri-suites, I watched the first act of a Bollywood epic. No popcorn, although I drank two Gatorades after experiencing a bit of light-headedness on the stairs. Blood loss, I thought. Need fluids. That in itself was a concern. Two hours since he'd left. Rodrian's phone was in my left back pocket; my phone was in the right. The house phone, which seldom rang anymore, was on the edge of the chair. Nothing was ringing.

For a brief time after he left, I'd stretched my senses out, trying to detect the traces of my Sophia in him. It was a faint glow that diminished while he drove away. Of course, I'd never done clinical trials with that aspect, either. All I knew now was that I couldn't feel him. It didn't matter that I had no way of knowing if I should.

And, not being able to feel him, I began to think the worst.

Blood rush was dangerous, even under controlled circumstances. Didn't Pontian tell us that? And what was going on between me and Rodrian if it wasn't blood rush? I'd seen the high in his eyes, I felt it with my empathy. Rodrian took more this time than he had before. Could be because he thought he needed a bigger dose of my essence. Could be because he was growing tolerant to the rush and needed a bigger dose to get the same effect. Look at nicotine. One cigarette was all it took to hook someone and I was confident blood packed a bigger punch than a Newport.

It was hard not to think in pharmaceutical terms right now, and definitely hard not to consider terms like tolerance, knowing dependence could follow close behind.

And the terms abuse and addiction lurked nearby, waiting for their opportunity.

How about it? Feeling guilty about helping Rodrian run off to certain death had a wonderful way of distracting me from worrying about Shiloh.

A bang downstairs signaled Toby's return and I ran to his room. About time he got back. His cheeks were smacked pink from the cold air, and he smelled like dirt.

It was a good, earthy smell that explained why I hadn't been able to reach him on the phone. He'd been playing outside in the woods, wanting some nature time before leaving the Stocks. I supposed the city Werekind didn't have the luxury of rabbit runs in their backyards.

"You want me to go help?" He looked ready to run out the door, even though we had no idea where to start looking.

I shook my head. "What good would it do? Besides, I don't want to be alone. You mind staying here? I mean, you don't have to hold my hand or anything. Just be in the house? In case?"

"Aw, girl..." He hooked a long arm around my neck, treating me to the other scents that lingered in his clothing—crushed leaves and wintery chill. "I'll be right here, in case you need me. I have to pack, anyway. Not that it will take long to do that."

"Pack?"

"Oh." He looked sheepish and grinned. "I'm, uh, gonna stay at Dally's for a few days."

"That's great!" I hugged him again. "Taking things to the next level?"

"Maybe. For now, it's to give Mr. Rodrian less to worry about with Shiloh's thing coming up."

I wanted to chuckle at his use of mister to refer to Rodrian but now really wasn't the time. "And Tanner's wolf?"

He sighed. "Coming with me, like always."

"Still haunting you, huh?"

He shrugged. "One day, it'll get gone. I know it."

Bethany appeared in the doorway, carrying a tray.

"He'll get his chance, Sophia." She shook her head. "I daresay sooner rather than later, the way things are going around here."

Great, I thought. Just what I always wanted: a harbinger.

Once I got back to the den I pulled out Rodrian's phone. Checking his call history, I saw Marek's number. The duration was only a few seconds, too short for an actual conversation. Rodrian still looked for his brother to help. It proved he wasn't confident enough to do this on his own.

Then I noticed the time of the call. He'd made it before Caen called. Before he drank from me. Could mean nothing, or everything. But it remained that it didn't occur to him to try Marek again before rushing out the door.

Should I try Marek? What would I say to him? Marek had Brinked and, like Pontian, could detect thought. Would he suspect what happened with Rodrian earlier? Would he understand?

I doubted it.

The memory of Rodrian's mental touch, the disconnected pleasure I felt when he urged me to unfeel the pain of his teeth—always, always left a wake of guilt and shame, and I didn't mean the simple Catholic kind. Being with Marek never caused me to doubt myself like this. Doing those things were wrong because Rodrian was not the man I should be with.

Marek had been more than my lover. He was my soul mate. Just thinking the words made me sad because I truly meant them. I'd only ever loved with the surety of destiny backing me up, a submersing and encompassing complete love. When I was seventeen, it had been Jared—sweet, messed-up Jared who loved me back with a desperation not unlike someone clinging to a ledge, trying not to fall.

Marek had loved me the same way, I realized, which was why he was so irreplaceable. Maybe the Sophia made me such a screwed-up case. I had been fortunate to find Marek, or to have been found by him. But it wasn't exactly as likely as hitting the Powerball. Fate doesn't keep tossing us second chances like that. Lightning, like Marek, wouldn't strike me again. He wouldn't let himself love me, ever again. Part of me felt the same way about him.

But another part didn't.

That's why the guilt, the shame. I didn't love Rodrian the way I loved Marek. I thought we could make a go of something less committed, but Rodrian didn't deserve that. I didn't give myself over to him, because I was holding back for another Marek. And Rodrian wasn't Marek, no matter how hard he tried to be.

He wasn't doing it for my benefit—he was a Thurzo, dealing with the staggering loss of the head of his family. No one lived a hundred twenty years in his big brother's shadow without squinting in the bright light once the shadow dis-appeared.

Rodrian had been having a hard enough time of it on his own without me screwing everything up for him. Holding everything together had been hard enough before he tasted my blood. I hung my head and rubbed my eyes, my guilt and shame nearly suffocating me.

I'd known my blood did things to him. At first, I wanted to believe I was doing him a favor, but now I realized what had really happened. Blood rush had made him think he actually could be Marek and assume his position and his power. He shouldn't have gone after Shiloh alone but he did it anyway because it's what Marek would have done. And Rodrian honestly thought he could handle it.

That had been Marek's downfall. Arrogance. Except where my blood had saved Marek, had held him back from a terrible Fall, Rodrian wouldn't be so fortunate. My blood and the power it gave him would only make a man like him reckless.

My throat constricted. Someone needed to go after Rodrian. Sliding open his phone again, I thumbed down to Greco's number. My heart boomed in my ears.

"Security." His voice was curt yet polite. He didn't waste words. The sooner he knew a problem, the sooner he could fix it.

"Gian." It was all I got out before my voice threatened to break.

"Where are you, Sophie?"

"Home."

"Where is Rodrian?"

Shit. I didn't know why I still hoped he was with him. "You don't know?"

"I'm coming out there."

"No! Find him. He went after Shiloh." I told him everything I knew, trying to be logical and sequential. Instead, the story flooded out in one huge um-filled run-on sentence. He had to interrupt me several times for clarification.

"Stay home," he said. "Don't leave, don't let anyone in you don't know."

"Okay."

"We'll find him. It'll be all right."

God, I wanted to believe him. I hung up and pressed Rodrian's phone to my mouth, wondering what doom awaited him. Blood rush rarely led to happy endings.

I took out my own phone, intending to break my date with Eirene since I was home bound, and her intended chauffeur was on his way to God only knew what.

Her phone went to voice mail, and I redialed. She answered on my third attempt. "Sophia. I didn't expect you to call so early."

"I have to cancel." Hurriedly I explained Shiloh's disappearance and Rodrian's departure. I left out my concerns about Rodrian's addiction to my blood, and my role in his possible demise. She already suspected I was incompetent; no use removing all doubt now.

"You shouldn't be alone." Her tone was compassionate but firm. "I can hear your distress. I will arrange my own ride and come out at once and we will wait together for their return."

I could have cried. I really needed a friend and, for once, she was being what I needed. "Okay. Please hurry."

"I will." I hung up and huddled on the couch, feeling completely alone for the first time since moving into the Stocks.

After all I'd done, I deserved to be.

Headlights swept the house like a search light, freezing like frost in the slender windows flanking the front door.

"Eirene's here, Toby." I called down the hallway toward the guest suite.

He poked his head through the door. "Okay. I'm going to get washed. Holler if you need me."

The door closed with a staccato echo that tripped out into the foyer. I really needed to lay runner carpets down here.

I wiped my hands on my pants and pulled open the door. Eirene and Dorcas stood motionless. They must have run up the steps.

"Where's your car?" I leaned through the doorway, scanning the driveway, but didn't see the vehicle.

"He parks out of the way, so as not to impede the arrival of others."

"Oh." Plenty of room in the driveway. It wasn't like I had to set a folding chair outside to save a parking space.

"Come in."

Immediately Eirene's expression tightened, her nose wrinkling with discomfort. "Sophia. You must have a dog in here. The smell is overpowering."

"I'll tell the housekeeper to change air freshener." I really didn't feel like entertaining her complaints, and I had no intention of letting her meet the "dog". "We can sit somewhere the dog doesn't go."

I led her toward the dining room and its formal parlor but as we passed the den, she paused, pointing to the half-open door and fireplace beyond. "That room looks very inviting."

Remembering the wards, I steered her away from the den and toward the open arches of the parlor. "Don't I know it. Barney's favorite pillow is in there. He's old, you know, and sleeps by the fire a lot. You'll just get covered in dog hair. We'll be more comfortable in here."

"Dorcas, find the staff and let them know we'll have tea." Before I could protest, Dorcas disappeared into the for-bidden kitchen. Bethany would have my head tomorrow, I thought.

Eirene raised a placating hand. "It is acceptable custom for servants to seek out servants of other households. Do not look alarmed. Once you select your personal servant, you will see how convenient is the practice."

I silently disagreed.

A short while later, Dorcas reappeared, carrying a laden silver service. I breathed a quiet sigh of relief; at least Bethany didn't come in herself, wearing the stern look that reminded me of hot water and harsh detergent. I'd be spared until morning light.

I lost no time in telling Eirene everything I could about Shiloh's call for help.

"So Rodrian went to look for her. I just don't have a

good feeling." It was more than a not-good feeling; the entire time I was telling Eirene about what was going on, I was struggling to keep a clear head. Not groggy, but murky. Opaque. Kind of the opposite of tipsy, when your thoughts were clear but your mouth was incapable of producing clear speech.

I had difficulty corralling my thoughts. It was like trying to scrape gravy together with my fingers. Could it be from the earlier blood loss? I couldn't ask Eirene and I couldn't risk dwelling on it. Anemia affected me in a strange way since the Sophia emerged and I only hoped it wouldn't impair whatever help I could offer now.

"I'm sure he will find her in a place she frequents. Children run toward the familiar when they need comfort."

"I don't know." I shook my head. "Shiloh has new friends lately and neither I nor Rodrian has met them. What if they are behind this?"

My gut nagged my head, trying to spark the leap of intuition. Something was missing. Something that should have been apparent all along. Something that seemed to be clouded.

I strained at the clues but it felt as if I couldn't think past a certain point. I just couldn't get to that conclusion. How much blood had Rodrian taken? My head swam, my thoughts were muddled. Sighing, I sank into the striped loveseat near her, feeling defeated. "I'm so worried I can't think straight. This *déjà vu*-ey feeling is keeping me from seeing things clearly."

Her dark eyes glittered like obsidian, cold and hard and completely not matching the soothing tones of her voice. "You must relax now. You are not alone. I will help you see the truth. We will find the answers together."

I nodded, breathing deeply and forcing my muscles to loosen, pushing my shoulders down.

Her voice continued its soothing drone. "You have great power but anxiety restrains it. We will combine our strength. We will surpass this minor obstacle."

I closed my eyes and drifted into the Sophia's core, lulled by the comfort Eirene exuded. I heard footsteps and a thump of swinging door as Dorcas came in from the kitchen and her power came up on my Sophia radar.

Immediately I pulled barriers, instinct warning. Dorcas' power was gigantic, no longer the sphere I'd en-countered during the barrier practices. It loomed, mammoth like a storm front, uncontained. It was all wrong.

I focused on maintaining an even breath and calm expression. I failed. Dipping my head I rubbed at the creases between my brows. My poker face sucked.

"Sophie?" Eirene's voice held polite concern.

"Just worried. Shiloh is so young, so scared. Who knows what trouble she might be in?" Real alarm spread through me, providing emotional clues I couldn't fake if I needed to. I permitted it to tremble my chin and waver my words, enforcing the impression I was deeply distressed over Shiloh.

As I chattered, I added a thicker under-layer of barrier and used the Sophia-sight to explore the boundary of Dorcas' power. The rail-thin matron stood passively near the door, but her boundary extended far past her body, like the bloated abdomen of an engorged tick. It was darker than her usual dark, reddish black and toxic. It moved, stretching and receding.

It wasn't right.

Eirene fluttered her eyes and sipped at her tea, pausing her soothing stream of near-whispered comfort. As I watched her, I felt my alarm fade.

Dorcas' power loomed as menacing as ever. I should still be alarmed.

When Eirene smiled, she showed teeth, white and gleaming.

Teeth. Threat. A flash of predator. *Déjà vu* smothered.

Her comfort snapped like a string, connection broken, and common sense trickled in.

"What are you doing, Sophia?" Eirene's voice held no comfort now. No tone, no expression. Her words were flat and empty.

"I—I'm having a—a panic attack."

"You are a poor liar."

That elicited a genuine response. "Look, Eirene, if I knew you were going to be so cold, I wouldn't have asked you to come over."

"Why didn't you call Marek?"

I felt as if I'd been struck. Right now, he was the last one on my mind, even though he was perpetually the first. The blow she dealt with that one simple statement knocked me off center and I almost lost my shielding. "He's not on my list of emergency contacts."

"I paid him a visit." She set her empty cup down on its saucer. Dorcas remained immobile. "Or rather, my associates did."

Her empty tone disturbed me. She smiled again, as if sensing my discomfort and enjoying it like a sip of fine wine.

"Why?" Warily, I glanced from Eirene to her servant and back. "Why the sudden interest in Marek?"

"It's not sudden." Amusement colored Eirene's voice. "I've always been very concerned with him. It wasn't until very recently I learned of his brother's family. I must admit, the discovery was a delightful one."

I stood, knowing I had to move without knowing why.

"Sit down." Eirene's black eyes flashed with a glint of cold white light.

I sat and forgot I'd risen. The impression of a clouded truth pressed at my gut sense, twisting my insides and manifesting physical pain. Helplessly, I endured it. Worry. Panic. Shiloh.

"Pontian was ripe for the picking. His dislike for Marek was easily distilled into animosity. It drove the hunt."

*Not Shiloh! Danger here!* My instincts screamed, a flood of liquid buzz. Fight or flight. *Flight!* "Hunt? What are you talking about?"

"Sophie..." She said my name like a lover, let it fill her mouth and spill from her lips, tasting the sound of my name as if she held my essence in her mouth. Eirene slid over onto my seat, sharing the cushion and pressing close. "Who am I? Who am I, really?"

I leaned back, away from her face. "You're Eirene. Sophia Eirene."

"Am I?" Her smile was a seductive secret, an all-knowing spread of lush lip and smooth skin. And I—

*Sophie!*

A mental scream filled my head as I rocked backwards under the force of an empathic shove, a warning to run.

Bethany!

The signal had Bethany's power behind it but she herself was gone, nowhere on my radar and all I could think was *run—run now!*

Ripped out of the snare of Eirene's compulsion, I snapped to my feet, looking down at her surprised expression and the cold white light trapped in her eyes. I watched the white flash into Sophia blue but it was too late. I saw. I knew.

Eirene was vampire.

Her surprise rotted into haughty rage and she crouched on the cushion like a beast before the springing attack. "Only now you see the truth. Sophias are not so wise, after all."

"Wise enough." I fought to remain calm. I sucked at remaining calm. "I revoke my welcome. Leave my home."

"Silly child," Dorcas said. "You cannot banish us by invoking a superstition."

Eirene's brows drew cruel lines over her eyes and she smiled with malicious glee. "Didn't Marek teach you anything?"

I had a hundred snotty retorts to that question but my wisdom proved its worth. It told me to raise my barriers and run. I bolted into the dining room and charged through to the kitchens. "Bethany! Vampires!"

The kitchen was black and I charged through the darkness. My foot caught on something and I tripped, sprawling face first and hitting something soft with my shoulder and chin. Peering through the darkness lit only by the lights of appliances, I strained to see what I tripped over.

Bethany. Eyes open, mouth slack. I reached for a pulse. Nothing. I reached with my power.

Nothing. Dead. My Sophia sight showed her body was cocooned in a black fog the color of Dorcas' power.

I never felt her go. I never—

A hiss rattled behind me and I clambered to my feet, racing once more, having no idea where I'd end up. This was what I got for never learning to cook. The kitchen and service rooms beyond were completely unknown to me. I ran through hallways and pushed open doors, looking for a way out of the house.

Rounding a corner, I emerged through a door in the foyer. Great. I'd run in an effing circle. Eirene strolled from the dining room, hands clasped in genteel delight. "You are entertaining. I enjoy watching you run through the rooms. How your blood crashes through your veins."

I backed away, pounding heart stuttering my breath. "I have holy water."

"Useless. Now, give me your death while you ride on the waves of terror. You intoxicate me. Give me your death and the sweet taste of Sophia."

A growl sounded behind us. "Give me a break."

She whirled at the sound of Toby's voice as he stepped from the den. "Were!"

"Right here, you pampered pig. You think you could shoot dirty pool with me here? Think again." Watching her, he flicked his hand at me.

I understood at once and edged away, feeling behind me for the wall.

"You will pay for your insult." Eirene seethed with rage, the whites of her eyes ringing the silver gleam of her irises.

"I just quit my job so I don't know when I can pay you."

"Insolence!" She whipped a look at me. "Stop there."

I bolstered my barriers and her compulsion slid past, ineffective. Carefully I continued toward the door. "Toby. She's vampire."

"She's trash." He snorted his derision at her. "That's what she is. She's rude, she's old, and she messed with the wrong people."

"How dare you!" Anger stripped away her humanity, revealing the wizened ridges of vampire. Beauty and culture vanished, leaving only ugliness and a corpse-like appearance: brow ridges shoved out, hair thinned, skin shriveled. "You will regret that."

"I regret it now. Boy, your outsides are uglier than your insides."

She forgot me and turned her full fury on Toby. I hoped he knew what he was doing.

I spun toward the staircase, focused on getting up to my room, behind those wards. Dorcas stood on the steps, still and staring, wearing a broken smile. Only one alternative: through the basement and out through the service entrance. I yanked open the basement door, slamming it shut before taking the steps two at a time. A floor-shuddering thump made me pause on the stairs.

"Toby!" I screamed.

He yelled a single word. "Run!"

I ran.

The automatic lights came on as I entered the gym, and I dodged the equipment, tripping my way to the showers. I ran through the shower room to the far side; be-yond the sink and stalls was the boiler room and its service door. I prayed it would open easily.

The grounds crew used the boiler room for storage and for access. It had to be open. I flipped the light switch and they popped on, illuminating the cool rooms.

To a dead end. The door was no longer there. Only a smooth sheet of concrete that didn't match the rest of the wall.

*No. Crap. No!*

I pounded my fists on the remains of the exit. Rodrian said he'd made some security enhancements after the Were attack. Oh, God. He'd sealed the door to eliminate unauthorized access.

He had sealed my doom.

As I backpedaled, I heard the upstairs basement door shatter and splinter.

"Sophia," Eirene called. "Let's be civil. Come die for me."

Only one place to go.

I ran to the pool. If worse came to worse, I could always drown.

No place to hide. I circled the pool, wondering if the trees were enough, knowing I was trapped, and circuited back to the door. Reaching up, I pulled the necklace Marek had given me out of my shirt. I gripped the smooth pendant between my fingers and concentrated. Marek couldn't save me, but maybe a higher power could. *Blood of Isis, protect this one...*

Hope bloomed and exploded in a flash of inspiration. I yanked the necklace, snapping its chain, and focused my Sophia power on it a moment before flinging it across the pool. The stone thunked onto a plastic storage box. I pulled up my barriers, as thick as they'd go, and took a deep breath, hunching into the corner by the control panel.

The door crashed open with the violence of a hurricane, shattering the glass. Eirene stepped through daintily, one deliberate slipper at a time. She never glanced toward the corner where I huddled and sipped at the air, statue-still.

"You are very good, Sophia," Eirene said, her voice as cultured and refined as the day I met her. She didn't sound like she wore her vamp face anymore; maybe she had lips again. "Very powerful. It would have been easier if I hadn't taught you how to use your power but you had to trust me. You give thrilling chase. It will make a powerful death."

She slowly tread deeper into the room, approaching the pool and veering away from me. I remained still, wanting to spring but holding myself back. *Not yet. Too close.*

"You have nowhere to run," she said. "Only one door, and you won't make it past me. Oh, I shall linger over you. I shall sip at your life and relish the flow of your Sophia into me. I see what it had done to Stolus' eldest son and I suspect it is responsible for the younger son's rise in power as well."

She was on the far side of the pool now, edging closer to the wall and the cabana box against it. Slowly, I unfolded myself and slid up the wall, feeling my knees protest.

Eirene stopped a few feet from the far wall, her back completely toward me. "I will consume you and I will be unstoppable. I will rule and I will conquer and I will not be denied!"

She flung open her arms and the cabana box exploded, the sides ripping away, revealing nothing but vacuum hose coiled within. It slid down into loose piles, spilling shapelessly onto the floor around her feet. Eirene leaned and picked up something from the mess.

My pendant.

She screamed. Voices and voices and voices screamed and clawed against my barriers. I steeled myself against the sensation and slid toward the panel. Just a few more inches.

"You!" She spun and saw me, spitting in rage. "You warded this trinket! Deceiver!"

I sprawled the last of the distance to the control panel

and cranked the dial to maximum UV intensity and flicked the switch, flooding the room with a supernova of sunshine. The heat glared down on my neck and I squinted.

"What have you dooo—!" Her voice rose higher and higher, ending in a shriek. Rage erupted, engulfing me and scorching my barriers, corroding them like acid. I pushed all I could into my shields, desperate to keep her hate from destroying me.

The sunlight showed no mercy. She smoked. She blistered. She flaked until her crumbling body disintegrated into a heap of smoldering ash. Marek's necklace lay in the mess, glowing from the extreme heat.

My nose stung from the smell, acrid and cloying. No wonder Buffy preferred a stake, I thought. Burning vamps was stinky work. Covering my nose and mouth with the neckline of my t-shirt, I fanned the air in front of me. "And stay dead."

I heard the door open. Unwilling to take my eyes off the smoldering mess lest it stand up again, I quickly reached out my awareness. There was no DV power.

"Toby," I said. "Are you all—"

Behind me, a tongue clicked in disapproval. "Sophia."

It wasn't Toby's voice. It was many voices, speaking in discordant unison. The noise of it jangled through my head. I jerked around.

Dorcas hovered in the doorway. "Eirene, my Eirene. What has this wicked Sophia done to you?"

She glided toward me and the pile of Eirene. I'd never seen Dorcas move like this, never heard this voice. *Oh, eff, another vampire! I can't fight another! I can't throw the switch from here!*

Wait. Not vampire. The UV lights were on.

What was she?

I watched her warily as she approached the greasy ashes, which still gave off faint wisps.

"Do you know how long I've had this child? She's been mine since her young mortal days. I've invested centuries. Centuries since she turned to vampire, and rose to new levels of ability." Dorcas glared at me. "I expended vast amounts of power cloaking her nature from you fools. And you turned her into useless dust."

The closer she got, the blacker she felt. All Eirene had ever said was that she was unique. I never questioned it, just accepted it. Was that Eirene's compulsion, making me forget?

There was no more compulsion now. Dorcas didn't hide

in her shadow anymore. Now I sensed her. She had a negative aura, like a black hole's event horizon. There was a void around her, through her. It ate life and energy as it passed near.

I backed up. Things that went in black holes tended not to come out again.

"What are you?" I whispered.

"Disgusted, is what I am." She sounded like an aggravated school teacher. "All that work, wasted."

Dorcas seemed to have forgotten the ashes, and now looked very interested in me. Bad stuff. She continued her boneless glide, and I paced back to keep from getting closer to her voidy feeling. Trying not to trip, I felt my way around a pot of pampas grass, putting it between us. As she drew up alongside it, the grass perished. Just drooped and ceased to live.

She hissed a scratchy *ahh*, as if she'd taken a big drink of water.

"I am of the Unseen. I am of the Balance." The voices rose and fell with the cadence of a litany, the sounds of Dorcas worshiping herself. Her mouth never moved. The words seemed to form themselves in the air around her and in my head.

"I am darkness. I am the Anti-Life. I am an ending. I collect screams of pain. I bring dreams of despair. I am the agony of childbirth. I am the grief of death. I am the pleas of the forsaken. I take where fools are doomed to give and give again. I am the moment between life and death. I am Truth."

"You are evil." Backing up, step by careful step, I didn't dare to leave her out of my sight.

"Evil is a shallow word. It is a coward's word. I am power. I am the love of the Self. I am the love that lasts. I am part of the Balance. There is no good or evil. There are

322

only shades of Truth."

I was running out of room to maneuver. She backed me into the far corner, where there was no door. No escape. "What are you going to do to me?"

"Ah..." Her voices sighed and she reached out a hand toward me. The gesture was tentative, a caress of the air around me. The bloody blackness leaked from her, the same color of her power core. Circling around me, she continued her examination and corralled me. "What will I do with you?"

Desperately, I reached out as hard as I could to see who else was in the house. The strain of the effort ripped a laser beam of migraine through the front of my skull, and it was all for nothing.

I sensed no one. I was on my own. I sank inside, and stared at the thing that had been masquerading as a vampire's servant.

"Nothing," she said mildly. "I shape, I do not avenge. I collect pain, not retribution. I am merely...curious. What might *you* be?"

Dorcas unfolded, splaying out many arms, like Kali and calamari. With the speed of a striking viper, arms flipped out, wrapped around me, pulled me into her void. The artificial sunlight dimmed like a wicked eclipse, blackness fitting like a hood. I couldn't breathe.

Too fast to wonder if I was a goner.

The room returned. I was on my knees although I didn't remember falling. I didn't seem hurt. Dorcas glided away from me, murmuring to herself in her jangle of voices. "No, no. She won't do. I must find another. In a city this large, it won't be a task."

She bent to regard Eirene's remains once more before glaring at me with a contemptuously bored look. "Such pity. All that, wasted."

Her image began to shimmer like heat waves coming off a distant summer highway, and she faded, as if she'd simply wished herself to be elsewhere. As she disappeared from sight, her voices echoed. "Wasted."

Exhaustion finally overpowered my adrenaline-fueled instincts and I sank onto a chaise under one of the potted palm trees. I didn't feel too much like moving. I sprawled and I boiled in the noon-strength sun and hoped Rodrian would get home before I developed melanoma.

Turned out it wasn't Rodrian that found me.

I heard Toby shouting my name long before the door flew open. He charged in wearing a cut high on his cheek-bone. The blooming bruise on his temple hinted at a blow that would have killed an ordinary person.

By then, I was cooked and ready to get into the pool, ashy film on the water or no. I vaguely worried about the scum clogging up the filter and how much it'd cost to have the water replaced and I waved limply from the chaise. "Hey, bud."

"Sophie! Are you okay? Yuck. What did I just step in?"

Toby stopped and looked at the bottom of his sneaker. He leaned over at the dusty pile, touching his fingers first to the ashes, then to his nose. And sneezed. "Is this her?"

"Yeah."

He rubbed his fingers together before scrubbing his hand on his pant leg. "Wow. You killed her."

Didn't matter that she was a vampire. Didn't matter that she couldn't be saved. I didn't like knowing I had to kill someone to stay alive. I was trying very hard not to dwell on it. "Like a boss," I said. "You okay?"

He scraped his sneaker on the patio bricks. "I'm fine."

"Let me see your head." I pushed up on the chaise and flopped my legs over the side.

He backed up, waving a dismissive hand. "Where's the other broad?"

"Gone, I think. She just—faded." Another thing I was trying very hard to avoid thinking about. That, and the odd sensation in my head that felt like wind in a big, empty room. She'd done something to me. The scariest part about it was that I had no idea what it was and I had no one to help me with it. I had to keep it secret for now. "I have no idea what the hell happened there."

"I'll sweep the house just in case. Stay here in the sun." He turned and trotted away, still wiping his fingers. Guessed vamp dust was on the greasy side. I could only guess what it would do to the washing machine.

When he reached the door, I had an idea. "What time is it?"

"Nine-thirty."

"Hit the real-time switch for me?"

He shrugged and tapped the control. The sunlight wavered and reduced itself to morning glow, the heat rapidly diminishing. My perspiration chilled and I goose bumped. Reaching behind my chaise, I grabbed a towel from the table and huddled under it, trying not to shiver.

Nothing like a brisk winter morning to make you feel alive again. Toby let me come up after deciding the house was empty. Although he said nothing about Bethany, I knew he'd found her. His eyes looked haunted and hollow. All he said was he made a call from Rodrian's phone, which he'd found in the den.

Rodrian. Shiloh. They still hadn't come home.

I checked all our phones for missed calls or messages. Finding nothing, I went straight to my room and dropped into bed. Euphrates lay on top of my head, doing his best to hide me.

Rousing from a half-nap, I heard a car coming up the

drive and glanced at the clock. Three thirty? Already?

*Thank God. Rode's back.* With the sun safely up at least I wouldn't have to worry about vamps busting down the door. Well, this time, anyway.

"Toby!" I yelled his name but there was no answer. When I'd gone to my room earlier, I'd seen him heading downstairs wearing a very determined look on his face. He had a bottle of holy water in one hand and a roll of paper towels in the other. I imagined he was going to clean up Eirene.

*What a mess that bitch left.* I clamped a hand over my mouth when my giggle sounded like it was two notes away from hysteria.

I hurried to the foyer just as the car door was slamming outside. First thing I would do was crack him in the forehead with his cell phone. Maybe a red mark would help him to remember to keep it in his pocket. Breathless, I punched the disarm code, unlocked the locks and threw open the door to let Rodrian in. The bright sunlight was startling and I squinted into it.

"Thank God, you're..."

That was as far as I got.

It was Marek.

I pulled back, not out of fear but rather from sheer dumb surprise. Marek was the last person I expected to see on my porch. This was the first time he'd shown up here since I moved in. There wasn't time for me to gather my emotional front or put up my walls. There wasn't a chance for me to protest.

One look, one accidental touch of his power and I knew something was wrong.

I forgot how I'd worked so hard to learn to avoid his touch and instinctively reached out to him. His power wore a black oily-feeling shell as if polluted. I found the tiny cracks in his barrier and pushed through to find the part that was still him.

He felt like despair. Finality. Hopelessness.

Resolution.

"Sophie..." His voice was low and rugged, textured with pain, and he wrapped one arm around his waist, holding himself as if it hurt to breathe. His eyes were on fire, emerald to rival the cold winter sun.

He looked...disheveled.

That was all. Marek wore no coat, despite the bite of December air. His clothing looked rumpled as if he'd gotten dressed in a hurry and had thrown on the nearest things at hand. He wore a green sleeveless undershirt that had seen better days. A few strands of hair had worked loose from his pony tail, giving it a frazzled appearance. Beads of perspiration glistened upon his forehead.

Subtle things. But in Marek, they spoke volumes. He wasn't tapping into his Brinkage power to maintain his appearance. This was the first time since he'd become Master that I've seen him looking less than supernaturally perfect.

I didn't waste time thinking. Instinct awoke within me, the Sophia unfolding like a ball of fog. I didn't reason. I didn't guess. I merely arrived at the truth. *This is bad.*

"Help me," he rasped.

Marek fell forward, catching himself on the frame of the door. Quickly I went to his side, supporting what I could, urging him inside.

I ignored the panic and the worry that trickled into my chest as I noticed his bare arm. It was reddening in the sun. Crossing the threshold, I kicked the door shut behind me and walked him into the den.

"Toby!" I shouted again, my voice streaked with tension.

Marek could walk, though with great effort; his

breathing was shallow as if he would suffocate. I wouldn't be able to tell what was wrong with him until I could examine him. The sunlight from the foyer's high windows streamed in through the open door like an accusation, slicing through the otherwise darkened room. He sank into the sofa with a stifled groan.

"Don't move," I said. "You're hurt. Rode. Damn it, Rode's not back yet. Toby!"

*Shit. Shit. Shit.* I dug through the fridge behind the bar, looking for something for him to drink. With Shiloh's treatment rapidly approaching, Rodrian had begun to stock-pile synthetic blood around the house. For an emergency, he'd said.

Marek leaned back against the cushions, his head back, hair spilling down like a crooked curtain. His breathing had evened out, but it still sounded raspy.

"No. Don't bother." He raised a hand to protest. Pain slid across his face when he lifted his arm. The skin glowed an angry red, making him look like a Jersey Shore tourist.

Shit. DV couldn't be hurt by the sun.

I slammed the fridge shut and rummaged through the bottom of the bar, and found an ice bucket. Pulling a linen tablecloth out of a drawer I tore it into strips. I dropped the bucket into the sink and ran the water to its coldest. Best I could do. "You're burned. I'm going to cool it down. Looks like blood on your shirt, too. Show me the worst wounds first."

"The worst?" He laughed, a hard sardonic sound. "You can't bandage the worst."

I ignored the familiarity of that tone of voice. It brought back memories of when we first met, and memories of meeting Marek only made me feel powerless. Reaching inside me, I resurrected old habits and let them take over, becoming instead the bossy first aid queen I'd once been.

We weren't going to play the old games. I was going to fix him and send him home.

Nurse Sophie, that used to be me.

Still, it nagged at me. He'd burned in the sun. Marek hadn't been sensitive to the sun before. Moreover, he wasn't using Brinkage to spruce himself up. His power felt sick, unstable.

*This is bad*, Sophia whispered inside my head. *Something has changed again.*

And when a DV changed, it was never for the better.

I shuddered, the trickle of panic growing into a steady stream. I lifted the bucket out of the sink and cursed when I caught the edge in my haste, splashing the contents across the counter.

"Calm down," he said, and I felt him dampen down the tendrils of anxiety that constricted my throat. The panic drained down, leaving composure in its place.

The composure wasn't mine. If I hadn't experienced his calming compulsions in the past—if the timbre of his touch hadn't been so familiar—I never would have noticed his interference. I winced against the mental intrusion.

"Stop it," I whispered.

"I am sorry." I heard genuine contrition in his voice. "I had no right to do that. But I cannot bear for you to feel that way."

"That's fine. Thanks. Whatever. Just stay out of my head."

"I need you to keep your sense. I need you, Sophia. Don't abandon me now."

Carrying the bucket over to the couch, I sat next to him and wrapped a wet bandage around his forearm. He sucked breath in through his teeth at the sudden icy touch.

"What are you talking about, Marek? I let you in, didn't I? I never abandoned you. Not ever," I said flatly. Meeting his eyes, I tied the makeshift bandage with a tug.

"It's more than shelter. Sophia..." Marek's eyes dimly brightened as if he had a weak battery. He searched my face, tenderness and unspoken regret softening his mouth, his brow, as if he'd finally remembered who I was, who I'd once been to him. "I ask you. Take my heart."

Pressing my lips together, I retreated to the bar, unwilling to look at him and see the tenderness I'd prayed so long to see again. I wanted to look. I slapped the counter, hard enough to sting. Mad at him. Mad at myself.

"I can't do this! I can't help you if you talk like this. I can't help you if you keep touching me with your compulsion. You're hurt, and you need help. That's all I'm going to do. Don't ask me to love you."

"I'm not asking you to love me," he replied, his voice leaden. "I'm asking you to kill me."

Toby let me come up after deciding the house was empty. Although he said nothing about Bethany, I knew he'd found her. His eyes looked haunted and hollow. All he said was he made a call from Rodrian's phone, which he'd found in the den.

Rodrian. Shiloh. They still hadn't come home.

I checked all our phones for missed calls or messages. Finding nothing, I went straight to my room and dropped into bed. Euphrates lay on top of my head, doing his best to hide me.

Rousing from a half-nap, I heard a car coming up the drive and glanced at the clock. Three thirty? Already?

*Thank God. Rode's back.* With the sun safely up at least I wouldn't have to worry about vamps busting down the door. Well, this time, anyway.

"Toby!" I yelled his name but there was no answer. When I'd gone to my room earlier, I'd seen him heading downstairs wearing a very determined look on his face. He had a bottle of holy water in one hand and a roll of paper towels in the other. I imagined he was going to clean up Eirene.

*What a mess that bitch left.* I clamped a hand over my mouth when my giggle sounded like it was two notes away from hysteria.

I hurried to the foyer just as the car door was slamming outside. First thing I would do was crack him in the forehead with his cell phone. Maybe a red mark would help him to remember to keep it in his pocket. Breathless, I punched the disarm code, unlocked the locks and threw open the door to let Rodrian in. The bright sunlight was startling and I squinted into it.

"Thank God, you're..."

That was as far as I got.

It was Marek.

I pulled back, not out of fear but rather from sheer dumb surprise. Marek was the last person I expected to see on my porch. This was the first time he'd shown up here since I moved in. There wasn't time for me to gather my emotional front or put up my walls. There wasn't a chance for me to protest.

One look, one accidental touch of his power and I knew something was wrong.

I forgot how I'd worked so hard to learn to avoid his touch and instinctively reached out to him. His power wore a black oily-feeling shell as if polluted. I found the tiny cracks in his barrier and pushed through to find the part that was still him.

He felt like despair. Finality. Hopelessness.

Resolution.

"Sophie..." His voice was low and rugged, textured with pain, and he wrapped one arm around his waist, holding himself as if it hurt to breathe. His eyes were on fire, emerald to rival the cold winter sun.

He looked...disheveled.

That was all. Marek wore no coat, despite the bite of December air. His clothing looked rumpled as if he'd gotten dressed in a hurry and had thrown on the nearest things at hand. He wore a green sleeveless undershirt that had seen better days. A few strands of hair had worked loose from his pony tail, giving it a frazzled appearance. Beads of perspiration glistened upon his forehead.

Subtle things. But in Marek, they spoke volumes. He wasn't tapping into his Brinkage power to maintain his appearance. This was the first time since he'd become Master that I've seen him looking less than supernaturally perfect.

I didn't waste time thinking. Instinct awoke within me, the Sophia unfolding like a ball of fog. I didn't reason. I didn't guess. I merely arrived at the truth. *This is bad.*

"Help me," he rasped.

Marek fell forward, catching himself on the frame of the door. Quickly I went to his side, supporting what I could, urging him inside.

I ignored the panic and the worry that trickled into my chest as I noticed his bare arm. It was reddening in the sun. Crossing the threshold, I kicked the door shut behind me and walked him into the den.

"Toby!" I shouted again, my voice streaked with tension.

Marek could walk, though with great effort; his breathing was shallow as if he would suffocate. I wouldn't be able to tell what was wrong with him until I could examine him. The sunlight from the foyer's high windows streamed in through the open door like an accusation, slicing through the otherwise darkened room. He sank into the sofa with a stifled groan.

"Don't move," I said. "You're hurt. Rode. Damn it,

Rode's not back yet. Toby!"

*Shit. Shit. Shit.* I dug through the fridge behind the bar, looking for something for him to drink. With Shiloh's treatment rapidly approaching, Rodrian had begun to stock-pile synthetic blood around the house. For an emergency, he'd said.

Marek leaned back against the cushions, his head back, hair spilling down like a crooked curtain. His breathing had evened out, but it still sounded raspy.

"No. Don't bother." He raised a hand to protest. Pain slid across his face when he lifted his arm. The skin glowed an angry red, making him look like a Jersey Shore tourist.

Shit. DV couldn't be hurt by the sun.

I slammed the fridge shut and rummaged through the bottom of the bar, and found an ice bucket. Pulling a linen tablecloth out of a drawer I tore it into strips. I dropped the bucket into the sink and ran the water to its coldest. Best I could do. "You're burned. I'm going to cool it down. Looks like blood on your shirt, too. Show me the worst wounds first."

"The worst?" He laughed, a hard sardonic sound. "You can't bandage the worst."

I ignored the familiarity of that tone of voice. It brought back memories of when we first met, and memories of meeting Marek only made me feel powerless. Reaching inside me, I resurrected old habits and let them take over, becoming instead the bossy first aid queen I'd once been. We weren't going to play the old games. I was going to fix him and send him home.

Nurse Sophie, that used to be me.

Still, it nagged at me. He'd burned in the sun. Marek hadn't been sensitive to the sun before. Moreover, he wasn't using Brinkage to spruce himself up. His power felt sick, unstable.

*This is bad*, Sophia whispered inside my head. *Something has changed again.*

And when a DV changed, it was never for the better.

I shuddered, the trickle of panic growing into a steady stream. I lifted the bucket out of the sink and cursed when I caught the edge in my haste, splashing the contents across the counter.

"Calm down," he said, and I felt him dampen down the tendrils of anxiety that constricted my throat. The panic drained down, leaving composure in its place.

The composure wasn't mine. If I hadn't experienced his calming compulsions in the past—if the timbre of his touch hadn't been so familiar—I never would have noticed his interference. I winced against the mental intrusion.

"Stop it," I whispered.

"I am sorry." I heard genuine contrition in his voice. "I had no right to do that. But I cannot bear for you to feel that way."

"That's fine. Thanks. Whatever. Just stay out of my head."

"I need you to keep your sense. I need you, Sophia. Don't abandon me now."

Carrying the bucket over to the couch, I sat next to him and wrapped a wet bandage around his forearm. He sucked breath in through his teeth at the sudden icy touch.

"What are you talking about, Marek? I let you in, didn't I? I never abandoned you. Not ever," I said flatly. Meeting his eyes, I tied the makeshift bandage with a tug.

"It's more than shelter. Sophia..." Marek's eyes dimly brightened as if he had a weak battery. He searched my face, tenderness and unspoken regret softening his mouth, his brow, as if he'd finally remembered who I was, who I'd once been to him. "I ask you. Take my heart."

Pressing my lips together, I retreated to the bar,

unwilling to look at him and see the tenderness I'd prayed so long to see again. I wanted to look. I slapped the counter, hard enough to sting. Mad at him. Mad at myself.

"I can't do this! I can't help you if you talk like this. I can't help you if you keep touching me with your compulsion. You're hurt, and you need help. That's all I'm going to do. Don't ask me to love you."

"I'm not asking you to love me," he replied, his voice leaden. "I'm asking you to kill me."

I looked back at him in dismay as the truth slowly dawned on me. He leaned forward, firm purpose replacing the pain in his eyes. "I'm finished. You must end it for me."

Marek rose; the simple act of standing caused pain to ebb in waves along his power. Light from the foyer illuminated one side of his body, a split image of positive and negative, dark and light. Black and white and emerald green where his eyes wouldn't go out. "Kill me before I turn. The sun will fall in a few hours. Kill me, else I fall with it."

"No," I whispered. "How could you ask me such a thing?"

"You are Sophia. You are the only redemption I have ever known."

"I am Sophie," I said firmly. "I don't kill. Not even if someone really deserved it." We faced off for many long moments, each one unrelenting, unwilling to admit we couldn't change, even if it meant the demise of the other.

Marek sank back down into the couch with an uncomfortable sigh. "Where is my brother?"

The worry I'd set aside for Rodrian and Shiloh resurfaced.

"I don't know. Shiloh took off yesterday. Rode got a lead and he went after it. He never came back and he hasn't called. I'm scared," I said softly. "Can you feel him? Do you know where he is?"

"No." His eyes drifted half-closed. "He is...moving, but I can't tell where he is." A violent fit of coughing stole his words, a wet and painful sound. I winced when I saw the stain of blood on his lips. "It is distracting, this process of dying. My power isn't orderly enough to be any use."

"Shut up," I said. "You're not dying. You can't be."

He exhaled and leaned his head back again. "I apologize for not meeting your expectations."

"Marek..." I gingerly sat down beside him, against the arm of the couch, afraid I'd scare him off. "What happened to you?"

He laughed, ruefully, and let his gaze take me in. For the first time since he'd left to start The Crap That Almost Killed Me, we were having a real conversation.

Great. He was dying. Now we were talking. Talk about procrastination. Why couldn't he have done this before? Why couldn't he have looked at me like this, like I was actually in the room and I actually meant something, before it was too late?

It couldn't be too late. I didn't go through all this for a pile of *too late*.

"A curse." He interrupted my frustrated stream of thought. "A curse that was uttered centuries ago, a curse upon my grandfather and his entire lineage. How about that? I was cursed before I'd even been born. I told you I was damned. I never stood a chance."

"I don't understand. What curse?"

He drew a deep breath through his nose. Next would be the lecture. Déjà vu.

"My grandfather was a constable in Old Hungary. He once arrested a DV noblewoman for attacks upon young women. This countess paraded as an instructor of etiquette, and well-born families sent their daughters to her so she could teach them the ways of courtly life."

Marek rolled his head toward me. "She was a 'lution junkie with a mean streak you couldn't begin to imagine. *Vicious* is too soft a word to describe her. She committed blood crimes so atrocious they became legend, even among humans."

He paused as I draped a wet bandage across his other arm, watching my ministering hands with an expression I tried hard to ignore. If I acknowledged the tender regret warming in his eyes, I'd die with him.

"When my grandfather arrested her, she cursed him and his line. The Unseen had heard and her curse became bound by the darkest powers. He tried to push for a lesser sentence in order to appease her, to spare his family, but it was too late. Eventually she died in captivity. Or so they thought."

Marek sighed and closed his eyes. "They were deceived. She'd evolved. She'd been planning her own revenge all this time. We never knew. Why would we? There are no female vampires."

"The DV were wrong?"

"As we often are when it comes to underestimating the power of a determined woman."

I kept my eyes on the floor. I would not be distracted by pretty apologies now.

"And so, finally, she came for us. I was ambushed last night, by vamps who would avenge the insult against

Erzebet Bathory. I would Fall in the name of the Vampiress Irony."

He opened his eyes, soft green wedges of lime light. "The vampires succeeded. They overwhelmed me. They plunged me into a sea of deaths and I drowned. My soul was so weak, Sophie. I'm sorry. I couldn't hold onto my soul."

"No." I shook my head. Bathory. Female vampires. It was unreal, even against the starkness of my unreal life and my completely off-the-map week. I pushed my sleeve up past my elbow and held out my wrist. "Share my blood."

He closed his eyes again and whimpered. "No."

"Do it. You don't have to hurt me. I know my blood helped you before. It helped Rode..."

Deceptive calm settled his anguish. "You shared blood with Rodrian?"

Faster than I could follow it, his hand shot out, grabbing my arm and pulling me against him. The movement was too sudden for me to evade. He drew me close to his face and breathed me in. Tender regret vanished in a whip crack of jealousy. "What else have you shared with him?"

"Let me go!" I struggled against him, trying to push without pushing against unseen hurts or raw skin. Marek released me with a tug and I got off the couch. "In case you've forgotten, you don't own me."

He didn't look the least bit apologetic. "You will always be mine."

"You're not my keeper. I'm going to be happy with someone someday. Someone who loves me."

"I love you," he said. The anger in his voice didn't belong with those words, giving them new meaning. "I never stopped. I could not be with you any longer."

"Why not?"

"I'd hurt you. You deserve love, Sophie, and life, and

happiness. I couldn't give you those things anymore, and I wouldn't allow my damnation to taint you."

"You did hurt me, Marek. I won't forgive you for going to face the Master. Rode told me." I turned away from him so he couldn't protest. "You'd planned it all along. Everything's the way it is now because of the choice you made. You are where you are because of you and only you."

I went back to the ice bucket and picked out a thick cloth, squeezing it a little. The cold water made goose bumps charge up my arms as I walked behind the couch. Gathering his ponytail, I gently held it up while I smoothed out the cloth around the back of his neck. I tugged out the elastic and carefully combed my fingers through his hair, remembering the silk, how it had once felt against my skin.

Another selfish indulgence. Reluctantly I pulled my hand away. It wasn't fair. He'd been mine once. He should never have stopped being mine.

Marek leaned forward, covering his face with his hands. "I have made so many mistakes. I have done so much to regret. I die knowing that instead of the love you deserve, I give you pain, right to the very end."

"First off, you are not dying. Second, whatever else there is can wait." I dug the cell phones out of my pocket. Flipping Rodrian's phone open, I began beeping through the contact list. "I'm calling Pontian. He'll know what to do."

"You can't reach him." His voice was grim. "Pontian has Fallen."

A cold lump hit the bottom of my stomach as that particular hope hit the skids. "How do you know?"

"Because it was him that Irony sent to ambush me."

That name again. "A vampiress named *Irony*?"

"Yes. In life she was the DV Countess Bathory of

341

Hungary, my grandfather's cousin."

Why did that name ring a bell? I mumbled the name, trying to work out the sound. *Irony, Iron, I-ron...Irene?* "Irony. Spelled *E-i-r-e-n-e*?"

His derisive laugh confirmed my suspicion. "What a vain creature she is. *Eirene*, the Greek word for peace. The only peace that wretched thing will know is when her cursed unlife winks out of existence once and for all."

"Um..." I sat down beside him. "It did."

"What?"

"Eirene. She's, um, no more. She's an ex-vampire."

His gaze threatened to pierce me as he evaluated the words and silently awaited the explanation.

"Toby is wiping up her ashes right now, as far as I know."

"Toby? The young Were who tags along after you?" Some things never changed, apparently. Marek was ready to meet damnation but was still firmly entrenched in his prejudice against Weres. "Rodrian described him as much less useful. He killed a female vampire?"

I shook my head. "No. Technically, I did. It was Sophie, in the pool room, with the UV lights."

Marek stared at me with an open mouth, and I reached over and pushed his jaw closed and tried not to look too self-satisfied.

"So. You do have the ability to kill when it's justified."

My half-grin faded. "Not this nonsense again."

"You killed a vampire."

Shrugging, I made a face. "One, it doesn't count because she was dead already. Two, the sunlight did it, not me."

"It does not alter the fact. You can kill me before I Fall."

"I am not listening to this!"

"Do you love me?"

That floored me. I gave him an incredulous look. "How

could you even ask that?"

"It's important."

"And it wasn't important for the last, oh, I don't know, year and a half?"

Issuing a frustrated noise, he made a thin line of his mouth. "Tell me. Do you love me?"

With that, he silently commanded it from me.

"Yes." I glared at him as the word obediently slid out. "But not in the way you're asking."

The compulsion released me and I tasted surprise in his power. "Oh?"

I faced him and steadied my nerve for the truth. I'd killed a vampire, right? Certainly I was capable of telling my ex how I felt. God knows I'd practiced enough in my head. Final curtain went up. Deep breath.

"You betrayed me by risking everything we could have had together, and I still loved you. You physically wounded me, but I know it wasn't your choice. There was no reason to leave. The worst had passed. We'd survived the absolute worst that could have happened to us and I still wanted you. You weren't protecting me by staying away. You were strangling me. You cut me off from everything that mattered. That's how you hurt me."

My eyes stung and my voice trembled but I didn't retreat. This was no time to be weak. Looking at the man I would love the rest of my life, whether or not he was in it, I planted my resolve and faced him. This could be the last chance I had to tell him.

"I love you, Marek. I never stopped. I loved you as you walked out on me. I loved you when you blew me off me over and over every time I tried to be nice. I loved you as I cried and finally convinced myself you'd never love me again. I'd still give my life for you a thousand times over, without hesitation, without regret."

Looking away, I wiped away the bitter tears I couldn't keep from spilling until I could speak again. Apology gleamed in his unshed tears.

"I love you, Marek." I looked down at his plaintive face and brushed my fingers along his cheek. "But not enough to kill you."

The sun raced across the sky and the horizon reached up to catch it. Nature itself fought against us. The one day I couldn't let end sped to its death.

So did Marek.

"Sophie."

I couldn't look at him. If his eyes looked the way his voice sounded, I'd shatter.

Perched on a bar stool, I went through Rodrian's phone contact list, hoping to get someone useful to pick up. More often than not, I ended up poking the end button in irritation as yet another perky or sultry or far-too-familiar female voice answered the phone with a smile in her voice. Apparently Rode's phone was more of a little black book than a useful organization tool. What a slut.

*Two dents. I'll hit him with both phones when he gets home.* At least my survival instincts still worked. I mustn't have been as overwrought by panic and frustration as I had thought if I could still manage to be petty about Rodrian's taste in women.

"Sophie, please. Look at me." His mournful eyes held more than regret. "Sophie, it hurts."

Sympathy welled where his pitiful words poked holes in my armor. Setting the phone on the bar, I sighed. "Can my blood ease the pain?"

"It might. But it won't change the outcome, and I don't know what strength a Sophia's blood will give a vampire."

"Stop saying that. Can't you just kill yourself?" I asked in frustration.

"Suicide is damning. What is the point of dying with my soul intact if suicide will doom me to Hell?"

"It was just a thought."

"Glad to see you are still looking out for me, dear," he responded. "But there's no alternative. My brother is not here. There is no one else. You have to do it."

"Do you know any hit men?"

"Your Were might."

"Oh, ha." Why did people keep throwing that into my face? What Tanner did wasn't Toby's fault. "Can you compel him to come here? He can't hear me."

"I thought Weres had superior hearing."

"The room is warded."

A look of puzzlement drifted over his face, bunching his brows. "Why, exactly?"

"Rode showed me how he set a ward. Good thing he did. The lesson saved my life a few hours ago."

"But why, exactly, this kind of ward?" The puzzled look sharpened into suspicion. "What have you done with him in here?"

I knew exactly what we'd done in this room. If Marek couldn't figure it out, I sure as hell wasn't going to volunteer the information. "What kind of question is that?"

"He created a cloaking ward. I get no impressions of

either of you in here. All your actions are hidden."

"He'd never hidden from me in here."

"He can't. The ward is set to both of you."

"You make it sound like I did something intentional."

"Not you. Him."

I closed my eyes and counted to three. What could I say to that? "Can you just get Toby to come up here?"

"No." He sounded weary. "Cannot compel Weres."

I swore a bitter and creative oath. "Fine. I'll get him."

"No, you won't. You'll stay here."

I shot him an *oh yeah, right* look and got up. Heading straight for the door, I made it to the threshold before circling in a smooth arc and marching back to my seat. As I plopped back down onto the stool, I blew my cool. "You jerk! You compelled me!"

"And it took precious power to do it. Don't fight me. Just do what I ask. No one else can get here in time. Sunfall begins in less than an hour. It hurts, Sophie. Please."

"What about poison? Can you drink bleach?"

He sat up despite the pain it obviously caused—his clamped jaw couldn't mask his discomfort. His wide eyes couldn't hide his shock. "What? You want me to drink bleach? My. You really haven't forgiven me."

"Cut it out!" I slammed the phone down on the bar in frustration. "Don't you know how hard this is?"

"Yes," he said sadly. "I do." He leaned his elbows on his knees as he stared me down. "But if you don't kill me, I will Fall. I will die right here in front of you while you watch. When the sun is dead I will rise as vampire, and the first thing I will do is kill you. Then I will scare the living shit out of your buddy downstairs, which will undoubtedly kill him, too. I'll wait here for my brother and his children and I will kill them all. It's what Eirene wanted. I'll fulfill the curse. You'll die knowing you could have stopped it. Is that what you want, Sophia?"

He stood up and stretched to his full height. "Now stop fucking around. You will end this now. Bring me the sword from over our bed."

I felt a mental shove as he compelled me out of the den and up the stairs to my room.

I couldn't fight it. I tried to raise my barriers but his power had a stranglehold on me, a connection I couldn't block. My feet obeyed, even with my eyes clamped shut. I didn't have to open them to climb up on the bed and un-hook the sword from its place on the wall.

*My bed, not ours*, I thought angrily.

As I submissively returned to the den, I heard Marek talking on the phone. He spoke urgently, issuing instructions regarding business matters. With a raised hand, he stopped me at the door.

I tossed the sword onto the floor with a bang and crossed my arms, giving him the most evil look I'd ever worn.

"The paperwork has already been prepared. You'll find it in the safe at Chaucer's Square. Do you understand every-thing I've just told you?"

He listened as whoever was on the other line spoke.

"That's right. Oh, and brother..." He turned to look at me. "Take care of Sophie. She's going to need you when you get here."

His imperious tone softened and he swallowed, his throat moving painfully. "Goodbye, Rodrian."

He flipped my phone shut and, after a few long breaths, dropped it onto the bar. "He's on his way. They have Shiloh."

I said nothing. I couldn't speak. There was so much in that goodbye.

"He won't make it in time, Sophie." He sounded

subdued, not at all like the bossy prick who just commanded me to do his bidding. "I've made all possible arrangements. I did the best I could for my family. Now I need you to do what is best for me."

He let his gaze drift down to the sword.

"Please, Marek. I can't. I couldn't live with myself if I do this."

"You won't live if you don't," he spat back. "Do you care about anyone other than yourself?"

Before I made my angry protest, his knees buckled. He doubled over and screamed.

That scream. I'd heard it before. The night we had been brought to the Master, when Jared was killed. When part of Marek's soul was ripped away by the death of my best friend.

*Marek is dying,* the Sophia whispered.

He looked up at me, agony and desolation making ghosts of his eyes. I'd be forever haunted.

"Sophia, please! Guard my death!" He wrapped me in his power and submerged me. It was madness and pain and I drowned in the tidal flood.

I cried out, adding my terror to the flood.

"Do it!" He hissed and raised his hand to me, fingers curled into claws of pain.

I couldn't fight the grip he had upon my will. I bent to pick up the sword, and slid the wicked blade from its sheath. "Marek! Stop!"

"Do it!" Marek drooped to his knees, eyes burning with neon fire. His hair was loose, spread out over his shoulders like a veil of night. His features were tangled with pain, teeth sharp and fully drawn.

*His soul is fleeing,* cried the Sophia.

He blasted me with his power, putting the last of his strength into commanding me. Step by step, I slowly approached him, raising the sword in both hands. His compulsion was impossible to resist. Tears rolled down my cheeks as I stared down the steel blade at the face of the man I loved.

Muffled footsteps echoed from the hall. I heard the basement door open.

"Toby!" I turned my head and screamed, even as I lifted the blade and leveled it at the last beats of Marek's heart.

Marek pulled my eyes to him with a hiss. "Don't hesitate, love. Do it. I beg you."

His chest lay beneath the tip. I leaned on the sword.

"Sophie?" Toby called as he emerged from the basement. "I think I got her all, but I used the last of the pool shock."

"Help us!" I cried. The compulsion prevented me from turning my head.

"Soph? Where are you?" I heard his footsteps as Toby stuck his head into the room. "What are you doing, Sophie?"

I sobbed. The sword had punctured Marek's skin. Crimson spots welled, making dark stains on his shirt. Marek squeezed his eyes shut, biting down and willing the arrival of his fate.

"He's dying, Toby. He's making me do this. Save him!"

"I'll save both of you." The tone of his voice was more serious than I'd ever heard from him. A split second passed during which I realized with perfect clarity what he meant to do. By the time it registered, it was too late.

Toby rushed past me, hands extended, as he forced himself to begin the change. His arms were peeling and cracking, hands splitting with the emergence of claws. He threw himself on Marek.

The sword flew from my hands and clattered to the floor when they collided. The compulsion snapped off as Marek struck back, and they grappled, Toby's determination against Marek's overwhelming power.

Toby was no match for Marek, even as wolf. It was a suicide move.

I raised my barriers and scrambled away from them, kicking the sword out of reach. I'd save him. I'd draw off whatever damage I could and keep his soul for him. He didn't need to die. Reaching out, I summoned the Sophia and reached through my barriers to his power.

When I touched it, I drew back as if I'd touched a hot stove, adding layer on layer of power to insulate me against his power. He didn't feel like Marek at all.

Marek wrapped his arms around Toby, pinning his arms to his sides. His change didn't progress beyond his arms, and the only weapon Toby could have used, his claws, were impotent beneath Marek's hold. Toby snarled and struggled but was clearly outmatched.

So much anger in Marek, such rage spilling out at this interruption. Fangs bared, Marek struck at the tender skin between shoulder and throat. Black hair swung to cover his face, a curtain to hide the horror.

Toby's eyes rolled and he sagged, the fight draining out of him. Marek pushed him away and Toby staggered, dropping in slow-motion, first to his knees before sprawling to the floor. Discarded. Threat eliminated.

Marek raised his head and looked at me, panting. Toby's blood smeared his chin and cheek, giving him a murderous look. His down-turned mouth and drawn brows revealed the pain and exertion this last distraction had brought him. Nothing would stand between him and an honorable death now.

Desperately, I looked to the sword, where it had slid alongside the bar. I had to do it. Marek hadn't lied. He had evolved. If I didn't do it, we would all be doomed. Toby wasn't moving. It was all up to me.

*No*, cried the Sophia. *Not like this! This will not save him!*

I ignored her.

The sunlight that had been streaming into the room seemed to waver a bit before finally fading like stars at dawn. I lunged for the sword, landing hard on my knees as I reached for it. Grabbing the hilt, I twisted and raised it even before I got to my feet.

Too late.

Marek roared my name, fear and pain sharpening his voice. It cut through me, straight to the core of the Sophia who screamed back, filling me. He sank to his knees, arms wide, and looked at me with begging eyes before he collapsed onto Toby's body.

A noise began to grow from somewhere. It was a living thing, this noise. I didn't know if it was wind or voice or song. With the sound came a light, seeming to come from everywhere at once. Everything around me began to glow. I thought I'd begun to pass out but kept my feet.

My eyes streamed tears as the light reached an intensity that rivaled noonday. I couldn't hear anything but the rushing sound that filled the air and vibrated through me. A wolf howled, its lonely call blending with the wind, fading into the hurricane of noise. The rushing sound melted into a piercing scream. The scream exploded into a crack of thunder that shook the room before it echoed into silence.

Stillness. Darkness. Emptiness.

I dropped the sword and covered my face.

The front door slammed.

"Sophie? Marek?" Rodrian called from the foyer. His footsteps quickened and I heard him come in. "What's going..."

He faltered as he drew up behind me. I couldn't imagine what he must have thought to see Marek and Toby lying in a bloodied heap. I couldn't bear to touch his grief yet, not when I couldn't hold my own. I turned blindly to him and buried my face against his chest, sobbing.

"What is that?" He didn't sound grief stricken. He sounded...baffled.

A groan from the floor drew my attention and I pulled my face from him to look. Toby rolled onto his side, pulling his knees toward his chest. He'd survived.

Marek was gone.

Or...was he? Upon Toby's shoulder, looking cruel and defiant perched a tremendous raptor.

A falcon.

White feathers tipped with black Vs streaked a broad

chest and dappled its head. The bird stood larger and thicker than a hawk, almost chunky. The impression of power was nearly tangible.

With a cock of its head it dared us to come closer, raising a pale eyebrow. As we stared in disbelief, its eyes gleamed for a brief moment, a ray of emerald light. Wicked talons threatened to break Toby's skin as it gripped its perch, a pose of command and triumph.

The front door banged open again. The bird leapt into the air, unfurling massive wings and gathering air and height beneath them.

"Sophie?" Shiloh's voice echoed from the foyer. "Dad?"

We ducked as the falcon sailed out of the room. It circled the foyer once before darting toward the open door and the glow of sunset. Shiloh, seeing the huge bird aiming straight for her, squawked and dove out of the way.

Rodrian and I scrambled to the door as the bird found the open sky. With lazy wing beats, it climbed higher and higher, issuing one last scream before it sailed toward the bloody sunset.

Marek was gone.

There were no words. There weren't even tears. My grief and my loss, so great they transcended anything I'd ever felt, froze me. Rodrian hugged me to him.

"Sorry, Sophie," said Shiloh from behind us, breaking our trance. "I didn't mean to lose your bird."

I paced and fidgeted.

Maybe if someone had been passing by the office and stuck their head in briefly, they'd have thought that I was changing a CD or rearranging my desk or merely crossing the room.

If they were a fly on the wall, they'd have seen I'd been doing the same things for forty-five minutes. My patience had run out and my nerves cried for distraction. How long until they finished with Shiloh? How long until someone told me if she was okay?

I crossed to the window and pushed aside the sheer curtain, staring down at the bleak, wind-swept grounds. Ragged tufts of long field grass, determined to push through the harsh icy crust, looked yellow-brown and lifeless, dried frail stalks of abandoned life.

December was slushy and sleety, snow flurries one day and dry winter sun the next, layer upon layer of desolate weather. I regretted wishing for a white Christmas. Only a few days remained before the big day and I was sick of snow already.

Scanning the skies, I searched for a black and white falcon, so unlike the raucous crows that called laughingly from the woods. Sometimes it drifted over the barren trees, fighting the winds to fly determinedly along its chosen route. I watched for it because, oddly, it brought me peace. Whenever I saw it flying, I thought of absolutely nothing. White noise.

Not serenity—everything that creature represented was as far from serenity as anything could get without turning into a suicide bomber. The peace was more of an interruption of my constantly-racing thoughts.

It was the sign-off pattern of 1979 television. It was the flat-line of a telemetry unit. It was the last continuous exhale of a gently dying man. None of those things left room for individual thought.

A knock on the door broke my trance and Toby cleared his throat. One last time, I swept the fields with a searching glance. Seeing no one, I let the sheer panels fall back together.

"All done, Sophie. I did the best I could." He carried in Marek's sword and the wooden shield to which it had originally been attached. I flinched inwardly when I saw it.

I put effort into a smile but my cheeks felt too heavy to make it last. "Thanks, Toby."

"One of the hooks was broken. You really busted it good when you ripped it down. Anyway, I used some wire to secure the sword to the plaque but at least it won't fall and cut your head off while you sleep."

"Well, there's a relief. Thanks for that."

"Hey, no problem. I told you I was here to help you out." His goofy smile faded a bit and he scratched the side of his head. "It's kind of a relief to finally be moving out, what with all the vampire fighting and all."

"Toby..." I blinked and forced my throat to cooperate. "I can't thank you for what you've done. You've put up with a lot from Rode and Shy but, if you'd given up on us, I wouldn't be here. None of us would be here."

"I had a debt to repay."

"Now that Tanner is gone for good, it's me that has the debt."

"Naw, you don't. Friends don't keep score. Besides." He grinned over his shoulder at Dahlia, who appeared in the doorway. I knew she'd been lurking outside and had been ready to call her in. "I got something wonderful out of all of this."

"You are so cute together," I said with a smile.

"See, there you go again." Dahlia blushed and joined us, linking our hands. "Using words that have absolutely nothing to do with me."

"Aw, not true, baby girl," Toby said. "You're as cute as they come."

"Baby girl?" I laughed. I wasn't sure how old Dahlia was but she was no baby. "That's so—"

"Yeah. Cute." Her mouth twitched with a smothered smile. "Shut up."

"So you guys are going to make a stab at living together, huh?"

"Oh, it's just temporary," Toby said, and grinned down at Dahlia. "I mean, until I can get a place of my own and she can come live with me."

"I can't understand why you didn't want to stay at a safe house, hon," she said. "The Northridge den has a pool in theirs."

I thought it was funny that a DV knew more about Were stuff than an actual Were but Toby seemed to take it in stride. Dahlia had been in contact with two of the area werewolf den leaders, determining which would be best for Toby. Apparently not all dens were created equal. Last update, she said it was down to a matter of *job placement capabilities* and *freshmen handling*.

I just shrugged and tried to look like I understood. Sounded too much like college.

I sensed Rodrian's approach as he aimed for the staircase in the foyer below, as if I were watching an infrared thermograph. Or something. His intent to seek me out acted like a signal booster and the Sophia's "ears" pricked forward at the sound of his power.

Rodrian walked in, taking all of us in with a single look. Before Dorcas touched me, he would've scared the crap out of me by appearing so suddenly. He'd locked his power down; he could move like Ninja or fog when he shielded. Now, some new door was open in my head and I could feel Rodrian despite his barriers. I could feel everyone in the house, if I tried.

I wasn't trying now. Rodrian's essence bled through his shields and soaked me with his mixed feelings. I didn't need to see his expression. Weariness and relief were evident upon his face.

He licked his lips. "She's okay."

I sighed with relief and hurried toward him, slipping my arms around him and resting my forehead against his chest. He wrapped himself around me, letting his weariness slip away. I gently gathered it, folding it and storing it in the place I put all those miscreant feelings: somewhere down.

Leaning against him, I felt his heartbeat, inhaled his scent, and basked along his warmth. I gave him comfort; his presence comforted me in return. It was a balance.

Behind me, Toby shifted uncomfortably. My new heightened senses still excluded Were emotions but the way he cleared his throat tipped me off. "We're leaving, Soph.

Glad to hear Shiloh is all right. Maybe we'll visit soon."

"Toby." Rodrian halted Toby when he tried to leave and I pulled away. Rodrian's arm held me close and he didn't release me, so I just turned my face toward the Were and waited. "I know I didn't make things easy on you."

Toby's smiled faded. "You don't have to explain."

"I do. I should have trusted Sophie's judgment. She always manages to do the right thing. And now I realize, so do you. I didn't give you enough credit. I was foolish."

"You were watching out for your own. You got a family to take care of. That's not foolish. That's being a father." Toby's voice was even but I knew the investment he'd placed in the last word.

Rodrian nodded. "I can only repay you in kind. You protected my family. I'll consider you family and protect you in turn."

Toby ducked his head and breathed deep. "I'll have a den soon. Dally's helping me look for one."

I reached out and touched his arm. "We found you first."

"Family." Toby rolled the word in his mouth, savoring it. "Really?"

Rodrian nodded. "If you'll have us."

Toby smiled, the defensive hunch melting from his shoulders. He looked taller, stronger, somehow. "Family sounds pretty good."

Rodrian extended his hand and Toby grasped it.

"See you around, little brother," I said.

"Yeah." He grinned, rakish rogue-like and took Dahlia's hand. "See you."

They called out last goodbyes from the foyer, pulling the front door shut with a quiet clap.

Rodrian slipped his free arm around me once more, sliding his hand up my back, under my hair, along the back of my neck.

I relaxed in his embrace. "That was nice of you, Rode."

"I can't think about what would have happened if he wasn't here. I'd never be able to repay that boy."

"You don't have to. People don't do nice things because they want to be repaid. We do the right thing because it needs to be done."

"Even the hard things?"

"Especially the hard things." I pulled back and looked up at him. "Can we go see her?"

Nodding, he smoothed my hair where it had been tousled by his sweater. "She's different, though. Are you ready for this?"

Wordlessly, I lifted my chin. Everything she'd gone through had been for the purpose of changing her. I had to be ready, whether I wanted to be or not. Rodrian released me and led me downstairs to the clinic that had once been my garage.

Strangers in scrubs milled around the room, packing up equipment and boxing supplies in an efficient, impersonal manner. Rodrian had located a specialist in Colorado who dealt with hypolution and spared no expense bringing him in to sub for Pontian. He'd left late last night after completing Shiloh's treatment, leaving his crew behind to pack up. The corner of the room had a sliding curtain suspended from a track in the ceiling, shielding it from view.

I could feel each of the DV—their personalities, their intentions. A half-minute in the same room with them gave me more information than they'd share with their closest friends in a year. None of them could ever be strangers to me now. They were mine.

Each tried so hard to keep their power to themselves, knowing it would be inappropriate to approach me at the moment. Their hearts shone all the brighter for daring to hope my name.

I glanced warily around, feeling the strain of so many people, so much power. I concentrated on adding another layer of security to my barriers and slipped my hand into the bend of Rodrian's arm. Pressing against him, I tried to melt into his power, hoping his signal would distract me and block the others out.

He looked at me a moment before clearing his throat. "Thank you, everyone. We'd like a moment alone."

I nodded in relief. He thought I was nervous about Shiloh. Truth was, I was too crowded by all the DV. He didn't realize what had happened to me after Dorcas touched me. I wasn't going to tell him, either. It would only frighten him, and right now that was the last thing either of us needed.

One by one they left, and I felt the soul count decrease as they did. Eventually, it was me, Rodrian, and one other. The staff had all left the room, so I knew the final power was coming from Shiloh.

I was a stranger to the feel of her power. Would I know her anymore?

Rodrian reached to pull back the curtain.

"Wait," I said. "Give me a second."

I closed my eyes, knowing it would appear that I simply braced myself. I rolled Shiloh's essence through my mind, trying to prepare myself for seeing the results of her cusp.

Her power felt nothing like her. It was careworn, and exhausted, and mature. No confetti. No Justin Bieber. Nothing like I'd expected.

Nothing like I'd hoped.

She couldn't have emerged from any of this the same, free-spirited Shiloh I'd always known.

After a moment, I nodded. "Okay."

He pulled back the curtain to reveal Shiloh, sleeping on an elevated hospital bed. Her skin was pale, freckles standing out like flecks of paint. Deep bruises under her eyes made her appear older than her almost eighteen years. Rodrian leaned and kissed her gently upon her temple, and she roused. When she saw me, her power surged, although, physically, all she did was blink.

It was like an up-close sunrise on a roller coaster. Her power nearly crushed me. My mouth opened but no sound came out. I grabbed Rodrian's hand. A moment passed before he realized I'd taken a direct hit and he hurried to quiet her. "Shh, sweetie. Remember how I showed you how to pull back? Easy..."

Her surge lessened, wavering down to a more-controlled level. She struggled to exercise parts of her brain which until this point had remained humanly inactive. As she gained control over her fledgling strength, she closed her eyes, the exertion taking a rapid toll. "I'm sorry, Sophie. I...couldn't help it. Did you always feel so...wonderful?"

Rodrian's eyes flicked from Shiloh to me and back. "Your barriers are thin, honey. You'll learn how to protect yourself quickly, I promise. But for a while, it's going to be strange for you, getting used to sensing others. Eventually, it's something that you'll ignore without thinking twice."

"I'll never ignore Sophie," she said. Her eyes remained closed, and her voice grew softer, as if she were falling asleep. "She feels like...heaven..."

Shiloh's head wobbled against the pillow. I realized she'd lost consciousness when her power dimmed once more. I watched her in disbelief, unable to comprehend her strength. When she'd hit me with her full uncontrolled essence, it reminded me of the night Marek had overthrown the Master. She wasn't even trying, yet it had been all I could do to remain upright. If Rodrian hadn't distracted her, I might have collapsed.

Rodrian reached down, smoothing her blanket and taking up her limp hand. He raised it to his mouth.

"I know, baby." He murmured against her skin, eyes aglow. "I know."

Meeting my eyes briefly, Rodrian leaked a heartful of longing and guilt before releasing her hand and striding out. I watched the door close behind him and trailed his power back to the den, feeling his tumultuous brooding over-shadow his every step.

I pulled a chair closer to her bed and took up Shiloh's hand, whispering a prayer of thanks she had survived. I prayed and I thanked God and every power we'd all survived, somehow. I fell short of wondering what the future held for each of us.

Right now, the present was all I could handle.

I sat a while with Shiloh, watching her sleep and gently smoothing away some of the strain and the weariness from her brush-burned soul. By the time I left, the bruises had diminished and she rested more comfortably. The Sophia would be very busy in the next few days, as would be my unrefined parenting skills. Shiloh needed me to be a lot of things this week. I had to be ready to be them.

Rodrian needed me to be a lot of things, too. His only brother had been transformed into the Horus Bird right before me. We'd both lost him in that instant, when Marek changed form and escaped. We had both held onto hope against hope that we could bring him back from the edge of Brinking, that the Sophia could save him—

No. It wasn't the time for me to pity myself and my loss. Rodrian needed me, although I wasn't sure I had what he needed. Part of me really wanted to try.

With a deep determined breath, I released Shiloh's hand and pushed to my feet. It was time to start.

Closing the curtain once more, I lifted fingers of Sophia awareness and reached to touch the DV staff, letting them know it was okay to return. They appeared at once and I slipped out before their power crowded me.

The door to the guest suite stood open and I glanced in, thinking how quiet it would be without Toby living here anymore. I wondered how quiet it wouldn't be now that Brianda and her girlfriend would soon be moving in.

I liked this whole thing of not being alone anymore. It was easier to deal with the gaps other people made when they left. The more DV, the merrier, I thought.

At least that was my thought until I approached the foyer and detected a strange DV signature. Rodrian was at the front door, talking to a stranger. Not one of the staff. Not one of the medical team. Curious, I went to see who it was.

Whoever it was, they didn't feel friendly. Business? Here?

Rodrian spoke with a tall, blond woman. The first thing I noticed were her legs, a mile long and stretching between a tight tailored skirt and next year's Pradas. Her power felt inquisitive, edgy, possessive. She didn't bother to hide her impression or the appraising glance she used to take me in. Rodrian's power felt tense and unsure, even behind his thickest shields.

Lots of ice here. Time to break it before my blood froze.

"Hi," I said and smiled, Sophie-sincere.

The blonde smiled back, teeth gleaming, and slid a hand up to her hip, rocking on one foot and angling the line of her body toward Rodrian.

Rodrian's mouth was tight, almost as tight as the coil of his power.

"Darling, this is Sophie. Sophie, let me introduce Aurelia." His voice almost disappeared behind the sudden booming pulse in my ears but his facial expression relayed the vocal cues I could no longer hear. "Shiloh's mother."

He pressed his lips together, once, before donning a pleasant mask. "My mate."

*Dear Lonely yet Hopeful,*

*Your letter strikes a harmonious chord within me. I can advise you with perfect clarity and absolute certainty.*

*You encounter the man whom you've loved so dearly, whom you always will. Love is not an illusion. When we love despite pain, despite anger, despite separation, we love justly and truly. You ask if you have nothing to lose.*

*If you don't strike down your hesitation and seize your opportunity, you will lose everything. Time runs away from us while we gaze longingly after hope. Time flees and urges us only toward our endings. Time works against us and cares only to steal away our chances of redemption.*

*Face him. Risk pain and persist past it. Don't spend any more time wondering if it would be right; you already know how right that love can be.*

*Don't wait. One day, time will sweep us up with mighty wings and hope will fly away. Don't allow yourself to be left behind, wishing*

*you'd done something.*
    *Be true to that love, which should never be denied.*

*Sincerely, Sophie*

THE END

## ABOUT THE AUTHOR

**Ash Krafton** is a speculative fiction author from the Pennsylvania coal region. If she's not writing, it's probably because she's distracted by all the cool junk on her desk or by the stacks of books that have grown up around it.

She writes novels, short fiction, and poetry for mostly adult audiences. (She's *mostly* an adult.). Some of those novel titles include:

### *The Books of the Demimonde: urban fantasy trilogy*

*Enter the world of the Demimonde.*

*Look outside your window. Same old town, same streets, same people, same stories you've lived all your life. Or... are they?*

*Sophie Galen is an advice columnist from the suburbs of Philly. Like many sensitive women, she's done her best to create a shelter for herself in order to live in a safe, predictable world, protecting her vulnerable self: her mind, her heart, her soul.*

*Then he came into her life and blew the walls in.*

*When Marek Thurzo arrived, he brought with him all the secrets she never wanted to know: the world outside was not what she thought. There were people and creatures and powers she'd never dared to believe exist and at the very center of this humongous supernatural web was one single person.*

*Her. The Sophia. The one hope for redemption for the Demivampire race.*

*Some days, she still can't wrap her head around the whole thing. Other days...*

*...she's ready to do whatever it takes to protect her Demivamps, no matter the obstacle, no matter the enemy, no matter the personal cost.*

*While meeting her deadlines, of course. Who says a girl can't multitask while saving the world?*

**Bleeding Hearts (Demimonde #1)**

**Blood Rush (Demimonde #2)**

**Wolf's Bane (Demimonde #3)**

## *WORDS THAT BIND: paranormal romance*

*Social worker Tam Kerish can't keep her cool professionalism when steamy client Mr. Burns kindles a desire for more than a client-therapist relationship—so she drops him. However, they discover she's the talisman to which Burns, an immortal djinn, has been bound since the days of King Solomon…and that makes it difficult to stay away from him.*

*Ethical guidelines are unequivocal when it comes to personal relationships with clients. However, the djinn has a thawing effect on the usually non-emotive Tam, who begins to feel true emotion whenever he is near. Tam has to make a difficult choice: to stay on the outside, forever looking in…or to turn her back on her entire world, just for the chance to finally experience what it means to fall in love.*

**Words That Bind**

She also writes New Adult spec fic as **AJ Krafton**. Her debut, THE HEARTBEAT THIEF (Victorian fantasy) is a little bit Jane Austen, a little bit Edgar Allan Poe, and a whole lot of stealing heartbeats in order to stay young and beautiful forever...

How far will Senza Fyne go to avoid Death?

**The Heartbeat Thief**

*"There was something smart, ominous, and romantic about this strange story..."*
Rated 4.5 stars on Amazon reviews!

## Join the Fictitious Initiative...

If you'd like an email whenever Ash (or AJ) has a new release, great giveaway, or special offer, you can sign up on her website or online at http://eepurl.com/wAm2T. Your email will never be shared and you can unsubscribe at any time.

## Thanks for reading!

Word-of-mouth is crucial for any author to succeed. If you've enjoyed reading this book, please consider leaving a brief review—just a line or two is fine, and it may help another reader decide to give this book a try.

And if you *really* enjoyed reading it, tell a friend. Friends share : )

www.ingramcontent.com/pod-product-compliance
Lightning Source LLC
Chambersburg PA
CBHW071205250626
47159CB00001B/214